Hyphanden's Box

Book Three of the "Stolen" Series

a novel by

K. A. Krisko

Table of Contents

Regional Map

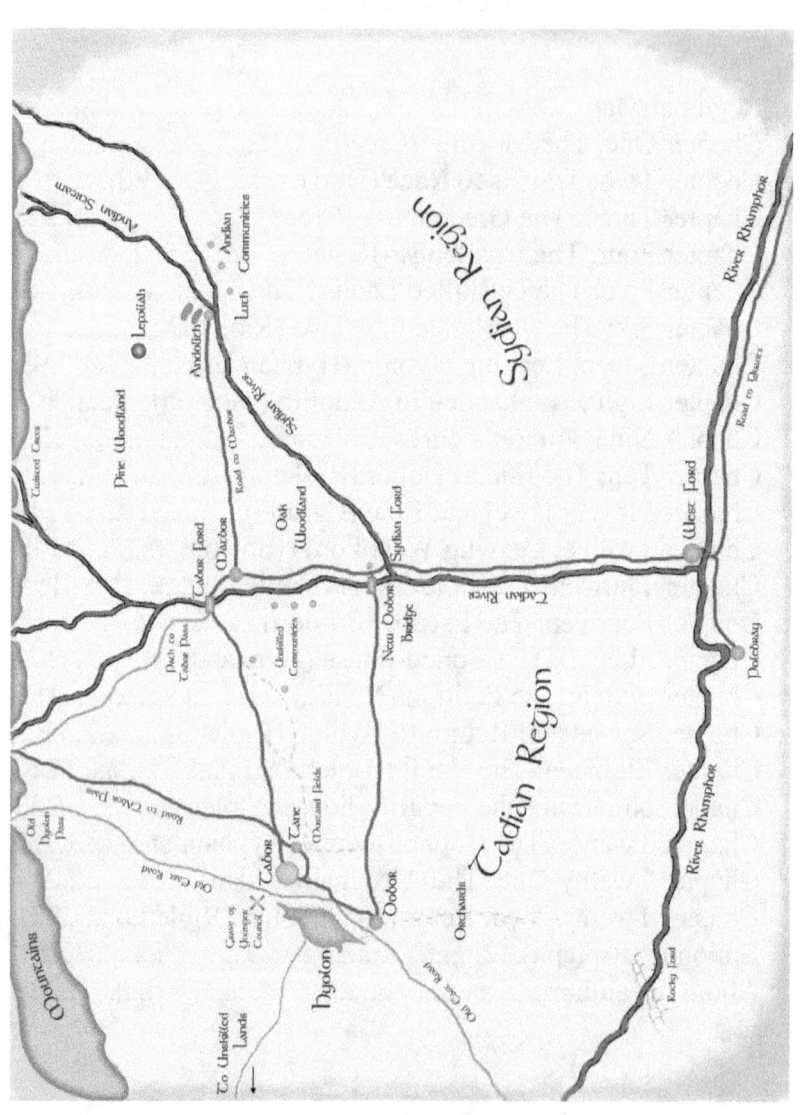

Chapter One: The Meeting (Creed)

The slow clop of hooves echoed through silent streets. Creed Ereptor rode a heavy dapple-gray horse bareback, the lines of its harness crossed over the back of its neck. Although the sprawling estates around him appeared deserted, their lawns dry and brown, their walls crumbling, he was on high alert. In his free hand he clutched one of his bows. Another was slung across his back, and a machete hung in a scabbard off the horse's withers.

It was late in the day, and the sun sank behind buildings wrapped in vines and cloaked with overgrown ornamental trees, drooping with purple and yellow flowers. A heavy odor of warm vegetation and perfume punctuated with decay permeated the air.

Creed turned the draft horse up a path no different in appearance from all the others. A rusting metal gate hung slightly askew. The stone walls enclosing the property were worn and moss-covered. But as Creed approached, the gates swung open on well-oiled hinges. He urged the horse forward, watching the lawn on either side dissolve from brown to lush green. An estate with large etched glass windows set deep in arches of granite wavered into view. Well-tended orchards peeked out from behind it, and a complex of other buildings took form to one side.

He guided the horse to the stables and alighted there with relief. The animal was one of his cart-horses, not a saddle-horse, and it was broad and round as a barrel. He was at the mercy of its bulging sides, and the ride from the north side of Tabor to Hyolon had been long. He stretched gratefully. Now safe within the Protections of the estate, he stowed his bows and unstrapped the machete.

1

Creed made his way from the stables to the heavy wooden front door, which stood ajar in the summer heat. The entryway led to a cool flagstone-floored hall with dark wooden doors on either side. He could hear the murmur of many voices ahead, drowning out the click of his boot-heels on the stones.

At the end of the hall was the great-room, well lit by large glass doors open to the backyard garden. A number of oversized high-backed chairs, all finely wrought and upholstered, were arrayed around a large stone fireplace, along with settees, hassocks and footstools. Many of these were occupied by a variety of persons, male and female.

Creed dropped his satchel near the fireplace and looked around for people he knew. The owner of the estate, Hyphanden Vrinal, sat with his back to the glass doors. He brooded with his fingers intertwined, his head lowered, his gaze from beneath his brows fastened on the stones of the hearth. He was tall and slender, with dark hair going to gray, and the slight overbite and narrow face marked him as Vrinac. Despite his stillness, an aura seemed to hover about him, and his mood made his power seem dangerous. Creed thought better of disturbing him for the moment.

To Hyphanden's right sat Kwistocta, her eyes skipping quickly from one guest to another, a slight smile on her lips. She was clad in high-waisted trousers and a fine silken shirt that seemed to change colors as she moved. Creed made his way to her chair.

"Good to see you, Creed," she said. She rose, her height almost equal to Creed's, and clasped hands with him. "We had word you would be joining us. We'll be calling the meeting to order in just a few minutes."

Creed looked around for a place to sit. He claimed a large, high-backed chair next to his one-time neighbor Stolen, now a permanent resident of the Ruined City. Stolen was engaged in wolfing down a hefty sandwich. He gave Creed a nod and raised his eyebrows, but his mouth was too full to offer proper greeting.

There was a stir among the people nearest the entryway and Creed saw two people, strange in appearance, enter the great-room. The first was a young woman, short of stature and slender. Despite the heat, she was dressed in a high-collared formal blouse with

2

sleeves that came down across the backs of her hands. Her face was beautiful and extremely regular, and her skin was smooth and unblemished. But her skin tone graded to deep gray, and a mane of what appeared to be chestnut-brown leaves cascaded down her back.

The second person was even smaller and thinner than she was, and walked with a jerky bounce, as if unsure of his balance. His face was similar in appearance to hers: extremely regular, but stiff, with prominent cheekbones and gray skin tone. His leaf-like hair stood up like a brush and was striped front to back in the yellows and reds of autumn maples, with the greens of spring growth arching back over his ears.

Hyphanden unlaced his fingers and glanced up for the first time. "Marsavrina, Skadar, welcome. Have you seen Kerdahl?"

"He's close behind us," Marsavrina replied in a musical voice that sounded like the vibration of wind across a reed. She turned and offered a hand to Stolen. Stolen clasped her fingers briefly and Marsavrina then offered her hand to Creed.

"It's nice to see you again. Skadar is doing well, as you can see," she said. "We are infinitely grateful to Stolen for growing him a body of his own. He's learning to adjust it to his own tastes."

Creed took the proffered hand and stared at Marsavrina. "Well met. You're looking very good, but that hair has to go." He grimaced, nodding at Skadar.

Marsavrina smiled stiffly. "Give him time. He hasn't had a body of his own for a while. How was your travel?"

"Fine," Creed said. "But I'll have to make my stay here brief and hope Ladon doesn't question me when I get back. I'm supposed to be picking up a wagonload of glass from Dobor for our greenhouse. I had to leave the wagon at Betar's and ride one of the cart-horses."

"It's too bad Rioletta couldn't come," Marsavrina said. "I'd like to tell her personally how much I appreciate her part in our rescue."

Hyphanden glanced questioningly at Creed, but Creed shook his head. "Ladon's been keeping her close this winter. Andor too, for that matter," he said. "I think he's afraid of what they learned while they were here last year. He's only let them go to Matbor,

3

and to West Ford when old Stetsordahl requested Rioletta personally. She met Nikal there."

"She learned nothing that is not our right to know, as part of our culture and history," Hyphanden said. "The truth should never be Forbidden. But you can at least bear her a message, perhaps some books?"

"Of course," Creed said. "She likes books. Cardon brings them when he can. He's freer to travel. Ladon figures he's already ruined, I guess."

Several of the other Outcasts came in to the great-room from the back. Mynador sat down across from Stolen and Creed on the far side of the fireplace. She was an upright and stern-appearing woman, some years older than Hyphanden and Kwistocta.

Stolen leaned towards Creed, rotating an apple in his hand to find the spot he wanted to bite. "I don't care for her," he said in a low tone, nodding at Mynador. "She's always staring at me. It makes me uncomfortable."

Creed shrugged. "You look a little unusual, my friend. I'd think you'd be used to it by now."

Stolen turned his attention to the apple. Creed could see that he was quite thin, thinner than he had been the summer before after having grown a new body for Marsavrina. Apparently the strain of growing a second body for Skadar over the winter had taken its toll. Leaves mingled with his hair and poked out of his sleeves. Creed knew Stolen could still take nourishment from the sun when he had to, and he assumed the extra leaves were there to facilitate that.

A wiry individual with long dark hair paced impatiently behind the chairs. He repetitively juggled several small objects in his right hand in time with his strides. Creed glanced over his shoulder in irritation as the sound of pacing boot steps neared him again.

"Duri! You're driving me crazy!"

The man juggling the objects in his hand halted. Hyphanden looked up at him and raised his eyebrows. "Yes, you should stop that, Duri. You realize Chasan used to do that?"

Durigon Cautes slipped the small talisman-stones he'd been worrying back into his pocket and grinned. "Creed, well met! I

4

have some trade goods you'd be interested in. Talk to me after the meeting!"

Creed returned a skeptical look. Despite Duri's help at the Crypt the year before, Creed had little use for him.

The conversation abated abruptly as Kerdahl hurried into the room. Kerdahl was young, and a Traditional. Creed knew that he had been banned from Tabor after refusing to swear allegiance to the First Chosen following the coup in which the Elder Council had been deposed. He had fled Tabor with Stetsordahl, grandson of the leader of the Elder Council. The two had ended up in Hyolon, guests of Hyphanden. Despite their differences, the two had remained and become valuable members of the Outcast community.

Someone vacated a chair for Kerdahl. Hyphanden cleared his throat.

"I've asked the Council and other members of the community to meet here today to hear news from Kerdahl. We're fortunate to be joined by Creed of Andolith as well." He gestured to Creed. "This news concerns the whereabouts and actions of Rudon, who betrayed us last year at the Council-house."

"We have heard nothing of Rudon all this winter," noted Caladoc. Creed had met Caladoc the year before. He was a member of the deposed Second Chosen who, with Cayondahl, had also joined the Outcast community. "Surely there's little concern. He's taken himself off elsewhere with his rogues."

Hyphanden scowled. "That I doubt. The Hyolonal have continued to behave strangely, operating in ordered ranks rather than infighting among their own clans. Besides, he's dangerous and must not be forgotten. Let's listen to what Kerdahl has to say."

Kerdahl loosened his collar nervously with a finger. "I've been able to obtain information about Rudon and his rogues on an infrequent basis, as you all know. The latest concerns the Hyolonal and Rudon's interaction with them. As Phando said, they've continued to behave in an unusual manner. Before the incident at the Council-house last year, we had observed them to operate in family groups or clans, with temporary cooperative ventures that fell apart quickly. But last year all the clans came together, apparently under the direction of Rudon. We assumed this accord

5

would quickly fall apart after Rudon failed to deliver, but it has not. They continue to function as a unit, operating under a phalanx of rogues Rudon's designated as generals, who provide direction for the clan leaders."

"Still, they can't be particularly dangerous," Cayon observed. "They have no Skills, unless you're implying that Rudon has managed to teach them some."

"No, he has not taught them Skills of which I'm aware," Kerdahl said. "But the mystery of how he's coercing them to behave has been solved. He's been using a Forbidden Technology."

A murmur ran around the room. Forbidden Technologies were not unknown. Occasionally small questionable devices found their way into trader's bags, but there was no general use of them even in the Outcast communities. Those who were strong in Skills tended to substitute Skills for Technology. Creed had only seen borderline devices such as the mapping device Rath of Luth used.

Hyphanden raised a hand. "This is something we've suspected since we found out that Rudon used such devices to manipulate the Younger Council," he said over the murmurs. "What more have you heard, Kerdahl?"

"He must have many more than the few he provided to the Younger Council. The rumor is that they're antiques from before the Dispersal."

"We've heard of these devices," Caladoc said. "But it's said that in the old days they were used along with talismans and Skills. They can't be very effective with the Hyolonal."

"While the Hyolonal are Unskilled, they're at least somewhat susceptible to mental suggestion," Kerdahl said. "Those with the devices also have talismans, and Rudon is able to pass messages through them. The interface isn't constant, but it's enough."

"This is why both certain Technologies and certain Skills were Forbidden in the Charter, and specifically were Forbidden to be used in concert with one another, although the Traditionals dispute this interpretation," Hyphanden said.

"I do not dispute it," Kerdahl said. "Although I disapprove of your methods, it's well known you've gained knowledge that would lead you to confirm such suspicions."

6

Creed raised his eyebrows. Rioletta would be interested to know that Kerdahl, a staunch Traditional, now agreed at least in part with Hyphanden's version of the events of the Dispersal.

"Surely Rudon can't present much danger to us, though," Cayon persisted. "It's not escaped our attention that you've learned a few Skills this past winter, Phando, as Kerdahl intimates. You're more than a match for Rudon, especially with the rest of us backing you. I'm sure we could have bested him and been done with him last summer when he attacked us as we rode to the Security House. It seemed to me you held back your strength then."

"I do not deny that I've become familiar with some unusual Skills," Hyphanden said, "but I choose not to use them, except in extreme circumstances. I seek knowledge for its own sake, not to increase my personal power or to wield it over others as does Rudon."

"I can hardly think of a more extreme circumstance than Rudon's attack," Cayon argued. "But Rudon must suspect the extent of your power. He hasn't dared come to this area of the city. Besides, what would he want with us?"

"Don't underestimate him," Hyphanden warned. "Power is increased through strong emotion: fear, anger, grief, desire. I have none of those to motivate me. I have never blamed my Outcasting on anyone but myself, and I've made a good life here. But Rudon has often allowed his emotions to blind him. He doesn't care who he hurts in his quest, and it's obvious what he wants: the Key to the Crypt of Souls and free access to those minds so he can learn the secrets of the Forbidden Skills quickly and increase his own power."

"And then what?" Creed asked. "Suppose he did get access to the Crypt. He couldn't hold more than a couple of minds within his own at any time, could he? He'd be a powerful Sorcerer if he could use what those minds knew, but most of you here have practiced the Forbidden Skills. Would he really be so much more powerful than any of you? And if he was, what of it?"

Hyphanden nodded. "A fair question, Creed. Ultimately, I believe, he desires revenge, against the Elder Council specifically or against the Council system in general. I suspect he'll eventually attempt to seize control of Hyolon, and after that, with a cohort of Sorcerers acting in concert with his devices, I suspect his plans reach as far as Tabor. He would undoubtedly love to sit in the Council-house and hold court in the Chapel of Trees."

"He's gathered some powerful rogues around himself," Kerdahl put in. "I know of Fellodon of Ankara and Losino of Kyelon, as well as others."

Creed was lost, although everyone else nodded and murmured around him. "Who are those two?"

"Fellodon and Losino were both members of the Outcast Community in the past," Hyphanden said. "Fellodon was clumsily Stripped when he was Outcast in Ankara, but Losino retained all his Skills. Neither of them cared for my leadership, and each challenged me and lost. It seems significant to me that Rudon is gathering such people to him. I suspect a plan is beginning to come together."

"What would you suggest we do, then, other than remain alert and gather as much information as possible?" Cayon asked.

Hyphanden glanced at him. "For one thing, I'd suggest we make an effort to discover more about the Forbidden Technologies, so we're not taken off-guard. One solution may be to send someone to seek enclaves where the Forbidden Technologies are still in use. It's rumored that there are places to the west where a few hidden societies exist."

"Who would you suggest for that mission?" Cayon asked skeptically. "Unless you know more than you're saying, these communities exist in rumor only, and we have no way to locate them. We certainly can't walk around asking for them."

Duri cleared his throat. "I'm a jump ahead of you there, Cayon. I've got a pretty good idea where some of these communities are. I've traveled to borderlands where unusual technologies are commonplace, and where the rumors are stronger. Tales are told around the fires at night of those who use the Technologies to their advantage and regret. I'm bored here anyway, and I'd like to travel. If I've got a mission and I'm not just drifting, so much the better."

Creed sat back. Perhaps there was a use for Duri after all, and a mission that would take him further away from the Sydian sounded good to him.

"What do you think, Kwistocta?" Cayon asked. "Is Duri trustworthy enough? Can he function with those two extra minds he's carrying, away from the protections of Hyolon and your guidance? He'd have to keep it secret, or there are those who would consider him dangerous and imprison him, if not worse."

Kwistocta smiled. "He's done very well partitioning Malbec and Chasan. They are only partial minds, after all, and have virtually no volition of their own. Duri's quite capable of taking care of himself, or themselves, as the case may be."

Cayon spread his hands in a gesture of acquiescence. But Creed spoke up again. "Then your plan is to send Duri to investigate Forbidden Technologies, and what else? Continue to monitor Rudon's activities until he puts some plan into motion? Or move against him to put him down for good before he musters a force powerful enough to cause real trouble?"

Hyphanden tapped his fingers together in deep thought. Finally he shook his head. "In one way I'm loathe to leave him to his own devices, but we don't have enough information to move against him decisively. We have a good inside source through Kerdahl, and I think we should continue to rely on him while we wait to see what Duri can discover. But I don't think Rudon will sit still forever. We need to prepare. I propose we come up with a plan for guarding those areas of Hyolon we most want to protect, including our own estates. In the meantime I'll search further for relevant information. Give me a little time. Ironically, Rudon's betrayal may have provided us with the means to overcome him, as well as a source for the kind of information I desire."

Creed glanced quickly at Kwistocta. Hyphanden obviously referred to the minds they had taken with them from the Crypt. Creed knew Kwistocta was uncomfortable with the idea of using those minds, but her expression did not change. He suspected she and Hyphanden would deal with the issue out of the public eye.

Gomphos of Lubgroten made the motion to adjourn and Mynador seconded it for the Council. Hyphanden rose and fetched several bottles of wine while Kwistocta brought glasses, a signal that the formal part of the meeting was over. The community members broke into smaller groups for conversation and discussion. Creed and Stolen remained near Hyphanden and Kwistocta at the fireplace. Since Creed would spend the night, there was no need for him to vacate the comfortable chair. He could feel the ache in his muscles from the draft-horse ride.

Caladoc offered Hyphanden a hand as he took his leave. "Be careful with your explorations," he said grimly. "While your information has been useful, furthering it is no doubt not worth the risk to your mind. In this I agree with Kwistocta. We will need you when this affair comes to a head. Rudon must not be allowed to become some de facto ruler of Hyolon, nor must we allow purposeful harm to come to the First Chosen, no matter our past disagreements with them."

Hyphanden grinned at Caladoc's warning. "I assure you, I'm in little danger. Your fears are exaggerated because you have little understanding of the Forbidden Skills. I promise you I won't disappear into some dark hole in my own mind. Go safely, and stay alert!"

Finally only Hyphanden, Kwistocta, Mynador, Kerdahl, Creed, and Stolen were left in the great-room. They gathered closer around the unlit fireplace to share a final glass. Kwistocta poured the last of a bottle.

"Well, Phando, as you're probably already aware, I came at the time of this meeting only by coincidence. My real mission was to bear a gift," Creed said. He pulled his satchel to him and rummaged in it for a moment, then handed a small cloth-wrapped object to Hyphanden.

Hyphanden carefully unwrapped it until it lay exposed on his palm. It was a flat, diamond-shaped translucent stone with beveled edges and a lavender hue, no larger than the palm of his hand. He stared deep within it.

"The Index to the Crypt of Souls," he whispered. "I have not seen it since before I was Outcast. I was aware Rioletta had obtained it, but I thought she passed it off to Nikal of Dobor."

Creed nodded. "She did. Old Stetsordahl gave it to her, but she thought it was a bad idea to keep it in the same place as the Key. She gave it to Nikal and he took it with him to Dobor. But when we agreed that I'd try and stop in Hyolon on my way to Dobor – that is, our Younger Council agreed – Rioletta contacted Nikal, and he met Betar south of Tabor and gave it to her. She had it for me when I got there."

Hyphanden turned the stone in his hand. "So now I will know exactly who inhabits the Crypt of Souls, and who inhabits my own box, here. I haven't accessed the minds of any but Stelaphandon since that first day."

"Just having the Index doesn't make it safer to access any of the minds," Kwistocta said stiffly. "Besides, you can't access the ones in the Crypt without the Key, and that is safe in Andolith."

"Right," Hyphanden said, glancing at her. "I only mean to see if I can ferret out why the minds are in the Crypt, how many are there, and how long they have been there."

There was an uncomfortable silence. Kerdahl hurriedly set down his glass and turned to Mynador. "You didn't speak during the meeting, Mynador, but I know you've been doing some exploring on your own. I'm sure Creed would be interested in what you've found out."

Hyphanden carefully re-wrapped the Index in its soft cloth and set it to the side. Creed turned his attention to Mynador.

"Many years ago, when I first came to Hyolon, I roamed throughout the area," Mynador began in her rasping voice. "I discovered a secretive community outside the walls to the northwest. I believe them to be descended from the same stock as the Hyolonal. They maintain the Unskilled language and many of their traditions and superstitions. They subsist by herding animals, hunting, and trading with communities farther west and north, crossing through the old Hyolon Pass in the Rimron. Also they broker trade between the Hyolonal and traveling tradesmen."

"This is how the Hyolonal move goods out of the city. We knew they had to have some intermediary, given their poor relationship with the Skilled," Kerdahl explained.

Mynador nodded curtly. "Books are much in demand for trade, because they're fragile and apt to be ruined and thus command a high price. I suspect the Key passed through their hands at some point, although where it came from I do not know. The Hyolonal always seek new places where books might be found. The Council-house is known to contain libraries, and thus is a desirable target, although so far they've only accessed it once, last year."

"Many of them saw the interior and now covet what it contains," Kerdahl put in. "Rudon has promised them their take of the contents in exchange for their cooperation. He's guided them to other places in the city that they've despoiled with his help. Rudon is a known Skill-breaker; it's one of his special talents."

"A pity," Hyphanden said. "I've been providing them with some competition and gathering books and other items myself. In the past we left them where they lie, as the most important places were Protected in ways the Hyolonal couldn't penetrate."

Mynador continued. "It's also rumored that this community brokers children, and I've harbored certain suspicions. Most recently I've confirmed that they trade with the Woodsmen, but I'll say no more until I have reliable information."

She rose suddenly and swept a long cloak around her. "It's growing late. Creed, it's good to see you again. Please bring my regards to Rioletta, Andor, and Cardon."

Creed rose to clasp hands with her. After she was gone, Stolen gathered his own things. "I'll stop by tomorrow morning before you leave, Creed. I'll come over with Duri and act as referee!"

"What, have you made some bargain with Duri?" Hyphanden asked in surprise.

"Creed's curiosity got the better of him," Stolen answered. "He's agreed to tolerate Duri in exchange for a chance at some of his trade goods."

"Early, then, Stolen," Creed warned. "I have to make time tomorrow, or Ladon will suspect me when I return."

Chapter Two: Travels to Race (Duri)

Duri strode quickly along the streets of Hyolon, west of the city center. He was on foot and leading both his saddle horse and his pack-horse, which was laden with his personal belongings and a fair amount of small trade goods. The trade goods were mostly common antiques from the Ruined City, but there were a few items of real value stowed deep in the bags. He would ride once he was out of the city, but in the narrow lanes of the west side it was easier and more efficient to walk.

He had been cautioned to leave the city on the east and travel around it either to the south, bypassing Tabor and Dobor by staying close to the city itself, or to the north, through the deep woods along the foothills of the mountains. But Duri was not a cautious man, and he had chosen to cut straight through Hyolon. He was well acquainted with the back streets and byways after a restless winter with the Outcasts, and although he remained alert and employed some Stealth and Concealment Skills, he was confident he could get through without encountering the Hyolonal or any other unsavory characters.

Truthfully, he was glad to be getting away. Being cooped up in Hyolon did not agree with him. There was little for him to do, and the novelty of carrying the partial minds of two Sorcerers in his own, struggling to keep them partitioned and under control, had worn off.

His mission was to travel to the lands he had visited as a youth, where Unskilled societies utilized technologies rare in the regions around Hyolon. If he was able to make contact with users of the Forbidden Technologies, he was to learn as much as possible, particularly about communications devices such as the ones Rudon had apparently obtained.

The clatter of the horses' hooves abated as he reached the outskirts of Hyolon, where the streets turned from paved to dirt. The buildings of the city disappeared behind overgrown trees and vines. He wound his way between low, crumbling walls of stone, once the delineators of gardens plots. Sometimes he caught furtive movement from the corner of his eye or heard a whistle unlike that of a bird. But he was unalarmed, if alert: the Hyolonal had learned to stay away from him and his knives, and rogue Sorcerers rarely traveled the streets. The only other dangerous creatures in Hyolon were Cardon's stray toothed horses, but they hadn't been seen for several months.

He mounted his saddle horse once the area opened up and kept a regular pace, steady but not fast, sustainable for both his horses and himself. He was good at pacing himself, having learned his own limits over the years, and he arrived at an acceptable campsite while still not overtired.

Duri disliked using campfires while traveling alone. They attracted attention. Instead, he opted for a quick meal of bread and cheese. Duri was wiry and could survive on limited food if necessary, although preferably augmented by some liquor. He had a quick pull at a flask before settling in for the night. He felt quite content to be traveling once again, responsible for none but himself and the minds he carried within his own, with an edge of alertness clearing the dullness of boredom.

He was up early. He bore generally west, with Hyolon at his back. The further west one got from the Ruined City, the fewer Skills the settlements evinced. They began to rely on technologies not Forbidden, but generally forgotten on the east side, where Skills could make up for the lack. If you traveled far enough, you'd arrive at places where Skills were almost unheard of, and a few tricks could earn you some money and some respect.

The area around Hyolon was mostly oak woodland. But the line of the northern mountain range, the Rimron, bent to the south as it passed Hyolon, and Duri's path rose gradually. After several days he was riding through foothills, where good trails followed the meadows of shallow valley-bottoms and large pines began to appear. Occasionally the road wound through fingers of forestland, or up over one ridge or another. Other paths appeared, striking off mostly to the south, and the road became more firmly packed, with bits of pavement near settlements.

Other than to take a few meals at roadside inns, Duri did not stop except to sleep. Ten days after he left Hyolon, he arrived at the top of a rise, on the far side of which the road ran sharply downhill. He paused and viewed the valley before him. There was a fair-sized city below with stone towers and well-made buildings laid out in a regular pattern. He could hear the hum of machinery and saw a few motorized vehicles on the roads entering the city. His horses were unused to motor-carts, but they were well trained, and Duri could exert some calming influence if necessary. He settled himself for the trip down the hill and gave his saddle horse its head.

The city was called Race, and was within the purview of Toramondon, the New Settlement outside the Ruined City of Toralon. It was populated, Duri knew, by a mix of Unskilled and minimally-Skilled non-Sorcerers. There was an inn on the edge of the city, and Duri stopped there. He booked himself a room and led the horses around two motor-carts parked nearby so they could examine them before stabling for the night. The roads in the city were carefully paved: the carts were not powerful, and would be useless on rough roads and steep hills such as those around Andolith and much of the Sydian region. They had a limited range, and were used strictly for transporting goods and people within the city limits. The more powerful vehicles of legend, those that burned combustible materials for fuel, had been banned during the Dispersal, and in places like Hyolon their rusting hulks sat camouflaged by vegetation, home to rats and cavity-nesting birds.

After a rest and a wash, Duri went out to stroll around the city in the evening cool. He walked slowly, orienting himself and bringing long-disused memories to the forefront of his mind. He had been here before, but it was long ago, when he was a young man traveling with the traders. He stopped at a café with an outdoor balcony and sat near the rail, savoring a beer and dinner.

The lights of the city came up slowly, and Duri took his time, enjoying the bustle and activity. He paid for his meal, nodded to the cashier, and slipped out into the night. He was careful not to attract attention or stand out in any way. Occasionally he stopped to look in the window of a shop, and at each intersection he paused to read the street signs, digging in his mind for memories.

15

His wanderings took him to the southern district of the city, along winding streets once nothing more than cow-paths, now paved into respectability. The lights were fewer here, the people scattered. Duri stopped at the window of a small shop, took a few steps back into the street and viewed the building as a whole. It was as he remembered it, virtually unchanged.

The shop was closed, but Duri stood near the window, a pane of glass covered with wire mesh, and with his face pressed close he could see into the dark interior. It was a shop much like the one his foster-family had once owned, full of knick-knacks and curiosities, and sometimes other things for the discriminating purchaser. This particular shop belonged to a man by the name of Porbruten, or had when Duri had last visited it.

After a minute Duri turned back the way he had come and walked to the inn, taking care to remember each turn. He had a final beer in the downstairs bar, then climbed the wide stairs to his room.

In the room, Duri extracted his knives to store them safely for the night. He generally carried three knives at all times: the large obvious one on his belt, with which he was quite adept, a smaller curved blade tucked into a supple sheath within the waistband of his trousers, and a similar one in an ankle sheath. These hidden two were his fighting knives, and it was with these he was most skilled. Knives were good weapons; he had only to extract one and point it in the direction of his opponent, touch the tip to flesh, and with a gentle push, he could inflict a great deal of damage. There was no throwing, cocking, aiming, or nocking involved. If he wanted, he could slice with it: a motion back and forth within a single second could lay a person open. Or he could feint and threaten without inflicting true harm, as he had done with the Hyolonal or during his fight with Creed at the Polebray.

Creed! He had beaten Duri senseless when they were sixteen, but Duri had come away from that experience having learned several valuable lessons. First, he was not well suited to life in a small village like Andolith. So he had gone to live with the foster family who had introduced him to trading and traveling. Second, he would never be able to defend himself through strength and size. He would have to rely on speed and skill, so he'd learned the fighting knives, and had become adept enough to earn the admiration of those who'd taught him. Third, he had preferences that would never be acceptable within the societies in which he lived and traveled. If he wanted to maintain his freedom, he would have to learn a certain restraint. He had sought out information that allowed him to compartmentalize his mind, and it was this that had prepared him to accept the minds of Malbec and Chasandahl into his own.

With two knives stowed within easy reach and one repositioned in his ankle sheath, Duri lay in the dark awake, planning his strategy for the following day. But once he had made up his mind he fell asleep quickly and slept well, without reconsidering the decisions he'd made.

Duri did not rush to Porbruten's place the following morning. It was a morning of heavy shopping for the local populace, and he preferred to have Porbruten's ear to himself. Instead, he hired a cart to take him to the central shopping district. The vehicle was an open-sided two-seater with a short bed in the back. It hummed along over the paved streets at a top speed about that of a horse's canter.

"Handy device," Duri remarked to the driver as they zipped around a corner. "We don't use them where I come from. I suppose everyone has one here."

The driver shrugged. "They're handy enough around town, but they take energy to run, and they can't travel far without refreshing. And they can't run over rough roads: not enough torque. We've all got horses and wagons for real work. They say the ones they used before the Dispersal were more powerful, but there's none of the fuels they ran on anymore."

"Oh, I expect there is some," Duri said casually. "It's just hard to get."

"Hard or impossible, without the Forbidden Technologies," the driver agreed. "You've got to have fuel to get fuel. It's a cycle with no beginning. But anyway, those Technologies were banned, and for good reason. We do just fine with what we have now."

"You think there's anyone who still uses those Technologies?" Duri asked. "Where I come from, there are Sorcerers who try out

17

the Forbidden Skills and are banished for it, if they don't kill themselves first."

The driver glanced at him. "Oh, there's tales, of course. But I think it'd be harder to use the Forbidden Technologies than the Forbidden Skills. You only have to learn the Skills. You don't have to solve the problem of how to get to them and make them usable."

"Not as easy as all that, but I take your meaning," Duri said. "And I suppose you'd notice pretty quick if someone was driving around in a high-powered cart with smoke coming out the back end."

The driver snorted. "That you would. Will you be wanting a pick-up?"

"No, I'll walk back and take my time," Duri said as he got out. He slung his satchel over his shoulder. The driver nodded and pulled forward to where several people with heavy bags gestured to him, and Duri crossed the street to a café to get his breakfast.

He spent the morning wandering around the city center, staring in the shop windows, but mostly listening to what was going on around him. A little Concealment served to make him less noticeable. He caught a number of conversations, but none drew his interest particularly. In mid-afternoon he began to make his way south towards Porbruten's shop. The morning crowds had thinned and the streets were quiet, with only a few carts trolling for customers.

A small bell on the door jangled as Duri entered. The shop was packed with shelves, cases, stands, stacked boxes, and even items hanging from the ceiling. It had an interesting odor, a combination of dust, mold, spices, and leather. Duri's eyes traveled quickly over the interior and found what he was looking for at the very back: a doorway behind a glass case and a small sign next to the door advertising potions. Conventionally, medicines were substances that worked without the application of Skills. Drugs could also work without Skills, but their effects could be changed by Sorcerers, and some of them were dangerous. But potions and brews were useless without the application of Skills by a Sorcerer or Healer. Race was peopled by the minimally Skilled and the Unskilled. Thus, it was unusual that a shopkeeper would advertise

18

potions, and likely that Porbruten himself was Skilled in some way.

In a few moments Porbruten himself appeared from a back room. He looked much as Duri remembered him, if a bit older: stocky, paunchy, round of face, and likely with a minimum of three knives hidden upon his person. He smiled in greeting and rubbed his hands together, but Duri noticed that the hands never left the vicinity of his beltline, where he was sure a knife was sheathed.

Porbruten did not have the look of a Vrinac, but there were other cities to the east. Duri thought it likely he had either been Outcast from one of them, or had developed Skills he was not allowed to use as a non-Sorcerer, and had eventually been banned from or voluntarily left his homeland. Just a few high-level Skills would impress the denizens of an Unskilled town and even those with minimal Skills of their own, and an enterprising person could make a good living in that manner, although it was considered unethical in Sorcerer societies.

"What can I help you with?" Porbruten asked. There was no reason he would remember Duri. Duri had been a boy in his late teens last he had been in the shop. "You're from out of town, I see. A nice vest you have there, in the style of the Toquant. I have some similar myself. Perhaps I could interest you in one or more?"

Duri smiled indulgently. "I'm more interested in knives, myself. I'm always on the lookout for sheaths and lock-backs, anything new and different."

Porbruten raised his eyebrows. "I'm a bit of a connoisseur myself," he said. "I've got some very pretty scribed blades over here. But perhaps you're more interested in knives as tools?"

"Knives with specific uses, anyway," Duri replied. "I don't care what they look like, as long as I can get them out quickly and do my business with them. I'm sure you know what I mean."

Porbruten chuckled nervously, but he smiled again and walked quickly to a case near the back of the shop. Duri followed him and studied the contents of the case with one eye on the potions advertisement.

"Pretty, but also pretty standard stuff," he commented. "I'm looking for the more unusual."

19

"Yes, well, I keep the more expensive and unusual stuff in the back. No use showing it around to those who aren't truly interested," Porbruten said.

"I imagine you have a number of unusual items," Duri said. "You're not from these lands. You're Baldrian, or I miss my guess."

Porbruten leveled his gaze at Duri without comment. Duri could see the muscles of his jaw working; he was definitely nervous now. Baldrian had been only a guess, but he could see, and feel, that he'd come at least close to the mark.

"I'm Sydian, myself," Duri continued casually. "Originally from Andolith, though I haven't lived there for years."

"You're a Sorcerer?" Porbruten said, licking his lips. "I could feel it when you walked in."

"No, not a Sorcerer, though I've obtained a few Skills on my own."

Porbruten relaxed a little. "But you have the feel of a Sorcerer. You were not inducted?"

"Not inducted and not trained. I have no mark; do you want me to show you?" Duri smiled. "The Andolith Sorcerers are marked on the back of the hip."

"No, no," Porbruten raised his hands. "Of course, that wouldn't prove anything anyway. Not all Sorcerers use a physical mark. But I have nothing to hide. I use my few poor Skills only for good, to help the people of the town with their little illnesses and problems."

Duri snorted. "I use my few poor Skills to help myself, and I suspect you do as well. But no matter; it's nothing to me. I've been traveling long, away from my own kin, and it's refreshing to meet someone of similar mind."

He reached into his shoulder satchel and extracted a bottle of wine. "Let's share a drink! I'll wager you haven't had good Tadian wine in a while."

Porbruten eyed the bottle for a long moment. "Vrinac?" he finally asked.

"Vrinac made, yes, but not from Tabor," Duri said. "From Hyolon, and some tasty stuff it is. Come, haven't you an opener?"

20

"Hyolon?" Porbruten grunted. "You are an interesting fellow. Well, come then, come to the back. We'll share a drink and some talk. I do admit that I miss good Vrinac wine and the only news I get of the region is sporadic at best."

Duri followed Porbruten behind the glass case and through the doorway into Porbruten's quarters, which were nearly as crowded as the shop. They made their way into a cluttered sitting room, attached directly to a crowded little kitchen, and Porbruten gestured for Duri to take a seat while he fetched an opener for the wine. He returned with two glasses and happily poured them full.

"Well, then, a traveler, a trader, a knife-fighter, and a user of Skills you are, with contacts in Hyolon," Porbruten said, raising his glass. "But what has brought you to my little shop, I have not discerned as of yet." He swirled the wine briefly, took a large mouthful, and relaxed back into his battered armchair with a sigh.

Duri raised his glass in return and settled back himself, crossing one leg over the other. The hem of his trousers rose, exposing the hilt of one of his knives protruding from his ankle-height boot. "I'm a traveler and trader, as you've noted, and bound to no one but myself. I make and hold contacts where it serves my purpose, and, like you, it serves my purpose to deal in the unusual and unexpected. I've traded books from Hyolon, and I have some with me now, as well as the wine. Unusual knives are a favorite of mine. Let me show you this one. As a connoisseur, you'll appreciate it."

Duri pulled the blade from his ankle-sheath with a practiced motion, flipped it over, and offered it hilt-first to Porbruten, who took it and examined it in detail.

"Yes, it's unusual, and well-balanced. The shape of the blade marks it as Tadian, but I don't know what the hilt is made of."

Duri took the knife back with a smile and re-holstered it. "It's an antique, and likely from Hyolon. Also from Hyolon, and sometimes from other places, I obtain small antique devices, which amuse me until I find a buyer. And there are many other trinkets I've dealt in over the years. It strikes me it could be valuable for us to collaborate. Your shop is in a handy spot, not far off my regular route."

Duri leaned forward and poured more wine into their glasses. "I see the possibility of a partnership. I could spend my time locating goods, send or bring them to your shop, and you could vend them from here."

"Yes, yes," Porbruten said shrewdly, "but what did you mean about the small antique devices?"

"Ah, I'll show you one some time. I believe I brought one along, but I may have left it at the inn where I'm staying," Duri said offhandedly. He smiled to himself. He knew from his previous visit that Porbruten had a penchant for devices. "But let's talk about some of the goods I saw in your shop. Perhaps I could move a few of them for you."

Duri deftly guided the conversation to a discussion of Porbruten's goods, and from there to where he had obtained them and his trading circle and contacts. Meanwhile, he kept the glasses full, Porbruten's somewhat more than his own. It was powerful wine, specifically chosen for this purpose by Hyphanden, but Duri had learned to send the intoxicated parts of his mind into exile in the partitions reserved for Malbec and Chasan.

"I'm not Baldrian, not quite, as you so astutely guessed," Porbruten slurred. "Actually, I'm from Portria, which as you might know is a satellite community of Baldria, split off when the maximum number was reached. Now, I was not seen as promising in the area of Skills. No, no one would sponsor me to train for the Council. But I was always fond of unusual things, you see, and so I eventually obtained a book from just such a trader as yourself, and from that I learned a number of interesting tricks."

"Interesting tricks not sanctioned for use by non-Sorcerers, I imagine," Duri prodded.

"Not sanctioned for use by anyone, Sorcerer or not," Porbruten laughed. "Specifically, I learned some aspects of Conjury."

"Ah, a Forbidden Skill," Duri nodded. "Conjury: to make something from nothing. Of course, that's an exaggeration. Nothing can be made from nothing."

"Oh, exactly!" Porbruten giggled. "Nothing can indeed be made from nothing! But from very little, one can create the illusion of substance, or of life. Quite impressive to those who know

22

nothing of it, who have no Skills! It's how I made my money when I first arrived here, having been, er, encouraged to seek my fortune elsewhere."

"Of course," Duri said. He dug in his shoulder satchel and extracted his mapping device. "Look, here's the device I was talking about earlier. Take a look; what do you think of it?"

Porbruten leaned forward and took the device. It was immediately apparent to Duri that he was familiar with such things, for after only a second he pressed the button that activated it, and did not seem at all alarmed when it came on.

"Yes, yes, I've seen such things before," Porbruten muttered. "Not quite Forbidden Technology. Borderline, because it can communicate with other such devices and does so automatically when it is on. But it can be turned off. Also, its communication can't truly be enhanced by Skills, so it is quite harmless, in the manner of the meaning of the Charter."

"Which makes it easier to trade and travel with. But such devices fascinate me. Had I lived in the time before the Dispersal, I'm sure I would have had all manner of them."

Porbruten heaved himself unsteadily to his feet and made his way into a crowded room behind them, where he rooted around for a few minutes. When he re-emerged, he held something in his hand, which he extended to Duri.

"Take a look at this, then. It didn't work at all when I first got it, but I'm a bit of a tinkerer."

Duri held it cradled in his hand. It was of a size that fit neatly in his palm. His fingers curled over it naturally to access a row of buttons along the side of the face. A slot at the top could have held a lanyard. It was made of some black material, with a few colored inserts. He knew immediately what it was, for he had seen illustrations in books in Hyolon and had it described to him a number of times. It was a communication device, one of the ones Hyphanden blamed for the downfall of Hyolon and for the Dispersal, a device that remained, of its own, permanently connected to others, and also linked the minds of the users in a human-device interface that provided for almost instantaneous communication mind-to-mind.

23

"Turn it on! Turn it on!" Porbruten urged. "It works just fine, even seems to be communicating with other such devices, although where they might be I have no idea. I've rigged it so it drops its communication when it's turned off, contrary to the way it was designed. I had a feeling it could be tracked here if it was always on. Here."

He leaned forward and punched a button on the face, and the little device began to vibrate slightly in Duri's hand. The face glowed faintly, and a series of numbers scrolled by, followed by what appeared to be a kind of map. Duri stared down into the face, and as he did he felt a wave rise out of the device and probe into his mind. Curious, he did not deny it entry, but allowed it to flow into him. The wave rippled through his consciousness, and into all the recesses of his brain like flowing water, even into the minds of Malbec and Chasan where they dwelt, and Duri felt a sudden awakening, a stirring of memory, a coalescence of all of the knowledge he held. He sat transfixed, listening to the voices of the minds within his, and then, quite suddenly, he became aware of voices outside his, voices far away, minds ebbing and flowing like waves against the shore.

The feeling was cut off quite suddenly. Porbruten had punched the button on the front of the device again, and the screen went blank.

"Now don't get sucked into that thing," Porbruten laughed. "If you like it, there's more where that came from!"

"I like it," Duri said in a whisper. For even though the device had been disabled, the minds of Malbec and Chasan had not retreated to their partitions. They had, in the space of half a minute, become completely integrated with his, and he knew he had access to all of their Skills, all of their knowledge, and in fact their consciousness, whole and complete now as though they had not been damaged. He was himself, and yet he was them as well, a person in triplicate, and the power he felt was more intoxicating than the wine.

Chapter Three: The Greenhouse (Creed)

It took Creed a full five days to make it from Dobor back to Andolith with a load of glass panels packed in his wagon. Nikal had helped him build an upside-down-V-shaped wooden frame, and they had mounted it in the wagon so the panels leaned with their tops close together lengthwise in the bed. The frame had several layers, so the smaller panels were underneath the larger. Each panel was wrapped and bound; but still, Creed had to drive very slowly and take the bumps in the roadway at a crawl to avoid breakage. It was hard work. He always had to be on alert, scanning the roadway for uneven areas and holding the horses off their natural pace. It was a relief to pull into the village in late afternoon.

He drove directly to the communal gardens, where a frame had been erected in anticipation of the panels' arrival. Cardon, Morcah, and several others soon arrived to help unload, having seen him drive in. The unload was short if nerve-racking: they had built a tall scaffold, and from this swung a cable hoist, with which they removed the entire V-frame from the wagon bed, glass and all, and deposited it carefully on the ground.

Creed took the horses to the stable. It was past dinnertime by the time he'd brushed them, examined their feet, fed and watered them, and wiped the sweat from the harness. He slung his pack over his shoulder, took his bow, and trudged through the village to Andor Acaladon's house.

He walked in without knocking, threw his gear on the floor inside the door, and fell into a large chair.

"Happy to be back?" Andor asked, ministering to a pan on the stove.

Creed let out a long breath. "What a miserable way to travel. I swear I'm not going back for another load. Ladon can send someone else."

25

"He's likely to send you east for a load of roof-slate, anyway. But the important thing is, did you get a chance to take care of your little errand?" Andor glanced self-consciously towards the front door, which stood open.

"Sure," Creed said. "Got all sorts of news. Brought some stuff for Rioletta, too, some books. But I'm hungry and I'd rather not tell it twice. Maybe after dinner I can get a quick wash and we can go on over to her house."

"We should get Pateret and Morcah, too," Andor said. "And Cardon. After all, they all know what you were planning to do."

Neither Morcah nor Pateret had been allowed to go on the journey the preceding year to the outskirts of Hyolon, where Cardon had intended to find the bodies of the Younger Council. During that journey, the group who accompanied Cardon met the Outcast Council and freed the minds of Marsavrina and Skadar from the Crypt of Souls. Although their adventure had generally been kept quiet in Andolith, the Council-members were aware of all the details, and Morcah and Pateret were disappointed to have missed the opportunity. Morcah was expected to become Leader of the Council someday, and to all appearances had accepted the role of a Traditional. But he and Pateret had supported the secret plan to send Creed to Hyolon during his trip to pick up glass, and both of them supported Rioletta's continuing research into the lost pre-Dispersal culture and history, despite Ladon's disapproval.

"Maybe we should get together in the Council-house, then," Creed suggested. "Rioletta's place would be a little crowded."

"No, we don't want anyone to overhear us. Ladon has a suspicious mind. If he saw us all meeting there he'd probably join us, and we wouldn't be able to talk openly."

"We could meet here, but you have to walk right by Ladon's to get here unless everyone sneaks around through the woods, and if someone sees people doing that, they'll be suspicious for sure."

"Well, your place is out, since you live in a bachelor-house," Andor said, dishing Creed up a plate. "Cardon lives with his mother, and Morcah lives in the family household."

Creed shrugged and sat forward to eat. "Pateret's place, then. It's larger and out of the way. No one will bother us there."

26

"You know Pateret doesn't particularly like guests," Andor said. "But I guess she'll suffer company for your story. I'll go around and tell everyone while you eat. I'll be back in a while."

Creed served himself another plate while Andor was gone, then shed his travelling clothes and bathed. About half his wardrobe was at Andor's house, so he was able to choose clean clothes and more comfortable shoes. Andor returned just as he pulled on his breeches.

"Pateret agreed to host our little meeting. Morcah's bringing a mini-cask to celebrate the greenhouse. Are you ready to go?"

"Do I look ready to go?" Creed asked.

Andor grinned and moved closer to him, running a hand up his bare chest. "No. Don't know why you bothered with those breeches. We've got a few minutes."

Pateret lived in one of her family's houses outside the main circle of the village, tucked back a short distance into the woods. By the time Creed and Andor arrived, the others were already there. Cardon and Morcah stood outside, looking out over the Sydian and sharing a smoke. Cardon himself didn't smoke: he said it reminded him of the drugs and potions he'd taken. But Morcah had discovered smoking at the Polebray and enjoyed it, and Cardon had recently brought him a sampler of Mahquant smokes as a gift.

The door stood open, and Creed could see Rioletta inside at Pateret's table, studying a book. She had become increasingly withdrawn over the winter and spent most of her time alone, reading and writing notes to herself. Rioletta often confided in Andor, sometimes in his presence, so Creed knew this was partly to avoid Ladon. He knew Ladon had refused to allow her to pursue what she wanted to study, and that he'd denied her requests to travel when and where she wanted.

Rioletta looked up and closed the book, with a finger in it to mark her place, as Creed and Andor entered the house, followed by Cardon and Morcah, still trailing a little smoke.

"Rio!" Creed said. "Brought some things for you. But first, I have a question: do you know what Woodsmen are?"

Rioletta narrowed her eyes and let the book fall closed completely. "I know the stories, much as I know the tales about the Lefollah. Where did you hear about Woodsmen?"

Creed grinned. "From Mynador, and a little from Stolen. I'll tell you the whole story in a minute, but I never found out what they are. I gather they're not firewood cutters, though."

"No," Rioletta said. "Woodsmen show up in a number of myths and tales. They're described as resembling human beings, but smaller, short and round-bodied, with spindly arms and legs. They supposedly don't interface with human society, although of course the tales are about times when they did. I've encountered them in amongst the stories I've found of the Lefollah."

Creed sat in one of Pateret's armchairs and dropped his pack to the floor.

"They supposedly have a peculiar Skill," Rioletta continued. "They're Translocators. That is, they're said to be able to project an image of themselves to some far spot they can see, or perhaps even only imagine, and then transfer their corporeal body to that spot. So they can move great distances very quickly. They disappear and show up suddenly in unexpected locations, and it's said they find great amusement in this. They sometimes appear to humans who are in compromised positions in the woods, and then disappear so quickly that the person is never sure what he actually saw, and can't prove it to his companions. Any prints found in the snow or mud suddenly disappear, and they can't be tracked. Of course, this is all legend. Now, what's the story you heard?"

"Mynador mentioned the Woodsmen while she was talking about a community outside the city who broker trade between the Hyolonal and antiques dealers," Creed explained as the others arranged themselves around the room. "She said they were rumored to broker children. She said they trade with Woodsmen, but I didn't understand what she was talking about. I asked Stolen the next day, but he didn't give me a very good description. His language isn't always the best. He just called them 'beings'. One thing he said: he knows very little about where he came from, but he does know that he was brought to the Lefollah by Woodsmen."

"That is interesting," Rioletta said. "The old stories portray the Woodsmen as baby-snatchers of bad children, threats to make kids behave. But if the Lefollah exist, there may be others we don't know about who exist as well, and the legends could be based in truth. That could explain how the Lefollah obtain human children when they want them."

"Perhaps Stolen was an unwanted Hyolonal child," Pateret said.

"But he has well-developed Skills," Rioletta said. "As far as we know, the Hyolonal don't. Maybe he was kidnapped by the Hyolonal and then sold."

"Shear speculation," Morcah said. "We'll never know unless someone finds a Hyolonal who's willing to tell the story and who knows it in the first place."

"Most likely," Rioletta agreed, "but it's interesting guesswork, anyway. I'd love to know where Stolen came from and who his parents were."

With a round of beer from Morcah's cask, the group settled in to listen to Creed's story of his arrival in Hyolon and the meeting at Hyphanden's house, including the new information about Rudon and his rogues. He told them about the plan to send Duri to the western communities to see if he could locate enclaves of people with knowledge of the Forbidden Technologies.

Andor raised her eyebrows. "Hyphanden trusts Duri with a scheme like that?"

"Kwistocta does, anyway," Creed said. "And of course Duri's a natural traveler and trader. Take a look at these. I got them on trade from him." Creed reached into his pack and removed a small leather bag.

"You traded with Duri?" Andor sneered. "Did you have to have an armed guard as an intermediary?"

Creed shrugged. "I can hold my temper to get things I'm interested in. Besides, he's different now that he has those two minds in his. He knows a lot of Skills, and I'm not so sure I'd want to mess with him. He seems changed, somehow. Anyway, Stolen was there to referee, and Kwistocta was lurking around as well."

"Kwistocta is hardly one I'd describe as lurking," Rioletta said, "but I'm sure she could have stopped any disagreement between the two of you quite quickly."

Creed grinned and carefully spread out a number of arrow tips on the table. They were tiny and multi-colored, finely wrought and translucent.

"Bird points," he said. "Take a look at them. They're much lighter than steel ones. No offense, Morcah. Your mother makes great arrow-points. I'd never trade my elk points! The weight gives them power. But these are made of a type of glass, and they can't be beat for small game. The edge is sharp enough to cut you if you just lay a finger on them. Don't know where Duri got them, he wouldn't say. He gave me a few arrows to haft them, too."

Creed pulled out several shafts and laid them on the table. They were slender and inflexible, of an unfamiliar material. In addition, he had a couple of small knives of the same stone as the bird points.

As everyone crowded around the table to examine them, Creed leaned back in his chair and reached into his pack once again.

"These are from Hyphanden, Rio," he said in a lowered voice, as he handed several small, thin volumes to Rioletta. She took them and flipped the cover of the top one open. Creed looked over her arm.

"*Regards, from Stelaphandon*," was written inside in a scrawling, old-fashioned cursive. She snapped the cover shut.

"Did Hyphanden like the Index?" she asked. She covered the books with the one she'd brought.

"Of course," Creed answered. "Kwistocta a little less so. There's some tension between them. Phando told me privately that she gets upset every time he accesses Stelaphandon's mind, so he usually doesn't tell her anymore. And he hasn't told her that he's accessed a couple of the other minds a time or two, either. I heard him lie about it while I was there."

"I don't blame her for her apprehension. It's a dangerous practice," Rioletta said. "As a Loremaster I appreciate his thirst for knowledge, particularly about the background of the Dispersal, but it's a risky way to obtain it. And he should not be lying to Kwistocta."

"Granted, but I think he's developed a good relationship with Stela," Creed said. "Their minds mesh easily. He's discovered

30

something he thinks is important, but he wouldn't tell me. He wants to tell you in person."

"I wonder why me?" Rioletta mused.

"You know there aren't any other Loremasters in Hyolon. Your kind is rare. That's probably part of it. He feels like he has some kind of connection with you."

Rioletta sighed and slipped the books into her satchel. "Even if Stelaphandon is trustworthy, the others might not be. At least he can't access the Crypt of Souls without the Key, which ought to be comforting to Kwistocta. He can only access those in his own box."

"Yes, Hyphanden's box," Creed said with a grim smile. "Who knows what he might learn from it? The question is, do we want to know?"

The group fell to discussing Rudon's possible plans and the confirmation that he was using Forbidden Technology to control the Hyolonal.

"Kerdahl's relaxed a little bit," Creed said. "At least he's revealed to Hyphanden and the rest of the Council that he has a contact within Rudon's rogues."

"I wonder who Kerdahl's contact is?" Rioletta mused. "He never told me."

"Better we don't know," Andor said. "The fewer who know, the safer the person. But I'll wager it's someone Kerdahl knew personally who was Outcast at some point, likely a relative. It's not unusual for a family to keep in touch, despite Outcasting. A true Outcast would be a natural ally for Rudon, especially if there was some trauma associated with it, like Skill Stripping. Such people become rogues more often than those who escape Outcasting intact. Rudon would trust a person like that, but family ties might make for a stronger allegiance."

Morcah unbuckled a round leather case he'd carried in with him and brought out another small cask of his family's beer. This was darker than the first brew, and stronger. With glasses refilled all around, they discussed the new glass plates and the greenhouse plans, and the prospect of having some fresh vegetables during the winter months.

"All hail to Andor, who opened the door to trade with Dobor," Morcah said, raising his glass.

"And Rioletta, who's maintaining it," Andor replied with a grin.

"I won't be, if I don't get to see Nikal a little more often," Rioletta said morosely, fingering her talisman and the Hyolon amplifier around her neck.

"Any chance Stetsordahl will call you back soon?" Creed asked sympathetically.

Rioletta shrugged. "I don't know. Nikal asked him to intervene last time. Stetsor's taken a liking to me for some reason, perhaps because I brought him news of Hyphanden. I think it makes him feel better to know that Phando's had a good life. I brought him news of his grandson, too, of course. I promised to tell him if I heard anything else."

"Stetsor the younger is fine," Creed said. "I saw him at the Council meeting at Hyphanden's."

"I'll pass it on when I can," Rioletta said. "I hope for another trip of that sort. Stetsor arranged for a nice room in an inn near the river, and Nikal and I crossed the Rhamphor one day and rode down towards Polebray. Everything was on Stetsor's bill."

"I wonder how Stetsor's getting his money, now that he's not leading a Council?" Creed mused.

"I think he has a bit socked away," Rioletta said. "The First Chosen allowed him and the other Council members to collect their belongings from the Council-house. That was probably a mistake on their part."

"Any rumblings of a return to Tabor?" Andor asked.

Rioletta shook her head. "I don't think it's going to happen. The First Chosen is firmly ensconced there now, and business is proceeding as usual. Trade is probably better than it was, given the integration of the Council of Tane. Most people probably don't care enough about the change in power to support an uprising."

Several rounds of beer later, Creed began to drowse in his chair. Andor ruffled his hair to awaken him. He looked up at her sleepily.

"You're exhausted. Why don't you go on home? I'll be there in a bit."

"To your house?" Creed asked.

"Of course," Andor said. "Don't forget your pack."

Creed heaved himself up. The stress of the last few days, coupled with sleeping out, eating strange food, and drinking quite a few beers, was taking its toll. He took his pack, now divested of the dangerous books from Hyphanden, and slung it over one shoulder. He closed Pateret's door behind him and stood for a moment letting his eyes adjust to the dark. There were still lights in most of the windows in Andolith, and he navigated towards them, with the hulk of the Contemplation to his right.

Suddenly a dark figure stepped out in front of him. Creed stopped short, a burst of adrenalin focusing his senses. He dropped his pack instantly and reached for his bow, but he had left it at Andor's and it was not slung over his back.

"Good evening, Creed," Ladon's voice said from the shadows. "Glad to see you made it back. It took you a day longer than I'd figured it would."

Creed let his breath out. Ladon was no danger, but he was Creed's uncle, an elder in his family, and the Leader of the Elder Council as well. Creed had hoped to avoid him, at least until he was well rested. Ladon was a Negotiator and Interrogator with a reputation for prying information out of people, and Creed was vulnerable even when not exhausted and intoxicated.

"The going was hard," Creed said. "The road's a lot rougher than you ever notice when you're not carrying glass. I figured it was better to take my time and arrive here with a full load of glass rather than risk any breakage."

"And you were successful, I hear. I'll take a look at it myself tomorrow. We'll get a group together to put it up and work on sealing the joints. I thank you on behalf of the people of Andolith for your service. I'll recognize you at the next public Council meeting." Ladon bowed slightly.

"You're welcome," Creed replied. Now he felt guilty for avoiding his uncle, who apparently only wanted to thank him.

"Interesting group of people you're leaving there," Ladon said more casually, looking over Creed's shoulder. "The Younger Council: Rioletta, Andor, Pateret, Morcah. And yourself and Cardon."

"My best friends, welcoming me back and celebrating the fact that the glass arrived intact," Creed said diplomatically, wishing he hadn't had quite as much beer. It occurred to him that Ladon must have been watching for some time to know who was in the house.

"Ah, yes, of course. How's Nikal of Dobor?"

"Good, fine."

"Adla Kathreftis? You saw her, I'm sure."

"Yes, she's good. She sent special greetings to Cardon."

"Interesting! And Edeowie of the Council?" Ladon probed, naming the Council-members of Dobor and pausing just long enough after each for Creed to answer him automatically. "Palagon? Tektal? Stektal? Stolen?"

"Fine, fine, fine, fine… " Creed stopped and swore an oath under his breath as he realized he'd agreed that Stolen was fine.

"I think you and I need to talk," Ladon said, clapping a heavy hand on Creed's shoulder.

"Ladon, I met Stolen in Dobor," Creed lied. "He and Durigon Cautes have been trading in the area to support the Outcasts. They just happened to be at Nikal's when I got there. They're not Outcasts themselves, neither one of them, nor are they Sorcerers. They travel freely, and I didn't see any reason I shouldn't have a drink with old friends, or at least one old friend."

Ladon let a moment go by while Creed held his breath. "What if I looked in your pack? Anything I might find interesting?"

Creed quickly picked up his pack and handed it to Ladon. "No, only glass arrow points I traded for with Duri. You're welcome to look at them, or I'll show you tomorrow."

"Well," Ladon said after another moment, "you're tired and your mind is addled with beer, so it's difficult to know if you're telling me the truth or not. If I discover you went to Hyolon, I'll be more than a little upset. Go on now, I'll want to hear news of Stolen in the morning."

Creed hurriedly headed off towards Andor's house, leaving Ladon behind. He could only hope Ladon wouldn't listen at Pateret's house. Going back to warn them would be too suspicious. But they had ceased talking about Hyolon, anyway, and had been discussing other more mundane things when he left.

34

Chapter Four: The Challenge (Rioletta)

Rioletta banged around in her kitchen irritably. She'd been up late the night before at Pateret's, but as usual she hadn't been able to sleep past dawn. She'd been in a bad mood lately anyway. She had only been able to see Nikal once that winter, and that had only been due to the intervention of Stetsor. Her talks with Nikal through the talisman were brief and unsatisfactory; she didn't seem to be getting much better at sustaining the connection. Nikal had told her many times that her mind was apt for Monitoring and Viewing, but she was beginning to think he was just flattering her. She fingered the amplifier she'd picked up in Hyolon. It snuggled up against her talisman on the chain and glowed a faint blue around the edges, but it didn't seem to improve communication. Nikal had looked at it again in West Ford and said he wasn't sure what it actually was.

The books she'd received from Hyphanden, or Stelaphandon as it might be, sat unopened on her kitchen table. She knew she wasn't going to have time to read them that morning. All the residents of Andolith were expected to turn out to help assemble the greenhouse. She couldn't very well leave them lying around, though. Ladon had been increasingly suspicious of her and it wouldn't be beyond him, she thought, to have a quick look in her house.

She pulled a small wooden chest out from under one of the kitchen counters and put the books in it on top of a pile of other documents, scrolls, and records she wasn't supposed to have. It wasn't a very secure hiding spot, but she had few options in her little cottage. What she really needed was a locking Skill on the chest, maybe with an alarm that would be translated through her talisman to alert her if anyone was trying to get into it. But she wasn't good at lock Skills. For that, she'd have to go to Pateret.

35

It was still early, but Rioletta headed for Pateret's house anyway. Perhaps she'd be up. As she neared the house she saw Pateret come out of the door, shouldering a pack.

"Good morning," Rioletta called out. Pateret looked up and pulled the door shut. "Are you going to the greenhouse raising?"

Pateret shook her head. "The wind machines. It's maintenance day."

"Oh, yes." The wind-machines had to be checked each week, or more often if the weather was bad. They were vital to Andolith, and had to be oiled, examined, and maintained routinely. "Do you mind if I walk along with you? I have something I want to discuss."

Pateret nodded and turned to the path that led behind her house and wound around the southern foot of the Contemplation. The two walked in silence for a while in the cool of the morning. The trail became more narrow and rockier the further from the village they went. It wandered up a narrow drainage, then began a series of switchbacks up the face of a ridge looming behind the Contemplation.

Rioletta's breath came shorter as they climbed. She watched Pateret walk steadily ahead of her, leaning forward against the weight of the pack with her hands hooked into the shoulder straps. It had been nearly two years since Pateret had been burned in the conflagration that claimed her aunt's life at Tabor, and few obvious traces of her scars remained, but she habitually wore tight leather gloves with the fingers cut short and a high, snug white collar beneath her pastel shirt. Her pale blonde hair had grown back, although it was not as long as it once had been.

Pateret stopped suddenly and looked up the trail. "You know, it's funny. Creed told us about those Woodsmen he heard about in Hyolon, and it reminded me of something. Two weeks ago I was up here and I heard a strange sound. It was very close and staccato, like a woodpecker. I turned around and saw just a flash in the woods. Then the sound seemed to come again, but from a distance away. I couldn't figure out what it was. It was odd."

"Did you see anything else?" Rioletta asked.

"No. I had a creepy feeling that I was being watched, but I think it was just my imagination. It was probably some bird." Pateret readjusted the pack and started off again.

Eventually the trail leveled out and they arrived on top. Rioletta stopped to catch her breath and looked up at the wind machines.

The towers were higher than the tallest trees of the forest below, with feet sunk deep into the bare rock of the ridge-top. Huge vanes, each as long as five men laid foot to head, swung down dangerously, changing the tenor of the constant wind. Each tower had three vanes. Rioletta understood enough to know that more caused interference from the eddy of air behind each vane, decreasing the efficiency. The towers were enclosed, so even in the winter the mechanisms were protected, and Pateret, or others of the Latrocin family, could work inside the shaft of the tower or in the small room below in relative comfort.

Pateret pulled out a leather roll of tools. Many of the larger tools were kept in one of the rooms beneath the first tower, but she had brought a few of her own favorites with her.

"Nice craftsmanship," Rioletta noted as Pateret unrolled the leather on a ledge of rock.

"Some of these were specially fashioned for me. Others are antiques, passed down through my family since before the Dispersal," Pateret replied.

She approached the northernmost tower and unlocked the door leading into the tower shaft and machine room with a key from a set she carried on her belt. The machine room was down three steps, bored into the rock, with the feet of the tower embedded on either side of it. Pateret disconnected the machinery within and set the brake for the vanes.

Rioletta sat down on the top step. "I was wondering if you could help me work a locking Skill," she said.

"Probably. Is it something difficult to lock?"

"No, it's a little wooden chest. I'm just not very good at lock Skills."

Pateret glanced at Rioletta swiftly, but did not reply. She worked steadily but not hurriedly, checking the joints and hubs and each tooth of each gear for wear. With a fine file, she buffed out a few burrs on a gear tooth or two, blew the slivers away, and wiped the gear clean with a rag. Then she reset the mechanism and allowed the machine to re-engage the blades to return it to service.

"Who is it you want to lock out?" she finally asked. "It makes a difference as to what kind of lock Skill to use."

"You can guess," Rioletta said wryly. "You've seen what things have been like for me this winter."

"So you want to keep Ladon out."

Rioletta sighed. "You can refuse if you want and I won't hold it against you. I don't mean to make you into a conspirator."

Pateret opened the room beneath the second tower, disengaged the vanes and performed the same tasks there as she had at the first. Rioletta patiently let her do her work. She watched Pateret disable several Protections and unlock a cabinet that was disguised to look like part of the rock. From inside she removed another key. Then she moved on to the third tower.

This tower was slightly different: it was sunk into the rock where a lip rose to one side, and thus the door was smaller and lower. Pateret knelt to access the lock. Of course, this tower was different for another reason as well, one not so obvious. Rioletta knew it was where the Key to the Crypt of Souls was stored. The book had been hidden in a Concealed compartment in the rock with multiple Protections around it. The Protections had been set by several members of the Council, each providing his or her own shell of Skill. It would take all of them, or else a very accomplished Sorcerer and Skill-breaker, to find and retrieve the book.

Finally Pateret turned to Rioletta. "Are you going to help raise the greenhouse?"

"Well, yes, I guess I'm expected to," Rioletta said.

"Then I'll stop by this evening. And if you need help linking an alarm to your talisman, I can help with that, too."

Rioletta smiled. She hadn't been sure Pateret would agree. Pateret often had to think things over carefully, but Rioletta had noticed that she often came down on the side of stretching the boundaries.

It was much faster going down the path than it had been going up. Rioletta reached the bottom in a few minutes, passed Pateret's house and the waterwheel, and followed the Sydian down to the gardens.

The greenhouse took shape slowly. Rioletta pitched in where she could, sorting connectors and reading directions. By lunchtime, the sides had been placed and connected to the frame. The work was hard and exacting, and everyone was ready for a break.

Those not working on the building had prepared lunch. Rioletta, Andor, Creed, and Cardon made their way along a line of tables set up in the garden. With laden plates, they moved towards the bank of the Sydian to find rocks to sit upon.

"Morcah!" Rioletta called. "Join us for lunch!"

Morcah shook his head. "Thanks, but I'll take lunch with Pateret. She should be done with the wind-machines by now."

Rioletta nodded. Morcah was in the habit of taking lunch with Pateret, and no doubt he wanted to relax in the cool of her shaded stone house as well. It was a warm day, and his black hair and dark skin absorbed heat. He had stripped down to his lightweight under-singlet, but still she could see that he wiped sweat away from his forehead as he hiked back to the village.

Ten minutes later, Rioletta was surprised to see Morcah hiking up the trail to the ridge where the wind-machines were set. A section of the trail was visible from the gardens, before it wound behind the Contemplation.

"I wonder why Morcah's going up to the generators?" she said, nudging Andor. "Do you suppose there's something wrong?"

Andor squinted at the machines. "All four of them are spinning. Maybe there's some minor problem. You know how Pateret is. She'll work at it until she gets it exactly and precisely right. Morcah's probably bringing her lunch and a drink. If there is something going on, he's the one to help her fix it."

Rioletta turned away to finish her lunch. Upstream, she could see Ladon and Tannon, who had been eating together by the water-works. Ladon rose and the two of them began to make their way back down to the garden. Rioletta sighed. That was the signal to get back to work.

But at that moment she heard a yell from the distance. Ladon and Tannon stopped in their tracks and turned towards the village.

39

A number of other people paused and looked as well. There was a stronger shout.

Ladon and Tannon began to run towards the village. Others began to run up the hill from the gardens. Rioletta joined them, not knowing what she was running towards, following Ladon's lead towards the Latrocin compound.

As she neared Pateret's house, Rioletta saw Morcah coming down the last part of the trail from the wind-machines. He carried Pateret's limp body in his arms. Ladon and Tannon reached him, but he shouldered them aside.

"Get Charnia!" Morcah yelled. He brought Pateret around her own house to the door and shoved it open with his foot. He carried Pateret inside and laid her on the couch. He smoothed her hair away from her face and bent over her, listening to her breathing.

"Do you know what happened?" Rioletta asked. She took Pateret's wrist to feel her pulse. She was relieved to see her chest rise and fall. "Perhaps she's had a reaction to an insect bite, or some other illness has come over her. But she seemed fine when I was up there not long ago."

Morcah puffed, still catching his breath. "The Key to the Crypt is gone, Rio. This was an attack, not an accident."

Rioletta turned sharply to meet his eyes. "How do you know?"

"I haven't trained to be a Sorcerer for nothing," Morcah snapped. "I managed to keep my head together well enough to check the area for my own safety. She was lying right outside the third tower. I could see the niche standing open. Besides, I set one of the Protections myself, and I could feel that it was broken."

Rioletta turned back quickly to Pateret, trying to concentrate on the situation in front of her rather than dwelling on the implications of the missing Key. Pateret must have been attacked just minutes after she left. She realized with a jolt of adrenalin how close she must have come to being assaulted herself.

Charnia pushed her way past the onlookers who were beginning to gather around the doorway, with Cardon carrying her bag. She bent over the couch.

"A Skill, and something else more deadly and more physical," she said. Rioletta grabbed a short stool and positioned it for the old Healer to sit upon. Charnia leaned forward and examined Pateret

40

more closely, running her hands gently down Pateret's arms and around her neck and head.

She pointed out a small wound on the top of Pateret's shoulder, near her neck. "Something has been inserted here, possibly a poison."

Charnia examined the area without touching it, squinting as she did so. "Someone knocked her unconscious, then inserted some object here. It seems an odd thing to do, if the idea was simply to get her out of the way. Why she wasn't killed outright, I'm not sure, but we must certainly remove this if we are to save her."

Cardon reached for a small, sharp steel knife in Charnia's bag.

"No!" Charnia cried sharply, throwing her hand out to stop him. "I perceive a Skill placed upon this object: a cruel one, and abhorrent. It's one I haven't encountered in many, many years, but I recognize it still. The touch of a metal blade will kill her. And yet, the object itself will certainly kill her slowly. It must be removed."

"But how are we to remove it, then?" Cardon asked, quickly putting the knife away. "Can you call it out, or cause it to remove itself?"

Charnia shook her head. "I have not that Skill, even if the object would respond to such a request. It must be cut out, and quickly, but we cannot use metal to do so. Undoubtedly her assailant meant it thus: that we would kill her ourselves, or be unable to save her. Thus her death would not be at his hands. I will have to consider what we are to do."

But Rioletta jumped up suddenly. "Creed's bird points!" she exclaimed. "They are made of glass and stone, and he had knives of the same material. Will they work, do you think, Charnia?"

"Yes, glass or stone will work, I believe," Charnia said. "But blades of such material, with no metal attaching them, are extremely rare. Fetch them quickly and we shall see!"

Rioletta turned and ran from the room. Outside, Creed stood nearby.

"Creed! Your bird points! Or better yet, the glass knives you got from Duri – do you have them?"

41

"They're still in my pack," Creed replied, slinging it off his back. He dug in the pack and gave the knives to Rioletta. She hurried back inside and handed one of them to Charnia. It didn't appear to have any metal at all upon it, having been hafted with a strange binding material fastened without bolts or screws.

Charnia looked it over quickly and ran a finger along it. The blade was exceedingly sharp, and a thin line appeared on her skin. Quickly she made an incision in the place where the mark was visible upon Pateret's shoulder, and using the tip of the blade, scooped out a tiny capsule. Cardon received it on a piece of leather and wrapped it securely.

"There is little more we can do at this point," Charnia said to Morcah and Pateret's family, who had gathered around. "Cardon and I will stay with her and provide her with such medicines and potions as we can. I'll see what I can discover about this object and its effects. We'll examine her for any further hurt that has been done. It's possible a person vindictive enough to do this has left other wounds."

"I'll stay, too," Morcah said. "Perhaps she'll gain enough consciousness to give us a description of who did this to her."

"It's obvious who it must have been, Morcah," Rioletta said as she rose from where she knelt next to the couch. "If the Key is gone, it was most likely Rudon himself. Rudon is a known Skill-breaker. I doubt many others would have the capacity to break a series of Protections in the time in which he must have done it. Any description would be useless at this point, anyway. He is doubtless on his way back to the Ruined City, with the Book."

"Then we should ride after him!" Morcah said heatedly. "Several of us with good Skills will be a match for this monster. I'm ready to go! Let's not allow him to escape!"

Rioletta put a hand on his arm. "You haven't met Rudon, Morcah, but his Skills are such that he could overpower all of us in this village at once."

"Riding after him is bold, but also stupid," Cardon agreed. "Morcah, rushing off after Rudon is not the way to avenge this injury. Even if it's not Rudon himself, it's almost certainly one who is associated with him. It could even be a group of rogue Sorcerers. They have Skills we can't anticipate or imagine. There are others who are stronger and will be more able to confront him than we are, although our help would surely add to their strength." He glanced at Ladon, but Ladon turned away from him.

"Some of you should go and finish the wind-machines," Ladon said, addressing Pateret's kin. "Do not go alone, although I suspect the perpetrator is long gone. I want to assemble the Councils to discuss this matter. We'll meet in an hour in the Council-house."

Ladon turned and strode away towards the village, but Rioletta caught up to him. "If we can't ride after Rudon, then at least we know where he's going. Hyphanden and his Council must be notified at once!"

"I will not notify Hyphanden of anything," Ladon said. He continued to walk. "He is an Outcast, and I have no business with him. This is a member of our community who has been attacked, and it is our business alone."

"It is far more than our business, and we will have to involve others if you intend to bring any justice to Rudon. He will go to the Ruined City and be out of our reach. Hyphanden must know. He is the only one who can help us."

"I will not request help from an Outcast," Ladon sneered. "The Councils will meet and discuss what we are to do, but it will not include any interface with Hyphanden or any other of his ilk."

"Hyphanden has not shown himself to be anything but honorable," Rioletta said angrily. "Do you deny the help he provided us last summer?"

"Whether or not he provided you with help is open for debate," Ladon snarled. "The task you undertook was Forbidden. I did not give permission for it, and Cardon's ills could have been solved in another way."

"Exactly how? There was only one solution, the one we took. Besides, our actions freed others who were imprisoned!"

"Imprisoned through their own actions and faults. And now, as you yourself told me, Hyphanden has in his possession and accesses at will those "others", as you call them. I will allow no further contact with him."

"If you won't notify him, I will!" Rioletta fumed, brushing past him.

Ladon grabbed her roughly by one arm and spun her around to face him in the village square.

"You are in contact with Hyphanden?" he demanded.

"No, but I could be!" Rioletta replied.

"You are not to contact him or any other Outcast in any way," Ladon commanded. "You yourself know that it is an Outcast who has done this!"

"Rudon is no associate of Hyphanden! He will go to the Crypt of Souls. He is well aware of how to open it, and now he has the means at his disposal! Do you really want to risk him freeing hundreds of minds that have been contained since before the Dispersal? Hyphanden may be able to stop him, but not if he doesn't know. If Rudon accesses those minds, his power will be unimaginable! Do you not know that he holds a grudge against the Council at Tabor?"

"It is not our business what happens to the Council at Tabor," Ladon said. "We have involved ourselves in their business once already. We will go no further."

"Many innocent lives may be lost if Rudon is not confronted," Rioletta argued. "You're the one who opened our trade relations with communities in the Tadian from whom we've been estranged for generations! Do you now abandon them to their fate? Do you now suddenly regret your policies?"

Rioletta became aware as she spoke that a crowd had gathered around them as they argued in the square. But she was not dissuaded. The argument with Ladon was long in coming.

"Yes, once when I was new to this position I made the decision to ride to the aid of the Elders of Tabor, and Tereret was lost," Ladon replied, his voice husky. "I will never forgive myself for that. She was one I had known since childhood, since infancy, a member of my own Council. I will not make the same mistake again. It is the policy of this Council not to become involved in the affairs of others, and I forbid contact with the Outcasts, even and including in this situation."

"You make this decision in the absence of the rest of the Council," Rioletta pointed out.

"The Elder Council sees clearly the path we are upon," Ladon asserted.

"A path that refuses to ally with defenders against the attacker of one of our own people? Is this truly the path upon which you wish to lead Andolith? Can you ignore the information the Younger Council is now aware of, the changes that have come upon this region in recent years?"

"Nothing has changed," Ladon insisted. "The interpretation of the Charter is still clear. The path you suggest turns us away from a tradition that has guided us for more than a hundred years, and it will not be done under my leadership!"

"Then I Challenge your leadership!" Rioletta shouted. "Let it be decided by the whole of the citizenship of Andolith!"

Ladon blanched and fell silent. Rioletta felt an immediate surge of regret. She had not truly meant to Challenge Ladon. A Challenge was a formal event, provided for by the Charter of Dispersal, and the outcome could result in either the overthrow of the Elder Council, or the Outcasting of the Challenger and any who supported her.

Ladon stood stiffly before her. "You are relieved of responsibility to me. I accept your Challenge, as I must according to the rules enumerated in the Charter," he said formally.

"Ladon, I do not desire leadership of the Council," Rioletta said, calming her voice. "Even if such a Challenge were affirmed, I would not take it. I only want consideration of a different path. The times that are coming will require it, as this event plainly shows."

"You have made the Challenge, and thus the direction this community will take is in the hands of the people. But if the Elder Council prevails, I will not be tolerant."

"I understand," Rioletta said bitterly. She turned abruptly and stalked off towards her house, her heart pounding. Andor quickly joined her.

"The Younger Council will support your Challenge," Andor said. "Ladon's direction must change. I believe we will be able to show it sufficiently to the citizens of Andolith, and prevail."

"I did not intend to Challenge him," Rioletta said. She realized she was shaking.

"It's not surprising, given how he's treated you this past winter," Andor said.

45

"He's only trying to protect the citizens of this village. He bears the loss of Tereret hard. It seems there has been an air of chaos around me all my life. Perhaps it would be better if I were to leave Andolith and the Council anyway."

"Don't be a fool," Andor replied. "Abandoning Andolith to its fate when you truly believe you see a different way would be irresponsible. The Younger Council has seen many things Ladon has not, and whether the time to turn our course is now or will come later, our direction cannot ever be his."

"You have no obligation to me." Rioletta turned to face Andor at the corner of her house. "I made the Challenge alone. I do not expect anyone to stand with me. It would be best if you stood aside, or with the Elder Council. You have a good life here, as do Morcah and Pateret. Don't ruin it by picking up my problem. It is mine alone."

"I was with you in Hyolon," Andor pointed out. "I know what led you in this direction. I rode with you to the Grove of the Lefollah. You are right, change is in the air, and we must rise to face it before it comes upon us. It is no longer possible for us to stand alone in isolation from one another. We must stand together, or Rudon and others like him will take advantage of our seclusion and we will fall, one community at a time. Now is the time to face Rudon, before he obtains what he desires, and we can do so only with the help of Hyphanden and the Outcast Council. We will stand with you, and should we lose the Challenge, we will ride with you to Hyolon to support the Outcasts."

"Whether we lose or win, we will likely ride to Hyolon," Rioletta pointed out. "You cannot speak for the rest of the Younger Council, but I appreciate your support."

"Will you contact Hyphanden now and warn him, as you said?" Andor pressed. "Have you indeed been in contact with him?"

Rioletta hesitated. "I have not been in direct contact with him, the way I communicate with Nikal," she said. "But I'm sure I can be." She went to a shelf in her front room and removed a talisman carved as a small dog, curled up, with bright, jeweled eyes. It was an antique from Hyolon, given her by Hyphanden.

She sat down heavily upon a chair and stared at the talisman. She had never used a talisman to communicate with anyone but Nikal, but she was fairly sure this one had been primed for communication with Hyphanden. From time to time, when she thought about him, as she had done a number of times over the winter, she could feel his presence as though he stood in the room. She looked into the little dog's eyes and cleared her mind.

In a few minutes she looked up at Andor, who had remained silently by the door.

"Hyphanden has been warned," she said. "And I will be welcome in Hyolon if my Challenge does not succeed."

Chapter Five: The Unskilled Lands (Duri)

Duri rolled off Porbruten's couch the next morning feeling sick. His carefully constructed inebriation partition was gone, as were all the partitions in his mind. Without them, he suffered from the full effects of Hyphanden's particularly powerful wine.

Porbruten was not to be seen. Duri got to his feet and poked around in the kitchen, looking for something to absorb the acid in his stomach and take the taste out of his mouth.

"*Nice hangover you've got us,*" Malbec growled in his head.

"*I hate hangovers,*" Chasan whined.

"Shut up," Duri said, then realized he probably didn't need to talk out loud to himself. "*Shut up,*" he thought deliberately.

Porbruten was fortunately a connoisseur of good bread, and Duri soon found several solid, square rolls and some hard cheese. The water from Porbruten's tap was cold, clear, mountain spring water. He sat down on the couch with a tall glass and a sliced roll filled with cheese. Soon he began to feel a little better, although his attention kept jumping from one part of his mind to another, and his view of the world seemed to alternate between Chasan's, Malbec's, and his own.

When he was done with his breakfast, he checked to make sure all his knives were secure, straightened his clothes, slung his shoulder satchel, and made his way out of Porbruten's quarters into the storefront. He scanned the contents of the shop briefly, then moved to the big glass knife case in front of Porbruten's door. The case was locked, but he soon found the key hanging behind the small "Potions" sign. He slid the back glass door aside and took each knife out. Then he carefully examined the shelf and bottom of the case. His fingers slid gently over the worn fabric put down to cushion the blades until he found the latch, just like in the case in the West Ford shop where he'd been apprenticed. He felt the shelf

49

release as he pressed the latch, and carefully pulled it up on hidden hinges.

In the hidden compartment were two more devices like the one Porbruten had shown him the night before. Duri stowed both of them in his satchel. He closed the lid and re-arranged the fabric. He put each knife back exactly as he'd found it, after having a good look at the blade and hilt, the hafting technique and grind, and any inscriptions or scrollwork on the blade or handle. A few of them gave him clues to their origins, and he mentally catalogued them.

Duri took a quick look around the rest of the shop, but nothing else caught his eye. He opened the front door carefully without allowing the bell on the door handle to ring, and closed it quietly behind him. He walked to the inn rather than hiring a cart, hoping the morning air and exercise would clear his head.

"You'll want to check on the horses," Malbec suggested. *"Never trust an inn."*

"I've been here before, and I trust them," Duri snapped. Nevertheless, he found himself at the inn's stables. The horses were in good shape, rested, groomed, and fed. His tack had been carefully hung away from rodents and his saddle blankets had been set out in the sun to air and dry. Duri checked their feet, but the hooves had been picked clean, and the yard was sandy and dry.

"I told you so," he reproached Malbec, accidentally out loud. A stable-hand gave him a funny look, and Duri scowled in reply. He retreated hastily to his room.

He washed up, swallowed some headache powders, and laid out a change of clothes. *"That green shirt is nice,"* Chasan suggested. *"I prefer the brown one,"* Malbec contradicted. Duri preferred the brown one as well, but when he looked down he discovered he was wearing the green one.

"Damn," he swore to himself. It was obvious that something would have to be done.

He sat down on his bed and removed the two devices he'd taken from Porbruten's place. The feeling he had had the night before when he'd turned Porbruten's on had been exquisite, and it occurred to him that with a little work he might be able to use it to more fully integrate Malbec and Chasan. Then again, he wasn't sure that was what he wanted to do. The idea was a little scary.

He weighed one of the devices indecisively in his hand for a moment, then punched the button on the front. Once again he felt the vibration, and the map flashed onto the screen. He kept his thumb over the power button, and allowed only a few seconds to pass while the waves of connection washed through his mind. With some effort, he punched the button again, and shuddered as the device shut down.

It took a few moments for him to return fully to his surroundings. Turning the device off was unpleasant, but he felt a certain smoothing in his mind, a calming of the two others within him. It would certainly be worth experimenting with, and this was, after all, part of what he'd been sent to find. He would return with valuable information for Hyphanden and the Outcast Council if he could figure out specifically how the devices worked.

Deep in the night hours, after Duri had finally convinced him that he was truly interested in trading Forbidden Technology, Porbruten had made him a promise. If he was good on his word, he would eventually arrive at the inn. Duri availed himself of the inn's library and chose a book to read under a tree in the yard, where chairs and tables were scattered about for the use of guests. He checked several times to make sure he'd picked up one he, himself, wanted to read. He looked up every time he heard a cart or horse arrive. By noon Porbruten was not there and Duri had lunch in the dining hall. He was beginning to wonder if he was going to have to make another trip downtown when he heard Porbruten's voice and saw one of the valets lead a stocky horse around to the hitching rail.

It took only a few minutes for Duri to call for his horses and pack his gear. He was ready before Porbruten had finished a noontime beer.

Porbruten led them out of town for a short distance, then turned aside on a well-maintained paved path cutting obliquely along the side of a ridge. The horses' hooves clacked on the stones, but they maintained a good pace despite the incline. At the top of the ridge they came to a pavilion with seats and tables.

"City park, nice view," Porbruten gestured. He was somewhat less talkative this morning. He rode past the pavilion and off the pavement onto the grass. The signs of civilization faded quickly away, and pines began to fill in around small meadows. Grey rocks poked out of the thin soil, and they encountered occasional clear mountain streams.

"This place we're going, will they be accepting of us, or should I be prepared to defend myself?" Duri asked.

Porbruten laughed. "Oh, they know me well enough! I've brought trade goods to them for years. They can't obtain some of this stuff themselves, being not only completely Unskilled but also users of questionable Technology. Besides, they shouldn't present any problem for a true Sorcerer."

"I'm not a Sorcerer," Duri said once again.

"*But we are,*" Malbec chortled. "*You have all our Skills now, both mine and Chasan's. We could show this charlatan a trick or two.*"

"*Now's not the time,*" Duri thought.

"*And what if I think it is? I've been itching to do something. This living without a body is getting old. Let's see what I can do!*"

Duri rode along for a moment, but barely a twitch bothered him. After a while he grinned. *"It seems I retain majority control over my body."*

"*Hmmph,*" Malbec grunted, but he fell silent.

Porbruten had been musing. "On the other hand, they're a picky lot. They want no truck with Sorcerers, have some sort of superstitious beliefs about the Skilled in general. They tolerate me only as a trader and a source of information. It won't do for you to be obvious with the extent of your Skills."

Duri digested that information and wondered how not to be obvious. He ended up simply hoping that the Unskilled couldn't sense his powers. He had had contact with many of the Unskilled during his travels, but he wasn't particularly familiar with their culture. He'd never been to a settlement that was strictly inhabited by the Unskilled. Neither Malbec nor Chasan were any help on that front.

They rode throughout the afternoon, through a succession of meadows and pine forests. Duri used his own mapping device to

52

track their progress, but it was not a complicated route, and he could easily remember the way even without a marked trail.

"We'll camp over the next rise," Porbruten said. "There's a nice valley with a stream for the horses and the ground's not too soggy. Tomorrow we'll come over this range and start down. There are a series of ranges in here, like wrinkles. Rough country."

The campsite was good, as Porbruten had claimed. Porbruten drank generously from a couple of flasks he'd brought, but when he offered one to Duri, Duri declined. The combination of vigilance and the shifting viewpoints and competing thoughts within his mind were exhausting, and he needed a good night's sleep unaffected by alcohol. He considered whether rather than integration, he could re-create at least one partition in his mind, but as soon as that thought formed, Malbec yanked his attention like a short leash.

"Oh no you don't. No partitions for us. You don't know what it's like to be closed down like someone in uneasy dreams until you're wanted. We're staying right where we are now. And you can't hide your plans from us! We know everything you know or imagine. Relax and enjoy it. Think of all the Skills you've got now: all the Skills of an inducted Younger Council Sorcerer of Tabor, plus a few of the Forbidden Ones. You don't want to put that on the shelf, now, do you?"

Duri quit arguing for the time being, but the original rush of exhilaration had passed, and now it was beginning to rub his mind raw. He couldn't risk trying to use the stolen devices in Porbruten's presence. He thought about Hyphanden, who had originally taken Malbec's mind and the mind of Marsavrina into his, with little preparation. Hyphanden had managed to hold those minds apart for long enough to be able to store them in his box, but now Malbec had experience with having been partitioned and stored, and Duri had not near the mental discipline of Hyphanden or Kwistocta. More unhappily, his thoughts turned to Cardon, for whom even short-term storage of the minds from the Crypt had nearly proved disastrous.

The following morning Duri awoke feeling a bit better, although he couldn't tell if it was because he was more successfully ignoring Malbec and Chasan, or because they were both more fully integrated with his own mind. They crested the mountain range early in the morning. The wind was chill, but they paused for a minute to look over the landscape. In front of them and far below, trending to the west, lay a deep, broad basin. Beyond the basin another range equal in height to the one they had crossed rose sharply, and beyond that the tops of a series of other ranges could be seen.

Far below, Duri could see what appeared to be a small settlement with a few trails winding in and out of it. A light haze hung over the basin. Tendrils of smoke rose from a few chimneys.

They started down the steep slope and soon found a narrow trail which became more developed as they worked their way through boulders and over rocky fields. Eventually they reached the basin floor. The trail continued towards the settlement they'd seen from the top of the ridge. They wound among gullies and hills of gravel washed out from the mountains by flash floods and heavy rains. To their right, ridges of multi-colored eroding minerals sloped down.

The road passed a pile of rusting machinery, and around the end of the next ridge they encountered a ravine obviously excavated by human action. At the head of the ravine stood a small factory with the appearance of a distillery. Several chimneys protruded from its roof, and there was a heavy, biting odor in the air. No one appeared to be working there, but the area behind the factory and closest to the ravine was piled with black slabs and chunks of a dark platy material, excavated from the hillside. A row of metal barrels lined the side of the building.

"Forbidden Technology: extractive mining," Duri noted.

Porbruten grunted. "It's Forbidden, as you say, but hardly worth bothering about. It's only for the use of this village and for minor trading, nothing on a large scale."

Duri turned his attention to the village unfolding before them. It was quite a bit larger than it had looked from above. The ground here was folded into low ridges, and many of the houses and other buildings emerged to view only at certain angles. Where the Skilled tended to build small, efficient houses with gabling, shutters, and other exterior decorations, these houses were long and low, simple and drab on the outside. They had real glass windows, though, and Duri saw sun-plates similar to the ones used in Andolith.

He became aware that they were being watched. There were two towers, one on either side of the street, and behind the windows of these towers people moved stealthily. More people watched from ground level, some from behind windows, some standing on covered porches near doorways. Children peered around corners at them. The low, flat roofs gave access to vantage points and positions of superiority for the residents. There were a few ladders leaning here and there. Any activity that had been taking place in the town seemed to have ceased completely.

"Don't worry, typical behavior," Porbruten said quietly. "We'll go straight to Kladeth the Trader's house. Things will get back to normal soon."

Duri remained on high alert as they rode through the village. In the background, he heard unfamiliar sounds: mechanical, similar to the sounds the wind machines and water mill made, but different in quality. But he saw nothing out of the ordinary besides the pervasive haze.

Porbruten turned them down several lanes and alleyways and eventually reined his horse to a stop in front of a low building that appeared to house either a very large family, or perhaps more than one. There was a large dirt yard in the front and multiple doors and windows, each with its own walkway and décor consisting of pots of multi-colored flowers, small statuettes, benches and stools, and other personal items. A number of bicycles of different sizes leaned against the wall. A pack of medium-sized dogs menaced from the corner.

Porbruten dismounted and tied his horse at a hitching-rail. Duri followed suit. By the time Duri turned back to the house, the top half of a heavy wooden door had been opened, and a man leaned on his elbows on the bottom half. His expression was inscrutable. He seemed to welcome them with a half-smile, but his eyes were veiled. From what Duri could see of him, the man was powerfully built, although somewhat short.

"Kedith!" Porbruten greeted the man enthusiastically. He offered a hand across the doorframe, and Kedith took it briefly, without changing expression or uttering a word. "We've come with trade goods, a few unusual things from Hyolon," Porbruten continued. "Thought we'd give you first shot at them. This is Durigon Cautes of Andolith, my new trading partner. Is Kladeth around?"

"Inside," Kedith said, and held the bottom half of the door aside. Porbruten entered and Duri followed, passing Kedith in the narrow hall. Duri noticed Kedith sizing him up, looking, perhaps, for weapons hidden on his person, but the knives were well disguised.

The dark, narrow hallway opened into a large room resembling a tavern, with a kitchen at the back, a glass door leading into a courtyard beyond, and a number of well-used heavy wooden tables. A fireplace of large stones was set into the wall. Another hall led back to the left. The back door was open to the courtyard in the heat of the day, but it was relatively cool inside due to the heavy construction of the walls. It was hazy, from smoking herbs rather than a fire. The acrid smoke caught at Duri's lungs, but he tried not to cough to avoid insult.

Several other people sat around the tables, including a man closely resembling Kedith. A brother, possibly even a twin, Duri guessed. He wore a heavy chain around his neck with an amulet on it, as did most of the Unskilled men. He stood up from where he sat with a friendlier expression than Kedith had given them, and enveloped Duri's hand in a powerful handshake when Porbruten introduced him.

"Welcome to my house, Durigon Cautes," Kladeth said. He introduced several brothers and other men of the town. The men nodded as they were introduced, but did not rise or offer their hands. Nor did they smile. A few women studied them from the darkened corners of the room, but they were not introduced.

"We saw your horses as you crested the ridge this morning, so your arrival is not unexpected," Kladeth said. "We could quickly identify Porbruten, even from a distance. But you we could not identify. Some of the men gathered here in anticipation of your arrival. You are of the Skilled, we can see. We do not often welcome the Skilled to this town."

"I am of the Skilled, but not a Sorcerer. I'm a trader like Porbruten and make my living traveling and bartering," Duri said.

"I bring goods not often found in this area. Porbruten suggested we offer them first to you, in exchange for such interesting things as you might have, before offering them to the people of his town. I took this as a measure of his esteem for you and your trade relationship."

Kladeth snorted. "Well spoken, but we know better. Porbruten trades where he can get the best deal. Nevertheless, we will look at your goods and hear what it is you're interested in. But not now. We are not given to rudeness, even towards the Skilled. We will make a meal and have drinks and smoke, and there will be time for trade later."

Duri and Porbruten sat down upon a wooden bench at one of the large tables across from Kladeth. "Scorcha!" Kladeth called. "Bring us beer! Two mugs for the new arrivals!"

A young woman, perhaps in her late teens, darted into the room from where she had apparently been lurking outside the door in the courtyard. She quickly removed two large mugs from the kitchen cupboards and set them in front of Duri and Porbruten.

"My eldest sister's child," Kladeth said, jerking a thumb at her. "Porbruten, what news of Toramondon? We have heard little lately. This spring there was word of the retirement of one of the Elder Council. Has any action been taken in that regard? Changes in the Councils always concern us. Who knows what issue a new regime might choose to take up for political gain?"

As Porbruten launched into a discussion of the politics of the Toramondon Council, Duri's eyes followed Scorcha from the kitchen to the cellar door and lingered there until she returned up the stairs with a pitcher of beer. Despite Kladeth's dismissive attitude, Duri felt a jolt of adrenalin when she was introduced. Her build, the shape of her face, and the shape of her eyes was different than that of the Skilled around whom Duri was used to living, but the exoticness of her appearance and dress only made her more attractive to him. He caught her eye as she poured him his drink, and smiled encouragingly. She returned the gesture, and lowered her eyelids as she moved away. Duri kept his eyes fastened upon her, and in a moment she glanced at him again. This time he purposefully turned his attention to his beer, but the game was on.

As the conversation continued, he checked her location from time to time, and often found her gaze upon him, to his satisfaction.

Porbruten was in his element, the center of attention, and Duri sat back and let him do the talking. Meanwhile, he took in the structure of the house, the people who came and went around the circle of men at the table, the women and children who ebbed and flowed in the room, dressed in their exotic clothing. Slowly, more of the village's men began to join them. The smell of broiling meat wafted in through the open courtyard door, and more pitchers of beer appeared. Smoking stuffs of various types were passed around as well, and as evening fell the room became more hazed with smoke and darkened with shadows. Lights set on small ledges around the walls were lit and exuded a faint acrid odor, as well as a hissing sound. Devices of various sorts sat upon tables and shelves. Everything seemed mechanical.

Duri made his way out into the courtyard to find the outhouse, and when he returned he chose a different seat at a small round table near the fireplace in a dark corner. Scorcha brought him a new mug of beer and a plate. He gestured to her to sit down. With a glance at her uncles, engrossed in Porbruten's tales, she quickly pulled a chair up near him at the table.

"So, you have come to trade the goods of the Skilled," she said, leaning towards him in the rising noise. "Did you only bring things to interest men, or do you have goods of interest to women?"

"I do not forget women when I trade," Duri said. "In Skilled society women are of equal status as men, and it would be foolish of me to confine my trade to one gender or the other. Tell me what it is you seek, and we'll see what bargain we can strike. I will pay well for...certain things."

"Indeed," Scorcha said. "Then perhaps we can trade, but it will have to be out of view of my relatives, for they would never allow me to trade with a strange Skilled man. I am hardly allowed to converse even with humans."

"As for that, I am not so strange," Duri said, "and I am certainly human."

Scorcha laughed. "You are of the Skilled, not human! At least, you are not of the pure lineage of humans, although I admit you

58

may have human blood. I'm interested in what differences there may be between us! But if you want to trade with me, later, out of earshot of my relatives, show me some token, so I know you'll meet me and keep your word."

Duri did not reply to Scorcha's strange assertions regarding his ancestry, but dug in the pocket of his vest and extracted a tiny box, an antique of Hyolon, with an etched rose in its silvery metal top. He slid it across the table, and Scorcha quickly covered it with her hand. She examined it in the light of the fireplace, with her shoulder to the room.

"Very pretty," she said. "I have not seen its like. What would you like me to bring you in trade?"

"What can I not get from your uncle and the other men of the village that I can get from you?" Duri asked. "I'm interested in technology."

"I have no technology to trade. What other?"

Duri shrugged. "You can bring only yourself, if you wish. I, too, am interested in our differences and similarities. But I would also be interested in books, histories and the like," he added, thinking of Hyphanden. Surely a Loremaster would be interested in whatever history of the Unskilled Duri could collect.

"The men will not trade you books or histories of our people. But I have some children's books of stories and some schoolbooks I might be willing to part with. I will bring them, and I will, of course, bring myself!"

Scorcha rose quickly from the table and disappeared down into the cellar. She reappeared a few moments later with more beer. Duri watched her as she made the rounds, pouring Porbruten and Kladeth full mugs along with the others.

"Careful, careful," Malbec scolded in his head in a gleeful tone. *"We know where you're going with this!"*

"I don't care for her," Chasan whined. *"She's not my type."*

"Shut up," Duri thought savagely. *"You're dead. I'm not."*

"I'm not dead!" Chasan howled.

"You are nothing but the imprint of your mind on the substrate of mine. What I do with this body is my decision and mine alone!"

"And I concur!" Malbec joined in. *"See if you can't get us some more of that smoke. If we're lucky, we'll have a fine time tonight. But be careful; she could be tricking you."*

"As for that, Chasan can stand guard," Duri replied. *"That way you and I can pay attention to other things."*

Duri pushed himself away from the small table and sat down on the end of the bench next to Porbruten, who was engaged in telling a story as amusing to the Unskilled, it seemed, as it was to the Skilled. Duri smiled indulgently, but the hour was getting late, and he was beginning to wonder if they would trade that night, or wait until the morning.

Suddenly Kladeth set his mug down heavily on the wooden tabletop. "Now, then, Porbruten, let's see what it is you've brought. It's been a while since you visited us. It may be we can trade for a few small trinkets such as you usually bring. And let us see what new things your partner has brought."

Porbruten rose with a nod and made his way back out through the dark hallway to the split door. Duri followed him.

"What shall I bring in?" he asked as Porbruten untied his saddlebags and unbuckled the bags from each other.

"They make their own beer, as you can see, but a few bottles of wine would go over well," Porbruten whispered, slinging one bag over his shoulder by the loose strap. "Also, they make their own medicines, or can trade with other Unskilled for them, but they are unable to make potions or brews and are short many of the common drugs."

"Potions will be of little use without a Sorcerer to administer them, but some drugs can be used by the Unskilled. I've brought a few."

"Bring them, then, but hold them back until you negotiate for what it is you truly want. They're aware you'd not come here if you didn't want Forbidden Technology or at least that which is borderline. They have little else to trade."

Duri chose a few items from his pack-horse, gathered them together into a single bag, and followed Porbruten back to the kitchen. The men had drawn off to the sides of the room, leaving one table open and clear, and Scorcha was just finishing wiping it down. Porbruten laid his bag on the bench and rubbed his hands together with a grin.

"Now, I will show you what I have to trade, and you may make offers upon my goods," Porbruten said. "But Duri will hold his goods until he hears what you offer. That way neither of us plays our hand. Fair?"

Kladeth grunted, with a glance at Kedith, who stood further back in the shadows. Porbruten bent to his bag and began to remove items, which he laid out quickly on the table. Kladeth and the others observed impassively until he was done. Porbruten stood straight and motioned to the collection. Kladeth and several others moved forward. Several of the women craned to see over their backs as the men handled and passed the items.

Kedith appeared with a few items from one of the rooms down the hallway and began to set them out as the men discussed the worth and value of Porbruten's goods. Porbruten took some of the items quickly and set them aside, but others he looked at and then shoved back across the table or waved away without examining at all. Duri could not distinguish what most of the items were, much less what caused Porbruten to accept or reject them.

Kedith disappeared and came back with a few more items, removing the ones Porbruten had rejected to another table, Duri assumed to be re-used in negotiations with him. There was little talking, the trading was swift, and he found it difficult to follow exactly what was going on, but he tried to keep up with the action and the movement of items back and forth across the table.

Suddenly Porbruten stopped and stood straight. "No good! Much of this I have already in my shop. I cannot sell it now, and won't be able to sell more of it. I see no deal here. Show me something I can make a profit on, or I will take back what I've brought."

Kladeth and Kedith stood straight as well, and crossed their arms. Several people looked disappointed, but all Porbruten's goods were tossed back onto the table, and Porbruten pushed the pile of items he had begun to set aside back towards them. There was a heavy silence for a few moments, then Kedith disappeared down the hallway again. He returned with several items, and Porbruten bounced on his toes.

"Yes, this is more like it. I can always sell these, if you keep me supplied with fuel. Show Duri how they operate; we'll see which ones I want."

Kedith picked up a metal canister. He attached what appeared to be a lamp to the top of it. There was a plunger on a cap on the side of the container, and he pumped it in and out a number of times. Then he opened a valve near the top of the lamp and held a match close to a sock under the hood. There was a hissing sound and within a few seconds the sock began to glow with a bright white light. Kedith adjusted the valve and the lamp began to burn more steadily. The light was by far the brightest indoor light Duri had ever seen, despite the odd odor and hiss.

"Impressive, eh?" Porbruten said. "What will you trade for two of them?"

Kedith shrugged. "You weren't happy with our wares before, Porbruten. Perhaps we should hear what your companion wants to trade. Is this what you came here seeking?"

Duri glanced at Porbruten. "It's similar to the small stove I carry, but the fuel must be considerably different. I'm sure I could move a few of those. I would trade some good Tabor wine and some Sydian drugs for them." He reached into his bag and set a couple of bottles and flasks on the table. Kladeth reached for them and examined them with interest, then pushed two of the little lamps his way.

"The wine looks good. The drugs interest me," Kladeth said. "For what would you trade the rest of what you brought? More lamps?"

Duri shrugged. "These things are really Porbruten's specialty. I seek other items."

"What, exactly?" Kladeth asked, crossing his arms.

"Antiques, mostly," Duri said. "Old technology, from before the Dispersal. For example, communications devices."

Kladeth and Kedith jumped up, and their hands went to their sides, where long, cruel-looking knives hung close to their legs.

"Rudon!" Kladeth shouted.

"What? No!" Duri glanced around quickly. The rest of the men had drawn back to the walls of the kitchen and formed a tight group. Porbruten was hemmed in by several of them, and the room was silent, all attention focused on Duri. Several of the men were obviously concealing weapons behind their legs and backs.

"You are an envoy of Rudon!" Kladeth spat, leaning forward to glare at Duri from a foot away.

"I know the name," Duri said calmly, "but he is no friend of mine, nor have I come here on his account, nor do I know of this place through him. I know nothing of what he may have done to insult you, but I assure you I have no part in it. My request is innocent."

Kladeth growled at him, his hands braced upon the table. "Innocent! You are a Sorcerer, and a compatriot of that wood demon!"

Duri shook his head again. "No. I have nothing to do with him. And I repeat: I am no Sorcerer, only one of the Skilled. I don't know what I've asked that's alarmed you. I am only a collector of strange artifacts. If you have none to sell or trade, then so be it."

Porbruten stepped forward and cleared his throat. "Truly, Kladeth, I would bring no one here who I believed meant you harm. What good would it do me? I would lose a valuable trading resource! You know me better than that!"

Kladeth relaxed a little. He rolled his shoulders as though loosening them. He pushed himself back away from the table. "The wood demon Rudon came here last year. He took advantage of us, as the Skilled have often taken advantage of the People."

"That is interesting," Duri said. Out of the corner of his eye, he could tell that the rest of the men were moving about a bit, relaxing, returning to their tables. The crisis, whatever it was, had apparently been averted. "What did he do?"

"He also requested that we provide him with these antique communications devices," Kladeth said. "He gave us time to collect what we could find from along our trade-route, and then returned. He brought drugs and wine, spices, fabrics, and other fine items to trade for them. He brought potions too, to heal our sick."

"Sounds like a good deal," Duri said cautiously.

Kladeth leaned forward again. "That night the baby-snatchers came. They took none of our children, but they prodded them in their cribs and left them terrorized. In the morning all the devices were gone, along with all the trade goods Rudon had brought."

"Baby-snatchers?" Duri glanced at Porbruten.

"The Skilled call them Woodsmen," Porbruten said. He cleared his throat. "They are the stuff of legend."

Kladeth crossed his arms and scowled deeply. "You think we speak of children's superstitions?"

Duri shook his head. "I myself have seen creatures deemed to be only legend. I have no reason to doubt you, nor any doubt that Rudon conspired to defraud you."

Kladeth returned to his seat across the table from Duri and Porbruten. "We have nothing else to trade this evening," he said casually. "I will take the wares you have laid out in exchange for the lamps. A final round, then, and afterwards I will direct you to an adequate camping place for the evening."

Another mug was placed in front of Duri, and he sipped it slowly while Porbruten gathered the goods, including a canister of fuel, into his bag. When Porbruten was done, Duri rose and bade a formal farewell to Kladeth's household. He followed Porbruten out the door, and they repacked their horses in the dark.

"Well, that did not go well," Porbruten said as they rode through the streets towards the outskirts of the village, heading towards the camping spot Kladeth had described. "Who is this Rudon?"

"Rudon is an Outcast Sorcerer of Tabor and a resident of Hyolon," Duri said. "Until last year, he was a trusted compatriot of the Outcast Council. However, he betrayed them. The story is long and complex. I was aware he'd obtained some antique devices, although I know little about how he intends to use them. My interest is personal. I had no idea he got them in this area, nor do I know about any alliance with the Woodsmen."

"Nor do I know," Porbruten mused. "I haven't been here in more than a year. It's too bad. Often I get a room to sleep in for the night. They wanted us away from them, that's for sure. We'll have to make our bed outside for the night."

Duri fell silent, thinking of Scorcha. It was unlikely she would meet him now. In his head, Malbec mourned the lost opportunity as well.

"I would have shown them what a true Sorcerer can do, had they attacked us," Malbec growled. *"That room would not have been a match for us."*

"Me, not us," Duri replied. *"It was my body in jeopardy, not yours. Don't be a fool. Besides, I have no knowledge of how to channel your Skills. It's likely nothing would happen at all. Remember, you've been unable to act through me so far."*

Porbruten pulled his horse aside and they made their way down alongside a stream to a grassy place. They had come far enough from the village to be up against the foot of the range, but not far enough to pass the factory, where, Duri now surmised, the fuel for the lamps was distilled. A few trees came down close to the stream. Porbruten immediately threw his belongings on the ground and pulled the saddle off his horse. Duri moved a short distance away and reorganized his packs and bags. The encounter with the villagers and their rapid dismissal had unnerved him, and after some consideration he decided reluctantly that he would sleep better if he left his horses saddled and ready to go. He dropped their bits to the side so they could graze and drink more easily, and pulled out a blanket to sleep on.

Porbruten rapidly began to snore, and Duri was glad he had set up his own camp a distance away. He sat down on the blanket and pulled out one of Porbruten's devices. He turned it on, his finger hovering over the power button. This time he knew what to expect, and he felt more in control. The feeling was still exceedingly pleasant, but he managed to concentrate on the map displayed on the front. Soon he figured out where his own device was depicted and how to enlarge and shrink the scale of the map. It was true, he saw: not a single device was depicted in the area they were in. If there were any at the Unskilled compound, they'd been disabled.

He hit the power button reluctantly and lay down on the blanket. A few insects bothered him, but he waved them away and tried to ignore the buzz. Suddenly, however, he became more alert: a movement and a rustle alarmed him, and he reached for the knife at his belt.

"Duri!" came a soft whisper, and he quickly sheathed the knife.

"Over here," he replied in a low voice, and in a moment he could see a form in the dark.

Scorcha dropped the reins of the horse she was leading and sat down upon the blanket next to him. She unslung a heavy satchel from her shoulder. "Here," she whispered. "I've brought you a few things."

"I didn't think you'd come," Duri said, weighing the bag in his hand, "after all that in the kitchen."

Scorcha laughed. "You can't blame Kladeth after what Rudon did," she replied. "He wants nothing to do with the Skilled."

"So it seems." Duri lit one of Porbruten's lamps and adjusted the flame. "Show me what it is you've brought."

Scorcha pulled several books from the satchel and tossed them onto the blanket. "Schoolbooks, histories, and fairy-stories," she said. "If you're interested, you may have them."

"I'll pay," Duri said, turning the books over to look at them in the light. "They'll be of interest to someone, if not high value."

"Kladeth would be angry if he knew I gave you such things. He says if the Skilled don't know their own history, it's not up to us to teach it to them. The Unskilled, the People, did just fine until the Time of the Sorcerers. We were strong, smart, and able to develop technologies that gave us good lives. We knew that some of the technologies caused damage to the land, but we also knew we were smart enough to develop fixes for those problems. But we didn't get the chance. The Sorcerers came and began to mix with our kind, and things changed."

"How so?" Duri shoved the books aside and lay down on his side on the blanket, supporting himself on one arm. Scorcha lay down as well, facing him.

"The Sorcerers were weak. They used their Skills to get what they wanted, but they had little technology. They didn't know how to use their hands and minds to find fixes for problems in the world. They fell into temptation easily. But once they began to mingle with humans, they became stronger of will and mind. They were slowly able to take over leadership and control, and a new race of beings was born, the Skilled, like you. Only a few, like my people, resisted integration, and remained pure."

66

"This is a story I've never heard before," Duri said. "It's worth as much to me as the books. Tell me more."

Scorcha shrugged. "Kladeth is convinced that the Sorcerers caused the downfall of society and the Dispersal by using human technology for their own designs. When they used the communication technology of the Unskilled, their minds became open to the minds of others, and they began to revert to a kind of group thinking. But there were those among them who were strong enough and aware enough to resist this, and see if for the evil it was. This was the cause of the Dispersal and the Forbidding of certain Skills and Technologies, which has driven us into a life of exile and lowered our standard of living."

She shrugged. "So I've been taught, anyway. There is more in the books, if you care to look. We have been taught that you are not human and that we should stay away from you. But Porbruten is funny! I've always loved to listen to his tales. I've been in this village my whole life, and I wish to see other places. Kladeth will surely not permit me, but I may go anyway. If I go, I'll have to know how the Skilled and the Sorcerers behave, how like and unlike us they are."

"I'm happy to teach you," Duri said softly. "I think you'll find we are more alike than we are different."

He reached for the knob on the lamp and turned out the light. In the dark, he moved closer to Scorcha.

Just as the dawn was breaking, Duri carefully pulled himself free of the blanket, leaving Scorcha wrapped within and still sleeping. He pulled on his clothes and shoes in the brisk morning air. He walked back into the row of trees where his saddle horse was rubbing its neck on a trunk.

"You should pack up and ready the horses," Chasan said sullenly.

"Why?" Duri asked sleepily.

"In case someone notices Scorcha missing, you idiot!" Chasan hissed.

"Oh, calm down," Duri smirked. *"I promise I'll find someone more to your liking somewhere. I can be flexible, I suppose."*

Nevertheless, he patted the horse on the rump and fitted its bit back into its mouth. He stowed the few things he'd brought out in his saddlebags, and checked the pack horse and its bags of trade-goods as well.

He stretched, looking out over the low valley in front of him. It was early, and Porbruten would sleep for some time yet. He had time to return to the blanket with Scorcha. But he thought he heard a distant sound. He squinted down the trail towards the village.

A group of horses burst over the rise in full gallop, with Kladeth and Kedith in the lead. As they saw the camp they began yelling, and several of them brandished firearms.

Duri leapt to the saddle immediately. Scorcha jumped up from the blankets naked, and Porbruten rolled sleepily to his feet. Porbruten Threw a clumsy Blocking Skill, hardly strong enough to do anything but rock several of the villagers in their saddles. One of them drew a long firearm and pointed it at Porbruten. There was a huge bang, and an object flew out of the firearm and struck Porbruten directly in the chest. Duri blanched as Porbruten disintegrated before his eyes as though blown apart from the inside.

Kladeth pulled alongside Scorcha, who gathered the blankets around herself, but Duri did not pause to see what might transpire. He spurred the horse to a gallop along the edge of the forest, trying to gain the trail. As he looked back over his shoulder, he could see that several of the men pointed firearms of different sizes at him. Vaguely he heard Malbec clamoring in his mind, but he had no time to think. The horse stumbled and Duri lurched forward over its neck. He pulled himself back to the saddle, but the men had gained on him, and turning his back upon them seemed more deadly than turning to face them. He reached for the bridle and jerked the horse around and in a moment he looked directly into the barrels of the firearms, into a death he had no idea how to escape.

Chapter Six: The Challenge Part Two (Rioletta)

On the evening of the Solstice, Rioletta went to visit Ladon at his home. The village was quiet: many people were at the Polebray, celebrating the final evening. The Challenge was set for two weeks after the Solstice, to give those who would attend the festival time to return.

The door stood open. Rioletta knocked on the frame, and Ladon turned from his task and regarded her with a look of resignation.

"Ladon, I'd like to talk about the Challenge," Rioletta said. Ladon stepped to the doorway, but did not invite her in. "I truly did not intend to offer a formal Challenge. It was a poor choice of words, nothing else."

"You made the Challenge, and I'm bound to hear it," Ladon said. "If you're suggesting I call it off, you're wasting your time. I cannot do so. The rules are clear."

"I did hope you would call it off," Rioletta admitted. She thought Ladon sounded almost gleeful at her discomfort. "I'm sure there's some protocol for when a Challenge has been issued in error or the Challenger wishes to withdraw it."

"You know the Charter as well as I do. There's no such protocol."

"Don't you think it would be better for the community to be relieved of this stress?" Rioletta tried. "It's distracting us from our ability to govern."

"No, it's time for the future direction of Andolith to be put to a community vote," Ladon said with a note of finality. "Then the people will be able to relax knowing what decisions we're likely to make in any given situation, rather than being subjected to random and unusual conclusions."

Rioletta turned away. At least she had made the attempt. Ladon was still angry with her and unwilling to listen. She was sure some provision could be made for calling it off, but he wasn't willing to explore that possibility. He was certain he'd prevail.

"Rioletta," Ladon called as she began to walk away. "Did you contact the Outcasts?"

"Yes," Rioletta said. There was no point in hiding it now. "Hyphanden knows Rudon has the book and he's prepared to protect the Crypt as best he can."

"Has anything happened there?" Ladon asked.

Rioletta hesitated. "No, not that I've heard."

Ladon nodded and turned away, pushing his door shut. Rioletta walked slowly back through the village to her own house. Perhaps Ladon thought the lack of any incident in Hyolon meant that her insistence on immediately contacting Hyphanden was exaggerated. She hadn't told Ladon that she'd had no contact with Hyphanden since that first message about the Key.

She now had to accept that the Challenge would go forward. If that was to be the case, she needed to prepare. If the Challenge couldn't be avoided, she might as well throw every argument she had into it and put forth the best case she could. Besides, from what she'd heard, although Ladon seemed confident, it was far from obvious which side would prevail.

Many people in the village now treated her with stiff formality. Most of those in Ladon's generation seemed resolved to support the Elder Council. Yet there were some who had told Rioletta they would staunchly support her. The Younger Council had thrown in their lot with her. Morcah, though the most Traditional of the Younger Council, was furious with Rudon, and still ready to ride to Hyphanden's aid in Hyolon. Andor had not backed off from her initial support. Pateret, despite her injury, was lukewarm about the Challenge, but she did not say anything against it, either. Aliora and Creed would support Rioletta, as well. All in all, the village seemed so evenly split it was difficult to tell how the Challenge would eventually resolve.

At home, Rioletta pulled the chest out from under her kitchen counter. She might as well use every source available to her. She pushed the volumes from Hyphanden to the side and began to sort the rest of the documents into piles by subject matter. Soon she had run out of room on the table, and began to use the chairs and counter top.

She looked up at the sound of a rap on the door frame. Cardon stood in the doorway.

"Good evening," Rioletta said. "Come on in."

Cardon put his hands into his pockets and walked into the room looking self-conscious. He looked around at the piles that covered every available space. Rioletta quickly removed a stack from one of the armchairs.

"Have a seat. Would you like a drink?"

Cardon slouched into the chair. "Sure."

Rioletta fetched him a beer and a glass. Cardon took a swig from the bottle, then poured the rest into the glass slowly. He watched the foam as it settled.

"Just out for a walk around the neighborhood?" Rioletta asked. She cleared another chair for herself.

Cardon nodded. He put down the empty bottle but continued to stare at the glass. Finally he looked up for the first time into Rioletta's face.

"Well, no. I mean, I came because I want to tell you something."

"Something that makes you uncomfortable, apparently," Rioletta noted. "I hope by now you know I'm unlikely to be judgmental."

"Yes, but I have to beg you, once again, not to disclose what I'm about to say to anyone else. I know I've made this request before and you've honored it, except when lives or safety were in danger. This is nothing like that. I'll reveal it myself soon, but there's a reason I ask."

Rioletta spread her hands. "As you say, it's nothing you haven't asked before, and I answer as I've answered before: I'll keep your secret unless it becomes ethically impossible."

Cardon shook his head slightly, as if denying what he himself was about to say. "Rio, I'm leaving Andolith. For good this time. I'm taking Justah and my mother. I can't stay here with those Leaves around, knowing Justah's being watched, knowing how close the Lefollah are, barely half a day's walk. I have to take her

71

someplace where she'll be better protected, where I'm not living in fear she'll disappear at any moment, of her own volition or someone else's."

After a momentary shock, Rioletta was not truly surprised. But they had grown up together and been through a lot, and it was difficult to imagine Andolith without Cardon.

"Where are you planning on going? Back to the 'Quant? Skyros and your mother's relatives will certainly welcome you there."

"No! That life is a hard one, and not one I'd wish for my daughter. Justah needs the guidance of those more knowledgeable than we are here in Andolith."

"Surely you're not thinking of going to Hyolon," Rioletta said. "That would be no place for a child, and would hardly be safe with Rudon on the loose."

"No, no, I'm not going to Hyolon, although I've no doubt Hyphanden and Kwistocta would welcome me there. I'm going to Dobor."

Rioletta let a long moment go by before she replied, as the pieces fell into place. "Adla Kathreftis."

Cardon nodded. "Yes. Of course, she's a Sorcerer, and committed to the Elder Council of Dobor. She can't marry, and I wouldn't ask her to give up her position. Nor can she take on the responsibility of a child. I'm well aware of that. But she has agreed to set me up with a house in a good location for my mother and for school and child-care for Justah. Justah will be much safer there. And as for Adla and I, we'll see what happens in the future. I have no vision of that, only the knowledge that this is an opportunity I may not get again."

"Yes," Rioletta agreed, although internally she vacillated from happiness for Cardon to an unfounded jealousy. "Adla is a wonderful person, very Skilled. Of course it will be safer for Justah, and it will be good for Lida to be near a larger community where there are shops and facilities only a short distance away. But I'll miss you here, Cardon. I've never imagined Andolith without you."

Cardon pushed himself out of his chair and knelt next to Rioletta's, taking her in his arms. Wordlessly, he laid his face on

72

her shoulder and held her tightly. Rioletta breathed deeply, trying to forestall her own tears as she realized it might be the last time she held him that way.

"You know I care a great deal for you, and you've saved me more than once," Cardon finally said, pushing back to look her in the face. "Our lives have been intertwined, and our minds are open to one another. I'll miss you a great deal, and so will Justah and Lida. It's just that this is the right thing to do. And after all, you'll visit Nikal, won't you? I'll see you then." He smiled determinedly.

Rioletta nodded. "It is the right thing to do, I know it as well. But when are you leaving? And why are you so determined to keep it a secret?"

Cardon threw himself back into the armchair. "I'm a disbarred Sorcerer, and my right to vote at all is questionable at best. My decisions are forever suspect due to the Skills I've accessed. But I don't think Ladon will try and rob me of my vote while I remain a citizen of Andolith, and it would look odd to do so at this point, right before the Challenge. However, should it be known that I intend to leave, a case could be made that my vote not be counted. So I'll wait to reveal that I'm leaving until after the Challenge, and I will vote with you, Rioletta. I could hardly do otherwise. But my intentions must remain unknown."

"Don't inconvenience your family for this," Rioletta said. "Your vote will most likely not be the deciding one."

"Perhaps not, but I intend to cast it," Cardon said. "Only Lida knows of this move, none other, even Justah. And should things not go your way – although I'm sure they will – you can travel with us if necessary."

"Thank you." Rioletta swallowed. She was trying not to think of what would happen if the Challenge failed, or indeed, if it succeeded. Either way, her life would never be the same.

Cardon seemed to catch her apprehension. "Things will work out," he said encouragingly. "You know many of the villagers are on your side. Times change, and to ignore information is folly, although to accept it is often frightening. You mustn't think this is your fault, any of it. It's been brewing from many quarters for a long time. It's a fact that over the last few years there have been more and more Outcasts from each Council. Certainly there's a reason for that, a gathering of the desire to seek knowledge that has previously been unobtainable to us."

He sat back and picked up his glass. "I'm glad you know about the move now. I feel a weight lifted off me. Soon all this will be over, and we'll see the future more clearly."

"Soon this will be over, yes, one way or the other," Rioletta said, "but then we must face the fact that Rudon has the Key to the Crypt of Souls, and that Hyphanden, Hyolon, and perhaps many more are in danger."

During the next two weeks, a stage was erected in the village plaza near the sundial. There was scant guidance within the Charter about the process of the Challenge itself, but Charnia, who had been designated the Coordinator, had contacted the few other villages she knew of where a Challenge had been held and had garnered a few suggestions.

Witnesses, Charnia told Rioletta, were to be allowed on either side. Witnesses need not be residents or voting members of Andolith. In accordance with the Charter, all members of both Councils would receive three votes, which could be split in any manner desired. Everyone else would receive one vote, except Charnia, who would receive two. There was no guidance regarding subsidiary communities such as Luth, which was beholden to Andolith for its Sorcerer Council, but it was agreed that such communities had a vested interest in what occurred, and thus any of their residents who showed up and were of voting age would be allowed half a vote. Charnia had decreed that all votes would be taken by open tally rather than by secret ballot.

Two days before the Challenge, a small group of riders entered the village from the direction of Matbor. Rioletta's house was within view of the road, and she heard the hooves of the horses and the jangle of bells on their bridles as they arrived.

She stepped out her open door and immediately recognized the big horse belonging to Stetsordahl Vrinal, the Leader-in-Exile of the Elder Council of Tabor. He was accompanied by Lindordahl, another of the Tabor Elders, and Fendant of the Second Chosen, as well as several pages. The group stopped before her door, and two of the pages jumped down to steady Stetsor's horse and help him from the saddle.

74

Stetsor adjusted the formal tunic he wore and offered a hand to Rioletta. "I trust the Council-house will be open for visitors?"

"Of course!" Rioletta said. "Although if you prefer, we can most likely put you up in an empty house, of which there are several in town."

"Perhaps Ladon will favor me with one of those, then," Stetsor said, nodding over Rioletta's shoulder. Ladon was hurrying to meet them.

"Are you here coincidentally, or to view the Challenge?" Rioletta asked.

"To view the Challenge. I've never seen one," Stetsor said, a slight smile playing on his lips. "It may be in my interest to learn about such proceedings and observe how things go. And I might have a thing or two to add. Witnesses will be allowed?"

"They will be."

Ladon arrived quickly and greeted Stetsor, turning his shoulder towards Rioletta. Rioletta withdrew both in deference and because of the obvious snub, and Ladon led the party away towards the village center and the Council-house. Rioletta watched them from her doorway. She could not fathom what Stetsordahl might say, or how it would be taken by members of the community who remembered Mosse's feud or by others who resented the loss of Tereret during Andolith's rescue of the Tabor Council.

The day of the Challenge dawned bright, hot and clear. The actual event was to be held in the late afternoon, when the trees would begin to cast shade on the village as the sun lowered, but with enough time to hear all witnesses before dark fell.

Rioletta had not slept well in days, nor could she eat. She had stopped poring over her books: there was nothing left for her to learn that could be of any use. She had not consulted with the rest of the Younger Council, although she knew they had met without her. She had made the Challenge herself, on behalf of herself as a private citizen and not a Council-member, and they were therefore only witnesses, although they would take the stage as part of the Council system.

Rioletta made several trips back and forth to the stage to bring her books and documents. Cardon met her and carried an armload of books, but she didn't feel like talking, and she simply thanked him after the final trip. She paced nervously inside her house, looking out from time to time towards the village center. People were beginning to gather, and she could hear voices rising and falling.

Finally the appointed time drew near, and she went to the plaza. She mounted the stage via a set of steps built against one side. The rest of the Younger Council was already there. The noise of the crowd hushed when she arrived, but soon resumed, since the Elders were not there yet. Scanning the crowd, Rioletta saw the Training Cadre in front, and near the back Stetsor and his entourage. There were a few people from the surrounding communities, include Rath of Luth. Rioletta fingered the black talisman at her neck. Nikal knew about the Challenge, of course, but he had been unable to break away from his duties in Dobor to support her. Her hand traveled down into the pocket of her tunic, where another talisman rested. Carefully, she drew it out and set the little carved stone dog on the table near her books. The jeweled eyes glowed in the sun.

Finally Charnia arrived and the crowd hushed. Ladon helped her up the steps to the platform. She hobbled out to the front of the stage importantly, holding a sheaf of papers, while Ladon, Amidon, and Boradon seated themselves opposite the Younger Council.

Charnia raised her arms for silence. "We are gathered here today to hear a Challenge brought by Rioletta Eris, inducted member of the Younger Council of Sorcerers of Andolith and its subsidiary communities, against the leadership direction of the Andolith Elder Council. This Challenge shall follow the procedures laid out in the Charter of Dispersal and such other procedures as have been agreed to in advance by the Councils."

Charnia lowered her arms and there was a musical sound in the silence as several metal bracelets slid back down to her wrists. "No limit shall be placed on either side as to the number of witnesses each may call to support his case. When all witnesses have been heard and all parts of each case laid out to the satisfaction of the Challenger and the defendants, an open vote shall be taken of all voting-age residents of Andolith and its subsidiary communities. The Challenge shall be affirmed or denied according to a strict tally of these votes."

She stopped and looked around. No one offered a question or stirred in the audience. Charnia stepped back between the two Councils and turned to Rioletta.

"Rioletta Eris, state the circumstances of your Challenge."

Rioletta rose reluctantly. She was not comfortable speaking in front of large crowds. When the Younger Council addressed the populace of Andolith, she preferred to pass her ideas on to Morcah, who was a natural speaker. But it was her Challenge. There was nothing for it but to state it as clearly as possible.

"First let me say that I issued this Challenge in haste and anger over the wounding of my fellow inducted Sorcerer, Pateret," Rioletta said, with a gesture to Pateret to remind the crowd of what had happened. "There were perhaps other means through which our disagreement could have been settled. However, once the Challenge was issued, Ladon was bound by the Charter to hear it in a formal proceeding. My objection to Ladon's direction was, and remains, his dedication to a strategy that I believe to be too isolationist in the face of a regional threat and an outside attack on one of our own Sorcerers."

She paused and glanced at the Elder Council. "Ladon's focus is on the protection of Andolith and its subsidiaries, an admirable goal and one I support. However, there comes a time when such strategies must be re-evaluated in the face of larger issues that have the capacity to affect us all. Thus the central question of my Challenge is this: do we continue to follow the strict Traditionalist and isolationist strategy laid out for us by Mosse Amwiska and her predecessors, and followed to a large extent by our current Elder Council, or do we allow ourselves to become more open to the communities of our region, not only in trade, but also by coming to the aid of those we wish to protect from possible overthrow by persons whose practices we would find objectionable."

She glanced at Charnia, who smiled and nodded at her. With the central question of the Challenge laid out, it remained for her to state her position and support it with evidence. "We cannot afford to sit by while others are in danger. Eventually their conflict will come to us, and their distress will become ours. This requires us to

77

toss aside old conflicts and suspicions for the greater good. This is not unprecedented: the Elder Council itself agreed to go to the aid of the Council of Tabor just two years ago, despite our previous disagreements, and we have recently solidified trade relations with Dobor. Our only true disagreement is how fast and how complete this change in direction should be."

Rioletta paused. The next part would be more controversial, but she had decided she couldn't shy away from it. "A second part of this Challenge concerns the ability of our Sorcerers to use and access information and Skills that previously have been unavailable to us. While I do not advocate using the Forbidden Skills, I advocate the collection and study of documents and books heretofore restricted, in order that we might make our decisions on the most complete information possible, whether or not that information agrees in strict terms with the ancient ideas expressed in the Charter of Dispersal."

Rioletta looked over the crowd. Most of the residents did not yet realize what she meant. She turned back to Charnia, who motioned to her to be seated.

Charnia turned to address Ladon. "Ladon, as Leader of the Elder Council and the specific focus of the Challenge, please provide us with the background that informs your decision-making."

Ladon rose and stepped to the edge of the platform. Rioletta knew she was at a disadvantage: Ladon was comfortable speaking before the people he had guided all his life. He appeared relaxed and unworried. She knew if she were forced to rely on speaking style alone, she would lose. She could only hope that circumstance would overwhelm personality.

Ladon put one hand in a pocket and casually paced the edge of the stage as he spoke. He took them back to the days of the Dispersal and told the story of how all the Councils of the old region known as the Surin met in Hyolon as their world began to deteriorate around them and decided on a drastic course of action that ultimately saved their lives. He reviewed the Charter and its articles and orders and related how each had flowed from necessity. He pointed to the success of Andolith and other communities in the more than one hundred years since the Dispersal.

"I fully acknowledge that not all information followed us from Hyolon to our communities," Ladon told the crowd. "That which was left behind was that which led us into deterioration. Those Skills that were Forbidden or Restricted were those shown to be dangerous to the integrity of the individual, to damage minds, to destroy the fabric of families and communities, to cause people to forget their responsibilities. Those Technologies that were Forbidden were those shown to be destructive to the environment, without the balance necessary to allow us an infinite existence on this world."

Ladon had stopped pacing and now stood on the edge of the stage, emphasizing his words with gestures. His voice rose with passion and intensity.

"We have followed the Charter closely as a Traditional society, and we have lived a good life here in Andolith. We have little crime, little illness, good food. None of us wants for anything. Our lives are satisfying and complete. We have art and craft, we have recreation and leisure. I acknowledge that Mosse Amwiska's policies were extremely isolationist, and that I have opened our village to wider trade relations for the advancement of our comfort and health. But in general I follow her Traditionalist philosophy. The Charter guides me closely, and I do not question its wisdom, having seen the success with which we have existed for more than a century."

Ladon ended his statement and looked around for a moment before sitting back down. Now Charnia turned once more to Rioletta. "Have you a rebuttal?"

Rioletta nodded and moved her chair closer to the table. She did not rise again, but flipped a few pages before beginning. She glanced at the talisman that weighted her papers. She would soon reveal things that most of the community did not know, information about the Younger Council's travels that the Elder Council had elected to conceal. She needed to work up to it carefully and logically.

"Ladon is right in many things," she began. "Our life here is good, and no one wants to disrupt it for the worse. Ladon has been a skillful Leader, and prior to that was a valuable second on the Elder Council. I am beholden to him for many things, as are we all. I don't wish to bring drastic or calamitous change upon Andolith. Our differences are minor in scope, very minor.

"However, I have traveled during the last several years and encountered things previously unknown to me. This began with the task I was set at my Induction. Recall that the task was set by Mosse Amwiska herself. Therefore, it is reasonable to believe she wanted me to discover at least some of the things I've learned."

Rioletta looked up as a slight murmur ran through the crowd. "None can deny that the Lefollah were unknown to us before Stolen. This is knowledge that was not brought out of Hyolon, for a reason we do not yet understand. Why was this information hidden from us after the Dispersal? Is it possible that Mosse knew something of this, and had a desire to bring it to our knowledge again? Recall that she was a Loremaster, and had been one for nearly half the time since the Dispersal. Ladon is not a Loremaster, nor are any of the rest of the Council except me. Perhaps she didn't divulge her reasons to Ladon, but consider the Task I was set. Is there another reasonable explanation for why she set it? Unfortunately, she died before she could pass on the reason for her actions."

She paused for a respectful moment at the mention of Mosse's death, and saw a few others in the audience glance up at the Contemplation.

"Following my discovery of the Lefollah, we abandoned our isolationist policies and rode to the aid of Tabor. Ladon, therefore, accepts the necessity of interfering in the doings of others when our interests are at stake. I will show that our interests are indeed at stake in this case."

Rioletta rose again and stepped closer to the edge of the stage, her hands clasped behind her back. She glanced purposefully at Ladon, who crossed his arms. She was about to reveal to the audience where the Younger Council had been after the Polebray the previous year, and she knew he must have guessed her intentions. It was a bit of a gamble: she would reveal that Ladon and the Elder Council purposefully concealed certain information from the community at large, but she would also reveal that she had been in Hyolon, in the company of the Outcasts, and she wasn't at all sure what kind of reception that information would get.

During the next twenty minutes, she slowly paced the edge of the stage as she carefully reconstructed the circumstances that had led her, Cardon, Andor, and Creed to Hyolon the year before. She described the people they had met, the actions they had taken, and the decisions they had made, as well as the results of those decisions. The audience was silent. Only her own voice echoed in the village square.

Finally she concluded with the meeting the previous fall in which the Elder Council had decided to tell the community that the four of them had stayed with the Tabor Security Guards Betar and Luridos, friends of Rath of Luth, rather than revealing where they had actually been.

"I would now like to call some witnesses for my side," she told Charnia.

Charnia consulted a list she held. At her signal, Cardon made his way to the stage. Charnia seated him near the front of the platform, across from Rioletta.

At Rioletta's request Cardon related his story, starting with his indiscretion with Marsavrina and the birth of Justah. He told of his association with the Younger Council of Tabor and his weakness in falling to the temptation of the Forbidden Skills. He confirmed what Rioletta had related about their time in Hyolon, including the Crypt of Souls. Cardon was a better speaker than Rioletta, and Hyphanden and the rest of the Outcast Council came out sounding reasonable and normal, to her relief.

When he was through, Charnia dismissed him and called for a break. The crowd broke into conversation and many wandered off to the Council-house, where food and drink had been laid out. Rioletta retreated to the side of the stage where the rest of the Younger Council gathered.

"Ladon's argument is powerful," Andor said, shaking her head, "but many of these people have never heard our story of Hyolon and the Crypt of Souls. I hope it will open their eyes to what's going on in the world at large. But it may instead

81

overwhelm and confuse them, and make many want to withdraw all the more."

"It's a gamble," Morcah said, "but one that's necessary to take. Many may also realize that Ladon picks and chooses what information he allows to be known by the people of Andolith, and they may wonder what else he's concealed."

Rioletta nodded, grateful for Morcah's support. Pateret seemed ill at ease. Rioletta knew that she disliked crowds and attention. But she had remained on the stage with the rest of the Council, and that seemed to Rioletta to be symbolic of her resolve.

After the break Rioletta was permitted to continue calling witnesses. She called Andor and Creed, both of whom had also been at Hyolon, and asked only that they give their own points of view to corroborate what Cardon had said. Charnia turned to Rioletta as Creed left the stage. "That is the last witness you have requested for this section of the Challenge. Are there any last-minute additions?"

Rioletta paused. "Yes," she said. "I call Rath of Luth."

There was a stir in the audience as people turned to find Rath in the crowd. Rioletta knew she was taking a chance. Rath was of Ladon's generation and moreover had been a close companion of Ladon for the last year. But Rath would tell the truth, even if hesitantly, she was sure, and if her testimony came out on Rioletta's side, it might sway some who voted due to loyalty to their generation.

Rath made her way up to the stage and was seated in the chair across from Rioletta.

"Rath, you followed us to Hyolon after the Polebray last year," Rioletta said. "Please relate to us what you saw there and what the people you met were like."

Rath cleared her throat and turned to face the audience. "I was treated courteously by the Outcast community. I was not imprisoned or forced to stay against my will. I found Hyphanden and Kwistocta to be reasonable people, who did not seem to be damaged despite their admitted use of the Forbidden Skills for many years. I found Hyphanden to be well-read and their household was well-kept and comfortable. Their actions were well thought out and reasonable. Their society was orderly and mirrored other communities. I saw nothing that would lead me to suspect their motives or ability to form correct conclusions."

"Thank you, Rath," Rioletta said. Rath glanced at Ladon before making her way down the steps.

Ladon had not requested to call any witnesses. Instead, he would call upon members of the Elder Council in the next part of the Challenge, in which supporters of each side could question and debate those of the other.

"We will break for dinner, and afterwards continue with the debates and open testimony," Charnia said with a sweeping wave of her arm.

Creed came up to the edge of the stage near the Younger Council and offered Andor a hand. She jumped off the edge, and Morcah followed. But Pateret lingered near Rioletta's table. Rioletta saw that she stared fixedly at the little dog talisman weighting her papers.

"Pateret! Come this way, we'll go off the back," Rioletta called to her. Pateret seemed to startle, then turned and hurried to the side of the stage, where she accepted Morcah's aid. Rioletta jumped off by herself, although Creed offered her a hand. He grinned when she refused.

"Perhaps you'll want some help getting back up, then," he said.

Rioletta forced herself to drink something, but could not eat. Her stomach roiled. She found herself simply wishing it was over, whatever the outcome. Finally she heard the call from the stage and they returned to their places.

"Now we'll turn to debate and open testimony," Charnia began when everyone was seated. "Ladon, since you called no witnesses, it's your turn to open the debate."

"I'll call Amidon," Ladon said. Amidon stood and approached Rioletta's desk.

"Rioletta, I've heard your claim that your ideas are very close to those of Ladon and the Elder Council," Amidon began. "But isn't it true that you advocate a structure of education and instruction for the Sorcerers that is more in line with the Tabor Council? Don't you in fact advocate that we study all the Skills, Forbidden and otherwise?"

"I advocate that we use all information that becomes available to us to make our decisions, whether or not it has been passed down to us through the Charter. If information becomes known to us even by accident, I say we must use it, lest our decisions be uninformed."

"But if the information we have now has allowed us to make appropriate decisions throughout the last hundred years, of what use is this extra information you propose to use, except to cause confusion and disruption?"

"Are you not interested in the truth, in all its complexities?" Rioletta countered. "Knowing the truth can only help us make sound decisions. Decisions based on falsities cannot be sound."

"Not so," Amidon responded. "If the information is constructed so as to make the decision sound, what matter whether it contains the absolute truth or not? If it serves us as it is, why concern ourselves with further details that the founders of our society thought trivial and unimportant? They have set us along this path, and it has served us well. There's no need to repeat the mistakes of the past."

"Those details the Founders thought trivial and unimportant may indeed be important at this point in time. We cannot rely on a document written more than a century ago, whose authors are long dead," Rioletta argued. "At some point we must re-examine its tenets and assure ourselves that they still mirror reality as we have come to understand it. This can only be done if we are in possession of information that either corroborates or refutes it. We must gather and use other information to make our decisions sound, and not rely on a single document."

"Then you admit that you advocate the indiscriminate use of any information you or any of us may come upon, including such texts as may be found by your Outcast Council in Hyolon, despite being unable to identify the author or that author's agenda."

"I admit that I think many such texts may be valuable. I think information should not be discounted simply because it suggests a different path than the Charter."

"In fact, you have read some of them yourself. And they have affected your judgment to the point where you issued this

Challenge in haste and anger, as you yourself admitted," Amidon said.

Rioletta felt her jaw tense. "I have read some of them, yes. But you previously heard testimony from my witnesses. If my actions and perceptions are distorted by what I discovered, then theirs are also distorted, as they are in agreement with me. And these witnesses include not only the members of my own Younger Council, but also at least one of your generation."

"Ah. I sum up your position thus: you have read texts and tracts Forbidden to you in your search to discredit the Charter; you have mingled with Outcasts with damaged minds; you have issued a serious Challenge in haste and anger, as you have admitted; and you find yourself more knowledgeable about how to make decisions than the Founders of the Charter, whose words and actions have successfully guided us over the last hundred years," Amidon said smugly, with a glance at the crowd.

"And I sum up your position thus," Rioletta shot back. "You don't care about the truth, but will blindly accept lies and pass them on to others. You are unwilling to admit that societies change and that our situation cannot remain the same forever. You are unwilling to use information readily available to you to help you make sound decisions to guide this community successfully into the future. You blindly follow the Charter as though it contains the answer to all questions, as though it can foresee the future. It is a valuable and historical document, but it is not infallible or even strictly the truth. We all know that truth is filtered through the eye of the beholder, and that words often cannot adequately describe our meaning. And this is why I issued this Challenge: to lead from a wider base of knowledge, one grounded in evidence and not in legend and tradition."

Amidon turned and bowed slightly to Charnia, who startled slightly. She had been listening with rapt attention from her chair. Now she rose again.

"Ladon, do you call any others to debate?"

"I reserve my right to call others, and open the floor to any who wish to speak," Ladon said.

Charnia turned to Rioletta. "Is this agreed?"

Rioletta nodded. "But I reserve my right also, to call members of my Council and others to debate or answer questions for me."

"Done," Charnia said. "We will open the floor."

A number of people from the community rose and approached the stage to ask questions, but Andor and Morcah were able to field them for Rioletta, giving her a break. Aliora, Creed's older sister, questioned Amidon once again about his statement that the truth did not matter if the falsity seemed adequate to do the job. Amidon clarified that he believed the Charter to hold the most succinct truth regarding management of society, and that he had not meant to imply that the Charter was a falsehood.

Finally no one else stood and approached the stage. Charnia rose again and moved to the front. "Is there anyone else who would like to speak before we move on to closing statements?" she asked.

"Yes!" A voice rang out from the back of the crowd. Stetsordahl Vrinal stood, one hand raised. "I am not of Andolith, but I request that I be allowed to speak as an interested and affected party."

"So be it. Approach the stage," Charnia said, with a slight smile.

Stetsordahl walked slowly around the edge of the crowd and stood before the stage.

"Many years ago, it was I who Outcast Hyphanden Vrinal and his cousin Kwistocta from my First Chosen Council, in strict accordance with the Charter," Stetsor began. His voice rose in power and volume as he spoke, and he turned slowly until he faced the crowd rather than Charnia upon the stage.

"Also I cast out another Sorcerer who practiced the Forbidden Skills, Rorudon Buradoc. But while I drove Hyphanden and Kwistocta from the city, Rudon I imprisoned and attempted to Strip his Skills. I was quite sure that despite the necessity for Outcasting, Hyphanden would make an honorable and successful path for himself. I was equally sure that Rudon's path would be ruinous. Unfortunately, Rudon's practice of the Forbidden Skills allowed him to successfully partition his mind, and many of his Skills were not Stripped before he was banned from the city, with a warrant on his head."

The crowd shifted and murmured. Some of them were familiar with Stetsor from his rescue two years before and from his infrequent visits to Andolith, but most of them were unaware of this part of his past. Skill-stripping, although authorized in the Charter, had not been practiced in Andolith for many years.

"Recently I learned that my prophecy regarding the paths of these individuals has come true," Stetsor continued. "My own grandson sought refuge in the Ruined City following the coup in which my Council fell. Despite our differences, Hyphanden graciously accepted him into his community. Also two members of the deposed Second Chosen abide there. They would not do so if they did not find the Community to be orderly. Indeed, one has become a member of their Council, although he maintains his Traditional ways."

Stetsor paused and scanned the crowd. "Last year Rudon betrayed them. I have little doubt that he seeks access to this Crypt of Souls and the minds therein, in order to garner power for himself such that none of us have ever seen. I say now that he must be stopped! He has already visited damage upon your village through his unwarranted attack on one of your Younger Council."

Rioletta leaned forward, trying to hear Stetsor's words. The murmur of the crowd grew louder once again. Charnia stepped forward and raised her arms. Stetsor paused until she regained control.

"This is not the time to sit back and hope that the battle will not come to you. This Challenge was issued, I am aware, because of Ladon's refusal to communicate with Hyphanden and the Outcast Council, or to seek help from elsewhere following the theft of the Key. I am eternally grateful to Ladon for his decision to go to the aid of my Council and for all he has done for us in the years since our ousting. But I caution you: his reluctance in this instance will not serve you well. The loss of Tereret was a tragedy, and one I regret, but you must be prepared for what is coming; and if you do not have the strategies and information to react, I fear you will not survive."

Stetsor ended abruptly, turned, and walked back to his chair at the back of the crowd.

"If there are no other requests, we will move to closing statements," Charnia said. No other rose to speak.

Ladon went first. He reminded the residents of the successful chain of Councils in Andolith, of their good life and of the principals embodied in the Charter. He would not forsake them, he said, and he had dedicated his life to guiding Andolith successfully into the future. He was willing to negotiate with the Younger Council in future decisions: he was not unreasonable. His tone was calm and friendly, and he presented himself as an experienced leader, one who could be trusted and relied on to make the right decisions.

Rioletta was permitted to have the last word. She reiterated her respect for Ladon, but pointed out Amidon's words. After all, a Council consisted of all its members, not only the Leader. This Challenge was about the direction of the entire Elder Council. She could not now ignore the knowledge she had gained, and she had been set upon the path she followed by none other than the Elder Council itself, who now disputed her right to that knowledge. And finally, her position was not outlandish: she was supported by the Younger Council and by many witnesses who wanted only the best for Andolith and their families who lived there.

At last Rioletta sat back down. There was nothing left now, nothing more to say. The argument would fail or stand on its own.

Kestrella propped up a board to keep score, and Charnia organized the vote. Each person was to pass in front of the stage and announce his or her vote. Then the vote would be tallied and the Challenge either affirmed or denied. An affirmation would go to the Challenger, a denial to the Elder Council.

A long line formed in front of the stage, and one by one the residents of Andolith stated their votes. In many cases, it was as expected. In some cases, it was a surprise. Rath's half vote went to Rioletta and the Younger Council. Finally all the residents had voted. The scoreboard, although too full to tell for sure at a glance, appeared to show a very slim margin for the Elder Council. But the Council-members had yet to vote. First the Elder Council voted, and each of them gave all three of their votes to themselves. Then the Younger Council voted, and each of the members did likewise, except Morcah, who awarded one of his votes to the Elder Council. Only Charnia was left to allocate her two votes.

"I award one vote to the Elder, and one vote to the Younger," Charnia cackled. "Kestrella, count the votes!"

Kestrella carefully counted the tick-marks on the board and wrote the final tally at the bottom. Charnia checked it, and then turned to the assembled and hushed crowd. She raised her arms, bracelets jangling, and let a dramatic moment pass before she spoke again.

"The Challenge is…affirmed!"

There was a stunned silence in the crowd. Rioletta looked swiftly at Ladon, who blanched and then slowly met her eyes. They remained, eyes locked, as the noise from the Andolith citizens rose around them.

Charnia shouted for silence.

"Rioletta Eris, your Challenge is affirmed!" she announced again. "Come forward and pronounce the fate of the Elder Council!"

Rioletta tore her eyes away from Ladon's and rose slowly. She walked to the edge of the platform without feeling her limbs, as though she had gone numb. She had thought of this eventuality, although she had scarcely dared to believe it might occur, and she was prepared at least to some extent.

She cleared her throat and waited for the crowd to hush completely. "As my Challenge has been affirmed, it falls to me to determine the short-term future of the Andolith Council system and the direction this community will take," she began bluntly. She turned to glance at the Younger Council. "There will be no Outcasting. The current Elder Council will now become an Elder Council of Advisors, consisting of Ladon, Amidon, Boradon, and Charnia. Their duties will include maintaining the new trade agreements and serving on the Regional Trade Council, providing such leadership as is enumerated in the Charter of Andolith during the period of turnover, and otherwise supporting the Andolith communities. Morcah, if you will, please accept the leadership of the new Sorcerer's Council. That Council now consists of Morcah, Pateret, Andor, and myself. For the time being, and into the foreseeable future, the two Councils will function as an Integrated

Council. As for myself, I will immediately recuse myself from any decisions affecting the future direction of Andolith. The Councils are charged, as a first duty, with preparing the current Training Cadre for induction as a Younger Council as soon as they reach the prescribed age and level of experience."

She turned to Charnia. "I have nothing else."

"Very well." Charnia addressed the residents. "The Challenge is adjourned. Further information will be posted over the next few days upon the Council-house door."

The crowd began to disperse, and Rioletta returned to her table to collect her books and documents. She was quickly surrounded by the Younger Council, soon to become the ruling Council of Andolith.

"A good call, and fair," Morcah said, "but I'm not yet ready to lead Andolith. I'll need to rely strongly upon Ladon."

"We will set it up to be so," Rioletta said. "I have no intention of completely disrupting the Council system or throwing Andolith into chaos."

Cardon, who had jumped up on the stage, collected an armload of her belongings. "Shall I bring these back to your place for you?"

"Please," Rioletta said.

Cardon leaned close to her quickly and whispered in her ear, "I guess my vote did count after all!" Then he hopped off the edge of the stage and headed for her house.

Rioletta turned to collect the rest of her belongings. Pateret stood near the table, once again staring fixedly at the dog talisman. As Rioletta watched, she reached out and took it, enclosing it in her hand completely.

Rioletta stepped forward. "I'll take that, Pateret."

"I don't like it," Pateret said, not releasing the talisman.

"I'm sorry. Give it to me and I'll put it away," Rioletta said. She put out her hand, but Pateret did not make a move to return the dog.

Rioletta took Pateret's hand and pulled the little talisman out. She dropped it in her tunic pocket. Pateret turned quickly away and went to join Morcah. Rioletta stared after her for a moment. It was a very odd encounter.

Ladon stood next to her when she returned her attention to her papers.

"Congratulations," he said, offering his hand, palm up in a gesture of deference. Rioletta took it, and he held on while he spoke. "It appears my time has passed. It's early. I'd expected to lead the Council for many years yet. I cannot say I'm happy with this outcome, but it has been done according to the Charter and as fairly as I think it can have been done. I appreciate your discretion in appointing an Integrated Council. I hope I'll be able to be useful in such a position."

"As I'm sure you realize, you'll continue to lead the Council in all but name for quite some time yet. Morcah isn't ready to assume full leadership. Things will continue much as before."

"But I guess you'll travel to the Ruined City to try and determine what's happening with this Rudon. Morcah will have the power to send others as well, to involve us in all sorts of conflict in regions far from here. It's not something I look forward to."

"As for involving us in conflicts in other regions, it was you who agreed to go to Tabor to free the Elder Council there. In many ways that precipitated all of this."

"A decision I have regretted since," Ladon said. "The saving of the Elder Council was not worth the life of Tereret, when the Council might have been saved by others at some other time."

Rioletta sighed and removed her hand from his. "I hope you and I can work together, Ladon. But I'm very tired and would like to go now. Undoubtedly we'll spend a great deal of time together in the coming days as we decide on our new organization. For now, good night."

Rioletta's house was empty when she arrived, the armload of books Cardon had brought dumped on one of her tables. She shut the door behind her. She did not feel triumphant, only empty and alone. She fingered the black talisman around her neck, but dropped it after a moment and instead pulled out the talisman from her pocket. Many times during the debate she had felt Hyphanden's eyes upon her, through the jeweled eyes of the little dog. Now she stared at it, and it seemed she could feel the intensity of Hyphanden's mind. She would see him soon in person. There was much she wanted to ask, much she needed to know.

Chapter Seven: Leaving Hyolon (Hyphanden)

Hyphanden sat in the kitchen with his elbows on the table before him, fingers interlaced, chin upon his knuckles, staring fixedly at the box. Kwistocta was away visiting Mynador, otherwise he would never have brought it out. They had argued repeatedly about his use of the box and the seven minds inside it, and in one corner of his brain he knew she was right: accessing those minds was dangerous, even though he now knew who each of them were.

The Index lay beside the box on the table, glowing faintly. He'd managed to access enough of it to get basic information about everyone stored in the Crypt: name, age, gender, year of internment, basic charges and circumstances of internment. But the inner recesses of the Index still eluded him, and Stela had so far refused to help him access it. Stela was cagey with his information, driving bargains in exchange for his Skills and knowledge. Sometimes he wanted to get drunk, or walk around Hyolon reminiscing about the city in its heyday. Hyphanden had accommodated him as much as he could, but recently their relationship had soured.

The Index had been the cause of that. Hyphanden could read Stela's basic dossier clearly enough: Stelaphandon, age 46, male, member of the Inner Circle of the Elder Council of Hyolon, interned in the Year of Dispersal. Charges: murder of a Council-member. Means of internment: murdered via Skill, mind removed by Trophandra of the Elder Council and interned to stand trial.

Stela had immediately become defensive when Hyphanden revealed what he knew and sought to question him about the circumstances. They had argued, and Hyphanden hadn't taken him out of the box since. The others in the box were interesting as well, of course. Two were only partial minds, and he had gleaned all he could from them. One of those gave him the shudders: she had been a truly evil person, devoid of conscience. One of the complete minds was more than four hundred years old, and that one fascinated him, but it seemed to have faded during its time in the Crypt, and seeking answers within its matrix was difficult at best. Stelaphandon was bright and alert, but Hyphanden had intended to leave Stela alone, perhaps permanently.

But today he had an excuse of sorts. There was a specific question he wanted, no, *needed*, to ask. He opened the lid of the box. Inside was a honeycomb of twelve cells, three deep by four wide. Within seven of the cells was a silvery semi-liquid substance, similar to the material in the actual Crypt of Souls. It was upon this substance, which could easily change from liquid to a fine mist and back again, that the maps of the minds were written and transported.

As soon as he opened the box, the stuff in one of the cells began moving of its own accord, twisting and oozing, going to mist around the edges. Stelaphandon was itching to be out. Hyphanden leaned forward and his eyelids drooped as he concentrated. Moments later, a cohesive ball of mist arose from the cell and floated in front of his eyes for an instant before disappearing as though it had been sucked in. Hyphanden jerked slightly, then sat back in the kitchen chair. When his eyes opened fully, he saw the world as though from two points of view.

He rose and went out through the large glass doors to the back garden and orchard, as he often did when possessed of Stelaphandon. Stela enjoyed being outside, and Hyphanden could pace in the garden and mutter to himself undisturbed.

"Well, Phando, greetings," Stela said inside Hyphanden's brain. *"I assume we're alone, or do I get to endure another bout with Tocta when she sees me in here?"*

"We're alone," Hyphanden said shortly, speaking aloud. "I have no wish to disturb her. But she's gone for only a brief time, and I've brought you out not for pleasure, but to ask you a specific question."

"I see. So I'm to be stuffed back in the box when you've got what you want from me? How pleasant."

"When I've got more time we can talk or go where you wish," Hyphanden promised. "But I've been thinking about something, and I have nowhere else to turn with this question. I suspect the use of a long-discarded Skill, one that was Forbidden even in the time before the Dispersal. Who would have knowledge of such a thing?"

"You presume that I would. But you pique my interest; what is it?"

"I told you before about the attack on the young Sorcerer in the village of Andolith. The Key to the Crypt was stolen at that time, and the Sorcerer rendered unconscious. Do you recall?"

"Of course. You told me the thief had implanted a device in her carrying a Skill that would cause her death if it were to be removed with steel, but cause her death by poisoning if it was not removed. That Skill was circumvented by a clever Healer who used a stone blade."

"Yes. But a question remains in my mind: why do such a thing? It was a clumsy Skill, easily detectable by any Healer worth her salt. Charnia is old and well known. Rudon would surely have realized she would find the implant and circumvent it. So why bother at all? What was the point?"

"I perceive that you have an answer yourself. And I concur: the implant was quite probably a ruse, a distraction from the real Skill that was placed. And if this is true, you are correct: it has been Forbidden for many, many generations."

"As I thought. Of course, Rudon rendered Pateret unconscious in order to access the Key and have time to break the Protections placed upon it. He had probably been watching the area, possibly through proxies such as the Woodsmen. Once he knew where the Key was located and the door had been opened by Pateret, he would have had little problem breaking the remaining Protections. He's a prodigious Skill-breaker, and I used him well when we first arrived in Hyolon."

"Mmm-hmmm," Stela muttered. *"To my advantage, and your own detriment."*

Hyphanden paused for a moment, but decided not to probe that statement further until later. "The Andolith Council is not highly Skilled in Protections. Nevertheless, he would have needed

95

some time undisturbed. But afterwards, he could have simply left Pateret unconscious and made his escape. Instead, he implanted the device. Anyone finding it would know it had been placed there during the attack, and Charnia was bound to find and remove it."

"The question would occur to the Healer: why was it there?" Stela said.

"If it carried a heinous Skill on it, the Healer who removed it would look no further for an answer. She would assume she had circumvented its purpose. But I suspect it was there for another reason: over time, it slowly infused another Skill into Pateret's body. It did this without the necessity for Rudon to be there himself, and by the time it was removed, its duty was done."

"The Skill of which you speak is generally used on animals, as people are aware of it unless it is infused while they are unconscious, such as in this case. We called it View Possession, in my time."

"Describe what it does. I know it only from brief references in books I've discovered in the city. I have no details."

"Its purpose is to allow the implanter to View as though the person is a talisman. The question is, why would Rudon want to be able to View Andolith after successfully removing the Key from there?"

"That I have not figured out yet," Hyphanden admitted, "but you confirm my fears. Rudon is, I believe, using Pateret as a Viewing talisman."

"What's led you to this conclusion at this point?" Stela asked. *"You hadn't reached this conclusion when you first told me about the incident."*

"No, but I have more information now. I have Viewed the Viewer, so to speak. Rioletta Eris, who issued a Challenge under the Charter to her Elder Council, is in possession of a talisman of mine, through which we can communicate and I can View and Monitor. She took it with her to the Challenge hearing. There I twice Viewed Pateret, who expressed dislike and suspicion of my talisman. She could feel my presence, and even though I'm not personally acquainted with her I could see that her behavior was unusual."

96

"Ah. And the conclusion of the Challenge hearing? I have some familiarity with such things. They were in practice before the Charter of Dispersal was written."

"Rioletta prevailed. What she will do now I do not know, but it's probable she will come here at some point."

"Excellent!" Stela exclaimed. *"I hope you'll pull me out for the occasion. You know I find her interesting."*

"I'm not so sure she finds you interesting, but we'll see. But there is something else I need to know: how to break the Skill. We certainly cannot leave Pateret with such a Skill upon her."

"No. I can perhaps break it, but my memory of View Possession is tenuous. I had limited familiarity with it, only having studied it as an acolyte. The Skill-breaking is in itself Forbidden."

"Can you teach me how? Give me the knowledge! With the Andolith Challenge affirmed, I may have better access to their Council."

"Hmm," Stela mused. *"I'll make you a deal. You carry me with you to wherever you go to complete the Skill-breaking, and I'll guide you when we're there."*

"How am I to arrange that?" Hyphanden asked.

"Don't know," Stela said with a verbal shrug. *"I'll look forward to your solution."*

Hyphanden fingered the talisman hanging around his neck. "Kwistocta is on her way back." He turned towards the house, but hesitated. "I have another question, a matter of curiosity."

"Of course," Stela replied cynically. *"Anything for you."*

"I've been musing over the Key. Nikal of Dobor picked it up at the Polebray. It was inscribed by Likendahl, one of Nikal's ancestors and the founder of Dobor, and it seems Nikal was drawn to it. But I wonder how Likendahl's Key came to be at the Polebray in the hands of book-brokers in the first place. It seems like it would be a Protected item, not something that would have been left lying around Hyolon after the Dispersal. Have you any ideas?"

Stela considered. *"The method of opening the Crypt was a matter of Special Knowledge, passed on from generation to generation through the Elder Council, with a single physical Key and no written record. But in Trophandra's time it was observed that the old Key was becoming brittle and worn. It was nearly four hundred years old at the time. So Trophandra proposed, and it was accepted by the Council, that a number of Keys be created, one for each member of the Inner Circle, of which there were four: myself, Trophandra, Likendahl and Erendak."*

"So Likendahl's key was a replacement for the original, and it was somehow lost during the Dispersal, or perhaps afterward."

"I don't know for sure, because by the time of the actual Dispersal I was dead, so to speak. I would guess that it was lost in Hyolon, rather than afterwards, though."

"Why would you make that guess?" Hyphanden glanced around, his hand still on his talisman, to make sure Kwistocta had not arrived yet.

"Because I have access to some of your memories. You spoke of breaking the Protections on a number of estates with Rudon when you first came to Hyolon. Were you aware that one of those estates was Likendahl's?"

"No," Hyphanden said. "Which one?"

"A large white rock construction west of this neighborhood. Later you decided it was too far away from the rest of the estates you intended to use for the community, and Rudon sealed it up again."

"With his own Protections, of course," Hyphanden nodded. "And at some point he must have returned there."

"Likendahl was a collector of books. My guess is that Rudon bribed the Hyolonal with trade goods, including Likendahl's expensive books. He passed the Key off to the Hyolonal unaware of what it was, and they traded it to an antique broker who brought it to the Polebray."

Hyphanden laughed. "So Rudon had the Key in his hands and never knew it! But you said there were four such books created. Where do you think the others are?"

"Are you contemplating finding one and emptying the Crypt so Rudon cannot have it?" Stela asked cagily.

"No! All right, I admit to you, since you can read it yourself, that the thought has crossed my mind. But I would like to gather the books together to prevent others from getting ahold of them and thus having access to the Crypt in the future."

98

"I see. Well, my own Book is most probably gone for good. In our travels through the city, we observed that my estate has been looted, since I left it Unprotected due to circumstances beyond my control. Trophandra probably hid hers in this estate, but I don't know where. It's also possible she took it with her to Tabor. I wouldn't know. As for Erendak, I suspect Likendahl took his book and hid it, since Erendak couldn't do it himself."

"Because you killed him," Hyphanden stated flatly.

"I assure you, I did not go to him with the intention of killing him," Stela said testily. *"If I had, I would have Thrown a Skill at him instead of risking a hand-to-hand encounter, during which he died a physical death, making it impossible to retrieve his mind-map. It was Likendahl who confronted me and in his rage Threw a deadly Skill at me. Fortunately for me, my mind-map was retrieved by Trophandra and stored for future access. But I was never retrieved for trial."*

"I would like to know more about your encounter with Erendak," Hyphanden said, "but now we must go, or you and I will have an encounter with Kwistocta."

Hyphanden went back inside and sat down at the table. Stela gave him only a moment of resistance. He stowed the box beneath the counter. Then he grabbed a book and threw himself into his favorite chair near the fireplace. Kwistocta was quite good at seeing when he had been in contact with Stela, even if there had been a short gap in time between her arrival and when Hyphanden had put Stela away. Kwistocta had, after all, been Stela's original host.

Kwistocta entered the house through the garden, coming down off the wall behind the estate. Hyphanden saw that she brought a package wrapped in paper, likely from Mynador. Mynador was occasionally able to obtain spices and minerals that could not be produced within Hyolon, usually in trade for wine and medicines.

"What are you reading?" Kwistocta asked as she opened the package and began to store the spices.

"An old manual, one I found in amongst the latest box of books we salvaged. It's an advanced course in familiarity with Forbidden Skills. I've found something interesting."

Kwistocta joined him in the great-room. Hyphanden told her about his suspicion that Pateret had been View Possessed, carefully leaving out his conversation with Stela and attributing his source to information he'd gleaned from the book.

"What do you intend to do about it?" Kwistocta asked. "Certainly Pateret can't be left in this state if this is true, both for her own health and because we don't want Rudon Viewing Andolith for whatever his purpose may be. Is there anyone in Andolith, do you think, who could be trained to break this Skill?"

"I'm afraid not. Skill-wise, the Traditional communities are very limited, and Andolith has been among the strictest. They've done themselves a disservice. Likely there are Sorcerers there who could have been quite powerful, but they don't have the training."

"Perhaps you could train them," Kwistocta suggested.

Hyphanden snorted. "I'm not personally acquainted with Ladon, but from what I've heard I suspect he has the ability to wield a great deal of power. But he would never agree to use a Forbidden Skill, even to break one, and he doesn't have the background to use it even if he was willing. I don't know much about the other members of the Elder Council, but I've heard they are even stricter than Ladon. That leaves us with the Younger Council. Cardon would probably be willing but too weak. Pateret can't break her own Skill, and Morcah has been trained as a Traditional. Andor I believe has the mind to learn it, and Rioletta has stretched her own mind by learning Restricted Skills of other communities. Either of them could be an aid, but not a lead in such a Skill-breaking."

"Then what do you propose?"

Hyphanden thought for a moment. "Even though the Challenge has been affirmed, there is to be a transition of power over time, and Ladon will continue to hold the reins. No one is eager to turn over complete control to the Younger Council, and Morcah will certainly need Ladon's hand for years yet. Even if he can be convinced that Pateret is under the influence of such a Skill, Ladon will not let her travel to Hyolon, of that I'm certain. Besides, such travel would be dangerous. Rudon would know she had left Andolith, and would wonder why. As she got closer to

Hyolon, he would guess at the purpose and possibly try to stop her arrival."

"Then what?" Kwistocta persisted. "You're not proposing going to Andolith yourself, are you?"

Hyphanden nodded. "I see no other way."

"But there's still a warrant on your head, Phando!" Kwistocta protested. "If you're caught outside the city, you'll be taken before the First Chosen, and who knows how Arvindahl and the others would treat you?"

"I could travel using the northern route and stay outside Tabor. Once I'm across the ford anyone who chooses to arrest me will have to negotiate an extradition, perhaps more than they're willing to take on. And I suspect I could elude any captors anyway. They might be surprised at the Skills I could bring to bear!"

"Still, it's dangerous. You haven't been outside Hyolon for years. Although few would recognize you, there are those who seek warranted Outcasts, and likely some keep track of the city and the comings and goings of its residents. They have techniques that could negate your Skills."

"Perhaps. But I see no other choice, do you?"

Kwistocta sighed. "No, I can't think of one at this point. Very well, then, Phando. But I shall go with you."

"No!" Hyphanden said. "There is no reason to endanger you as well as me. Rudon has made no move since he obtained the Key, but at some point he will. What if we are both gone, or arrested? What better time for him to make his move? One of us must stay and give the appearance that the other remains as well. And I know how to break the Skill. I'm the one who should travel."

"How do you know how to break the Skill?" Kwistocta asked. "Most trainee manuals don't include specifics about Forbidden Skill-breaking techniques."

Hyphanden hesitated, and Kwistocta picked up on it immediately. "Oh, I see. You're planning to use Stela's knowledge to help you break this Skill. Is that how you actually found out about it? Show me where it is in the book you're reading!"

Hyphanden closed the book, which had been lying open across his knee. "It's not in there. But this is for a good cause, and not for

101

my own interest. This is the very reason these minds are so valuable."

Kwistocta jumped to her feet and strode into the kitchen angrily. "Obviously there's nothing I can do to stop you or convince you, Phando. For all I know this idea about View Possession is some false idea planted by Stela to convince you to keep him within your mind and out of his box for longer, until he can get such a grip on you that you won't be able to return him. Everything you say is suspect as far as I'm concerned. You're speaking with Stela's mouth, and I want nothing more to do with it!"

Hyphanden sighed. He knew there was little he could now say or do to assuage Kwistocta's anger. In time she would relent and perhaps listen to the rest of his proposal. But her words had also planted a seed of doubt: could Stela have been leading him on for the purpose of spending more time in his head?

He got up and followed her into the kitchen. "You're right, Tocta, he could have been leading me on. But I had the idea that it might be View Possession myself, before I asked him about it. In the absence of any real information to the contrary, I'm inclined to trust him. After all, it was he who led us out of the Council-house during Rudon's betrayal, and he led us true, without asking anything in return and without questioning who you were or what you wanted."

Kwistocta sighed. "That isn't what I wanted to hear you say. I was hoping you would realize how dangerous this game is, whether Stela was a trustworthy person in life or not. I suppose you're going to continue with your plan."

"I'll access him as little as I can," Hyphanden promised, "but I do think he's our only hope for breaking the Skill on Pateret. Please don't be angry, Tocta. I'm doing this with the best of intentions."

"You're doing this because your "*best of intentions*" disguise your desire for interaction with Stela. I know it; but on the other hand, I can't think of any other way to get to Pateret and decide whether this Skill has been laid and how to break it if it has. When are you planning to go?"

"As soon as possible, and as quietly as possible."

"After you finish breakfast, then, let's make the necessary preparations. I want you to be as safe as you can be. Please contact me often through the talisman. I dislike and disagree with your use of the minds in the box, but I don't love you any less. I'll worry."

"Of course," Hyphanden said. "I'll go and return as quickly as I can. I have no intention of being gone for long. There's too much Rudon might try. I won't be brash or obvious. I'll go as secretly as I can and put my trust in few. I'll be back with you again in no time."

Hyphanden leaned over and kissed Kwistocta on the forehead with a smile. She looked up at him, but her eyes were veiled.

Chapter Eight: Hyphanden in Andolith (Rioletta)

For the first two days after the Challenge, Rioletta slept a lot and saw no one. But by the third day she was more alert and restless. She propped the front door open to allow the fresh air in, and started washing the dishes that had piled up in the sink.

Andor stepped into the open door frame and tapped lightly as Rioletta dried her hands.

"How's it going? I saw your door open."

"Well, I seem to have caught up on my sleep. What's going on with the Council?"

"We left you a notice," Andor said worriedly. "Didn't you get it?"

"Yes, but I didn't feel like joining you. It didn't seem appropriate and besides, I was too tired." Rioletta picked up the notice she'd found posted on her door the day before, informing her that the Council would be meeting that evening.

"Well, things actually seem a lot like before. Morcah took on chairing the meeting but not much else. Ladon seems to be settling into his new role, which doesn't in truth seem much different from his old role."

"Good. I intended it that way. I suppose before I leave I'll need to sit down with Morcah and hash out the details of how the Integrated Council should be managed."

"Before you leave? Have you made a decision, then?"

Rioletta hesitated. "Well, not really."

Andor had been leaning on the doorframe, but now she pulled a chair out from the table and took a seat. Rioletta sat as well, and leaned her head on one hand, with her elbow on the table.

"I know about Cardon's plans," Andor said. "He's slowly been letting a few people in on it."

"The best idea seems to be to travel with Cardon to Dobor," Rioletta admitted slowly. "I need a break from Andolith. I'd like to spend some more time with Nikal, and I'd like to find out what's going on in Hyolon with Rudon and the Key."

"We should figure out some way to keep in touch so you can tell the rest of us what's going on and we can make the right decisions without waiting too long."

"You mean like a communication talisman?" Rioletta smiled. "That's Restricted Technology, and it's not in Andolith's City Charter!"

Andor snorted. "Teach me. I don't care."

"It's a good idea, but I'm not sure I have the ability to develop a talisman on my own. Nikal is much better. But find something over the next few days that would work for you. We'll figure something out."

After Andor left, Rioletta picked up the three slim volumes Hyphanden had sent to her. She hadn't had a chance to look at them yet. She sat down and opened them one at a time, sorting them by date. The books were all journals belonging to a man named Erendak. She quickly discovered that he was a pre-Dispersal Sorcerer, a member of the Inner Circle of Trophandra's Council of Hyolon, and thus a member of the Surinate, the governing body of the region. He was not one whose name history had preserved: she could think of no city or village named for him or claiming him as its founding father.

The reading was difficult. Erendak's writing was often terse and obscure, as if he feared someone else might read the journals and he wanted his notes to be ambiguous. The journals were written in the days just preceding the Dispersal, and this would have been intensely interesting to Rioletta had Erendak spoken openly of what was occurring. Instead she was just able to glean that he was engaged in secret meetings with a group of powerful Sorcerers. He spoke of a Second Accord, but didn't record the details.

A few pages in, Rioletta came upon the name Stelaphandon. He was also a member of the Inner Circle, deeply involved in plans for the Dispersal. She wondered if this was the Stelaphandon rescued from the Crypt, and if so, why Stela would have led

106

Hyphanden to the journals of Erendak. Perhaps he had left no journals himself, and this was a way to pass on information about his own life.

Another passage intrigued her. Erendak's cryptic notes spoke of ordering the removal of the mind of a younger Sorcerer to the Crypt of Souls. It was obvious that he was uncomfortable with the decision, but felt it was necessary. It was also apparent that he feared repercussions from other members of the Council and community. At first, Rioletta wondered if the mind might have been Stela's, but instead it appeared to have been a woman.

"The crime is treason," Erendak wrote. *"There can be no doubt that revealing what she has discovered would derail the Dispersal. We cannot afford that at this point. All of us would be subject to Challenge and removal to the Crypt were our plans known. But I fear the effect this action may have. My own safety may be in danger."*

Suddenly she felt something rap sharply on her shoe. Startled, she looked down to find a Leaf perched on several of its bracts, tapping imperiously. She felt a chill run up her spine. She had lived in the company of the Leaves for most of her life, and there was no reason to be any more alarmed at them now than she ever had been. But this was different behavior, and it was in her house.

As she stared at the Leaf, it scuttled out the door and away into the forest and then stopped and turned back towards her. That is, it turned from the direction in which it traveled to exactly the opposite direction. She could not tell if it had a front and rear side. It was obvious that it wanted her to follow. Without a backwards glance towards the village, Rioletta walked off into the woods.

She hardly needed to follow the Leaf's course. With little variation, it headed along the well-known path to the Grove of the Lefollah. Rioletta was well familiar with it, although it had been more than a year since she had taken it. She paused only to tighten her shoes as she neared an area of exposed rock and steep slopes where the path became more difficult. The Leaf scuttled ahead of her over the loose cobbles on the trail.

The Leaf did not rest, and became agitated when she stopped. She arrived at the Grove several hours after leaving the village, sweaty and tired. It was just past midday, and the sun was hot where it broke through the canopy. The center of the Grove was open, with a large flat rock that Rioletta had used as chair, table, and talisman in the past.

Rioletta knew the Lefollah preferred to move about in the dark, and she suspected she would have to wait until at least sunset. She had brought no food, water, or entertainment, so it would be a long wait. But almost as soon as she stepped into the Grove, she noticed movement in the tree she identified as Hope, the Grove's leader and Stolen's foster-mother. Several long limbs from the lower branches of the tree reached forward, and Hope began to speak from within.

Rioletta's Lefollah language was a little rusty, but she quickly began to remember what the creaks, pops, and rustles signified.

"There have been changes within your village," Hope began unceremoniously. "We have watched and seen. You are required through our bargain to inform us when changes occur that might affect us."

"As I would have, had the changes affected you. But the transfer of power from the Elder Council to the Younger Council will have little or no impact on your Grove. Besides, I do not consider that the bargain still stands. Stolen violated his part of it in Hyolon, and you responded by revealing yourself to the Outcast Sorcerers and trying to capture or injure him."

"Stolen broke his part of the bargain, it is true. Those who revealed themselves at your Ruined City were cohorts of ours. The message had been passed that Stolen should be stopped if possible. His use of the Shape-changing Skills violates a compact much older than the one between you and us. But the rest of the bargain still stands, as far as we are concerned: you will inform us when changes occur that could affect this Grove and keep our location unrevealed, and when she is of age, the girl Shushte will be allowed to come to us and make a decision about her future of her own accord."

"I will honor that part of the bargain, but anything involving Stolen is removed from it. He is his own man and can't be forbidden from using his knowledge while he dwells in Hyolon, in the company of the Outcast Sorcerers."

"Then we will reserve it to ourselves to stop him if the opportunity presents itself. His use of the Lefollah Skills violates the oldest compact."

"Which compact is that?" Rioletta asked.

"It was not given to you to know; therefore we will not reveal it. At one time your people knew it, but they have chosen to forget. Much of it was already forgotten by the time of the Second Accord a century ago, but after that it was completely suppressed. We will not violate our part of the bargain, even if you continue to do so."

"I can't keep an accord I don't know about," Rioletta said. "If you want us to keep it, I suggest you acquaint us with it."

Hope hesitated. "It is true that your personal knowledge has moved beyond what your people have maintained over the last century. Therefore I will offer you another bargain: should you find the evidence for these two Accords within your own records, I will confirm what you find. The oldest occurred many centuries ago. The second occurred a little more than one century ago, when your people abandoned the cities. I cannot tell you more."

"Very well," Rioletta said, "should I discover evidence of either of these accords, I'll return to you for details. Is that all you wanted from me?"

"One other thing: a warning. You are being watched. I do not know the reason or source."

"You mean the village is being watched?" Rioletta asked with a prickle of alarm.

"No. You, yourself, are being watched. Remember that my Leaves are watchers in and of themselves, and we are aware of other watchers. I am not able to discern the source, but the feeling is there."

Rioletta remembered Pateret telling her of the feeling of being watched as the two of them climbed towards the windmills.

"Woodsmen?" she asked hesitantly. "We were attacked recently, and there's evidence that someone or something was watching us beforehand."

"No, I know the Woodsmen, and although they have indeed been in this area, the watcher of whom I speak is not one of them."

"Perhaps it's just my communication talismans," Rioletta said. "I have two, one of which I carry with me."

"It does not have that feel. This is different. I cannot tell you further, because I do not know."

"Then thank you for the warning," Rioletta said. "I'll be more aware."

Rioletta was back in the village by dinnertime, a little footsore. Cardon caught her as she walked out of the woods. He looked at her suspiciously; she was sweaty and flushed, and had obviously been walking for some time. He knew where the Grove of Lefollah was located, but other than shooting her a questioning look, he didn't ask where she'd been. Rioletta simply waved briefly and made for her house. With Hope's warning, everyone was now suspect in her mind.

She locked the house up and checked the windows and doors twice before going to bed. It was hot in the house with the windows all closed, but she didn't feel secure with them open. She lay awake for a long time, alert for any small sound, trying to figure out how she was going to determine who or what was watching her. Hope had identified her, in particular, not the village itself, as the one being watched. She couldn't figure out why, unless it had something to do with the Key. Could someone else be looking for it? Surely anyone associated with Rudon would know it was gone.

It was light by the time she crawled out of bed the next morning. She went into her kitchen in her nightclothes and fixed herself a cup of tea. Just as she was sitting down at her small kitchen table, she glanced up at the shelves over the window. The eyes of the little dog talisman were glowing and fading slowly, rhythmically, almost as if it was blinking.

Rioletta jumped up and snatched the talisman off the shelf with a jolt of adrenalin. She looked deep into its eyes and opened her mind to Hyphanden. Immediately she felt Hyphanden's presence, and his intentions tried to form themselves into words in her mind.

"Have you a horse?" he asked, without greeting.

"No, but I can borrow one and the tack if I need to," Rioletta replied.

"No, you can walk. Leave your village via the road to Matbor. Keep an eye out when you have gone a mile or so."

"An eye out for what?" Rioletta asked, but the connection had faded. She was generally unable to maintain communication with anyone for very long. But she did not need an answer to follow Hyphanden's directions. If he wanted her to search for something a mile from Andolith, she would do so.

She pulled on some clothes hurriedly and finished her tea in a gulp as she headed out the door. Her house sat within view of the road to Matbor, with the door to the northwest, while the bulk of the village sat behind the house to the southeast. Two hundred yards from her door she was out of view, concealed by the trees of the Riola.

Her feet, although sore from her unexpected hike the day before, found the packed smooth dirt of the road comfortable. It was becoming dusty with the summer heat and lack of rain, but the passage of many horses and wagons kept it tamped down. The north side was more heavily treed, and Rioletta walked closer to that side in the shade.

After fifteen minutes, she began to scan either side, looking for anything unusual. The more open, sunny south side was easy to scan, and she saw nothing. The north side took more concentration, but still nothing popped out at her. She examined the road itself as well, looking for something small, but found nothing.

A mile and a half from Andolith she was almost prepared to turn around, thinking she must have missed it, when she heard the snort of a horse. A hundred feet off the road on the north side, a large dark gelding champed in the trees, saddled and bridled. She could smell the heavy sweat as she drew closer. Then she saw him, seated on a log, holding the horse's reins loosely in one hand, his elbows resting on his knees.

"Hyphanden!" Rioletta exclaimed. "What are you doing here? You shouldn't be outside of Hyolon!"

Hyphanden rose to greet her with a smile, and rather than take her hand he drew her into a hug. "Yes, so I've been told. However, I've managed to make it here without arrest. I apologize for the poor directions. I've never been to Andolith and so I had to guess at how far I was from the village."

"Of course. But you should have let me know you were coming. I would've been better prepared!"

"There's a reason I chose to wait until the last moment, and also a reason I elected not to ride into your village, besides the fact that I don't know where you live. We must discuss it before we go further and decide what we're going to do and how we're going to do it."

"I would love to have you stay in town, either in the Council-house or in some other accommodation. But I fear Ladon would order an arrest and extradition. We could possibly circumvent that through Morcah's orders, but you would be vulnerable the minute you left."

"I don't fear Ladon, nor do I truly fear any contingent that found it useful to ride out to arrest an old Outcast. It's Pateret I want to avoid."

"Pateret?" Rioletta asked incredulously. "Why in the world?"

Hyphanden told her about his suspicions and his confirmation with Stela. "When I Viewed the Challenge proceedings, I saw Pateret's reaction to my talisman. If she is View Possessed by Rudon, and he was also watching the proceedings, he might have become aware of my presence there. That certainly would have disturbed him."

Rioletta sat by him on the log. "But why would Rudon want to View or Monitor Andolith?"

Hyphanden shrugged. "I'm not sure. I think it's you he's tracking. Remember there are certain requirements for opening the Crypt of Souls, and he may not have all the elements he needs. A Loremaster is almost a necessity, or one who has been specifically trained in Loremaster Skills. He knows full well he'll never get me, but Loremasters are few and far between. He doesn't have a lot of choice as far as the rogue Outcasts he attracts to him. He knows you are a Loremaster with Reading Skills. In fact, he undoubtedly found out quite a bit about you before we went to the Crypt. He might think you'd be vulnerable to kidnap or even coercion, given your recent disagreements with your own Council."

Rioletta shuddered, thinking of Hope's warning. "So of course you can't be seen by Pateret. Otherwise, Rudon will know you've left Hyolon, and he could use your absence to his advantage, though perhaps not to access the Crypt."

Hyphanden nodded and sat up, stretching his back. "I'm sore from riding. I'm not used to long trips on horseback. We need to think about how we're going to approach this. Is there any hope of smuggling me into town until we can formulate some plan of action?"

A few minutes later the two of them started back towards Andolith, leading the horse and keeping an ear out for any other travelers on the road. Several hundred yards from town Rioletta led Hyphanden off into the woods a short distance. Rioletta mounted the horse, with a boost from Hyphanden as his stirrups were set much too long, and rode off to the south, skirting the village.

She rounded the communal gardens, deserted in the heat of the day, and rode up along the Sydian. From just below the greenhouse, she followed one of the garden paths towards the stables. There she dismounted, led the horse along the longest barn to the end, and opened the door to the raceway. The stalls on this end belonged to Cardon, and he kept his Mahquant horses here. Rioletta quickly unsaddled Hyphanden's mount, which bore little similarity to the stocky, short Andolith horses, stowed the tack among Cardon's gear, and turned the horse into an empty stall with a bucket of water and some hay. She hoped anyone who saw the strange animal would assume it was a new acquisition of Cardon's.

With the horse taken care of, she made her way quickly back up the slope to the village and through the plaza towards her house. A few people were out, taking care of whatever business they had, and she greeted Lida near Cardon's house and the Polisher at the sundial, performing her daily ritual. She rounded the corner of her house and made straight for the road again.

Hyphanden had stretched himself out on the leaves of the forest floor, hands behind his neck. He rose quickly when Rioletta approached, and the two of them shouldered his saddlebags and satchel. They made their way to the very edge of the Riola, where Rioletta peered cautiously out at the village.

"That house there, with the open door, is mine," she whispered, nodding at it. "We'll go straight from here to there. If we're lucky, no one will see us."

113

The two stepped out of the woods and walked briskly towards Rioletta's door. The angle of the house concealed them well, and they stepped into the front room without incident.

"Huh. I wondered what you were doing sneaking around town with a strange horse," came a voice from the shadows. Rioletta started and Hyphanden brought a hand to his waist, where a knife hung in a sheath.

"Sorry, didn't mean to startle you. The door was open," Creed said. "I wanted to make sure all was well. Besides, I thought I recognized that horse as you came around the gardens, Rioletta. Phando, good to see you again so soon!"

Rioletta relaxed in relief, and Hyphanden reached out with a smile to clasp Creed's hand.

"Well, I guess we've been caught," Hyphanden said. "Perhaps it's a good thing! We're going to need some help and support."

"I can support you with some good beer, if you want," Creed said. "Let me go and fetch Andor and the rest of the Younger Council. We don't need to let Ladon know what's going on."

"No!" Rioletta said. "Andor perhaps, but not Morcah or Pateret."

Hyphanden quickly explained to Creed why he had come to Andolith.

"But if this is true, can you break the Skill?" Creed asked.

Rioletta looked sharply at Hyphanden. She had not thought to ask.

Hyphanden shrugged. "With a little help in the form of Stela," he said. "I brought him with me."

"Portable Crypt," Creed raised his eyebrows. "Great."

Rioletta crossed her arms, but said nothing. They could debate the wisdom of that later. First they had to determine whether or not Hyphanden's suspicions were even true.

Creed left with the promise to bring Andor and Cardon that evening. Cardon was necessary because he had access to the implant that had been removed from Pateret. In the meantime, Hyphanden bathed and changed from his riding clothes to something lighter and more comfortable. He explored her house carefully, looking over her books and documents and the other accoutrements of a Loremaster Sorcerer of Andolith. He also took the little dog talisman and pocketed it.

"I'll keep it with me while I'm here and return it when I leave. That will make it easier to contact me. The longer a talisman is in possession of its owner, the stronger the bond becomes, and the more powerful the connection."

"Maybe you can help Andor and I set up talismans before you leave," Rioletta suggested.

"Of course!" Hyphanden laughed. "A few Restricted Skills never hurt anybody!"

As evening fell, Creed and Andor arrived, and a little later Cardon. He brought the implant, wrapped carefully in leather.

Andor brought a main dish for an evening meal, and Creed brought the beer he'd promised. They laid out the table and made small talk about goings-on in Andolith and Hyolon. Hyphanden had never traveled that way before. He asked about the Grove of the Lefollah, the wind machines and water generator, the dwelling of Rath of Luth, and other subjects.

"We may not see much of Rath of Luth for a while, until Ladon forgives her for voting with the Younger Council," Creed said.

"Ladon will get over it eventually," Andor said with some certainty.

When the dishes were cleared away, Cardon put the leather packet in the middle of the table. Hyphanden did not touch it. Instead he went to Rioletta's back room, where she'd allowed him to stash his belongings. In a minute he returned, and Rioletta could feel a change about him.

Hyphanden sat back down at the table and carefully unwrapped the implant. It was cylindrical and metallic, with tiny slots along either end. He used a glass knife of his own to roll it around a bit, and Rioletta brought a light closer to illuminate it better.

"What do you think?" Hyphanden muttered. At first Rioletta thought he was asking them, but quickly she realized that he was speaking to the other in his head. He nodded and rolled the device around a bit more, then suddenly dropped the knife and took the thing up in his bare fingers.

115

Andor jumped to stop him, but Hyphanden raised his other hand, and she sat back down. Hyphanden brought the implant closer to his face and concentrated his attention upon it for a long minute. Finally, he replaced it on the leather patch and rolled it up again.

"It has the feel of the device Stela and I think it to be," he announced. "The View Possession Skill takes time to imbue. It must be infused slowly into the person to avoid notice or obvious harm. This device was created long, long ago – it's an antique. Its purpose was to infuse healing Skills that needed to be instilled over a set period of time. Rudon has co-opted it for his own purposes. I can feel his Skill about it. The Skill that would have caused it to release a fatal dose of poison if it was touched by metal has dissipated. It was a ruse calculated to distract from its true purpose. By the time it was removed, the View Possession had been imbued, and no one looked for anything else once it was taken out, believing they had circumvented the Skill." He glanced at Cardon.

"I should have searched further," Cardon admitted. "Or I should have had Charnia do so."

"I don't think you would have been able to detect this, as you're not familiar with it," Hyphanden said. "But now that I'm sure, what are we to do?"

There was a long silence in the room.

"Well, we can't very well kidnap Pateret, hold her down, and perform some sort of Forbidden Skill-breaking on her," Andor said. "It has to be something she does of her own accord, and with the permission of at least the Younger Council. On the other hand, we can't very well reveal to her what's happened. Who knows what Rudon would do? But she can't be allowed to be a walking Viewing talisman for Rudon."

"I'm not sure there's anything Rudon can do from this distance, but I'm not sure enough to feel confident. If we give Pateret too much time to think about it, Rudon will certainly View and find out I'm here. He probably has some access to her thought patterns, too. There's also the possibility that the purpose of this Skill is to lure me out of Hyolon, and if so, I don't want him to know he's been successful."

116

Rioletta frowned. "This seems very dangerous for you, Hyphanden."

Hyphanden shrugged. "I can only do what I think best, and keep an eye out for my own safety. I'm not in immediate danger. At the moment, the most important thing is dealing with the View Possession."

"Perhaps we can tell Pateret we believe she has some left-over effects from the Skill that left her unconscious, and that Charnia and I have been exploring means to remedy that," Cardon said. "We can get her to go along with our actions, and explain the entire truth later."

Andor shook her head. "Dishonest. I'd prefer not to do it that way, but I see little option. But she won't trust you alone with such a thing, Cardon. Charnia would have to be involved."

"Perhaps Charnia would go along with it," Cardon said. "I'm not so sure she wouldn't. I've found her tiresome in the past, but sometimes she surprises me. She split her vote on the Challenge, after all."

"If we perform this Skill-breaking without the knowledge of the Elder Council, and it is found out later, we will have truly burned all our bridges with them," Rioletta said. "They would be in the right to Challenge us again, based on the use of Forbidden Skills on a member of the Council. There is really very little way this Skill-breaking can be interpreted as anything but Forbidden. There's no room for argument about it like there is with some of the other Skills."

Hyphanden sighed. "Well, then, perhaps we'd better have Ladon in here. Without his permission, this thing will not happen."

"No, Hyphanden," Rioletta protested. "He's just as likely to call in a warrant upon you."

"It's worth the chance," Hyphanden said. "And if the arrest happens, it happens. I will not Throw Skills at Ladon or any other from Andolith." He rose and went back into the back room, pulling the heavy drape behind him.

Reluctantly, Rioletta was the one who made her way through the village to Ladon's door. She could see a light through the window, but no one answered her knock. Frustrated, she headed for his brother Tannon's house. She could hear the voices of many

117

people inside as she approached, a family gathered for the evening meal. She knocked tentatively on the frame.

Aliora answered and greeted her warmly.

"I'm looking for Ladon," Rioletta told her. "It's important that I speak with him."

Aliora nodded, and a minute later Ladon appeared at the door. He stepped out and they stood in the pool of light beyond the doorway.

"Ladon, a matter of some seriousness has come up, and I request your presence to discuss it," Rioletta said. "I would not call you away if I did not need your help."

"All right," Ladon said with a combination of grudging acceptance and superiority in his voice. "What do you want?"

Rioletta led the way through the village to her house without revealing to Ladon what to expect. As they stepped into the front room, the conversation ceased. Ladon looked around at Cardon, Andor, and Creed, and then his eye fell upon the figure seated in an armchair towards the back of the room.

Hyphanden and Ladon had never laid eyes upon each other, but as Hyphanden rose, the suspicion of recognition crossed Ladon's face. The two men stood staring at each other without a word. No one else spoke in the room.

Finally Hyphanden cleared his throat and took a step forward. "Ladon Ereptor, I have heard a great deal about you, even in Hyolon," he began. "I am Hyphanden Vrinal of the Outcast Council. I am a friend of several of your citizens, and it was I who accommodated them when they sought the Crypt of Souls. You and I have taken different paths in life, but in many ways we are peers, both Leaders of our Councils. I would be most pleased to make your acquaintance." He extended a hand, palm up in a gesture of respect. It would be the height of rudeness for Ladon to refuse it, and he did not, although his expression remained cold.

"Please, Ladon, have a seat," Rioletta said. "There's a reason Hyphanden is here. He's not traveling around risking his own safety for a lark. Please listen to what he has to say."

Ladon sat stiffly at the table, and Hyphanden pulled a chair in closer. Over the next half-hour he described, in as much detail as he could while softening the story a bit for Ladon's benefit, how he

118

had come to be aware of Pateret's attack and how his research had brought certain suspicions to his mind. He did not mention his practice of accepting Stela's mind-map into his own. Finally, he described the Skill-breaking that would be necessary to remove the View Possession. Hyphanden, as a Loremaster, was a master storyteller and possessed large amounts of information he could wrap into the telling. He had an organized mind, and his story wound along a logical route, doubling back to emphasize important points. Even a master debater would have had difficulty refuting him by the time he was finished, and Ladon sat in silence.

"Here," Creed said, "have a beer." He poured one for Ladon and another for Hyphanden. Hyphanden raised his glass briefly, took a long draught and smiled.

Finally Ladon spoke. "You present a reasonable and persuasive case," he said. "I can now see why certain members of my citizenry were enamored of you, and made the decision to trust you. I cannot say I trust you, and I am sore tempted to call in a warrant upon you. But neither can I say with certainty that you are damaged or insane due to your use of the Forbidden Skills. I admit to a certain surprise."

Ladon looked around at the others seated around the table. "I was raised and have lived as a Traditional. It has not been an easy path, and perhaps I'm disdainful of those who fell to their own temptations. There are things that have tempted me as well, but I have kept myself upon the Traditional path and tried not to succumb to selfishness. I admit to a certain feeling of superiority for that; but I will try and set that aside, and analyze the evidence you've presented on its own, disassociated from the presenter."

"That's all I can ask," Hyphanden said mildly.

"It seems that two choices lie before me, with little or no middle ground," Ladon continued. "I can allow an Outcast Sorcerer to perform a Forbidden Skill upon a member of my Council to remove another Forbidden Skill that endangers another member of my Council, with unknown consequences. Or, I can refuse, and allow that member of my Council to exist in a state of Possession, being used without her leave as a Viewing talisman. The consequences of this are unknown as well, both short-term and long-term. Neither of these choices is particularly attractive."

Ladon rubbed his hand through his hair and sighed. He rose from the table. "I must have some time. I wish I could consult with Amidon or Boradon, but I suspect that wouldn't be a good idea. In reality, of course, you could now overrule me, with Morcah's acceptance. But I infer from your request that you want my permission and acceptance, and I appreciate that and accept the responsibility you lay upon me."

He looked Hyphanden in the eye. "In the meantime, Hyphanden, I would, if I were you, not make your presence known in this village. There are those beside myself who would happily call in a warrant on you, in the hopes that it might further our relationship with Tabor's First Chosen or for other reasons. I make the promise right now that I will not do so, but I make no promise for anyone else."

"Understood," Hyphanden said. "I came prepared to camp if necessary, and if you prefer, I can remove myself from your village until such time as you come to your decision."

"That's not necessary. I'm sure someone can provide you with food, drink, and a couch for a few nights. Goodnight."

After Ladon left, Rioletta pulled the door shut.

"Congratulations, Phando," Andor said. "You've survived your first meeting with Ladon Ereptor virtually unscathed."

"With only a few pokes to my ego, re: falling to temptation," Hyphanden laughed.

"Until tomorrow, then," Andor said. She and Creed gathered up the dishes they'd brought and the empty bottles, and Cardon folded up the piece of leather around the implant and put it in his shoulder satchel.

When they were alone, Rioletta set to work making a bed for Hyphanden out of her couch.

"I was summoned to the Lefollah yesterday, to tell them what happened with the Challenge," she told him. "The leader, Hope, the one who raised Stolen, warned me that I was being watched. She also mentioned something about two historical Accords. She promised to give me the details if I could find the basic facts myself. Have you heard of either of these two Accords, ones that would affect the Lefollah?"

Hyphanden grunted. "Indeed, I've come across mention of both of them. It's something I thought you might be interested in. I'd be very interested in hearing what Hope has to say about them. They directly affect our history. You have read Erendak's journals that I sent you?"

"Parts of them. Perhaps we'll have time to discuss them tomorrow," Rioletta said. "I've given up any pretense of studying only the documents prescribed by the Council. I might as well satisfy my curiosity."

"Ah, one last thing before bed," Hyphanden said. He pushed aside the curtain separating Rioletta's back room from the front and re-emerged a moment later with a small, heavily decorated antique box. It was made of silver metal with a blue inset lid overlaid with intricate scrollwork. It also had a sturdy clasp and lock.

"Stelaphandon," Hyphanden said. "I figured you might not want him in your room tonight."

"No thanks," Rioletta acknowledged. "Did you create a new crypt just for him?"

"Just for travel. I didn't want to bring the whole box with all the mind-maps. This is easy to carry and snug enough inside that it can be inverted or shaken with no consequences. At least, I think so."

"Were you surprised by Ladon?" Rioletta asked him as he stowed the box in one of his saddlebags near the couch.

Hyphanden considered. "Perhaps as surprised by him as he was by me. But when I think about it, I'm sure he didn't come by his position easily, even if this is a small, Traditional village. He has given up much to get where he is, as he pointed out. It's unlikely he would be the leader of the Elder Council without the ability to weigh facts and make informed decisions. I admit to some fear that he'd just jump on me and throw me in a cell. Certainly he could physically overpower me if he so desired."

"But you could easily out-Skill him," Rioletta said.

"Not if others were in the immediate vicinity who I didn't want to harm. Most Thrown Skills are not that specific. There's slop-over, and they expand with distance. But anyway, it doesn't seem that it'll be necessary."

"No. In the past I've repeatedly been forced to go to Ladon with some problem or another, usually when either I or someone else didn't want to or feared to do so. And each time he's been reasonable and come to a sound decision, with the exception of after Pateret's attack. In many ways I wish I hadn't Challenged him."

"That took a lot of guts, or a lot of bravado, one or the other. It's not a common thing to do. But these things seem almost fated to happen around you. There have been others in history who were catalysts for change, like Trophandra. Don't worry yourself over it; it seems to have worked out well so far."

Chapter Nine: Pateret's cure (Rioletta)

For the second night in a row, Rioletta slept restlessly, waking at every small sound. In some corner of her mind she expected an attempt on Hyphanden's freedom, but there was little she could do to protect him other than stay out of his way should anything happen. But morning dawned uneventfully, and Hyphanden was dressed and lounging on the unmade couch when she came into the front room.

"Are you interested in learning about the Accords your Lefollah friend was talking about?" Hyphanden asked as she prepared them breakfast.

Rioletta nodded. "Erendak's first journal mentions a Second Accord."

"Yes. I know more about the First Accord than the second one, though. It's an agreement that was almost forgotten even by the time of the Dispersal, since which it's been completely suppressed. I've found only hints about it in old documents buried deep in some of the oldest houses in Hyolon. But most of what I know remains only in the form of stories."

"I've collected stories myself, looking for clues about the Lefollah," Rioletta said.

"There's often some kernel of truth within fairy tales. I asked Duri to pick up any interesting books he found in his travels among the Unskilled," Hyphanden said. "Which reminds me: I haven't heard from Duri in a while. Rumors have reached me about the disappearance of an itinerant pseudo-Sorcerer in the settlement of Race, just the kind of person Duri would associate with, and this concerns me. I hope nothing's befallen him."

"I suspect Duri can take care of himself, don't you?" Rioletta asked.

"Perhaps. But back to the Accords: the First Accord happened long, long ago, and as often happens, the passage of time has pushed it into the realm of myth. It was an Accord between the

Lefollah and the Sorcerers. The Sorcerers apparently agreed to provide the Lefollah with Skilled bloodlines from time to time to keep the Lefollah from becoming too sedentary."

"What does that mean?" Rioletta asked suspiciously.

"I'm not sure how it worked yet," Hyphanden admitted. "But in exchange, the Lefollah agreed to undo Skills that had gone awry which the Sorcerers weren't able to deal with. These probably had to do with Mind-sharing and Shape-shifting."

"Then the Lefollah and the Sorcerers were well known to each other and had ongoing contact at that time."

"Hmm," Hyphanden mused. "I don't know about ongoing contact. It was more likely very occasional, reserved for those in the Inner Circles of the Councils. Over time it became less and less frequent as the Sorcerers turned their interests to other Skills and forbade the ones that caused the most problems. By the Dispersal this Accord was practically forgotten and almost never honored."

"But Hope may have remembered it when she freed the Elder Council from the tapestries," Rioletta mused. "What about the Second Accord? Both Hope and Erendak have mentioned it."

"It happened at the time of the Dispersal, but once again I have little information. Less information, in fact: while the First Accord became the stuff of stories, the Second Accord was hardly recorded, and in the chaos of the Dispersal it was largely ignored or forgotten. Erendak mentions the Second Accord, as you noted. From what I've gathered, he made a bargain regarding the Crypt of Souls and the use of those imprisoned there."

"Do you think the minds in the Crypt were promised to the Lefollah to re-invigorate their line?" Rioletta asked incredulously.

Hyphanden nodded. "Stelaphandon has hinted at this, but he keeps his knowledge close. He knows I desire it, so he uses it as a bargaining chip to keep himself in my mind and out of his box."

"A good reason to keep him out of your mind entirely," Rioletta replied. Hyphanden grimaced and took a swig of hot tea.

It was mid-morning before Ladon appeared at the door. He greeted them formally, as he was in the habit of doing with Rioletta. Hyphanden rose and clasped hands with him, deferring to Ladon once again.

"I've made the arrangements, and my decision," Ladon said. "If you're willing, we will break this Skill. I cannot see how we can do otherwise. I will bear the responsibility of this decision myself, whatever the future consequences."

Hyphanden observed Ladon with a slight smile. "That's very liberal of you! It's too bad I didn't arrive before the recent Challenge. Perhaps it could have been forestalled and some other arrangement reached."

Ladon's jaw clenched. "I was obligated to hear that Challenge under the rules of the Charter, once it was issued," he replied. "I am not necessarily backing off my previous position. And I will not permit any member of this community to learn this Skill or aid in it. The onus of casting a Forbidden Skill shall rest upon you entirely, Hyphanden."

"No problem," Hyphanden said.

"Is it a problem?" Rioletta asked. "Is the breaking of this Skill apt to cause you harm from its rebound? The Tabor Younger Council suffered severe effects from their use of such Skills."

"I don't know," Hyphanden admitted, "but remember that I'm much more prepared to use Forbidden Skills than the Younger Council were, and also I assume I won't be Throwing it. I'll be in physical contact with Pateret. And I'll have the aid of Stela and his mental faculties to support me. I'm not worried."

"What have you arranged, Ladon?" Rioletta asked hurriedly as Ladon frowned at Hyphanden's comment about Stela.

Ladon turned to her. "I went to Charnia's house last night. She was actually delighted to help out. She agreed to go to Morcah and Pateret herself and tell them she's been studying the implant and believes that Pateret is suffering from some lingering effects. She told Pateret it was imperative to reverse these effects as quickly as possible."

"How did Pateret take that news?" Rioletta asked.

"She was somewhat recalcitrant. But Morcah convinced her, and Charnia left them with a tea containing a potion that causes some sedation, to be consumed this morning. Charnia told me she also added a potion that reduces one's ability to utilize Monitoring or Viewing Skills, in the hopes that Rudon will be limited in what he can observe."

"It's possible Rudon instilled some resistance to tampering with his Skill," Hyphanden put in. "That would explain Pateret's opposition."

"Hopefully her opposition won't be too strong. Morcah's to bring her to Charnia's clinic. Charnia will completely sedate her before you arrive," Ladon nodded at Hyphanden. "I'll allow Charnia, Cardon as her aid, Rioletta, and Morcah to be in attendance during the procedure. Morcah won't be informed of the true nature of the procedure until later. This skirts the issue of informed consent, but under the circumstances I feel Pateret is not in her right mind, and therefore we can't rely on her to make the right decision. So we'll make the decision for her, in the belief that she would wish it were she capable of understanding the issue."

"We must do this quickly, then," Hyphanden said. "I don't want Rudon catching on to what we're doing."

"Pateret should be on her way to Charnia's," Ladon said. "Rioletta can take you to a place to wait out of sight. Cardon will come and get you when we're ready."

Hyphanden dug the small box out of his saddlebag and sat down at the table as Ladon left. He flipped open the lid, revealing the silver substance inside. Rioletta watched as the silver disintegrated to mist and disappeared into Hyphanden. When he looked up his eyes had a sharper focus, and his movements as he rose were quicker and more decisive.

"Let's go," he said, shutting the box with a snap. He left it sitting on the table.

Rioletta led Hyphanden/Stela into the Syrola across from her doorway and around the north side of the village. As they neared the base of the Contemplation they were forced to scramble a bit to keep away from the village clearing. Eventually they passed behind the bachelors' house where Stolen had once lived, and there they waited amongst the boulders along the wall of the Contemplation. Ladon's house was visible, and Charnia's clinic further into the village itself.

Finally Cardon appeared near Ladon's house and motioned them to come. They walked swiftly to Ladon's back porch and hugged the wall as Cardon checked for residents out and about in the area. When he was satisfied, they skirted the side of the house and cut across a corner of the plaza to Charnia's back stoop. Ladon held the door ajar for them.

They passed through Charnia's personal quarters and into the front of the building, which she used as a clinic. The door was shut and latched and the blinds drawn, followed by heavy curtains to block out light and prying eyes. The front room was lit only by artificial light, and Pateret slumbered on a couch there. Morcah sat by her holding her hand, although she appeared unconscious.

He looked up as Rioletta, Cardon, and Hyphanden entered. An expression of some confusion passed over his face. He was not familiar with Hyphanden. He looked to Ladon instead.

"Morcah, we have requested the aid of Hyphanden to fully remove the effects of Rudon's implant from Pateret," Ladon told him quickly. "I have agreed to it myself. Although we did not wish to alarm Pateret, the situation is very serious. We will tell you more when the procedure is over, but we must begin now, without further ado. I ask you to trust me. I did not make this decision lightly."

Morcah gaped and then hurriedly moved aside as Hyphanden approached. Hyphanden sat down and leaned over Pateret. Almost tentatively, he took her wrist and studied her face. Then he sat back and looked at Charnia.

"I will need a vessel, some kind of container for the Skill to be temporarily drained into until it can be destroyed. Much as it was imparted over a period of time, it will have to be removed slowly, like drawing out a string. A disposable container with a tight lid would be best."

Charnia disappeared into her kitchen for a moment, then returned with a small wooden box. Inside it contained a waxy substrate much like the one in Hyphanden's box.

"Will this do?"

"Perfect!" Hyphanden said, studying it. "I'm surprised you have something like this."

"Hmmph," Charnia replied, but did not elaborate. Rioletta stared at the box in astonishment. Charnia was certainly full of surprises.

"This is going to take a little longer than I thought," Hyphanden told them. "Are you prepared to keep Pateret asleep?"

127

Charnia nodded. Hyphanden set the box on the couch near Pateret's head. As time passed, he appeared to fall into a kind of trance. His head nodded. Occasionally he muttered or passed a hand near her face. But nothing appeared to pass between them, and Rioletta became restless, quietly changing her position from time to time.

After more than an hour, Hyphanden suddenly sat up and snapped the box shut.

"It is done," he replied. "We won't know the results until Pateret wakes. I can only hope there's no underlying damage. I followed my own knowledge and Stela's as best I could, but it is not complete."

"Pateret's been asleep for a long time, and should be wakened as quickly as possible," Charnia said.

Hyphanden rose. "Then I'll go, if Rioletta will escort me back to her house. I'll need some rest."

Rioletta grabbed him by the arm. He looked drawn and unstable, and his eyes seemed as though they were looking inward rather than focusing on his surroundings. He stumbled as they made their way from Charnia's back door to Ladon's stoop and then into the woods.

Hyphanden stopped abruptly. He sat down heavily on a fallen log and leaned forward, resting his forehead on his arms across his knees. "The Skill was much more powerful and more unfamiliar than I thought. I know nothing else like it. It's very akin to the Shape-changing Skills no one has mastered in recent memory."

Rioletta grabbed his shoulders and kneeled down to look him in the face. "Do you need to get rid of Stela?" she asked. "I can run and get the box for you."

"I don't know. I'm not sure. Perhaps he can support me. I need potions, but I'm not sure you have the capacity to create them here."

"We can try if you can give us directions," Rioletta urged. "I can get Cardon or Charnia. We can help you back to my house and bring what you need."

Hyphanden shook his head slowly. "I should have thought of it before and brought something along. But I didn't know

128

specifically what I'd need, and now there's not time to brew and distill potions." He slumped forward, resting his head on his arms.

"There must be something we can do!" Rioletta said. "There must be some way to reverse this effect! What about the Lefollah? They are only a half-day's walk away."

"Yes," Hyphanden said weakly. "But I don't think I can walk that far without some potion to help me."

"We can ride," Rioletta said. "I'll go and prepare two horses now and bring them here. We will ride straight to the Lefollah." She jumped up, but Hyphanden grabbed her wrist and gripped her with the last of his strength.

"Don't leave me!" he begged her, looking into her eyes. A flicker of terror crossed his face.

"Hyphanden! I have to go! I'll be back as soon as I can!" Rioletta told him, prying his fingers off her wrist. She ran through the forest, avoiding rocks and downed branches, and made straight for Charnia's clinic. She burst through the door without announcement.

"Charnia! Hyphanden has been taken ill. He needs any supportive potions you can give me. Cardon, can you get us two horses saddled quickly? We'll ride to the Grove. Otherwise I fear the same fate as the Younger Council."

"I'll come with you," Ladon told Cardon, and the two of them hurried out the door towards the stables. Charnia turned quickly to her cupboards.

"Give him these," she said, pressing two stoppered flasks into Rioletta's hands. "They are not of a strength to counter the effects of casting a Forbidden Skill, of course, but they are supportive of the mind. And take this." She added a small paper packet. "This I take myself, to maintain my mental faculties as I age. Who knows? It could help."

Rioletta ran back out the door clutching the flasks and paper packet. Hyphanden, to her relief, remained sitting, supporting himself with legs spread and his arms crossed over his knees. Unceremoniously, Rioletta grabbed him by the back of the collar and pulled his head up. He looked barely conscious. She unstoppered one of the flasks and held it to his lips. He took a small sip, and then several larger ones. Rioletta put the flask down, opened the other one and fed him a few sips of that as well.

Hyphanden seemed to revive a little. Rioletta opened the paper packet. It contained a powder. She ordered Hyphanden to open his mouth and sprinkled it on his tongue, then washed it down with the contents of one of the flasks. He coughed a little, but supported himself in a more erect position.

"Those will stave off the effects for a short time, anyway," he confirmed weakly. "I'm surprised you had anything like it here. Charnia is an interesting old Healer."

Rioletta relaxed a bit. "There's more. You tell me when you feel you need it. Cardon and Ladon are saddling horses for us. We'll ride to the Lefollah and see if Hope can help us."

He smiled weakly. "For what bargain this time?"

Rioletta shook her head. "We'll worry about that when we get there."

Hyphanden closed his eyes. "Stop and fetch the box before we go," he said. "I do not know where in my mind Stela has gone, although I feel his presence. Perhaps later I'll have the strength to return him to the matrix."

Rioletta sat down beside him on the log and put her arm around his shoulders, supporting his head on her shoulder. In only a few minutes, Cardon and Ladon arrived, riding two saddled horses and with a third, Hyphanden's horse, in tow.

"I'll go with you," Cardon said as he and Ladon dismounted. "I don't much like the thought of being in the presence of the Lefollah again, but I'll ride to the edge of the Grove in case you need me."

Ladon pulled Hyphanden's arm across his shoulder and raised him bodily. Rioletta brought his horse close, and Cardon and Ladon together helped him to the saddle. Hyphanden settled himself and Rioletta and Cardon mounted their own horses.

Cardon had brought one of the Andolith horses for himself and another for her. These horses were smaller than the Mahquant horses of the plains, quick and agile in deep woods. Hyphanden's horse was big and solid-boned, but it kept pace well enough with the other two. They skirted the edge of the forest and Rioletta slipped off and went quickly to her house, where she retrieved the antique box. With Rioletta before and Cardon behind watching Hyphanden in case he should slip, they set a rapid pace. Moving much faster than Rioletta could on foot, they came within two hours' time to the Grove of the Lefollah.

Cardon helped Hyphanden dismount, and Rioletta gave him another draught of each of the potions. Then she supported him and walked him in to the middle of the grove.

Rioletta quickly began to address Hope in Lefollah, apologizing for waking her in the middle of the day. Hope began to stir. She sent forth a stream of Lefollah, much louder than Rioletta could speak, which sounded like a windstorm in the tops of the tress.

"You have brought a Sorcerer, one with the feel of one of the Old Ones," Hope observed. "Yet he is in crisis. He has cast a Skill far beyond his own art."

"Yes, one he cast for the aid of another," Rioletta said. "Can you right him? We have no other hope."

"The Skill he cast was a Breaking Skill, one intended to break Shape-changing or shifting," Hope replied. "Of course this is our specialty, and was reserved for those who followed our path long ago. It is not intended that the Sorcerers, who sacrificed their power, be able to use this. It is generally fatal when they try, and they do not advance far along the spectrum of shifting and changing."

"You mean it was reserved during the First Accord?" Rioletta guessed desperately. "You told me you would discuss the Accords with me if I could find out more about them myself. Well, this is my source of information. If he dies, that knowledge will once again be lost."

Hope hesitated. "Bring him closer to me. I can at least provide him with some aid."

Rioletta pulled Hyphanden closer to Hope. Hope bent forward and used some of her limbs to wrap him, probing and tapping at his chest and skull. Hyphanden grimaced, but stood still until Hope began to pull him closer. He staggered as she impelled him towards her, until she had forced him right up against her trunk. Although Rioletta could not see what was occurring, she could

131

guess that he was face-to-face with Hope's true self, an uncomfortable proposition at best.

Finally Hope loosened her grip, holding him and supporting him with just one limb.

"He is in possession of another mind," she said. "Do you desire that this mind be removed from him?"

"Can you cause it to go into a container?" Rioletta asked. "Or must you expel it into the void?"

"I can cause it to go into a container, if you have one," Hope replied.

Rioletta went to the edge of the Grove and Cardon handed her the box. She brought it to Hope, who took it gingerly with a large-fingered limb. A moment later, Hyphanden exclaimed as though in pain, and as Hope released him he fell to the ground. Rioletta ran to him. He supported himself on one elbow, the other hand to his face. Hope extended the box.

Rioletta took the box. She assumed Stela was back inside. The removal hadn't been a smooth transition, obviously. But despite his pain, Hyphanden's eyes seemed more present and focused. He looked up sideways at Rioletta.

"That was rough. But I feel more ordered in my mind. I don't feel as though I'm shutting down anymore."

"Yes, his mind has been ordered," Hope said. "It required that I place some of my own essence within it, for some of the connections were breaking apart."

Hyphanden looked up sharply. "I understand that," he said in amazement.

"And I found within your mind the knowledge you hold of the Accords," Hope replied. "Return here when you are well, and we will discuss these Accords and both the past and the future." Her trunk zipped suddenly closed, she snapped upright, and to all appearances she returned to the form of a tree.

Rioletta helped Hyphanden to his feet. Cardon brought the horses a little further into the Grove, and Hyphanden was able to mount by himself. He accepted another of Charnia's draughts before they began to ride again.

By the time they arrived at Andolith, Hyphanden could again hardly keep his seat. Cardon dropped them off at Rioletta's house and took the horses to the stables himself. Rioletta helped Hyphanden to the back room, where she laid him on her bed in the dark. She wanted him to be comfortable, and the couch was really too short for him to spend a night on when he was ill. She would take the couch herself.

After he was settled, Rioletta went to Charnia's house. Charnia told her that Morcah had taken Pateret to his place for the evening. The story had rekindled Morcah's anger at Rudon, and once again he had expressed a desire to travel to Hyolon and confront the rogue Sorcerer. Now, however, he was not constrained by Ladon, who had previously refused to allow him to go.

"I'll talk to him, and maybe Hyphanden can, too," Rioletta said. "There's no point in running off to Hyolon at this point. If the Outcasts need our help they will let us know and we can make an informed decision then."

Cardon stopped by the door, and Rioletta went with him to see Andor and Creed. They found Ladon there. He had described the events since the morning to them.

"How's Phando?" Andor asked.

"I think he'll be all right. He's sleeping now. We'll see how he feels tomorrow."

"Did he realize he was risking his life to save Pateret?" Andor asked.

Rioletta hesitated. "I'm not sure. In one way, he risks his safety every time he performs a Forbidden Skill or takes Stela into his mind, or even walks around the streets of Hyolon. He certainly risked his freedom coming here, and there's still the journey back. I think he's used to it. I'm not sure he realized how serious the Breaking Skill was until afterwards. But he might have; certainly he knew first-hand what happened to the Younger Council of Tabor. He told me he was willing to risk it anyway."

"The village owes him a debt," Ladon admitted. "One thing we might be able to do for him is work to assure safe passage back to Hyolon."

"I've thought about that," Rioletta said. "If Hyphanden can stay for a few more days, he can travel with me to Dobor. Perhaps you might allow a couple of other people to accompany us as well."

Ladon smiled. "It's no longer up to me. But I would be happy to suggest that Andor, Creed, and perhaps Aliora accompany you to Dobor. From there it will be up to you to get him to Hyolon."

Chapter Ten: The ride to Dobor (Rioletta)

Rioletta played host to Hyphanden for the next several days as he slowly began to recover. He visited Charnia several times for more potions and when the village was quiet he sat outside on Rioletta's porch in the shade reading some of her documents. Rioletta watched him carefully. She knew the Skill that had felled the Tabor Younger Council had taken a number of days to do its work. Gradually she became used to his moods, and the fear that a period of brooding foreshadowed illness began to disappear. However, she found that if she didn't pointedly offer him food he would often forget to eat as he pored over one book or another. All of this was enlightening to Rioletta: other than Mosse Amwiska, she had never been around another inducted Loremaster, and it was interesting to identify certain character traits in herself that were mirrored in Hyphanden.

Several days after the Skill-breaking, Rioletta stopped by Cardon's house. He was on his knees in the back room of the house, packing leather-working tools carefully into a large crate.

"The rumor has been spreading that you're leaving, Cardon," she told him.

"I thought it would," he replied with a laugh. "I made sure a few select people knew, and there's been no need for an announcement!"

"What's to be done with the house?"

Cardon paused and looked around. "It will sit empty until Ladon appoints it to someone, I suppose. It's not large, but it's in good shape, and there's this shop in the back for some craftsman to use. It will serve some young couple well."

"Will you miss it?" Rioletta asked.

"I suppose I will. I've spent my entire life in Andolith in this very house. But the leaving's been made easier by the events of the

135

last two years. I don't feel safe here, and the career I once thought I'd follow is gone. Dobor will be something new for me and I'm looking forward to it. At this point I'm just ready to go and be done with it."

Rioletta didn't pack much. Although she was leaving with no idea in mind of when she'd return, she was unwilling to abandon Andolith altogether and still remained, in name if not in practice, an Andolith Council-member and inducted Sorcerer. She contacted Nikal via her talisman, sitting alone on top of the Contemplation, and told him she was coming for a visit. He was eager to hear of Hyphanden's adventures: the two of them, after some initial tension, had gotten along well in Hyolon.

On the last day before they were scheduled to leave Andolith, Hyphanden discussed visiting the Lefollah again with Rioletta.

"I'm interested in the details of the Accords," Rioletta said, "but I'm not sure I'm interested enough to make that journey again, or to listen to Hope. She hints around at things, but rarely comes right out and says them. When she does say or do something straight out, she's often rough and selfish."

"I could go by myself," Hyphanden said. "I haven't listened to her as much as you have. Whatever she did to repair my mind gave me the ability to understand her speech. I don't need a translator."

"Can you find the way?" Rioletta asked. "And do you feel safe enough outside the boundaries of Andolith?"

"The way is fairly straightforward, and there are no settlements between us and the Grove, so I should be safe enough. I'm not afraid of the animals of the woods."

"Hope prefers to talk at night, so you might as well not leave until afternoon," Rioletta said. "Come back after you're done. It's almost a full moon, so you should be able to find your way. If you have to, you can wait until morning, but we're planning to start tomorrow by midday."

Despite Hyphanden's confidence, Rioletta was apprehensive. She realized after he left that he had forgotten to give her the talisman back, so she had no way to communicate with him. She wasn't sure he'd be able to find his way after just one trip through the Syrola, and that one made while he was deathly ill. She distracted herself with final packing and frequent trips to Cardon's house to talk about their plans. Finally, though, it was time to retire. She wanted to at least try to sleep to be ready for the journey the next day.

But her mind resisted sleep. She lay awake, occasionally changing position, and several times she got up and walked around the house for a few minutes before trying to resettle herself. Hyphanden had re-taken the couch after one night on her bed, and it was strange, after a week, to see the couch empty. In addition, although she no longer feared being watched by Pateret, she couldn't help but consider that Rudon might look for some other way to coerce or compel her.

She awoke with a start in the very early morning hours and realized that despite her initial difficulty, she must have drifted off. She could hear someone in the front room and tell from the rustlings that the person was settling on the couch. Relieved, she fell back to sleep almost at once, and did not awaken until it was light.

There was little time to talk in the morning. Hyphanden, still a secret to most of the town, left early with the intention of waiting for them down the road. Cardon's wagon had to be packed and Lida settled, the horses had to be fed and groomed, and last-minute preparations had to be finished.

In mid-morning the little party set out with a number of onlookers. Cardon had made the rounds and said his good-byes, but there were still many who had come to wish him a good journey, since he would not return to Andolith. There was some hope they'd see him at the Polebray or during his travels, but in reality there were those in town he would likely never see again. Others had come to bid Lida good-bye, and Alaxas brought her own children to bid farewell to Justah. Creed, Andor, and Aliora, who were traveling with them, waited patiently, holding their horses at the edge of the Riola.

The day was bright and all of them were in a good mood. Hyphanden joined them within half a mile. He joked with Creed and grinned his wolfish Vrinac grin, his dark eyes snapping beneath his heavy brows.

Andor chuckled. "Hyphanden, you should stop grinning like that. You'll scare small children."

"Nonsense," Hyphanden said, pulling close to Justah's pony and leaning in close to her. "You're not afraid of me, are you, Justah?"

Justah looked him full in the face and spoke a sentence in Lefollah. Hyphanden laughed out loud. "You see, she's not afraid!"

"That doesn't mean much, unfortunately," Cardon said. "She's not afraid of anything."

Once away from the town, they discussed their plans for travel again. They were headed for Dobor, but the question was, by what route? They had already decided to spend a night in or near Matbor and a second night camping along the Rhamphor Road, well away from Tabor Ford. However, the third night was up for debate.

Andor and Creed suggested that they bypass the new Dobor bridge and spend a night at West Ford, then backtrack the next day. Cardon wanted to cross the bridge late in the day and camp along the road to Dobor. Hyphanden was of a mind to go to West Ford: the road between the bridge and Dobor itself, although in name part of the jurisdiction of Dobor, was poorly guarded and Tabor bounty-hunters and brigands roamed there at will. Rioletta could not make up her mind. She saw the advantages of each and knew Cardon wanted to get to Dobor, but she was not in a hurry herself.

"Remember there may be a warrant out on your head, Cardon, as there is on mine," Hyphanden said. "You are known to have associated with the Younger Council and to have been with them near the time of their deaths. Their relatives are powerful people in Tabor, and they would probably like to question you. Likely they would prefer to have Justah for themselves as well, and raise her as a citizen of Tabor."

"But most Tabor residents won't recognize me. Camping is hard on Lida and I'd like to get to Dobor as quickly as possible. Going to West Ford will put us behind by almost a full day."

"I'm as anxious as you are to arrive in Dobor and to return to Hyolon. I've rarely been away from Kwistocta for this long," Hyphanden said, absently fingering the talisman around his neck. "We are cousins and were raised together before we became Tabor Sorcerers. But many of the First Chosen would certainly recognize me, despite the passage of time. We were well known to each

138

other. And remember that Tabor is not like Andolith. Andolith is a community of the Skilled. The Unskilled have a valuable place in Tabor society. They're often hired as bounty-hunters and security patrols. You probably encountered a group of them during your liberation of the Elder Council. They are quite keen to serve warrants, as the reward is often great."

"It seems to me that Hyphanden's safety overrules the convenience of arriving in Dobor a day earlier," Rioletta said. "Have patience, Cardon. We can take a good meal in a boarding house in West Ford, and you might even encounter relatives from among the Mahquant and Kirquant there."

They spent the first night at their usual inn in Matbor. After dinner, Hyphanden fell asleep quickly, his mind still exhausted by the Skill he had thrown. The rest of the group went for a few drinks at a nearby tavern, leaving Justah with Lida. They strolled around the town, browsing through the shops that remained open in the early evening. Matbor was known for its fine and brightly colored fabric, and much of the region's fashion came from there every year. Rioletta and Andor bought a number of shirts for themselves, and Cardon bought some for Lida and Justah.

The following day went much as the day before. The weather was good and they continued down the Tadian towards the Rhamphor until late afternoon. Andor turned them aside into the woods and they camped off the beaten track near a lushly vegetated spring. On the third day they worked their way back to the main road and continued south, occasionally passing other groups of travelers along the way.

Rioletta noticed that Cardon gazed towards the new Dobor Bridge as they rode by, but he said nothing. It was not close to the road upon which they traveled, but could be seen in the distance, arching over the Tadian, with a few people crossing over it. The path was now well-established, and a few vendors had set up wagons and huts at the crossroads to take advantage of the traffic.

In West Ford they took a couple of rooms at the inn by the river where Rioletta and Andor had found Cardon two years before. Since they were there, Rioletta and Andor thought it proper to pay their respects to Stetsordahl and Lindordahl, both of whom had settled in West Ford.

"I think it's probably not a good idea for me to show up unexpectedly at Stetsor's doorstep," Hyphanden said with a grin. "Forgiving he may be, but I prefer not to bring up old memories."

"Who knows? Maybe he'll want to see you," Rioletta said. "You can wait here and get a little dinner, and we can send for you if he does."

"Cardon, go ahead and get a meal with Phando," Aliora offered. "I'd like a chance to wash up. We can order a meal brought up for Justah and Lida, and I can sit for Justah for a while and give Lida a break. When you're done we'll trade places and I'll go down to dinner myself."

After unloading what they'd need for the night and stabling the horses, Rioletta, Andor, and Creed decided to walk to Stetsor's place. It would feel good to stretch their legs after several days of riding.

Just as they were leaving, Hyphanden called Rioletta aside. He pressed the little dog talisman into her hand. "I think I've had it long enough. The connection should be quite strong now."

Rioletta smiled and slipped it into her satchel. "Thanks. Maybe I'll use it if Stetsordahl decides he wants to see you this evening." She hurried to catch up to Andor and Creed.

It wasn't a long walk to Stetsor's apartment overlooking the Tadian. He greeted the three of them enthusiastically and sent one of his ever-present attendants for food and drink. Rioletta had learned to be forthright with Stetsor, as he seemed to be able to read between the lines when she left things out. She told him what had happened with Pateret and their suspicions about Rudon, and when the page was out of the room, she told him about Hyphanden's arrival and help.

She was not particularly surprised when Stetsordahl indicated he would like to see Hyphanden. She tried to contact him via the little dog talisman, but to her surprise it either did not work, or he was not listening.

"I'll just run back to the inn and get him," Rioletta said.

"Don't put yourself out for me and my whims," Stetsor replied.

"No, it's not that far. I'd like to see you meet again."

"Or I can go," Creed said, "or go with you if you don't like the thought of traveling through West Ford by yourself in the dark."

"Really, it's no problem," Rioletta said. "I'll be back in a few minutes."

She jogged down the steps from Stetsor's second-floor apartment. She moved through the smaller streets quickly, using a little Concealment, but West Ford was low in crime and she wasn't particularly worried. She went in the main door of the inn and quickly scanned the restaurant. It was dim, but she didn't see Hyphanden or Cardon, or Aliora for that matter. She trotted up the stairs and knocked on the door of the room Hyphanden, Creed, and Cardon would share, but got no answer. Then she crossed the hall and unlocked the door to the room they had reserved for the women of the party.

Aliora looked up expectantly as she came in. Lida and Justah were asleep, and Justah only stirred a bit.

"Where are Hyphanden and Cardon?" Rioletta whispered. "Stetsor wants to see Phando."

"I don't know," Aliora whispered back in an irritated tone. "I thought Cardon might come back and give me a break so I could go eat dinner, but he hasn't returned yet."

"You haven't eaten dinner?" Rioletta asked in surprise. "It's been more than two hours since we left."

Aliora shook her head. "Did you check downstairs?"

"I looked in the restaurant and didn't see them. There's a bar, but it would surprise me if they were just sitting there drinking without giving you a break." She glanced at Lida and Justah. "Come on, we can leave them asleep for a few minutes."

Aliora pulled the door closed quietly, and the two women descended the stairs once again. This time they walked through the restaurant deliberately, checking every nook and cranny. But neither Hyphanden nor Cardon was there.

Aliora approached the front desk to ask if they'd been seen.

"The tall Vrinac and the 'Quant?" the man at the counter asked. "They were here, sitting at that table by the back door. They ate and paid up, bought another round afterwards. I don't know when they left; didn't see 'em go."

141

"Thanks," Aliora said, turning to Rioletta. "Let's go check the bar."

They followed the hallway to the left of the main stair and entered a dark, smoky tavern. They threaded their way through the crowd behind the bar seats, but the two men were not there either.

"You don't think they just went out on the town, do you?" Aliora said in exasperation.

"That's all I can imagine, although it doesn't really sound like Phando," Rioletta said. "Maybe he's enjoying his few days of freedom from Hyolon. Why don't you order some dinner? If you don't mind, I'll go back to Stetsor's."

"Go ahead," Aliora said. "Check a few bars on your way. If those two come back drunk in the middle of the night, you'll hear me giving them a piece of my mind no matter what the time is."

"I'll join you in that," Rioletta said. She was slightly worried, although more exasperated. Before returning to Stetsor's, she went around the river side of the inn and checked the tables set up overlooking the water, where she and Andor and Cardon had talked before. But no one was there, and she doubted they were in the darkened stables. She returned to the main road and started back to Stetsor's. He would be disappointed, but maybe it would be for the best. She could imagine a meeting between the two turning ugly, and it would certainly be tense. Perhaps there would be another time the two could meet.

Chapter Eleven: Dwel and Rant (Cardon)

Cardon and Hyphanden threaded through the crowded dinner hall to a table at the back, near a servant's door that opened out into the stable-yard. The door wasn't used frequently, but when someone did come through, it allowed a rush of fresh air into the room. It was a favorite area of the hall for the Mahquant and Kirquant travelers.

Hyphanden, as he walked through the crowd to the table, attracted some attention. His appearance was obviously Vrinac, and except for Stetsor and Lindor and their entourage, there were few Vrinac in West Ford. But the back table was tucked in deep enough that the attention soon faded, and anyway, when he sat down he was not as obvious. They ate their dinners in peace, and then ordered another beer as dessert.

Cardon leaned back in his chair and looked around the room. It was dark in there, and hard to make out the faces of the 'Quants who frequented the place. He was eager, now that they were in West Ford, to see if he could find a relative or friend who could take a message to Skyros, who had helped him during his recovery from the Shape-changing draught. He wanted his kinfolk to know he was moving to Dobor. Perhaps it would be easier to stay in touch with Lida's clan when they were further south and out of the Syrola.

He heard Hyphanden grunt and turned back to him. At first he saw nothing unusual, except an expression on Hyphanden's face and an odd rigidity of posture.

Then he noticed the gun stuck up against Hyphanden's back just below the armpit, and the man sitting next to him, casually leaning forward out of his chair, whose finger was on the trigger.

Hyphanden's right hand lay on the table, and Cardon noticed his forefinger twitch. The man jammed the gun against Hyphanden harder.

"Don't even think about it," he growled. "Any Skill you Throw at us is sure to catch many others and do them damage. I can likely pull this trigger before I'm disabled anyway. It'll kill you and probably go right through to your partner here."

Cardon moved his head slightly to look over his shoulder, and found a man of similar appearance standing directly behind him. He felt the hard muzzle of another gun press against his shoulder blade.

"There's been a warrant on your head for many years, Hyphanden Vrinal," the first man grinned. "The First Chosen will pay me a handsome bounty to bring you in. As for this other one, if he's in your company there's likely a warrant on him as well. Perhaps we'll get lucky and get a real prize."

The man reached around with his free hand and grabbed the talisman Hyphanden wore on a chain around his neck. With a brutal snap, he broke the chain, leaving a mark on Hyphanden's neck. "So you can't call your buddies," the man said.

Still keeping the gun up against Hyphanden's side, he reached into his vest pocket with his free hand, deposited the talisman, and withdrew two short sashes of yellow material with large bulky clasps at the ends. He tossed them on the table.

"Go ahead, Rant," the first man said. Rant quickly stuck his firearm in the waistband of his pants, picked up one of the sashes and fastened it around Hyphanden's neck. Then he took the other one and fastened it around Cardon's neck, pulling it tight with an adjustment hidden in the clasp. Cardon felt an odd sensation, as though his ears had suddenly become stuffed up.

"These will keep you from using any Skills," the first man told them. "True, it'll run down within a couple of days, and neither of us have the Skills to recharge it. But we'll have you in Tabor and in front of the First Chosen by then."

Rant laughed sharply. "No Skills to recharge it, in fact no Skills at all. But it doesn't seem to be much of a disadvantage, does it, Dwel?"

"Now we're going to get up and go outside through that little servant's door," Dwel said. "Quiet, like we're friends going out for a smoke. You don't want a scene, do you? We're better known here than you, I'll wager."

"A poor wager," Cardon said boldly. "I'm Kirquant, and many in here are my relatives. If I need help, they'll come to my aid."

Dwel snorted. "I've never seen you in here before, and if you knew any of these men and women, you'd be sitting with them and not all by yourselves. Besides, most in here know us and our business, and few will risk their own safety to help strangers accused of a crime."

There was little choice but for them to rise slowly and make their way out the door, followed by the two Unskilled bounty-hunters. The stable yard was dark and cool. The river ran by to their right down below the bank, and the horses champed in the stables ahead of them. Clumps of cottonwoods overshadowed the yard.

Just outside the door, Dwel stopped them and clamped their hands behind them with metal cuffs. Then he searched them both quickly and thoroughly, removing everything from their pockets and the knife each wore at his belt. Dwel grabbed Hyphanden's cuffs and Rant took Cardon's, and twisting them cruelly, forced the two Sorcerers towards the stables. Cardon made a few attempts to twist loose, gauging Rant's control. His attempts only served to hurt his wrists.

When they reached the stables, Dwel opened a door leading to a small, dark room, and forced them inside.

"Sit down on the floor," he told them.

Hyphanden leaned his back against a wall and carefully slid down it to a sitting position. Cardon crossed his ankles and leaned forward to let himself down, trying not to overbalance with his hands behind him. Dwel quickly closed the door, leaving them in pitch-black.

The room had a pungent medicinal odor. Cardon guessed it was a preparation room used to mix salves and sprays for the horses. The floor was hard-packed earth and the walls the same thick beams as the stable. There was no window and only the small door Dwel had forced them through.

145

Cardon pushed himself back to his feet as soon as the door closed and began to grope awkwardly around the room, hoping to find something of use.

"What are these things around our necks, Phando?" he asked, forcing his own hands up behind himself to reach the top of what felt like a wooden table or counter. "I feel like I'm going deaf."

"Skill-blockers," Hyphanden said. "They rely on both technology and Skill to operate. The machinery is in the clasp. The Tabor Council has used them since the Dispersal to control Sorcerers they plan to Strip and Outcast. Dwel's wrong on one count, though. They'll run out in a few days only because they require mechanical recharging, no Skills necessary. He apparently doesn't realize that. If he did, well, he's Unskilled, and probably has a good knowledge of mechanics. He'd be able to keep these things going for as long as he likes, and have a Sorcerer at his disposal."

"So you have experience with these things? You know how to defeat them?" Cardon asked as he located a hoof pick and slid it off the counter and into a vest pocket.

"No, not direct experience. Stetsor allowed me to flee and didn't imprison me for Stripping. I was never trained in their use and I have no knowledge of how to defeat them."

"Could Stela help?"

"Perhaps, but he's drowsing in his box with our gear, not extant in my mind," Hyphanden replied.

"There's got to be something we can do, rather than just go along blithely to Tabor with these characters," Cardon fumed.

"If you've got any ideas, I'm happy to hear them," Hyphanden said. "I have none at the moment."

Cardon removed a flask from the counter in the dark, squatted down to put it on the floor, and knelt near it, struggling to open the top with bound hands. "You can't defeat these things with some of your Forbidden Skills? Even get a message through to someone?" He bent down and sniffed the open flask to identify its contents. "How far away can you communicate with Kwistocta?"

"From very far, if I have my talisman and amplifier. But Dwel took it. Distance Communication is a Skill, and these sashes block it like any other."

They could hear Dwel and Rant talking and the snort of the horses as they were led from the stables. A minute later, the door opened. Cardon sat back down on the floor. He had pocketed two hoof picks and two small flasks of horse medicines.

Dwel grabbed Cardon by one arm and dragged him up and outside. Cardon saw that one of his own horses had been fetched and saddled for him. "How are we supposed to get on the horses with our hands behind our backs?" he asked.

Dwel did not answer. He wrapped a thick leather belt around Cardon's waist and buckled it tight in the small of Cardon's back. Then he unlocked the cuffs and released Cardon's hands. He threaded the open cuffs through a ring attached to the belt in the front. He guided Cardon's hands back into the cuffs so his wrists were attached to the belt near his waist in the front.

Together Dwel and Rant helped Cardon to the saddle. They had fitted Cardon's horse with a halter and lead-rope, rather than a bridle. Hyphanden was similarly fitted with a belt, cuffed in front, and heaved up onto his own horse. With Dwel in front leading the horses and Rant in back, they started off through the dark down towards the Rhamphor, skirting the well-lit main road. From there they followed the Rhamphor upstream to its confluence with the Tadian and turned north along the eastern bank, climbing to the narrow residential alleys and lanes, the dark and less-traveled backways of West Ford.

Chapter Twelve: Leaving West Ford (Rioletta)

In the morning Rioletta was awakened early by a knock on the door. She scrambled out of bed and went to the door, opening it just a crack. It was Creed, and she opened the door wider.

"They didn't come back last night," Creed said. "I've been down to the stables. Their horses and tack are gone."

Rioletta was suddenly fully awake. "Their horses are gone?"

"And their tack, except for the bridles. Hyphanden's horse is missing, and one of Cardon's saddle-horses that he was trailing."

Rioletta glanced at the farthest bed, where Lida and Justah were beginning to wake. "Give us a minute, Creed, and we'll meet you downstairs."

Rioletta pushed the door shut. She and Andor and Aliora hurriedly dressed.

"We'll be back in a few minutes," Aliora told Lida. "Don't worry, everything's fine."

Downstairs, Creed was pacing impatiently in front of the counter. "We should have known something was wrong last night," he reproached himself.

"Let's not waste time berating ourselves," Rioletta said. "But I agree: something's happened. I can't see either of them being out all night on the town with their horses. And it's odd that they didn't take their bridles. I wonder what that means?"

"Easy enough to guess," Aliora said grimly. "It means someone else was leading their horses. There was no need for them to use the reins."

"The only thing I've been able to find out so far is from the stable-hands," Creed told them. "The horses were gone by the time they reported for work this morning, and someone has been in the prep room where they mix foot ointments and fly spray and the like. A few items are missing."

"What's missing, did they say?" Andor asked.

"They think a couple of hoof picks and some small flasks of hoof infection treatment. Not even potions or brews, but regular medicine."

The four of them stood thinking for a minute, but that news seemed to shed little light on events, if indeed it was even related.

"We're going to have to find people who were here last night and saw them at the restaurant, and ask them what they noticed," Andor said. "One or two of us should check the bars around town, in case they did go out and met some trouble. We should check the jail and the hospital as well."

"Agreed," Rioletta said. "Let's first see if there's anyone who can care for Lida and Justah for a while. That'll free the rest of us up to start looking."

The front desk clerk told them he could have his wife bring food for Lida and Justah and entertain them for a while. He had not been at the desk the night before; he was a morning clerk. But he agreed to let Rioletta and Aliora question guests as they checked out, as long as they didn't harass anyone. Creed and Andor went to the stables to get their horses. They would make faster time around town mounted.

Very few guests were leaving at that hour, and those that were had gone to bed early the night before. Several of them remembered seeing Hyphanden in the restaurant around dinnertime: he tended to stick in the memory. Fewer of them specifically remembered Cardon, who resembled the 'Quants who frequented the inn, although his hair was cut shorter. None of them recalled anything unusual. They shrugged as they made their way out the door, in a hurry to be gone. Rioletta and Aliora waited impatiently around the desk as the minutes crept by, occasionally talking with the clerk to pass the time. Andor and Creed were taking a long time, but eventually Aliora realized that the bars would not be open in the morning, and the two of them probably had to scout up the owners and bartenders at home to question.

In mid-morning, Rioletta questioned a heavy-set individual with an odor of stale beer about him as he checked out at the desk. He was obviously a traveling merchant of some type and hung-over, not happy about her questions. He did, indeed, remember seeing Hyphanden and Cardon at a table near the back of the restaurant around dinnertime and for some short time thereafter, but he thought they were gone by mid-evening. He had little else to add, except that he was curious, as were others, about the Vrinac. He said he figured the man was an acquaintance of Stetsor's, noting that there had been more Vrinac in town since the Tabor Council had set up residence in West Ford.

Rioletta thanked him, and he headed slowly for the door, arranging his money inside a leather folder. At the doorway he stopped and turned around.

"Hey!" he shouted as a means of gaining Rioletta's attention. He waved her over.

"There was one other thing I saw," he said thoughtfully, eyeing her from under heavy brows, straightening his beard with the fingers of one hand. "I don't know if it'll mean anything to you. But Dwel and Rant were here last night. They disappeared about the same time as your friends."

"Who are Dwel and Rant?"

"You don't know them? Well, I suppose they don't get up the Andian much. They're bounty-hunters. Unskilled, but employed by the Tabor Council to bring in Skilled criminals. They have means of controlling Sorcerers if they can take them unawares, at least short-term. They keep good tabs on who's out there and who's wanted at any time. Rant's some new lackey, but Dwel has been around for years, since before the First Chosen took over in Tabor, and he makes a good living at it."

"Thank you," Rioletta said, trying to keep her voice even. "Good travels to you, sir."

She hurried to where Aliora was questioning another guest and pulled her aside.

"I'm afraid we may have our answer," she said, and told Aliora about Dwel and Rant.

"We have to go after them at once," Aliora said urgently.

Rioletta shook her head. "They have a long head-start, and we can't guess which route they'll take. Besides, we have Lida and Justah."

"What are we to do, then? We can't just let them be taken to Tabor. If Hyphanden's warrant is honored by the First Chosen, he'll be Stripped at the very least. I have no idea what they might do to Cardon, but he can't be very popular in Tabor."

"I don't know," Rioletta said helplessly. "Let's get Creed and Andor and we'll talk about it. Meanwhile, we can get the wagon ready to go and get Lida and Justah packed. At the very least we know we'll be leaving here."

"I'll go to the stables," Aliora said. But as she headed for the door, she stopped and turned. "What about Stetsor?"

"What about him?" Rioletta said. "I don't think there's anything he can do to help."

"You could at least tell him," Aliora said. "He might have some insight into the First Chosen."

"We'll stop by on the way out, then," Rioletta agreed.

Andor and Creed arrived back at the inn not long after. By the time Rioletta had paid for their rooms and gotten Lida and Justah downstairs, and Andor had brought Hyphanden's and Cardon's bags from their room, Creed had harnessed the team and brought the wagon around to the front. Cardon's extra horses were led out and hitched to the clips on the rear of the wagon, and Andor led Creed's horse.

They pulled into a side alley after a short journey, and Rioletta ran up to Stetsor's apartment. He was taking an early lunch on his veranda.

"Just in time for a bite," he greeted her pleasantly. "Please, have a seat."

"Thank you, but we're on our way out of town. The others are waiting for me," Rioletta said. Then she told him why she had not been able to contact Hyphanden the night before, and what they believed had happened.

Stetsor observed her grimly. "That is a very serious thing for Hyphanden," he said. "The First Chosen are apt to be more severe with him than even the Elder Council would have been. Over time my feelings have mellowed, and after all, I allowed Hyphanden to escape to Hyolon. But the First Chosen were his peers, and in some ways they have felt themselves betrayed by him."

"Betrayed?" Rioletta asked. Stetsor's attitude only served to increase her alarm.

"Had he remained the Leader of that Council, it's likely they would have retained power. When he left, he took not only his own knowledge and Skills, but also Kwistocta's, leaving the First Chosen to fill the void with others from their Training Cadre. My Council later became convinced the First Chosen would be incapable of properly leading Tabor into the future, and we dismissed them and selected the Second Chosen. Had Hyphanden stayed, it's much less likely we would have made that decision. Thus the First Chosen suffered for many years because of him, in their view. Of course, in reality it was because of their own incompetence, but they will not admit that."

"What do you think they'll do?" Rioletta asked. "Is there anything you can do to help us?"

"I'll consider what I might do. I obviously have no love for the First Chosen, and would prefer that Hyphanden go free. As for what they might do, I imagine they'll try and Strip his Skills, if they can control him for long enough. Of course, doing so would destroy him at this point. But from what you've told me, Hyphanden might be able to muster forces unknown to the First Chosen, who, despite their disagreements with us, remain Traditionals. It may be that he will be able to rescue himself and Cardon. However, I'm also familiar with Dwel, who worked for us when we occupied the Council-house. I know he has devices and resources to control Sorcerers for transport, and if they were taken unawares, even Hyphanden might not be able to escape. Let me know what you find out. There is information that might prove to be our ally."

Stetsor narrowed his eyes as he spoke the last line, as though considering some idea.

"You're thinking of something," Rioletta said. "Is there anything I can do?"

"Not now," Stetsor said. "If worse comes to worse, I have some knowledge we might bring to bear against the First Chosen, and especially Arvindahl. I would have used it before now, except that I don't have enough evidence that it's true. But with your contacts, it's possible we could confirm it, at least beyond any reasonable doubt. I'll see what I can gather from my old notes. You should go to your friends now, and make haste to Dobor."

Rioletta thanked Stetsor and hurried back to the others. They started out along the northern road through West Ford, heading back towards the new Dobor Bridge. With any luck they would arrive at Nikal's house by evening, and Rioletta hoped the Dobor Council might be able to offer them some solution. She fingered the talisman around her neck, but the one in her pocket weighed heavily, a useless figure of stone.

Chapter Thirteen: Travel to Tabor (Cardon)

By morning Hyphanden and Cardon were far from West Ford and well past Dobor Bridge on the east side of the Tadian, heading for Tabor Ford. Dwel pressed them along at a good pace. The night was cool and the road clean and solid. The horses, although they had already been traveling for several days, continued through the night without flagging. Cardon remained alert all night, his mind racing, trying to formulate some plan or take some opportunity for escape. He tried a few Skills he could cast without the need for talismans or his hands, but all that happened was that he felt an uncomfortable tingle at his throat and pressure in his ears. He tried it short-distance, aiming for Hyphanden, but Hyphanden gave no sign he had sensed anything.

Hyphanden seemed to Cardon to be completely resigned to his fate. He even drowsed in the saddle, jerking awake occasionally as he started to slip. His complacency irritated Cardon. Hyphanden should at the very least be awake and paying attention, maybe concentrating on breaking through the collar's blockade to contact Kwistocta or Rioletta.

He knew Hyphanden was a Loremaster and that Loremasters were often given to study and learning rather than the practice of Skills. He'd heard Hyphanden claim that he felt little compunction to use his ample repertoire, and that Rudon was thus a stronger Sorcerer. And he knew Rioletta had a similar attitude: it was one of the things that irritated him. But he also knew that Hyphanden's Skills, both normal and Forbidden, far surpassed those of anyone else he knew, and that he'd gained even more Skills through his association with Stelaphandon. He was sure there must be something Hyphanden could do. It frustrated him that they had been taken so easily by two Unskilled bounty-hunters, when, given a few seconds of warning, they could have incapacitated them and made an easy escape. Certainly Hyphanden could have incapacitated the two even after they'd been held at gunpoint. He had demurred only because he disliked hurting or stunning people who weren't involved. But Cardon would gladly have taken Hyphanden's stun if it meant their escape from Dwel and Rant.

As dawn broke, Dwel turned them off the main road along a narrow track leading away from the river into the woods. They followed the track through the oaks and scrub for a couple of miles, taking one branch and then another as they came to places where several trails intersected. Eventually they arrived at a modest cabin of stone and wood, with livestock pens in the back and a small garden. The house was low-roofed and squat and had the look of the residence of an Unskilled.

Dwel led the horses around to the back. He and Rant dismounted and together helped Cardon and Hyphanden off their horses. They were soon joined by three men, one older and two younger, who Cardon assumed were the house's owner and his sons. Dwel spoke to them in a language Cardon could not understand.

They were led inside. One of the sons prepared a meal, and all of them ate while Dwel and Rant rambled on in their own language. Cardon concentrated on trying to eat efficiently while bending uncomfortably towards his cuffed hands. When they were done, they were shown to a small dark room at the back of the house and allowed to lie down on a couple of mattresses to sleep. The room was empty except for the mattresses. One of the sons pulled a chair up next to the door, a long gun across his lap. It was obvious they were to be guarded throughout the day while Dwel and Rant got some sleep elsewhere.

Hyphanden fell asleep quickly, despite having drowsed throughout the night. Cardon had been fighting sleep for some time. Now he gave in, reasoning that he might as well be rested for whatever was to come. Soon Creed would realize they had not returned and a search would begin. But what anyone could do now, a full night's ride behind them and with no communication, Cardon could not imagine. A wave of guilt swept over him as he thought of his mother and daughter, and also Rioletta. Once again

156

he had disappeared, leaving them with no way to know what had happened to him.

They were awakened at nightfall and fed again. The Unskilled men ignored them for the most part, other than to shove a plate close to each of them. Cardon was relieved to see that his horse had been cared for. It had been fed, watered, and groomed, and was saddled just before they mounted.

Cardon put a foot in the stirrup and stepped up as best he could while Rant shoved him roughly. Hyphanden did not ride as much and was more awkward. Rant heaved him up, cursing. "Step up, wood-demon! I'm not going to lift you to the saddle!"

Dwel had borrowed some lead-rope to increase the distance between himself and the two prisoners' horses. The horses were able to sort themselves more naturally into single file along the narrow track. Rant dawdled along behind them, sometimes humming or muttering to himself. When they reached the main road towards Matbor they turned north in the dark, keeping a good pace as they had the night before. At this rate, Cardon figured, they would cross the Tabor Ford before daybreak.

Cardon's horse responded to leg signals, and a little pressure from his knee brought it up alongside Hyphanden's. He was still irritated, but he craved some conversation. Hyphanden seemed more alert after sleeping all day. Cardon reasoned that perhaps he was still recovering from breaking the Possession Skill, and had needed the rest. Perhaps his lack of response was simply a function of exhaustion, mental or otherwise.

"So, have you had any more ideas?" Cardon whispered.

Hyphanden grunted. "Nothing occurs to me at this point."

"Have you been working on the sash?"

"I don't know how to defeat it, Cardon."

"Why didn't you do something when Dwel first accosted us in the inn?" Cardon fumed. "Your hands were free. You could have Thrown a Skill of some sort. I would gladly have suffered the consequences if it meant you could have escaped."

"You might have been willing to be stunned, but I doubt many of the other patrons of the inn would have felt the same way. Some of them might have fallen off chairs, been cut on broken glasses, struck their heads, or been otherwise injured. Then I truly would have been guilty of a crime: assault. And it would likely have been for naught. Remember, most of those other patrons were Skilled."

"So?" Cardon replied.

"So? Cardon, you know that the Unskilled have much hardier constitutions than we Skilled do. It takes much greater force to knock the Unskilled out, even the Hyolonal. Any force I could muster strong enough to seriously stun them would kill at least the weaker of the Skilled in that room. And these two, Dwel and Rant, are purebred Unskilled. They've maintained their language; it's an indication that they have remained apart and haven't integrated with us. There are a number of such societies, governed by strict rules regarding integration."

Cardon considered. Perhaps Hyphanden had had a reason for not responding with force after all. Dwel and Rant had approached them in a crowded inn purposefully: they knew Hyphanden would be reluctant to Throw anything that would harm others in the restaurant.

They rode along in silence for a while. But eventually Hyphanden allowed his horse to lag enough to come alongside Cardon's again.

"He's right, you know," Hyphanden said.

"Who? Right about what?"

"Rant. The wood-demon thing. It's not just a nasty name."

Cardon grimaced in the dark. He had no idea what Hyphanden was going on about.

"Do you want to know more about the Unskilled?" Hyphanden asked. "There are things I know about them, and about us, that might surprise you."

"If you want to tell it." Cardon was bored, and a tale would serve to amuse him for at least a short time, if the bounty-hunters would allow them to talk. He glanced back to see that Rant was well behind them. "I know they're said to have descended from the same stock as us, but lost their Skills along the way somehow."

"Which is untrue," Hyphanden said. "The Unskilled are hardy, inventive, creative, and have had much of their technology for thousands of years. It was they who created machines, developed sources of energy, discovered glass-making, and many of the other crafts we now rely on. But they've never had any Skills."

158

"That's news to me," Cardon said. "I've always heard they're a degenerate race, and that they got worse after the Dispersal."

"The Dispersal disadvantaged them more than the Skilled. Many of them resented the fact that we tried to limit their use of their own technology, even though by the time of the Dispersal it was obvious that many of their extractive technologies were seriously damaging the earth. Some of them withdrew to isolated communities, where they are forbidden from intermingling with the Skilled."

"But I know that some of them do intermarry and mix with the Skilled. In those cases, it appears that their children are Skilled, although perhaps not the most powerful."

"Correct," Hyphanden said. "The Council of Tane is an example: too much Unskilled blood dilutes the abilities."

"Why, then, did our ancestors intermarry with the Unskilled? What would have been the advantage?"

"Hmm," Hyphanden said. "I'm not sure you've got it. It was the technology and constitution of the Unskilled that attracted our ancestors and caused us to start to interbreed."

"The Unskilled with the Skilled," Cardon confirmed.

"No. The Skilled are the *result* of that interbreeding. The Skilled are cross-breeds. Our ancestors were the Unskilled on one hand, and another race on the other. These ancestors did not have the technologies or the constitution, of the Unskilled, and desired it."

"But what would the Unskilled get from breeding with these ancestors, then?" Cardon asked.

"The ancestors were Skill-users, obviously. Most importantly, they had potions and brews, which are much more effective at curing disease than the medicines of the Unskilled. The mixed-breed children had a desirable blend of strength, intellect, technological understanding, creativeness, inventiveness, and the ability to use Skills, although they were diminished in capacity from their purebred parents. Some of the Unskilled objected and remained a separate kind, and these are the purebred Unskilled of today."

"Not too separate a kind," Cardon noted, "if they could easily interbreed. They must have been closely related to start with."

159

"No." Hyphanden said. "They were not closely related." He paused. "You know, we have been thinking about things wrong. All of us, for many years, have gotten things wrong, in particular one branch of the Forbidden Skills. Shape-changing was never intended to be a short-term or temporary condition. It is something to be done over a very long period of time, and the changes are meant to be permanent."

Cardon squinted at Hyphanden through the dark. Once again, he'd apparently changed the subject in midstream.

"Many Sorcerers have died trying to Throw Shape-changing Skills or taking the potions they believe will help them acquire those Skills," Hyphanden continued. "That's because they're trying to do things much too fast. I's not something that can be used to, say, imprison an entire Council in tapestries, at least not without deadly consequences. It's to be used to create life-long changes, down to the core of the being, inheritable changes. For example, the way Stolen was changed. This is the mistake we have made. This is a thing I did not understand until recently. Now it's quite clear."

Cardon nodded. Hyphanden's sudden change of topic made more sense now. "Is this what you learned from the Lefollah when you visited them before leaving Andolith?"

"Yes," Hyphanden said, "or rather, this I confirmed. I knew, or suspected, much of it before. Our ancestors were required to change drastically to be able to interbreed with the Unskilled. These changes were made down to the very core, the maps of their minds and bodies, and were thus inherited by their offspring. It's a thing that cannot be easily undone, particularly at this point, so many years later."

"Then while the Unskilled remained in the same form as their ancestors, the other ancestors of the Skilled had some other form, and they do not exist anymore?"

"Oh, they exist." Hyphanden said with a short laugh. "Do you want to know who they are?"

"Of course," Cardon said.

"Are you sure?"

Cardon hesitated. Hyphanden's cautiousness unnerved him to some degree, but he did want to know.

"Yes, of course, I want to know," he said.

Hyphanden let a long moment go by before he readjusted himself in the saddle and leaned slightly towards Cardon in the dark.

"They are the Lefollah," he said.

Cardon's horse lurched in reaction to his inadvertent response, nearly unseating him. Of course, it was now obvious what Hyphanden had been working up to. All of the evidence began to come together in Cardon's mind: Stolen, a changeling, one of the Skilled, slowly turned to a Lefollah, and then, slowly, able to change himself back to a semblance of what he had been. The Forbidden Skill of Shape-changing and the mistaken belief that it was a Skill that could be used to quickly or temporarily change one's form, leading to death and disability in those who tried.

"Does Rioletta know this?" Cardon asked he regained his composure and settled his horse.

"No. I haven't had a chance to tell her," Hyphanden said. "I had hoped to have time during this journey."

"Why are you telling me, then?"

"Because I think it likely I will not survive this encounter with the First Chosen," Hyphanden said bluntly. "If I do survive, it's likely I'll be left seriously damaged. You cannot Strip all the Skills out of my mind without destroying me at this point. There are too many Skills, too integrated into the rest of my psyche. Your fate will most likely be less severe. I would like someone to know what I've spent most of my life laboriously uncovering."

A chill swept over Cardon. He refused to believe that the First Chosen would treat Hyphanden severely enough that he would not survive.

"There is more I would like to tell you," Hyphanden said. "Rioletta knows a little about the First Accord and the Second Accord, but now I know more than when we discussed them."

"Hey!" Rant yelled, bringing his horse forward. "That's enough talking! I don't want you two plotting and planning." He flicked the end of his reins, and Cardon's horse jumped forward and skittered around.

Dwel turned in his saddle. "Who cares if they talk, Rant? There's nothing they can do. Don't frighten the horses. The First

Chosen will be upset if one of them falls off and is damaged. They like their goods unscathed."

Hyphanden fell silent, and Cardon allowed his horse to drift away a short distance. They had bypassed Matbor along the riverbank and were nearing Tabor Ford, and it would be daylight within a couple of hours. Meanwhile, his mind was occupied unpleasantly with the thought that the Lefollah had in the far distant past been his relatives.

The road was deserted in the early morning hours, and when they arrived at the ford the four horses clattered across the bridge unobstructed. Dwel was pushing them now, but the horses were tired. Cardon ached from having his arms stuck in front of him. He tried rolling his shoulders and twisted from side to side to loosen his back.

Dwel turned off the main road along the edge of the first mustard fields of Tane. They passed the houses and estates of the Skilled brokers and mustard distributors. Further south they began to encounter the houses of the Unskilled who worked the fields and staffed the distilleries and factories where mustard sauces and other mustard-based products were produced. In the distance, Cardon could see a large factory looming out of the dawn.

Dwel led them into the yard of a house tucked back into the woods. Once again, their arrival provoked no overt surprise. Cardon assumed Dwel was either well known, or these were relatives of his and they had grown to expect his occasional arrival with errant Sorcerers in tow.

This time the house was occupied by a family with several young children whom the wife ordered to stay away from them. Hyphanden and Cardon were seated at a table outside and the wife quickly brought them food and served Dwel and Rant while the husband, a man named Byre, cared for their horses. Cardon noticed Byre running a hand over his horse and examining it carefully. He hoped it was admiration for a good horse, but began to fear that the payment for their occupancy of the house might be their horses once they were incarcerated in Tabor.

Since Byre worked in the mustard plant and the wife was busy with the children and household tasks, Dwel and Rant were forced to take it in turns to guard the two prisoners. Hyphanden and

Cardon were locked in a small storage room and provided with a couple of mattresses, much like the night before.

Once the door was closed, Cardon scooted closer to Hyphanden.

"We'll be in Tabor tomorrow," he whispered. "If there's anything to be done, we must do it now. Is there any way you can help me communicate through these collars? I've been told my mind is very open. Perhaps I could reach Rioletta if we can defeat these things for just a minute."

"Your mind is very open, yes, to reception, but as far as I know you aren't strong at sending messages. As for Rioletta, she is no better than average, and our communications have been brief even with the help of a powerful talisman. She was able to communicate directly with you those few times because she had recently been guided by Nikal, and his influence was within her mind. It was aided by your strong bond in those days."

Cardon sat back, frustrated. He realized that Rioletta and the rest of the group at West Ford would be searching for them by now. On the other hand, he didn't want to sit by and wait for a rescue that might not happen in time. He was less afraid for himself than for Hyphanden. Hyphanden had become a friend, and Cardon was worried on a personal level as well as for the future of Hyolon.

He crawled back to his mattress in the dark. If Hyphanden was unwilling to work to defeat the collars, the only other option was a physical escape. He bent at the waist, worked the belt up around his torso as far as he could and strained to bring his hands to his neck. He carefully examined the collar with his fingers. There appeared to be no latch or catch on the clasp, and the material was strong and smooth. He tried to rip it, but as he exerted more force, the collar began to beep.

"Hey! Quit fooling with your collar!" Rant's voice growled from behind the door.

With a sigh, Cardon leaned back against the wall. After a minute he worked his hand into his tunic pocket, and fingered the two hoof picks and the vials he'd stolen from the prep room at the inn in West Ford. He racked his brain for what he could use them for, going over all the preparations and brews he'd learned with Charnia.

Each vial was about four inches tall and flattened. Each was securely corked. He had managed to carefully work the cork off and smell them to determine what was in each one. They contained not liquid, but solid chunks. His nose quickly told him these were crystals used medicinally to treat hoof infections and the like. Cardon was familiar with them. They caused a purple stain if one didn't handle them carefully.

His association with Pateret had not been useless. Now he strained to remember what she had once told him: the crystals could be used to manufacture a low-level explosive, perhaps enough to distract Dwel and Rant and either injure them or escape.

Hyphanden seemed to be sleeping. Cardon crawled quietly around the little room, using his hands to examine whatever he could reach. He was in luck. He encountered a corner stacked with mops and brooms. The wife of the family kept her cleaning supplies there.

There was a wall of shelves, and Cardon began methodically removing the containers he found there. Most of them contained soaps and washing solutions, but eventually he found what he was looking for: a large bottle of a particular strong-smelling cleaning fluid. Next he found several empty bottles. He couldn't tell if they were clean or not, but he would have to take that chance. He located a stash of rags and chose several he could use as filters.

It was difficult work in the dark, although as his eyes became accustomed to it he found there was a little light let in from under the door and from around a boarded-up window in the back. He poured the crystals into one empty glass container and, using a funnel he'd found, poured the cleaning solution after it. He waited impatiently until he thought the crystals had soaked enough, then filtered the solution into another container through the rags he'd found. He carefully removed the cloth filter with its sludge and put the glass bottle in the corner of the room, hoping the wife would have the sense to dispose of it and not use it for cleaning.

The sludge would have to dry for some time before it was usable as an explosive. It would have to be carried very carefully until he was ready to use it. Also, he would need to throw it, which meant he needed his hands free.

While the sludge was drying, he sat back against the wall and pulled out the two hoof picks. They were flat, except for the tip, which was hoe-shaped. In the dark, he fumbled with the metal cuffs around his hands. They were made with a curved bar that slid between two other bars, and there was a ratchet keeping the bars from sliding apart. There was undoubtedly a release mechanism, but Cardon could not feel it or discover how it worked. But if the double bar was pried apart, he might be able to remove the single bar from it.

The hoe edge of the hoof pick was narrow enough that it fit between the double bars on the cuffs. Once again, he crawled around the small room, examining the shelving unit. It was crudely made, with boards nailed to a frame. The boards fitted together poorly. Cardon found a gap between the boards on a lower shelf and by kneeling as close to the side of the unit as he could, he was able to force one cuff down into the crack until his wrist lay flush with the board. Then he jammed the end of one hoof pick into the gap between the two bars and began to twist.

The cuffs were lightweight, but quite strong. Cardon could feel the two bars begin to separate, but when he released pressure on the pick, they snapped back together again. He readjusted the pick and tried again. Finally, he heard a satisfying pop and felt the rivet give way from one side.

That was enough. The single bar could now be pulled free from the ratchet. Cardon pulled his wrist out and relished the freedom for a few minutes. But the wrist would have to go back in and the cuff be readjusted to appear as though it was undamaged. His plan would be foiled if Dwel noticed the damaged cuff and used another pair to secure him.

He heard the doorknob rattle and scrambled to return to the mattress.

"What are you doing in here?" Rant asked suspiciously, sticking his head in the door.

"Trying to get comfortable with my hands hooked in front of me. You try sleeping in this position some time," Cardon growled, squinting in the light from the open door.

Rant grunted and pulled the door shut. Cardon adjusted himself on the mattress. He would try and get some sleep, but he'd have to wake himself again before evening to package his explosive crystals. Hopefully they'd be dry enough by then to replace carefully in the flask.

Chapter Fourteen: The Escape (Cardon)

Cardon was wide-awake and alert as Dwel led the horses out of the yard. They had been allowed to rest well into the night and started late. Cardon assumed the reason was to time their arrival in Tabor for early morning, before the town truly began to awake but late enough that the Council-house would be open and the prisoners could be taken straight in. Dwel apparently had a different route in mind than the one Cardon knew, for instead of heading back towards the main road, he led them south through the mustard fields of Tane. Cardon kept his bearings, figuring they would turn and come up the road that led between the fields and the vineyards. That road became paved near Tabor and continued straight to the southern entrance of the Council-house.

The moon rose three-quarters full, providing enough light for them to follow the trail and avoid overhanging branches and other obstacles. As they settled into their routine, Cardon pressed his horse forward. He pulled up next to Dwel, who jumped when he noticed Cardon. His horse shied away a bit.

"What?" Dwel growled, taking up the slack in Cardon's lead-rope.

"I'm bored," Cardon said. "My companion doesn't feel like talking. Talk to me for a few minutes. What's your connection to the First Chosen, or does it matter to you who's in charge in Tabor?"

"As for that, I don't care," Dwel said with some suspicion. "I worked with the Elder Council when they were there, and after the First Chosen came back, I continued the agreement with them. Nothing changed as far as I was concerned. Your business, your Councils and your Elders and your Youngers, and who's Chosen and who's not, mean nothing to me. There's no Skilled blood in my body and I'm not beholden to your governments. It's to our

167

advantage to work with you, because you pay better than most of us can do for ourselves, and of course, you hold the reins of control in this region. But your little disagreements about your Charter and your Skills, which ones of them you can do and not do, they don't interest me or concern me. I just do my job."

"We have limited contact with the Unskilled in Andolith," Cardon said. "Everyone in Andolith is Skilled. So I'm curious: you've obviously maintained a language apart. What's the history of that?"

Dwel readjusted himself in his saddle and glanced back over his shoulder at Rant. "The Unskilled have always been a people apart. Our language comes from a time when we didn't mix with the Skilled. Some of our people made a bargain that they'd mix with the race of Sorcerers in exchange for potions and brews and other favors. But those of the Unskilled who didn't go along with the bargain maintained their bloodlines and language, and we've always been stronger and smarter – at least in the ways of technology, maybe not in the ways of Skills."

"Our history doesn't teach us that. It's interesting what bits of the truth are found in stories and tales," Cardon mused. Dwel's story meshed more closely with Hyphanden's tale than did the stories of the Skilled. "How did you recognize Hyphanden so quickly at West Ford? He could be any Vrinac."

"I was looking for him. Arvindahl called me in. He's the Leader of the First Chosen, and he always calls me first when he has an important warrant to serve," Dwel bragged. "He told me he got information that Hyphanden had left Hyolon. He thought Hyphanden might end up in West Ford or thereabouts. I've been at this occupation for thirty years, and I remember when he was Outcast from Tabor. Many of us searched for him then, but he escaped to Hyolon too quickly. Arvin told me he'd reward me well if I could bring Hyphanden in. But I've never heard of you."

Cardon digested that information. Arvindahl must have contacts in Hyolon if he knew Hyphanden had left. If Rudon's purpose in creating the View Possession Skill was to lure Hyphanden out of Hyolon, Rudon could have passed on that information to the First Chosen. But it would be difficult to prove without more information.

"If you keep an ear to the news, you heard about the death of the Younger Council two summers ago," Cardon said. "I was a companion to them, but as far as I know I have no warrant. I fear your trouble will not be worth it."

"Of course I heard," Dwel said with a tone of surprise. "Also I heard of the kidnapping of the Elders by the Sorcerers of Andolith. Were you part of that group?"

Cardon grinned. "Yes, I was. So, perhaps there is a warrant on me. How about Rant? Has been in this job as long as you?"

"No," Dwel said, "he's new to my operation. My previous partner fell a few months ago crossing Tabor Ford and struck his head. He's not been able to work since, so I took Rant on. I'm teaching him the ropes. He's not so quick on the uptake, though. I'll find someone better eventually."

"Really?" Cardon said, seeing an opportunity. "That's funny, because we've been talking back there in the dark, Rant and I. It was you he said was slow on the uptake, and he said he intended to take your route and do business with the First Chosen himself. In fact, he's got some plan to discredit you in front of the Council this morning. Something to do with letting the rest of our party escape."

"What?" Dwel turned angrily. "Are you playing wood-demon's tricks on me?"

Cardon shrugged. "No reason for me to do that. I just figured you'd want to know what your supposed partner said."

Dwel slowed his horse and circled in the dark, letting Cardon's lead-rope go slack again. "Rant! Get up here! I've got a question for you and your big mouth."

Rant urged his horse forward past Hyphanden's. In the dark, Cardon rolled his wrist and slid the single bar out through the damaged ratchet. He reached into his vest pocket and pulled out the flask loaded with the dry filtered powder.

As Rant's horse cantered up, Cardon raised his free hand and threw the bottle hard at the ground. The explosion behind the horses' feet was loud and more energetic than he had expected. All four animals reared in alarm, but Cardon was prepared and kept his seat. He had a fleeting impression that Rant had fallen heavily from his horse. Hyphanden was further away and seemed to

169

maintain his seat. Dwel's horse staggered, probably injured. Cardon felt a flicker of guilt, but he had no time to consider. He reached forward and pulled loose the buckle on his horse's halter, and the halter fell away, trailing after Dwel's horse by its lead-rope.

Freed from its tether, the horse spun around and fled into the night. Cardon allowed it to run at first, keeping low and hoping its night-vision would guide it. After a few minutes he began to issue some commands, first with his knees and then with his voice. The horse's motion smoothed out and changed from a headlong flight to a controlled gallop. Its breathing became more regular and Cardon relaxed in the saddle, his free hand gripping the base of the horse's mane lightly.

Now he dared to look behind, but there was no one following him. He felt badly that he'd been forced to abandon Hyphanden, but he was sure he could be of more use free, bearing the information to others who could respond.

He slowed the horse to a walk and allowed it to calm before asking it to run again. They trended generally south and west through mustard fields and past houses and distilleries. He could see the glow of lights from Tabor to his right, and eventually they intersected the road that would lead them to the door of the Council-house. Cardon turned south, away from Tabor. If he was lucky, he'd reach Dobor by mid-morning, and Lida and Justah would be there with Adla and the rest of the traveling group. Nikal was sure to help, and he was on good terms with the First Chosen, or as good terms as could be expected, given that the Tabor Council had expressed an interest in annexing Dobor.

By the time the sun rose, he was feeling fairly confident. He was outside the boundaries of Tane and Tabor, in the open lands between those communities and the Dobor road. He stopped at an old ranch, abandoned but with a good well, and watered the horse. He spent some time working on the second cuff and eventually pried it open using an old bar of iron he found near the collapsing barn. He removed the waist-belt and threw it inside the old barn, glad to be rid of it. The marks around his wrists were red and raw from wearing the cuffs for so long, but they would heal, and it felt wonderful to have both his arms free.

The tight collar bothered him, but he knew of no way to remove it. He had no knife or other sharp object, and none was to be found in a quick search of the ranch. He decided he could wait until he was in Dobor. Perhaps Nikal would know how to defeat it. It was unfortunately bright yellow, and anyone seeing it would surely view it with suspicion, as yellow was the color traditionally worn by guards and prisoners.

Cardon remounted and turned his horse towards Dobor once again. There were few people on the road, and those he encountered didn't seem to give him a second look. By mid-morning he could see not only the looming southern buildings of Hyolon through overgrown trees, but also the hills of Dobor with their smattering of white, red, and blue roofs and stone-laid trails. Nikal's house was visible on the tallest hill. His mood rose as he urged the horse forward.

As he rode up the main street, he saw two horses he recognized outside the market. He pulled his horse up next to the hitching post and leaned on the saddle-horn. In a few minutes Creed and Andor exited the market and Andor saw him as she neared her horse.

"Cardon!" she cried, nearly dropping her bags. She handed the groceries off to Creed and ran forward. Cardon swung down off his horse with a grin and gave her a hug.

"Where did you come from?" Andor asked as Creed and Cardon clasped hands. "Where is Hyphanden?"

"I escaped," Cardon said, fingering the collar to bring her attention to it. "Unfortunately I was unable to rescue Hyphanden. He's undoubtedly at the Tabor Council-house by now."

"We're all up at Nikal's place," Andor said. "We came down to fetch groceries. Ride up with us and tell us the story, and we'll figure out what to do about that collar and Hyphanden."

It was a short ride from the market through town and up the winding lane to Nikal's estate on the hill. There Cardon was reunited with his mother and daughter as well as Adla, Nikal, Rioletta, and Aliora. He briefly told them the story of their capture at the inn and their travels from one Unskilled house to another. He described how he'd manufactured the explosive and used the hoof-picks to break the cuff, then distracted Dwel and Rant enough to escape.

"Cardon! That's very inventive – I'm proud of you!" Andor said. "Too bad you couldn't get Hyphanden away, though."

"We'll have to do something," Cardon said, readjusting Justah on his lap. "Hyphanden's sure the First Chosen will be brutal with him. He told me some things because he was afraid he wouldn't survive. We will have to act fast."

"We figured out what happened pretty quickly after your disappearance," Rioletta said. "We rode here as quickly as we could. Nikal was able to contact Kwistocta, so at least she doesn't think Hyphanden's dead. Of course she knew immediately when his communication with her was cut off, and she thought he might have been overcome by the Skill he'd broken. We'll contact her again soon with your information. We know she's working on a plan."

"What can Kwistocta do?" Cardon asked doubtfully. "She's warranted herself."

"We'll find out when we talk to her next," Andor said. "Right now we should work on getting that collar off so you can function. Nikal, don't you know how to disable these things?"

Nikal examined the collar. "We don't use these. The Dobor Council has never cared to enforce warrants against Outcasts and we don't pay bounty-hunters to bring them in. I'd say let's just cut it off and see what happens."

"See what happens?" Cardon exclaimed. "I don't like the sound of that!"

Nikal shrugged. "I have no better idea. We'll go slowly and if it hurts you we'll stop and figure out some other solution. But why waste time if we can simply snip it?"

Cardon reluctantly sat down on an ottoman in Nikal's living room, and Nikal fetched a pair of scissors, which he slid up under the snug cuff of the collar. He made a small cut, and Cardon felt nothing. Encouraged, Nikal tried a larger cut, then suddenly yelped and the scissors flew as he jerked his hand away. Cardon yelled at the same moment and grabbed his neck.

"What happened?" Andor asked, retrieving the scissors.

"Some kind of charge," Nikal said. "This thing seems to be run by a battery of some sort. There's a wire, or more than one, running through the collar."

"We'll have to drain the charge," Aliora said. "You've exposed one of the wires. We should be able to use that and pull the rest of the charge out. It's been operating for several days, it's doubtful that it has much of a charge left anyway."

"Or we could just cut through all the wires using a wire-cutter with wooden handles," Nikal said. "I have one in the stable."

"I don't like the idea of the wires being in contact with the cutter, which will be in contact with my neck," Cardon argued.

"We'll slip a piece of leather up there," Nikal suggested.

He and Aliora went out to the barn to fetch the cutters and an appropriate piece of leather. When they returned, Aliora slid a thick leather patch up between Cardon's neck and the collar and held it there while Nikal carefully slipped one blade of the cutter between the leather and the collar. Nikal bore down on the handle of the cutter.

The collar was cut through, and Aliora quickly pulled it away from Cardon's neck and tossed it on the floor, where it sparked and writhed like a snake. After a moment, Cardon could tell that he had suffered no ill effect, and in fact, he soon began to feel the return of his Skilled faculties.

"I've never been without my Skills," Cardon said. "It's an odd feeling. I'm relieved to be back to normal."

"We'll need to take care of those wounds around your wrists and there's a mark on your neck, as well," Adla said. "My house is small, but you and Lida and Justah can stay there until we can get you set up in the house in town. I'll work on your sores. They're not serious, and you'll heal quickly."

Nikal set the clippers and leather patch on a small table. "The next order of business is what to do about Hyphanden, then."

"We'd better hurry," Cardon said. "Dwel seems to be well-known to the First Chosen, and he claimed Arvindahl called him in and told him to look for Hyphanden near West Ford. If Arvindahl's that interested in Hyphanden, they might take action quickly once he's brought in."

"Grim news," Nikal said. "That means Arvin knew Hyphanden had left Hyolon. He's got some source of information inside the Ruined City, and we'd better let Kwistocta know."

Nikal rose and went to a desk in the corner of his sitting room, where he pulled out a sheaf of papers and a pen. "I'll travel to Tabor and petition for amnesty for Hyphanden. I don't think our Council will object. It seems ridiculous to call in a warrant issued thirty years ago. We don't believe in Skill-stripping either, which is brutal and often results in damaged Sorcerers running around. I can point out that Rudon is such a one: the Stripping of his Skills has resulted in the situation we now face in Hyolon."

"I'm not sure how I'll be received in Tabor, but I'm willing to go as well," Rioletta said. "Andolith does not Strip Skills either, and in fact we don't really Outcast errant Sorcerers."

"I can attest to that," Cardon said.

"But you can't, at least not in front of the First Chosen," Nikal pointed out. "It would be foolish for you to escape the bounty-hunters only to present yourself to the Council."

"I agree. Cardon, you'd better stay here until we know if there's a warrant for you or not," Adla said. "If we prepare the petition today, we can go around to the members of our Council and our Advisors and get their signatures on it. That will add emphasis."

"Then Rioletta and I will travel to Tabor early tomorrow," Nikal said.

"Only the two of you?" Cardon protested.

"We might as well go too," Andor said. "I'm a representative of the Andolith Council in good standing, and I don't expect Creed will let me go alone."

Creed grinned. "My sister and I will be happy to go."

"At least we'll be doing something," Rioletta said. "I feel better knowing that. Let's hope it's not too late, and that they keep Hyphanden for a while as they make a decision as to what to do with him."

"If we are too late, or unsuccessful, the future of Hyolon will be grim," Nikal said. "And eventually it will come to us. Rudon will not stop at Hyolon, and who knows what he'll be able to do

174

with access to the Crypt of Souls? Whatever it is, I don't want to see it."

Chapter Fifteen: The Council-house (Hyphanden)

When the explosion happened, Hyphanden's horse leaped in the air and then backed desperately away, pulling against the lead-rope tied to Dwel's saddle. It tossed its head back and forth in panic, but it was not wounded, and they were farther away from the bang than the others. Hyphanden grabbed the saddle-horn with his cuffed hands and managed to stay aboard. Ahead of him in the dark, he saw someone fall: Rant, he thought, and he heard the grunt and exhalation of air as the man's wind was knocked out. Cardon's horse streaked away to the south, going flat out but, he guessed, under Cardon's full control. Dwel's horse staggered around, its rear legs bloodied from the blast.

Cursing, Dwel threw himself from the saddle and grabbed the bridle to calm the wounded horse. Rant lay flat on his back in the roadway, gasping for breath. His horse pitched and bucked by itself, off in the scrub oaks. With his own horse shaking but stilled, Dwel strode over, took the reins of Rant's mount, and brought it back. Then he grabbed Rant by the shirtfront and hauled him to his feet.

"Are you hurt?" he demanded. "If not, take your horse."

Rant took the reins, still gasping, and Dwel handed him his own reins as well. Then he strode to Hyphanden's horse, reached up, and yanked Hyphanden from the saddle. Holding him by the collar, he delivered several quick punches to Hyphanden's face. Unable to defend himself, Hyphanden fell to the ground, where Dwel kicked him sharply in the hip.

"You've injured my horse, wood-demon!" Dwel shouted.

"I did no such thing," Hyphanden protested from the ground. "I had nothing to do with it. Don't you think I would have gone off with Cardon had I known what he planned?"

177

Dwel stood panting for a moment, one boot poised to continue. "I don't doubt you would have if you could have done it," he growled. "You've taken me for a fool this time, but I'll not fall for that again. I've been patient with you, given you good food and plenty of rest, but don't expect any of that from me anymore!"

He grabbed Hyphanden by the front of his shirt and hauled him up. Then he shook him so violently that Hyphanden rocked on his feet and staggered.

"I doubt you'll get any money for me if you bring me in dead, and less than you'd get otherwise if you bring me in damaged," Hyphanden reminded him as calmly as he could. "The First Chosen undoubtedly want me of sound mind and body to face my trial. If I'm not they'll have to feed and house me until I'm whole, and that will cost them money. They'll not trust you again to bring in a valuable warrant."

Dwel stopped shaking him and let go so abruptly that Hyphanden collapsed to his knees. He eyed Dwel apprehensively as the bounty hunter stared at him in the moonlight. He was thrilled that Cardon had gotten away, but less than thrilled about the beating he was receiving.

Dwel turned and went back to where Rant stood holding the horses. "Bring out a light," he demanded. Rant dug immediately in his saddlebags. He handed a light to Dwel, who turned it on and examined the bloodied back legs of his horse.

Dwel clicked the light off. "Let's get the Sorcerer back up," he said, his voice calmer. "Rant, you ride and hold his lead-rope. Keep him up close, now. I'll walk and lead my horse. We'll stop at the nearest ranch and see if we can trade. I know many people around here. We're near the Skole property."

Hyphanden was shoved back up to the saddle, where he adjusted himself as best he could. His hip throbbed from the kick, and he wiped his face and nose against his shirt shoulder, sure he was bleeding. His cheek felt swollen on one side as well.

Dwel turned off the road and led them down a long track towards a collection of buildings amongst the mustard plants. There was a light on, and soon he had successfully secured another horse. The sun was just tinting the eastern sky as they turned back onto the road towards Tabor.

178

When the sun was well up Dwel stopped at a roadside well, dismounted, ran up a bucket, and wet a cloth in it. He remounted and rode back alongside Hyphanden.

"Look at me," he commanded gruffly, and reached out with the cloth to wipe the blood off Hyphanden's face. Hyphanden was sure it was a gesture born not so much of compassion as of a desire to present his warrant in as good of shape as possible to the First Chosen, but he appreciated having the sticky blood cleaned off him anyway.

Soon they passed through the low wall marking the boundary of Tabor and made their way into the heart of the city. Hyphanden could see the Council-house with its buttressed arches and dark-tiled roof looming over the buildings for many blocks before they entered the plaza. Dwel led them clattering across the bricks to the west side of the Council-house, through an archway and into a courtyard with high walls. From there they passed through a second, interior archway after two guards cleared them. They dismounted and the horses were quickly removed by stable-hands. The three of them were led into an antechamber and bade wait there while they were announced to the First Chosen.

The antechamber was furnished with chairs and couches, and refreshments had been laid out on a long table against one wall. There were books and magazines for entertainment. Hyphanden had, of course, been there before, in the days when he himself had been an inducted member of the First Chosen Council. He was amused to see that some of the furniture remained the same, although the upholstery had been changed. He knew the route they would take when, and if, they were summoned to stand before the First Chosen. He knew they would either see one of the Council-members in his office, or have an audience with all of them in one of several chambers, though likely not the main hall.

In less than half an hour, one of the pages returned and told them the Leader of the Council, Arvindahl Vrinal, would see them in the Second Chamber, along with other members of the First Chosen. This was unusual, as drop-in visitors were often set an appointment and sent away, he explained, but he had passed on Dwel's message, and the Council wished to see them right away. He led them out of the antechamber and up a flight of stone stairs to a level of the Council-house where there were offices and private meeting rooms. A balcony ran around, allowing them to see down into the spacious main hall below. Even further below, Hyphanden knew, were the private chambers of the Council and their private audience hall, hidden beneath many Protections, where once the tapestry portraits of the Elder Council had hung.

The page led them to a door and opened it for them. Dwel stepped in first, took Hyphanden by the arm, and dragged him to a place in the middle of the room. There were several desks, armchairs, and couches around the room on a series of low tiers, and it was lined with tall bookcases filled with volumes. Dwel and Rant withdrew to the side, and Hyphanden was left facing a man he had not seen in thirty years.

Arvindahl Vrinal rose slowly from his seat and stepped close to Hyphanden, peering into his face as if bringing back a memory from long before. Arvin was stouter of build, shorter, broader of face and darker of complexion than Hyphanden, and several years older, an original member of the First Chosen. Hyphanden knew that he had been raised in Kyelon, to the northwest, and that his mother was a native of that region. Like Hyphanden, he had been fostered in Tabor as a boy and then attended the preparatory school for promising young Sorcerer-adepts prior to being assigned to the Training Cadre and eventually the Council.

Hyphanden met his gaze evenly. He had not been a friend of Arvin's. He had found Arvin abrasive. Arvin was not lacking in Skills, though, and he had the ability to form alliances and garner loyalty. He had been groomed to become Leader of the Council for a reason. But he had been usurped by Hyphanden, who, although widely seen as impulsive and overly self-assured, was well liked by his peers and the Elder Council. Later, Hyphanden had strayed and destroyed their unit, already damaged by the Outcasting of Rudon. Within ten years, the Elder Council had found the reconstituted First Chosen unsatisfactory amid rumors of dishonorable behavior and had rejected them in favor of the Second Chosen.

Arvin turned his face briefly to Dwel, his eyes still tracking Hyphanden. "Remove the cuffs," he ordered. Dwel scooted quickly over and unlocked the cuffs, removed them and the belt, and returned silently to his place. Hyphanden rolled his shoulders and felt his wrists.

Arvin continued to study Hyphanden's face. Then he turned once more to Dwel. "What did you do to him?"

"Ah, he tried to escape," Dwel said apologetically. "We stopped him, obviously, but not without a little trauma. One of my horses was injured seriously, will cost me a lot of money to get him treated."

Arvin narrowed his eyes and stared at Dwel, who shifted uncomfortably.

"Are you going to tell him about the one that *did* escape?" Hyphanden asked casually.

Arvin glanced swiftly at him, then crossed his arms. "There was another?"

"One without a warrant," Dwel assured him.

"Probably warranted," Hyphanden put in. "He was a compatriot of the Younger Council before their demise, and knew the location of their bodies. Later he also participated in the kidnapping of the Elder Council from this very house. He was once an inducted Andolith Sorcerer, named Cardon Ereptor."

"I know of him, then. Not formally warranted," Arvin said. "Still, I would have liked to question him. There is cause to hold him, and I would have paid to bring him in. As for your horse, Dwel, you were obviously careless, and you've brought this man in damaged. I cannot question him without being sure his mind is sound, and I will now have to wait until he has sufficiently recovered. That will cost me time, and I would dearly love to talk to him now."

Arvin turned back to Hyphanden and scrutinized him for a moment. He signaled to a page, who stepped forward quickly. "Take the bounty-hunters and make sure they're well-fed. I'll write a scrip for payment, and they can collect tomorrow," he said. The page nodded and escorted Dwel and Rant out of the room, leaving Hyphanden alone with Arvin.

"Well, Phando," Arvin said. "It's been a long time. Your warrant still stands as it was set out by the Elder Council after your Outcasting. I admit to an impatience to question you, to hear about your life as an Outcast and to find out how you came to be so

181

careless that you allowed yourself to be caught in West Ford by Dwel the bounty hunter. But you're an important prisoner and your treatment will certainly be scrutinized. It's an opportunity to demonstrate our policies to the people of Tabor. Therefore I will make sure we scrupulously obey all decorum as to your handling. There will be nothing to challenge us on, and we will proceed smoothly towards an end I already anticipate."

Hyphanden looked down for a moment, then met Arvin's eyes. "You and I were never friends, Arvin, but I confess to some confusion as to why you seem so eager to see me Stripped and disabled. I've not caused any problems for Tabor in the last thirty years."

Arvin snorted. "Your very existence causes me problems, Phando. You're way too close to the Elder Council and the Second Chosen now, and you've managed to drum up some sympathy for the Outcasts by taking in Caladoc and Cayondahl, among others. I don't need some conspiracy brewing in my back yard with the intent of overthrowing my Council. You know too much, and you guess at more. You've become dangerous to me."

He turned towards the door. A guard had appeared to take the place of the page. "Take this man to the secure chambers here in the Council-house. He is not to be taken to the jail. He is to be provided with medical care and food and drink. He is not to be treated as a common prisoner. Bring him books and other such entertainments as he might request. You are to keep me informed of his condition. Do you understand?"

"Yes, Councilman," the guard replied. "The collar is to remain on?"

Arvin squinted at Hyphanden again and nodded. "Yes, indeed. Nevertheless, you are not to send any person in to treat him alone. I don't trust that he cannot defeat the collar, with some time to contemplate its construction, and his hands are free, which doubles his risk."

Arvin turned abruptly, and the guard grasped Hyphanden's upper arm and led him from the chamber. Hyphanden followed without protest, his mind searching for the memories that oriented him to his position in the Council-house. They descended past the main level, past the street level and further down into the lower chambers. Hyphanden was shown into a small room equipped with a bed, desk and chair, and small sitting-area with a table and armchair. There was also a shelving unit, but no window, since they were far underground. The walls were of stone. There was a rug covering most of the floor.

The guard locked the door as he exited, and Hyphanden sat down upon the bed. There were several books and magazines, but he preferred to think and rest for the time being.

Shortly, the door opened again, and a man entered with a large satchel. A second man stood near the door with a well-armed guard behind him.

"I am Curatto, a Healer, originally of Ankara," the man said. He turned quickly to the second man. "Huri, please remove the control device. I wish to examine his neck and face, and I cannot do so with the device in place."

Huri entered with his own bag, which he placed upon the floor. From it he pulled a second sash, smaller in construction. He grabbed one of Hyphanden's ankles and quickly fitted the device around it. Then he stood and removed the collar from Hyphanden's neck with an intricate key, accompanied, Hyphanden noted, by a Skill.

"The ankle-piece works just the same," Curatto told him. "There's no need to go about with the thing on your neck, except for humiliation's sake."

Curatto attended to Hyphanden's facial wounds and the sores around his neck and wrists from the collar and cuffs. He briefly examined the dark, spreading bruise on Hyphanden's hip from Dwel's boot and prescribed a potion to be taken at regular intervals. He left the medicine in a flask, along with a cup, on a small table beside the bed.

Within an hour of Curatto's and Huri's visit, another page and a guard came to escort Hyphanden to bathe. He was also provided with several sets of clean clothes, and later he was fed a rather good meal, probably from the same menu as the First Chosen received.

He had plenty of time afterwards to peruse the magazines and books and to think. For all he knew, it could be his last night on earth, or at least his last sane night. For a moment he was sorry he

183

had ever left Hyolon. It was apparent now that Pateret's View Possession had been a ruse calculated to get him out of the way. But there was no use regretting the past. He had never regretted it before. Besides, relieving Pateret of the Skill was the right thing to do.

Finally the light slowly dimmed in the chamber, and Hyphanden lay down on the bed to sleep.

Chapter Sixteen: The Petition (Nikal)

Nikal sat in the courtyard of his house at dawn. All was quiet around him; no one else was up. He toyed absently with his communication talisman with one hand. His eyes were fixed on the barely visible silhouettes of the buildings of southern Hyolon behind the trees and hills of Dobor.

He sighed. He had left Rioletta just beginning to stir in bed. She had been here for just two nights, but she would leave for Hyolon today. He wasn't sure he could continue with a long-distance relationship built on a couple days here, a few days there. He wasn't willing to give up on it yet, but Rioletta needed to make a decision: was she going to remain in Andolith and resume her duties as a Council-member, or was she going to take a leave of absence or even abdicate her position altogether?

He heard the creak of the screen door and glanced over his shoulder. Rioletta came out onto the porch. Her long dark hair was pulled back into a silver barrette at the nape of her neck. She had dressed in high-waisted riding pants, short, supple leather boots, and a deep emerald green blouse that made her eyes look almost purple. Her long hair and deep-set dark eyes had been the first things Nikal had noticed about her in Andolith two years before.

"Were you able to contact Kwistocta?" she asked as she joined him on the settee.

"Yes. She was waiting for my signal," Nikal said. "She's anxious to put the plan in motion."

"I don't blame her. I'm anxious as well. Is everything set?"

"Yes. Mynador gathered some final information, and I passed on what Stetsor told us last night. Together, I think a case can be made to Arvindahl."

"Will Stolen travel?" Rioletta asked.

"No. He's not well-spoken, and it might not be safe. I think Kwistocta has planned another surprise."

"Very well. How are we to proceed?"

185

"We'll go ahead with our petition," Nikal said, "but if it fails, they'll be prepared to deliver the message. I hope, for the sake of privacy, Arvindahl sees reason and releases Hyphanden to our care."

"We'd probably best get going soon, then," Rioletta said, rising. "We want to be in Tabor as early as possible."

"And if we do succeed?" Nikal asked. "You're still planning to go to Hyolon?"

Rioletta hesitated. "Yes, Nikal. I'm sorry, it's where I think I need to be at this point. I know I need to make some decisions, but right now, with Rudon's threat, isn't the time."

Nikal nodded with no reply. He was wise enough to realize that pushing her might result in a decision he did not want. He followed her back inside and began to rouse the rest of his visitors. Within a few minutes all were dressed and mounted, and the little group of five wound sleepily down Nikal's hill in the half-dark. They stopped briefly at an early-morning café to pick up a breakfast that could be eaten on the road.

The morning sun was still low in the sky when they rode up to the south side of the Tabor Council-house and stopped in front of the annex archway. They were ushered in to the first courtyard, where guards speedily disarmed them as pages scurried to make their presence known to the First Chosen. Then they were led in through the second archway to the stable-yard, where their horses were taken, and shown in to the antechamber.

The entire First Chosen Council, including the Integrated Council of Tane, chose to meet them in the First Audience Chamber. Nikal's group was eventually led before an assembly of thirteen Sorcerers: the four remaining original members of the First Chosen, the four later replacements, plus the five Elders of Tane. Also in attendance were some of their Advisors and members of their Younger Councils.

Nikal was well known in Tabor, and Arvin greeted him coolly. Although negotiations had been ongoing between the two cities, Dobor's construction of a bypass bridge in response to Tabor's bid to annex them had angered the First Chosen. Nikal responded formally, and gestured to his group.

186

"May I introduce to you Rioletta, inducted Sorcerer of Andolith, Andor, inducted Sorcerer of Andolith, and Creed and Aliora, hunters of Andolith," he said.

"I'm familiar with Rioletta and Andor," Arvin said. "I believe both of you have been in attendance at the negotiations in West Ford." He rose from his chair and approached them. "But I hear Ladon has been deposed. Perhaps our relationship will change in the future. You are here, I expect, with some petition or another?"

"We are here to lobby for the release of the Outcast Sorcerer Hyphanden," Nikal said bluntly.

"News travels fast," Arvin replied. He returned to his seat and gestured to a collection of chairs nearby.

"We were informed of the event by Cardon Ereptor, who was kidnapped from West Ford with Hyphanden, but escaped," Nikal said, taking a seat.

Arvin sat back in his chair. "Hyphanden was not kidnapped. His warrant is good in West Ford. He was arrested. Perhaps the bounty hunters made a mistake with Cardon, but at any rate he would have been released if no cause was found to hold him once he arrived here. However, I find it likely some cause would have attached for his continued detainment. I see you have not brought him with you."

"We have not," Nikal said.

Arvin shifted in his seat and glanced at some of the other members of his Council. "It seems odd to me that you would arrive here with the stated intention of petitioning for the release of an Outcast. Your Council is a Traditional Council. Are they in agreement with this support of the Outcasts? Are they aware that you maintain relations with these people?"

Nikal ignored Arvin's insinuation. "As you know, Dobor does not warrant Outcast Sorcerers, nor do we Strip the Skills of those who are dismissed from our Council. We disagree with the practice in principle, as does the Council of Andolith. In addition, we are in frequent contact with Stetsordahl the Elder, who has indicated to us he wishes the warrant dropped. It is thirty years old."

Arvin snorted. "We are not beholden to Stetsor, and I care not that he wishes to drop his own warrant. We have taken up the warrants, and we will continue to fulfill them as we desire. Your

187

Councils may not support warranting Unstripped Outcasts, but the precedent is there, as well as for the Stripping of those picked up on such warrants. This practice follows directly from the Charter."

"Hyphanden is little threat to you at this point," Nikal argued. "He has remained in Hyolon for thirty years. He has no outside following, no political sway within Tabor or any community other than the Outcasts. There is no reason to Strip him or punish him in any way, except for your own revenge, or perhaps to suppress knowledge you believe he has about you and your Council. Turn him loose and allow him to return to Hyolon. I will personally guarantee that he will not come out again. If he does, I will not interfere again with the service of his warrant."

"You'll personally guarantee?" Arvin grinned. "What possesses you to care so much about this Outcast Sorcerer? I can see you petitioning for the release of an Outcast due to your policy against warranting, but to personally guarantee his activities is another matter. What was he doing in West Ford anyway? I'm well aware West Ford is the home of Stetsor, and I have my suspicions."

"What would it matter to you if Hyphanden was visiting Stetsor?" Nikal said. "I've told you Stetsor wants the warrant dropped."

Arvin shifted uncomfortably. "Are you confirming that Stetsor and the Elders are in direct contact with the Outcasts? We already know that two of the Second Chosen live openly in Hyolon. I'm sure the populace of Tabor will be interested to know that the Council they once trusted has been revealed as confidants of those who practice the Forbidden Skills."

"I confirmed no such thing," Nikal answered. "I only wondered why it would bother you. But we're off the subject. The Outcast Rorudon, who was once a member of your own Council and lived many years in Hyolon, has betrayed the Outcasts and now has in his possession the means to access Forbidden Skills beyond the wildest imaginings of any of us in this day and age."

Arvin interlaced his fingers and raised his eyebrows. "Rudon, eh? It's been a long time since I heard that name. He was the first of our Council to go. I recall he was Skilled in Protection-breaking.

But I say, good for him for betraying the Outcasts! That can only be a move that is seen as praiseworthy."

Nikal frowned. "I think you misunderstand. Already Rudon prepares to overcome and destroy the Outcast Council, and the Council feels he will not stop with Hyolon, but that his intention is to exact his revenge on the Councils of Tabor. In particular he bears a grudge against the Tabor Elder Council, but if he betrayed the Outcast Council which he sat upon for nearly thirty years, he will not hesitate to destroy others."

Arvin waved a hand. "I haven't heard anything about him in years. I doubt your story; he couldn't be strong enough or Skilled enough to pose a threat to us. As for the Outcasts, I do not care what happens to their community. It does not concern us."

Nikal studied the Council Leader. Arvin sounded oddly unconcerned to him. That was to be expected, though, if Arvin had actually been in contact with Rudon. "You may not realize the resources that are available to the Outcasts, particularly a Protection-breaker like Rudon. He has, over the years, obtained many documents that should have been destroyed at the time of the Dispersal, but for one reason or another were not. These have given him a great deal of knowledge regarding the Forbidden Skills."

"You seem to have a lot of information about Rudon," Arvin mused. "All of this through Stetsor?"

"You know that two of the Second Chosen fled to Hyolon after your coup," Nikal said. "Also I'm sure you're aware that two of their supporters, one of whom is the grandson of Stetsordahl the Elder, fled to Hyolon after refusing to pledge allegiance to you. They still dwell there, and thus our information is confirmed through independent sources."

Arvin grinned mirthlessly again. "Sources who would wish ill luck upon the First Chosen. And I note that none of them appear to have been in West Ford. If all of your information is coming from a warranted Outcast who has dwelled in Hyolon for thirty years, with no contact with the outside world and no means of assessing his mental health, I distrust the seriousness of it. It seems to me he is overwrought and exaggerating. I would not be seen to be taking advice from an Outcast, or consorting with one in any way."

"Are the other members of the Council not at all curious as to what Hyphanden has to say?" Nikal asked, glancing around the room. Arvin turned to his compatriots.

"We will question him closely before Stripping him," Regner said. "Any information he has will become known to us. He is fitted with a device to block Skills and will be unable to resist our inquiries. It's unnecessary to release him in order to get this information."

Arvin turned back to Nikal's group. "That's your answer. We will have plenty of time with Hyphanden."

"And if you discover that what I say is the truth, that Rudon poses a threat to Tabor as well as Hyolon? You will need his assistance and the assistance of the rest of the Outcast Community to defeat Rudon while he is still in Hyolon. If at that point you have damaged his mind, it will be too late to seek that assistance. The Outcasts would likely choose to join Rudon in their anger towards you."

"I'll take that chance," Arvin said.

"I request that you consider what I've said," Nikal said. "We will return to Dobor if you will not entertain us further, but I request audience with you again tomorrow, to give you time to consider and change your mind."

"Very well," Arvin said. "I will not refuse you. It's good for us to be seen negotiating with Dobor and granting free access to other Councils. Please accept my invitation to remain tonight in the Council-house. You will be well-fed and housed, and will not have to travel as far to make your plea tomorrow."

Nikal hesitated, but then acquiesced. "We'll accept your offer."

"Have you anything more to add to your appeal before we dismiss you?" Arvindahl asked.

Nikal looked down as though thinking, and absently rolled his communication talisman in his fingers. "As you know, Cardon Ereptor was in contact with the Tabor Younger Council, some of whom were, I believe, close relatives of yours. During that time he became acquainted with Rudon, who actively recruited the Younger Council. You must know Rudon attempted to exact revenge against the Elder Council at that time, using your coup as cover and impetus for the Younger Council's activities."

"This I know," Arvin said impatiently. "It is for this reason I would have liked to question Cardon. I am not immune to grief and was disturbed beyond what I can tell you by the deaths of these young people. It was not done at my order or suggestion, this I swear to you."

"I do not accuse you of such," Nikal said. "I bring it up only to emphasize that two years ago Rudon was already a force to be reckoned with, powerful and manipulative enough to deceive the entire Younger Council. Is it not unprecedented that an entire Council should fall to the temptation of the Forbidden Skills? Usually it is one or two."

"Unusual, but not unprecedented." Arvin smiled slightly but shook his head. "Your reasons are not compelling. Cardon is not here to speak for himself. It could be you are putting words in his mouth. But it doesn't matter. We'll get what we want from Hyphanden, and we'll have no problem standing against Rudon and whatever piddling minions he can muster from the Outcast rogues and the Unskilled."

Arvin rose as though to escort Nikal's group from the room, but at that moment a page burst in. "I'm sorry to interrupt," he panted, "but I would like to announce two new guests."

"Yes?" Arvin asked impatiently.

The page swallowed. "They are two exceedingly odd-appearing individuals, sir, but they introduce themselves as Marsavrina and Skadardahl Vrinal of the Younger Council of Tabor."

There was stunned silence in the room for a long moment, and Arvin lost the color in his face. Then he hurried out of the room. "We will meet them in the Main Hall!"

Andor turned to Nikal. "I wonder if we'll get to see this."

"I know where the Main Hall is," Nikal said. "Follow me."

Nikal led the way through the hallways up to the main level. Along the way he reached into his satchel and brought out the formal silver circlet of the Dobor Sorcerers and fitted it upon his brow. A number of pages and guards were running around in excitement. Only one challenged them, and Nikal raised his hand in annoyance.

"I am Nikal of the Elder Council of Dobor, here at Arvindahl's invitation," he announced.

The guard eyed the circlet, then bowed slightly and stepped aside. The group rushed past him and entered the back of the Main Hall, where Nikal directed them to an out-of-the-way spot behind the columns that supported the first-floor balcony.

The First Chosen and the Council of Tane reassembled quickly in the front of the Main Hall, talking in subdued voices amongst themselves. When they were seated, Marsavrina and Skadar were shown in. Nikal caught Marsa's eye as she passed by and nodded to her. He tucked his talisman back into his shirt.

Marsa approached Arvin and offered him her hand, palm down to indicate she held the power in that encounter. He took it in shock, scanning her face for recognizable features. She bore some purposeful resemblance to her old self, but her gray skin color and the extreme regularity of her features were uncanny. She had a kind of unnatural beauty that was almost unnerving. Skadar had toned down his hair color for the journey, but even without the unusually-colored leafy hair, his appearance was of something other than human.

Nikal beckoned to the rest of the group, and they moved further towards the front of the hall, keeping behind the columns.

"Arvin, Valdic," Marsa began in her reedy, musical voice, addressing her own relative as well as the leader of the Council. "We thank you for granting us audience. I'm sure this comes as somewhat of a shock to you, and we apologize for not letting you or our other relatives know before this time that we do indeed live, in a manner of speaking."

Marsa paused, and Nikal smiled at the shocked faces upon the stage.

"As you may have surmised, our bodies are deceased, but the maps of our minds have been transferred onto the matrix provided by these bodies. Many Forbidden Skills were used to create what you see before you. And, as you have also perhaps surmised, we have been living in Hyolon, for where else would have us? Thus, we come to you as emissaries of that community, to request the release of the Leader of our Council, Hyphanden Vrinal."

There was stunned silence in the room for a minute. "Do others of the Younger Council live as well?" Arvin finally asked, still staring at her.

"There are two other minds that were rescued in part, those of Malbec and Chasan. They currently survive as dependent parts of another individual's mind. I'm afraid the other four, Verdahl, Macar, Rousa, and Roriz, all perished, due to our own use of the Forbidden Skills at the urging of Rudon."

"How did this come to be?" Valdic put in weakly. "This is not something known to be possible. It is legend."

"I will tell you the details later, if it interests you. But now we have an urgent matter before us: the release of Hyphanden. His absence has been noticed in Hyolon, and Rudon presses his advantage. If Hyolon falls to him, Tabor will be in danger."

"So we have heard this morning from the Councils of Dobor and Andolith, who, I assume, are aware of your existence," Arvin said bitterly. Nikal stood quietly behind the column, but he felt a flush rise along his neck. In this Arvin was right: it was unfair that Nikal had known of Marsa's survival, while those of her own family had not.

"But despite our elation in finding you alive, we have no compelling reason to release Hyphanden, nor to accept your assertions that Rudon threatens our community," Arvin said more steadily. "We would most certainly like to talk with you and call for your other relatives to celebrate your existence, but I see no further need to discuss Hyphanden."

"There is more reason than you may think," Marsa said softly. "There are other matters I would discuss with you, but perhaps you would prefer to speak to us in private?"

Arvin frowned. "I see no reason to do so," he said. "The Council is quite aware of each other's business."

Marsa paused for a long moment. "Very well then," she said, but she did not begin, only looked at him with her strangely immobile eyes.

"What is it you want to say?" Arvin growled. "You've piqued my interest, I admit, but I warn you, it will not change my mind."

"Then I won't waste time," Marsa said. "I wish to talk to you about Torpekai, an Outcast of New Herion. Do you remember the name?"

Arvindahl paled a bit, but he smiled indulgently. "Of course. She was expelled from Tabor some thirty years ago or more, after she was discovered living amongst the populace here. She was said to have entered the Closed City of Herion, where Skills flow down the streets by themselves, and was thus Outcast. The Councils of Tabor honor the Outcasting of other cities."

Nikal crossed his arms. He knew at least generally what was coming next.

"Many would be very interested in knowing what she discovered in Herion," Marsa acknowledged. "I know that at around the same time, you had a child out of wedlock, after you had been inducted as a member of the First Chosen Council."

"So?" Arvin shrugged, with a glance at his Council. "Many Sorcerers, even inducted ones, have children. The prohibition is against devoting oneself to a family, not against taking lovers. Sometimes the safeguards fail. I'd be willing to bet there are a fair few running around who are the children of inducted Sorcerers, all unknown. Both Trophandra and Likendahl are known to have had direct descendants. You, yourself, had an illegitimate child."

"I know what became of my child," Marsa said. "What became of yours?"

Arvin shrugged. "I don't know. The woman vanished, and the child with her."

"I think you do know. The woman was Torpekai, and you'd been harboring her in exchange for access to what she knew about the Closed City and the Forbidden Skills required to enter it. The contents of that city must be very great. You could not protect her, of course, when she was discovered, as that would have meant revealing your relationship and the Skills you had practiced together."

"An interesting guess, but a guess only, and one made only because the time period fits," Arvin said with a sneer.

"Regardless of my guesses, I do have some facts. Torpekai fled to Hyolon. The Outcast Community did not exist then, but there were a few who gathered together and made their way in the city. She found protection with a woman named Mynador. The child disappeared. Torpekai refused to tell anyone what had become of it, or she did not know. Later, Torpekai was found dead. Mynador says she killed herself."

Arvin had been sitting with his chin resting upon one hand, evincing boredom, but at this he sat up and placed his hands on the arms of his chair. "I did nothing to precipitate that. When I found out, I had her body collected and returned to her family. I never knew what happened to the child. I did not maintain relations with the Outcasts."

Nikal smiled at Arvin's unwitting confession of his knowledge and involvement with Torpekai.

"I think you did," Marsa insisted. "You were involved in the Skill-Stripping attempt on your fellow Council-member Rudon."

Arvin gestured dismissively. "Once again, nothing you say is unusual nor any secret. Every change of Council, someone has to be trained to Strip Skills. I had an opportunity to practice on a powerful Sorcerer, albeit one of my compatriots. I hope to soon refresh my Skills in that regard." He glanced at the rest of his Council with a brief smile, but it was not returned. Traminec Vrinal shifted uncomfortably and averted his eyes.

Marsa kept her own eyes fixed upon Arvin. "I suspect you learned a great deal during that event, and I suspect there was a reason Rudon retained most of his Skills, a bargain of some type. Rudon is known to be a prodigious Protection-breaker, an ability quite useful for someone looking to enter the Closed City of Herion. It's likely that bargain included maintaining contact for mutual benefit, contact you continue to this day."

"It's likely, you have reason to believe, and so forth," Arvin burst out. "You have no proof, is what you mean! Neither has any other who has made the same accusation."

Marsa shrugged. "As I'm sure you've guessed, some of these accusations we have heard from Stetsordahl the Elder, who suspected improper behavior from you but had not enough proof to level charges."

"No, although he leveled allegations, and used them as an excuse to discharge the First Chosen," Arvindahl said bitterly. "Had he any proof, I'm sure he would have charged me with it then. But this is old news, and I fail to see what any of this has to do with the situation at hand. It is conjecture. The woman is dead and cannot bear witness, as you have noted. Stetsor and the Elder Council never found cause enough to bring any charge against me, and I admit to none of it. No one will believe some Outcast Sorcerer's story from thirty years ago, and the child is likely dead as well."

Nikal was listening with rapt attention. He glanced at Rioletta, but she was transfixed by the scene.

"No," Marsa said. "The child, a man now, is not dead, but alive and well and living in Hyolon. He has also lived in Andolith. It was put forward that he was a child born of Sorcerers who practiced the Forbidden Skills, which was truer than they knew at the time."

"I have seen this man!" Traminec interjected. "He visits the Polebray, where he races horses. He is of a very odd appearance, indeed."

Marsa nodded at Traminec and the rest of the Councils. "He goes by the name Stolen. It was he who grew us these bodies, from his own skin, and he who allowed us to regain our mobility and independence. He can bear witness to the fifteen or sixteen years he spent as an Outcast child, and the thirteen he spent trapped in a terrible prison in the northlands before the Andolith Younger Council freed him. His anger at his wasted childhood is great, and he would be most willing to tell his story to any who would listen, to bring back the tale of Torpekai, his mother, and to point to you as his father."

Arvindahl leapt to his feet, anger distorting his countenance. "You have no evidence this person is my son! I do not know what altered his appearance, but to intimate that it was caused by the practice of Forbidden Skills by his parents is ludicrous."

"This story can be corroborated by deposition from Mynador. Perhaps, under oath, a few members of your own Council could provide some corroboration as well." Marsa looked pointedly at Regner. "You gave the child to Rudon to dispose of, to do away with any evidence of your relationship with Torpekai. Rudon gave the child to the people known to us as the Woodsmen, with whom Mynador has established a relationship, and from whom she has

196

obtained this information. This explains why you are not particularly worried by Rudon's escapades in Hyolon. It's likely you think you'll benefit by his access to the Crypt of Souls, and that he'll learn more about access to Herion that way. But I note he did not tell you about our existence, so I hope you'll realize that Rudon reveals only what it's in his interest to reveal at the time."

Arvindahl remained standing, his fists clenched by his sides, glaring steadily at Marsavrina. Nikal suddenly became aware of the heavy silence in the hall; no one was moving at all.

"As far as proof or disproof of Stolen's heritage, I suspect a Skilled Healer in contact with both of you could verify he is your son," Marsa continued. "His appearance in Tabor would certainly cause a stir. Some might wonder how he came to look the way he does, if they did not take affront outright at your consort with an Outcast of Herion and your treatment of him and his mother."

"So you propose to blackmail me for the release of Hyphanden," Arvin growled, pacing the dais. "You assume I'll not take the risk that citizens of Tabor might believe this man to be my son, that the tide might tip against us if any of them cared about a thirty-year-old relationship and the unfortunate upraising of a child I had nothing to do with."

Marsa shrugged. "It is, of course, up to you. If we leave here today without Hyphanden, we will immediately make plans to reveal this information as widely as possible. Already an Outcast of New Herion has made contact with his old Council to warn them of Rudon's threat to the Closed City. Likewise, if we do not return to Hyolon for any reason, a plan is in place to reveal what we know here. Perhaps, in itself, it will not bring you down, but certainly it will add to any questions regarding your ability to lead Tabor into the future, and it will provide fodder for your opponents in the community. Would you risk the outcome of a Challenge? This would be grounds to bring one. You are bound to hear them and abide by the decision, unless you intend to set yourself up as a Councilorship and abdicate the Charter altogether."

Arvin glared at Marsa. "My position is secure. I have little fear that any Challenge would result in the return of the Elder Council."

Nikal whispered to Rioletta, "But I suspect a Challenge by the Second Chosen would be supported by a good number in the community, and they are surely waiting for a good opportunity to make one."

"Is Hyphanden worth the risk?" Marsa went on. "Smaller scandals than this have brought down Council-members before, and resulted in expulsions and Outcastings. How ironic if you were to be Outcast yourself! Would your own Council perform the Stripping?"

Arvindahl strode forward towards Marsa. "I must say, my joy at finding you alive has been tempered by your obstinacy. I no longer wish to discuss this with you, nor will I entertain any petition by others of your acquaintance. Remove yourself from my presence and from the Council-house at once! If you wish to visit your relatives, you will get no help from me in locating or contacting them. In fact, I suspect you to be an impostor, and that I will pass on to whomever I can find to listen."

Marsa bowed slightly, and together she and Skadar turned to leave. At that moment Arvin noticed Nikal and his group.

He pointed at them, and several security guards jumped up. "I will hear no further petition from you, either!"

Nikal gestured to his group. The guards escorted them hurriedly down to the antechamber.

"I hope Stolen isn't too upset that this secret had to be shared," Nikal said to Rioletta as they hurried down the stone steps. "He hasn't had much time to think it over. I wonder how long Mynador has known?"

"Mynador has suspected it since she met Stolen, I think," Rioletta said. "Torpekai of Herion must have been a powerful, if disturbed, Sorcerer if she managed to access the Closed City. I've never heard of anyone else who accomplished that, and lived."

"Is there any reason to think Rudon or Arvin has actually accomplished it yet, I wonder?" Nikal mused.

"I don't think so. I'll bet Rudon's planning to give it a try after he gets access to the minds in the Crypt. If he can find a pre-Dispersal Sorcerer with knowledge of Herion, he'll have a distinct advantage."

"Unfortunately, this revelation might have backfired," Nikal said. "We've made Arvindahl angry, but I'm not sure we've accomplished much else."

As they waited to be shown out, Perviridis, a member of Tane's Younger Council, appeared from a side door. He presented Nikal with a document.

"You offered your oath that Hyphanden would not enter Tabor or the territories of Tabor again, or that if he does, you will not dispute his arrest," Perviridis said. "Arvindahl finds it sufficient to guarantee and disregard a thirty-year-old warrant, which is, after all, of little interest to anybody. Please sign your guarantee, and I will bear it to Arvindahl. Hyphanden will then be released to your custody."

Nikal raised one heavy eyebrow and glanced sideways at his compatriots. He was under no illusion that his petition had been accepted, but it was a graceful way out for Arvin. He bent over a table and signed the form, then returned it to Perviridis, who bowed and strode out of the chamber. A minute later, two guards opened the exterior door and showed them out.

The group made their way through the inner courtyard, where they were reunited with their horses, and into the second courtyard, where Creed and Aliora's bows were hastily returned, along with a variety of knives the travelers had given up. As they repacked the horses, Nikal nodded to the inner courtyard. Two more horses were being brought out, and in a moment Marsavrina and Skadar appeared.

As Marsa and Skadar joined them, Hyphanden's big dark horse was brought out and saddled in the courtyard. Andor went over and gave the stable-hands Hyphanden's bridle, which she had brought along from West Ford.

Within a few minutes Hyphanden appeared at the doorway of the chamber. He paused as a guard removed a yellow anklet from him. He walked briskly to his horse and led it through the archway to the outer courtyard to meet the others.

"Well, I confess I'm confused," he said happily, addressing Nikal. "I'm practically being thrown out of here. They can't get rid of me fast enough. I assume you've made a successful petition for my release, but I can't imagine what might have persuaded Arvin to miss his chance to torture me for a while."

"The successful petition was made by Marsa," Nikal said. "But let's get out of here! We'll tell you about it on the way."

"You look awful," Rioletta said. "What happened?"

"The bounty hunter Dwel was less than pleased at Cardon's escape," Hyphanden said wryly. "I received some treatment last night."

"I have some medicines with me," Rioletta said.

"Forget it," Hyphanden replied. "I'm anxious to get away from this place before Arvin changes his mind, and curious as to what made him change it in the first place. Let's go, and I'll recover in Hyolon."

The group made good speed down the causeway to the south, through the commercial district of Tabor. Along the way, Nikal told Hyphanden about Marsavrina's confrontation with Arvindahl.

"That explains quite a lot," Hyphanden said. "I've wondered about Rudon's willingness to betray our Council. It hardly seemed that the temptation of the minds in the Crypt was enough, even coupled with a desire for revenge. But the temptation of accessing Herion as well might be enough."

"I assume that Rudon and Arvin must have agreed to lure you out of Hyolon," Nikal said. "Rudon would be rid of you, and Arvin could support the old warrants as well as rid himself of someone with dangerous information about him."

Hyphanden shook his head. "Rudon was almost certainly responsible for stealing the Key in Andolith himself. But this plot has all the hallmarks of Losino, a very crafty fellow who we know has joined Rudon. Losino is an Outcast of Kyelon. Arvin was raised in Kyelon and his mother is from there. It's possible they are known to each other or even related."

"What makes you think that?" Nikal asked.

"Rudon is a Protection-breaker and a Healer and charismatic enough to draw people to him, but he isn't the most organized person I've ever known. I've wondered about the complexity of the plot to imprison and steal the Elder Council during the coup of the First Chosen. It seemed to me to be a stretch to believe that Rudon himself made that far-reaching plan. Losino, on the other hand, enjoys complexity and convoluted plots. He and I used to enjoy playing strategy games together when he was part of the Outcast Community. I've missed that since he left. But now I wonder if he has been helping Rudon with his plans for many years."

"Bad news for those of us who wish to keep the Crypt away from Rudon, if that's so," Nikal said.

Hyphanden shrugged. "Well, we now know Tabor will provide Hyolon no help in this matter. We're on our own, for good or for ill."

Eventually they paused at a crossroads. One road wound out through the vineyards to the west, leading generally towards Hyolon, the other towards Dobor.

Nikal and Hyphanden clasped hands. "We'll pass all the news to Cardon. I'm sure I can make him feel plenty guilty about the beating Dwel delivered," Nikal told Hyphanden with a grin.

"Don't torture him, Nikal. You know he's sensitive enough as it is," Rioletta scolded.

"Ah, yes," Nikal said. He looked at her for a long moment.

"I'll keep in touch and see you soon," Rioletta said. She smiled and fingered her communication talisman.

With the late afternoon sun before them, the group turned west, waved goodbye to Nikal, and jogged down the road towards the towers of Hyolon, looming in the distance beyond the vineyards. Nikal waited a few minutes, then reined his horse to the south and settled in for his journey home, alone.

Chapter Seventeen: Return to Hyolon (Rioletta)

They kept their horses at a good pace as they passed through the vineyards of western Tabor. Rioletta saw Hyphanden fingering the talisman at his neck, which had been returned to him along with other small belongings taken by Dwel. The chain was broken, but Aliora had been able to make a temporary repair. Rioletta knew he was once again in contact not only with Kwistocta, but also with the rest of the Outcast community.

Rioletta herself was both relieved and excited. She had had a nice two nights with Nikal, and now she was off on another visit to Hyolon, where she had ready access to both interesting books and interesting people. She had kind of missed the intrigue of the previous year's journey. The Challenge had been excitement of a different sort, one she had not enjoyed at all.

Eventually the road narrowed and then became rough dirt. It was nothing more than a trail by the time it intersected the Old East Road. They turned at Hyolon's east entrance, a broad, paved avenue that passed between two huge buttresses built at the end of sweeping reaches of wall. Beyond, the view opened up to the downtown plaza. The group rode past buildings that had at one time been shops, offices, and inns, some now fallen to ruin, others fairly intact.

They turned north into the old neighborhood of Hyolon's elite and wound along curving streets until they arrived at the tumble-down gate protecting Hyphanden's estate. With a wave, Hyphanden released the Protection and the Concealment.

The gate closed behind them with a solid click. Hyphanden urged his horse up the drive to the front door of the estate, rather than to the stables. Kwistocta stepped out to meet them, and Hyphanden abandoned his horse and enfolded her in an encompassing hug.

They stood that way for a long minute, Kwistocta with her head buried in his shoulder. The others dismounted, and Creed discreetly took hold of Hyphanden's horse and led it away.

Finally they stepped back from each other, and Hyphanden kissed Kwistocta gently on the forehead, then grabbed her hand and folded it to his chest.

"Are you mad at me?" he asked, looking into her eyes.

"Absolutely," Kwistocta answered gently, with a smile that belied her words. "You're careless, and you make me madder than anyone else I've ever known." She laid a hand on the side of his face, still bruised and cut by Dwel's blows. Then she composed herself and turned to the others. "Let's get your horses unsaddled and your belongings inside. There's plenty of food, and others will be coming by to greet you. We'll have time to talk about things this evening."

"How's Stolen?" Rioletta asked.

Kwistocta sobered. "Bitter. His attitude has been poor lately anyway, and this revelation has not helped any. Creed, he'll be happy to see you. Perhaps you can spend some time with him. There's a lot for him to come to terms with."

Rioletta took her saddlebags inside and deposited them in the room she and Nikal had occupied once before. She would share it this time with Aliora. She rummaged for a moment in one saddlebag. Then she went to the kitchen, where she found Hyphanden momentarily alone. She placed a small, heavy box on the kitchen table.

"I forgot to return this."

Hyphanden picked up the box and weighed it in his hand. "Thank you. I hadn't even thought about it. Perhaps I'd best put it away somewhere. Tocta won't be too pleased to see it again."

That evening the Outcast Community, except those stationed on guard, arrived to welcome Hyphanden back to Hyolon. There was a great deal of food and wine and the large glass doors were thrown open. Many people sat out in the back yard and orchard in the cool of the evening. Others sat inside in the great room or hovered around the laden tables in the kitchen. Stolen sat off to the side most of the evening in conversation with Creed. It unnerved

Rioletta to see flashes of resemblance to Arvin in Stolen's expressions. She tried to refrain from studying him too openly.

Eventually the Council gathered in the great room. Kwistocta went over the most recent encroachments onto turf they had claimed as their own and the apparent testing of their strength by those they believed to be associated with Rudon. In Hyphanden's absence, she had put in place a carefully-constructed plan of rotating guards, interlaced Protections, and Misdirection.

"We've reserved our strongest Protections for our estates," she said. "They won't be able to strike here. The Museum and Security House we guard lightly, but it's obvious that Rudon has noticed our interest in them. The Council-house we watch from a distance, with plans to respond should any threat become apparent. Right now we believe Rudon has only two choices: a stealthy approach to the Council-house that circumvents our guards and the Alarm Skills we've set around the area, or a large-scale attempt to divert and scatter us followed by a physical assault."

"Rudon has many, many times the number of people at his disposal as we do, if you count the Hyolonal," Kerdahl said.

"'*Disposal*' is probably the right word," Cayon said. "I doubt he sees them as anything other than convenient trash."

"However he sees them, they are now well-organized and communication flows quickly through their ranks," Kerdahl said. "They've obtained a few firearms and some of the higher-ranking Hyolonal have been trained in their use. They're being drilled in the use of bows as well. In a direct confrontation, they'll hang back until we're tired or distracted, then press forward to cause physical damage."

"I certainly hope it doesn't come to a direct confrontation," Hyphanden said. "I have no wish to do damage to Rudon or to Losino and Fellodon. I've known Rudon for more than thirty years."

"Fellodon arrived here about twenty years ago," Kwistocta explained to the Andolith group. "He was borderline insane from the clumsy Stripping performed by the Council of Ankara. Rudon and I worked to improve his mind. It's not a surprise to me that he gravitated to Rudon when he left us."

"What about Losino?" Rioletta asked. "You mentioned him on the ride here, Hyphanden."

"He arrived about fifteen years ago from Kyelon, Unstripped. He and I enjoyed a little rivalry at strategy games, but after a while it got out of control. He challenged my leadership here and failed. I know he also enjoyed mapping the city and exploring with Rudon. His Skills were somewhat limited, but those he had were very powerful, with a kind of edge to them."

"The Council-house is their main target, of course," Cayon said. "Once inside, there are the Skills that went awry last year to contend with, bouncing around with no outlet. Rudon will have to enter with a set of Sorcerers who can protect themselves. I wouldn't expect more than a small group to attempt entry for that reason."

"At least he doesn't have the Index," Rioletta noted.

"I don't plan on allowing him to take the Council-house," Hyphanden said, "but if he does, he'll have no recourse but to experiment with whomever remains in the Crypt."

"I wish we had some method other than brute force to protect the Council-house," Cayon mused. "There are various Protections available for the Tabor Council-house, if one knows how to trigger them. Some of them can even be triggered remotely. It seems to me those Protections would likely have a precedent. Have you never come upon any hint of such Protections in your readings, Hyphanden?"

Hyphanden considered. "No, not in my readings. But it may yet be possible to discover whether such things exist. I hope Rudon doesn't strike too soon. I'm tired, and I could use some time for research."

"Of course," Kerdahl said. "We have things well in hand, and you can spend some time recuperating. I doubt Rudon will strike any time within the next few days, at any rate."

After the community had departed for the night, Andor, Creed, Rioletta, and Aliora remained in the great room for a final glass of wine. Kwistocta rounded up a few partial bottles and poured them out among the group.

"Hyphanden," Andor said, "you said you hadn't come across anything in your readings about any special Protections on the

Council-house. But you also said it might be possible to discover whether such things exist. Together, I take those two statements to mean you know some other source of information regarding the operation of the Council-house."

Hyphanden smiled and interlaced his fingers. "Very perceptive. Of course there's another source. Stelaphandon has knowledge of the Council-house's history and functions."

"Hyphanden, no," Kwistocta objected.

"He's hinted, but he hasn't told you outright?" Rioletta pressed him.

"Well, Stela's a bit cagey with his information. He wants something in return. Sometimes I can bargain with him, and sometimes I can't."

"You're too tired to use Stela," Kwistocta said. "You've had problems getting him out of your mind lately."

"I could try it, for just a few minutes," Hyphanden suggested. "If he isn't willing to tell me what I want to know, I won't bargain with him."

"Not tonight," Kwistocta said firmly. "Sleep and rest tonight. Think about it again tomorrow."

"I agree," Rioletta put in. "I appreciate Stela's help with Pateret, but it's still a dangerous diversion."

"Ah, still the Traditional, despite everything. I haven't managed to convince you yet," Hyphanden teased. "But there's more for you to know. In fact, Cardon knows more than you do about certain subjects! We'll have to spend some time and see if I can move you an inch further in my direction."

"You know, perhaps there's a good reason she remains Traditional despite everything," Kwistocta said impatiently. "Her world was disrupted and her stability destroyed when she was a young child. No one believed her then, and they discount what she knows now. Perhaps she turned to the ritual of the Traditions and the security of study to regain some sense of safety and some acceptance in her life."

Hyphanden looked disconcerted. "I didn't think of it that way. I was only prodding you, Rioletta, because I know you have a good mind and I enjoy the company of another Loremaster. I didn't mean to make you uncomfortable."

"No harm done," Rioletta said lightly. Internally, she felt a shock of recognition. She had to concede that what Kwistocta said might be true, although she had never realized it on a conscious level.

"Speaking of Cardon, what's going on with his errant horses?" Andor asked.

Hyphanden shrugged. "They disappeared for a while, and we were worried that Rudon might have co-opted them for his own purposes. But that doesn't seem to be the case. They've been seen roaming the southern part of the city. I have no idea how to control them. That's a set of Skills I haven't concentrated on, and I don't know anybody who has."

"I suppose they'll have to be dealt with at some point," Rioletta said. "Otherwise they might escape from the city. And they'll certainly make glass salvage dangerous if they're in the area near Dobor."

"Yes, but Rudon's a more pressing problem right now. Sleep and rest sound good to me. We'll have time to talk tomorrow."

Rioletta rose early the next morning. No one else seemed to be up, so she took Erendak's journals to read until the others rose. As she came down the hallway she glimpsed Hyphanden passing through the great-room from the other side. In one arm he carried a stack of books, and in the other hand he carried the small, jeweled box.

She stepped back a bit, her suspicions aroused. He continued on out into the garden. She watched as he crossed on a walkway between rows of kitchen herbs and flowers and passed underneath the fruit trees. There was a bench and arbor in a corner of the estate, backed against a crook in the wall.

From the kitchen Rioletta could see him set the box down gingerly on the seat beside him. After a final glance around, he unlatched the lid, opened it, and stared deep within.

But only a minute later, Hyphanden snapped the lid shut. He remained in the garden, staring at some point in the distance. Rioletta went out through the glass doors.

Hyphanden looked up guiltily as she approached and placed the box in his pocket. He pulled the books towards himself across the bench.

"I know what you were doing, Phando," Rioletta said. "There's no point in hiding it from me."

"I don't need to be nagged by you as well as by Kwistocta," he snapped.

"Well, then, I won't nag you. Did you find out anything about Protections on the Council-house from Stela?"

"Yes, and no," Hyphanden said, crossing his arms. His voice betrayed frustration.

"Let me guess," Rioletta said. "Stela does have information, but he wants to drive some bargain in order to reveal it."

Hyphanden laughed shortly. "And I refused the bargain. But if in the future I need the information, I might accept it."

"Be sure he actually holds the information before you take the bargain, whatever it might be," Rioletta warned.

"I would not take it lightly. The Protection Stela offers would close the Council-house to Rudon, but also to everyone else, probably forever. We would not have access to it again: not to its libraries, its labyrinths, or its secrets."

"And in exchange for how to trigger this Protection, Stela would want to take up permanent residence in your mind," Rioletta guessed.

Hyphanden glanced at her, but otherwise didn't acknowledge her guess. "But Stela does indeed share valuable information with me. Anyway, do you want to know what Cardon knows about the Lefollah that you don't?" he asked with a grin.

"Of course," Rioletta said. She stacked her own books on a small table near one of the garden chairs and looked at him expectantly. He obviously wanted to change the subject.

Hyphanden told her what he had told Cardon during their ride with Dwel and Rant. He watched in obvious amusement as Rioletta absorbed the information.

"But if this is true…" Rioletta shuddered as a memory of the Lefollah running naked without their shells came to her mind, "…you're saying I have a Lefollah for an ancestor!"

"As do we all!" Hyphanden laughed. "I know it's hard to imagine, but long and slow Shape-shifting, the way it's supposed to be done, changed our bodies forever, in an inheritable way, to make it possible for our ancestors to breed with the Unskilled."

209

"But when did this happen, and why? I can't imagine the desire for either group to interbreed with the other!"

"It was long, long ago, a time of chaos in the world. One group of Lefollah thought intermingling with the Unskilled would be the best recourse to allow them to survive into the future. They enjoyed the physical freedom, strength, and other advantages of the Unskilled. There was another group of Lefollah who thought disappearing into the forests would more likely be the best course of action. The two groups split. Those who would become the Lefollah of today concentrated on their Shape-changing and group communication Skills, to the exclusion of almost all else. On the other hand, our direct ancestors concentrated on the Skills that made them most useful and attractive to the Unskilled and produced the hybrid Skilled line from which we are descended."

"And at that time we began to forget the true Lefollah, maybe purposefully," Rioletta guessed.

"The Sorcerer Councils retained that knowledge, although by the time of the Dispersal hundreds of years later, it was confined to the Inner Councils. The Skilled entered into the First Accord, which you know something about already. The Lefollah had sacrificed their mobility and consequently became inbred over time. They needed the blood and intellect of the Skilled to reinvigorate their line, both physically and mentally. The Lefollah would be provided with children from time to time, unwanted children, who would slowly be changed to resemble their Lefollah ancestors closely enough that they could breed."

"That's abhorrent," Rioletta said. "The idea was to turn unwanted children into breeding slaves."

Hyphanden shrugged. "In exchange, the Lefollah provided access to certain Skills the Sorcerers could no longer practice. The Lefollah reversed Skills that had gone awry and helped the errant Sorcerers who Threw them regain their sanity and health."

Rioletta shook her head in disbelief. "But there's no mention of this in any of the histories I've studied as a Sorcerer Loremaster."

Hyphanden picked up a small bound booklet and handed it to her. "The Charter," he said.

"I've been studying the Charter for years, Hyphanden," Rioletta said disdainfully. "I don't need to see a copy of it to know what it says."

"Well, then, Article One, Section One – what does it say?"

"It covers the general make-up of the governing bodies of the cities and requires vestment of legislative and judicial powers in the Councils. Boring administrative stuff."

"Very good. And what else?"

Rioletta shrugged. "I know what you're getting at. The rest of the Section recognizes that Special Knowledge is held within the Councils of Sorcerers that isn't generally available to the rest of the public. That Special Knowledge has been interpreted to be our training and the intensive study of the Charter itself."

"In Tabor that section is a topic of spirited debate. Many believe there was a special, separate bank of knowledge into which Inner Council members were initiated at one time, which has since been lost. Since it's mentioned in the Charter, it seems that this knowledge was to continue even after the Dispersal. But it obviously didn't. The Dispersal was much more chaotic than was expected. Many groups barely survived, like the Andolith settlers, for example."

Rioletta crossed her arms. "I assume you have an opinion as to what this Special Knowledge is, then, and why the Dispersal was so chaotic?"

Hyphanden grinned. "Of course. The First Accord was undoubtedly part of this knowledge. But there was more: the Traditionals hold that the Dispersal occurred because the extractive technologies of the Unskilled began to cause serious and overwhelming damage to the environment."

"There's good evidence that this is true," Rioletta said. "There are huge damaged and destroyed areas that haven't recovered to this day."

"I'm not denying that. But haven't you ever wondered exactly how the Dispersal was accomplished? Can you imagine hundreds of thousands of people obediently abandoning their comforts and setting out into a veritable wilderness to establish primitive settlements, guided only by the Charter of Dispersal, a document they had only just been introduced to?"

211

Rioletta kept her arms crossed. She wasn't going to let Hyphanden twist her thinking about history, but he did have a point. It was hard enough to get all the citizens of Andolith to agree on any one thing, as had been demonstrated by the Challenge.

"According to Stela, in the days before the Dispersal the Councils of the cities discussed whether or not the environmental damage could be mitigated through regulation and voluntary compliance," Hyphanden continued. "They agreed it would be possible to engineer their way out of that particular predicament."

"Then why the Dispersal?" Rioletta asked impatiently.

"Because their problems were compounded by the invention of the communication devices, some examples of which you've seen yourself. When these devices were paired with amplifiers and talismans and with personal communicative Skills, they formed a network of instant communication that could not be turned off. This allowed everyone to remain in constant communication with each other, with virtually instantaneous message-passing."

"I've heard this theory of yours before," Rioletta said. "You think the devices precipitated the Dispersal, rather than the environmental problems."

"Yes, with confirmation from Stela. Some people began to send out messages that distorted the truth and caused people to behave in ways they wouldn't otherwise behave. The reliance on these devices caused people to begin functioning as kind of a hive-mind, losing their individuality. They were able to use Skills in conjunction with each other and increase the power of those Skills, sometimes for harassment, ostracization, and coercion. The Councils feared the people would return to a state more like the Lefollah from which they came, in violation of the First Accord, which reserved constant communication to the Lefollah."

"Distant Communication and Monitoring and Viewing were not Forbidden in the Charter," Rioletta pointed out.

"Because they can't be maintained constantly. They aren't much of a threat. Besides, the network only worked optimally when at least 5000 people, preferably more than 25,000, were involved in it. This seems to be some sort of critical mass."

Rioletta thought for a moment. The Charter set limits on the size of villages, with 5000 being the maximum size for an incorporated city, and 25,000 the maximum size for a collective of villages dependent upon a single Council.

Hyphanden nodded. "The only solution the Councils could see was to disconnect the devices and make it a crime to utilize those technologies in conjunction with communicative Skills. But that was easier said than done. They knew that turning off the network would cause widespread havoc, chaos, and panic, even rioting."

"Then how would the Dispersal have been managed? You yourself suggested that hundreds of thousands of people wouldn't readily obey an order to abandon everything they knew."

"Indeed, here's the crux of it, as I understand it now. The Council of Hyolon was responsible for enlisting help from the Lefollah to take over the communication network at the time of the Dispersal. They were to use their superior communication Skills to create specific messages prior to the final disconnection of the devices. These would suggest an emergency need to evacuate the cities and disperse into smaller settlements, and reinforce the Charter as the one document whose contents could be trusted and relied upon, in almost a religious manner. Erendak, whose journals you have, was conscripted to be the liaison with the Lefollah. He developed the Second Accord, which released control over the Crypt of Souls to the Lefollah in exchange for their help."

"I see. Another abhorrent agreement. It seems like things didn't go as smoothly as they expected, though," Rioletta said. "If such an Accord was made, then why does the Crypt still exist, and why was Stolen taken years later?"

"Because after the Dispersal the Crypt was not available to the Lefollah as promised. Trophandra was damaged beyond saving during the Dispersal as she tried to retain her personal memory of truth. The liaison Erendak was dead, Stela was accused of his murder, Stela himself was dead and imprisoned in the Crypt of Souls, and Likendahl was charged with the murder of Stela. Thus the Lefollah eventually fell back on the First Accord."

Hyphanden paused at the expression of dismay from Rioletta. "Yes, Stela is a murderer as well as a victim. He committed the act with a knife and caused a physical, unrecoverable death, but

213

Likendahl committed the act with a Skill, allowing Stela's mind-map to be rescued at the last moment, as Trophandra's last truly sane act. Likendahl was a brother of Erendak, and his motive was anger and revenge. Stela's motive was more complicated, it seems."

"And his action more permanent," Rioletta observed in distaste.

"I won't attempt to excuse it," Hyphanden said.

"Do you know what caused Stela to murder Erendak?"

"No. He has refused to tell me, so far. But certainly all of this adds a new dimension and interpretation to the Charter, doesn't it? It was a document intended to mislead and cover up the truth of the past."

Rioletta looked him straight in the eye. "Hyphanden, the Charter still holds. What Amidon said was right. If it guides us true, what matter that it doesn't contain every bit of information? Its principles are even more important now that I know more about the Dispersal itself. Communities must be limited in size and contact to prevent the development of a communal mind. The Skills must be Forbidden along with the Technologies to avoid serious consequences. We must remain independent so that we never again fall into the trap of losing our individuality. The Charter is still our guide, and I see now more than ever that it allows us to behave in ways that protect our individuality and our future."

"Bah!" Hyphanden threw down his copy of the Charter. "The Charter does nothing for your individuality, your future, or your behavior. How do you think Sorcerers managed to comport themselves in the days before the Charter existed? Do you think if this document was suddenly erased and all memory of its contents wiped from your mind, that you would run wildly around destroying the earth and tearing into the minds of others?"

Rioletta stared at him, startled. She had truly never thought of how the pre-Dispersal Sorcerers managed their cities with no Charter to guide them. "Of course not," she said reluctantly. "But if the Charter didn't exist, I expect some other document, some other series of orders, would soon be adopted, to provide society with some form upon which to build itself. Such a thing must have existed in the days before the Dispersal. The Sorcerers must have had Orders and Policies, at the very least."

Hyphanden sat back more calmly. "There's a difference between Orders and Polices, which are limited in scope, and a single overarching document not subject to revision or repeal. You do not need the Charter any more than I do."

"Perhaps not, but maybe I want the Charter," Rioletta replied. "The Charter is comforting to me, as I suspect it is to others, and it's accurate enough to allow us to build our communities upon it, whether it contains the strict or whole truth or not. Seek information for its own sake, Hyphanden; don't hope to change the world with what you alone know. One thing I have learned this past year: information is not wisdom, and the guidance of our people relies on more than data."

Hyphanden lowered his eyes with a pained expression, but then he looked back up. "Change comes slowly, and I can't expect it to happen all at once. I'm not discouraged! I am a Loremaster, Outcast or no, and the end of my seeking will be the end of my life."

Rioletta sat still for a moment, going over everything Hyphanden had just revealed to her. "So, Hyphanden, given all that you believe you've discovered, all you think you know, do you believe the Dispersal was a good thing or a bad thing?" she finally asked.

Hyphanden snorted. "Tell me this, Rioletta, given all you've discovered and all you think you know, was your Challenge a good thing or a bad thing?"

Rioletta felt a flush rising in her cheeks. She could think of no way to continue constructively, so she rose to leave. Hyphanden looked up at her with a slight smile, but she worried. The intensity of his desire for knowledge was dangerous, and the only others she had known with that kind of passion often ended up discouraged and isolated. She hoped he would forget it for a while, and concentrate on his recovery.

Chapter Eighteen: The Vault (Rioletta)

Later that day, Rioletta, Andor, Creed, and Aliora were introduced to the guard posts and spy points around the city. Stolen and Jamoy, a young Outcast with whom Stolen had become friends, served as their guides. While Stolen was taciturn, Jamoy was the opposite, good-humored and full of energy. By the end of the day the four Andolith citizens were foot-weary from following along. They prepared a simple meal from leftovers from the night before and sat in the great room reading and talking, with the garden doors open, until the sun was down and the city dark. Jamoy and Stolen joined them for the evening, as Creed had convinced Stolen that seeking company would be good for his state of mind. Kwistocta offered them a room for the night, which Stolen accepted, although Jamoy declined the offer and left after dinner for a night shift on guard duty.

Finally the first person made the decision to go to bed, and everyone else followed with a round of goodnights. Rioletta and Aliora talked briefly in the room they were sharing, but soon Aliora was fast asleep. Rioletta lay awake for a little longer, contemplating what she'd learned from Hyphanden, but soon enough sleep overtook her as well.

In the middle of the night she awoke to an earth-shaking boom. She sat up in her bed. Aliora sat up as well.

"What was that?" Aliora whispered.

"Thunder?" Rioletta suggested, but the sky had been clear and the stars bright when they had gone to bed. She checked the clock near her bed: only four hours had elapsed.

Aliora threw off the covers and went to the window, which looked out towards the stables to the east.

"The sky's clear. That was no thunder," she said. Just at that moment there came a second boom, and the sky lit up from somewhere to the west.

"This is bad," Aliora said, dropping the curtain. Rioletta hastily turned up a light and the two of them scrambled into their clothes. They could hear voices down the hallway, and by the time they made their way to the great-room, Creed, Andor, Stolen, and Kwistocta were already there. Hyphanden came in a few moments later. Creed clutched his bow. Aliora had her own bow over her back. Stolen held his machete in one hand.

"What's going on?" Rioletta asked.

"Those are explosions if I've ever heard them," Creed said. "I'll bet you anything it's Rudon's doing."

"Agreed," Hyphanden said. "You should outfit yourselves with whatever you need to do battle if necessary. We'll head in the direction of the blasts and try to find the night guards. We'll need to gather the Community."

As he spoke, he fingered the talisman and amplifier around his neck. Rioletta wished she could contact Morcah and request help from the Andolith Council, although it would be days before they could arrive. She could, however, contact Nikal. She drew out the black stone around her own neck.

A few minutes later they carefully departed through the garden door. There were Protections around the estate, but Hyphanden was on high alert anyway. Rioletta, as usual in a battle situation, felt useless. But she might function as a sentry and an observer, using her Skills in Concealment, Stealth, and Misdirection, if not a combatant.

Creed climbed the stile to the top of the wall first. Although the wall made attack from below during daylight less likely, they soon realized that at night they were silhouetted against the sky and vulnerable to long-distance weaponry such as firearms and arrows. But it was the quickest way to travel without dropping down into the streets of Hyolon, where the Hyolonal or others could be lurking around any corner.

There had been no further explosions, but as they hurried along the wall Rioletta saw a glow to the west. Another glow seemed to rise to the southwest in the heart of downtown, and in its light billows of dark smoke could be seen. They reached one of the turrets along the wall, and Hyphanden motioned them to stop.

218

"The bachelor estate is up and responding," he said. "Sanctacar was on guard duty near the Council-house. He'll be here in a few minutes to give us the news. We'll wait for him here."

"Can you tell what's burning?" Rioletta asked.

Kwistocta answered. "It's difficult to tell, but it appears to me that the tall building to the south is the Vault."

"I remember it," Rioletta said. "Rudon took us by there last year."

"Why would it be targeted?" Andor asked.

"A fire there would cut off safe access to the Museum. We've had guards stationed in the Museum because we know it was a place of special importance to the Dispersal-era Sorcerers. The guards have been accessing it through a secret entrance in the Vault. Those guards now can't return to us without leaving the building at ground level and passing through the streets, which is undoubtedly very dangerous at the moment."

"Perhaps the entrance is not so secret," Aliora said darkly.

"No," Kwistocta agreed. "The other fire appears to be between the bachelor estate and the Convention Center. I suspect it's taken out the section of wall we used to access that part of the city safely."

In a few minutes they heard someone scrambling up the steep broken rock from the greensward side of the turret. Creed aimed an arrow, but it was Sanctacar who appeared over the rim. Even in the dark, Rioletta could tell he was shaken. Sanctacar was young, an Outcast from Torbros, a city near Toralon.

"They've blown up the turret near the plaza just past the Convention Center," Sanctacar gasped as soon as he had gained the top of the wall.

Hyphanden gripped him firmly by the shoulders to steady him both physically and mentally. "Did you see anything?"

Sanctacar shook his head. "I was on duty along the base of the wall, walking the Greensward. Hadrost and Myloy were on the turret. I ran that way as soon as I heard the explosion, but..." He paused with a gasp. In a moment he regained his composure. "They are both dead. I found only scraps."

"Do you know of any other injured?" Kwistocta asked hurriedly.

"No. I haven't been in contact with anyone at the Museum. If they're smart they won't try and get to us using the streets, they're crawling with Hyolonal. I met Dacent and Jamoy at the remains of the turret. They were on guard at the Council-house. They say there's a horde of Hyolonal milling around there as well. I saw Kerdahl and a few others from the bachelor's estate heading that way."

"Cayondahl and Caladoc were on guard in the Security House," Hyphanden said. "I've been in contact with them, and they tell me they are besieged but are holding their own for the time being. We need to gather our forces and make a plan, but I fear we are already too scattered."

"I suggest some of us go to the Council-house and meet the guards and those from the bachelor's estate there and see if we can forestall entry into it," Kwistocta said. "That group should be Sorcerers who can Throw Skills and some guards for protection. We should send a contingent to liberate Caladoc and Cayon, if possible, and another couple to scout a route of escape for those trapped at the Museum. Those with fewer battle Skills should stay in the area of the estates and at least let us know if an attack is launched there."

It was quickly decided that Hyphanden, Kwistocta, Creed, Andor, and Aliora would go to the Council-house. Marsavrina and Skadar would provide protection for the estates, as they were not physically capable of battle. Stolen would join a group made up of others from the Community who would go to the aid of Caladoc and Cayon at the Security House. The force besieging them was reported to be mostly Hyolonal, with only a couple of rogue Sorcerers commanding them. Rioletta would go with Sanctacar, who was also Skilled in Stealth and Concealment, to the Museum.

"I doubt we've seen the last of the explosions," Hyphanden warned before they parted. "Losino is skilled at explosives. Remember that he's also a strategist. It's likely he has something else planned. Be careful!"

Kwistocta, Hyphanden and their group left to find their way to the Council-house. The rest scattered in other directions, leaving Rioletta upon the turret with Sanctacar.

Rioletta had met Sanctacar only a few times at Hyphanden's estate and had never spoken more than a few words to him. "I'm sorry about Hadrost and Myloy," she said as she followed him along the wall. "I know the Community is small and you're all very close."

"Hadrost was a good friend," Sanctacar said. "At least it must have been quick."

His voice quavered. Rioletta changed the subject, hoping to help him focus on the task at hand. "What do you know about the Vault and the Museum? I've only been there once."

"It's a complex of buildings around a plaza, like a little fortress. The Vault stands on one end. The building directly opposite is the Museum, one of the buildings left heavily Protected. There are many mysteries about it and the buildings that make up the two sides of the fortress. There are hints of secret passageways, storage facilities, rooms, and Concealed devices. We've always been interested in it, and we found a passage into it through the Vault that allowed us to enter at an upper level. This kept us off the street and away from the Hyolonal. But with the Vault damaged, there won't be a safe way for those at the Museum to leave. The Hyolonal can just wait outside and pick them off as they come out."

Sanctacar took a circuitous route along the wall-tops. Rioletta could see the towering Convention Center to her right, silhouetted against the sky. It had been one of the first buildings she'd noticed when she'd entered Hyolon the year before, a landmark that could be seen from miles outside the city.

Just as she laid eyes upon the Convention Center, there was another blinding explosion, and the building disappeared behind a huge tower of smoke. She and Sanctacar both crouched involuntarily. They were too far away from the explosion for any debris to reach them, but a few seconds later the shock wave rolled over them.

Sanctacar stood up and grasped the talisman around his neck as they stared in dismay at the devastation. A minute later he nodded. "Hyphanden and his team are all right; but no news of anyone else who may have been nearby. Come, we should hurry."

Rioletta took one last look at what remained of the Convention Center, silhouetted in the light of burning debris, then turned her back and rushed after Sanctacar. In a few minutes they came to the edge of the sprawling and complex plaza into which the main road from the east fed. The glow from the burning Vault was now much closer, lighting up the central district.

"We'll have to cross the plaza," Sanctacar said. "It's possible to skirt it if you go far to the east, but it's faster to go from building to building."

There was a large clock tower with an eccentric, geared clock face in the center of the plaza. Sanctacar led her to the arched doorway and massive dark wood and glass door, looked around, and then passed through as though it did not exist. Rioletta followed him without hesitation. She was able to see such things quite easily. They came into a small oblong foyer with no apparent outlet. There was a dusty replica of the clock tower against the far wall and Sanctacar quickly went to it, opened the glass, and turned the wheels in the clock face. Then he slid his fingers behind a narrow rim in the face and pulled the entire front of the clock open like a door. Behind it lay a passageway, and the two stepped through the narrow slot. Sanctacar pulled the clock-face door closed behind them.

They continued in the dark along a passageway that Rioletta could feel rise gently under their feet. Soon they passed an open exterior window, and she realized they were winding around the clock tower in a circular path.

About halfway up Sanctacar stopped. There was another door, this one made to look like a window with the lower half made of the stone wall. They stepped out onto the roof of the clock tower's support house. They hurried along it to one of the corners and from there crossed a cunningly-built bridge, almost invisible from the ground, to the corner of the roof of another building. They were able to continue from corner to corner until they reached the opposite side of the plaza and descended through a gated and Protected stairway. From there they continued along the streets.

Finally Sanctacar stopped, pressed up against the buttress of a brown stone structure, and motioned her in close.

"Just ahead is the plaza in which the Museum sits. We're facing its eastern wall, which is connected on one end to the Museum and on the other to a fortification that runs into the Vault. I propose we scout along the wall and identify where any of Rudon's forces are stationed, and then see if there's any way we can access a door or window."

Rioletta nodded and checked her Concealment. Dawn was coming and they were now able to see fairly clearly, although colors were still faded and gray. Together they crept forward, Sanctacar checking the building-tops above them every few seconds. As they reached the broad court in which the complex stood, he pointed out two sentries upon the rooftops, one on either side of the street down which they carefully moved. There were none visible upon the eastern wall of the Museum itself, but as they cautiously peered around the corner they saw a group of Hyolonal talking casually together a hundred yards away to their left and another couple standing near the fortification where it curved upwards towards the burning Vault.

"None around the Vault itself. They're all concentrating on the Museum," Sanctacar whispered. "I wonder why?"

"Likely they're afraid the building will fall," Rioletta said. "They must know that burning buildings often collapse." But she noticed that despite the passage of time since the explosion, the spread of the fire looked fairly minimal.

The Hyolonal to their left were holding spears and their typical fighting sticks, but at least two of them also had bows slung across their backs and quivers by their sides. These two were dressed differently and wore objects secured to their belts that Rioletta guessed were Rudon's communication devices.

She and Sanctacar made their way along the front of the buildings not far from where the group stood. One of them, with a crossbow over his back, seemed more alert than the others. He looked around from time to time, and often checked on the two sentries on the rooftops, sometimes signaling them as though to check that everything was okay. His eyes slipped over Rioletta. She stopped instantly, as motion could easily give away

223

Concealment. She had to remind herself that he was Unskilled, and thus unlikely to detect her Skills.

They paused again at the corner of the complex where the wall intersected the hulking structure of the black stone Museum. Somewhere in there several of the Outcast Community were trapped. A number of Hyolonal milled around outside the main door, where polished stone steps rose steeply between metal rails. The door appeared intact, and there was no sign of a rogue Sorcerer in the area. It appeared that the Hyolonal had been left with orders to keep anyone from leaving or entering the buildings, a task they were capable of doing in the absence of direct supervision, especially with the communication devices linking them to Rudon.

They continued on past the main entrance and down the west side, which was made of a series of interconnected buildings with a single pitched roof of dark brown tile. From this side they could see the fire burning within the Vault. Flames licked out the broken windows six or seven stories up and debris scattered the ground. But the force of the explosion seemed mostly to have damaged a foyer or large vestibule that stood out from the main building, once several stories high, now reduced to rubble with smoke pouring from its interior.

"That was the main entrance hall," Sanctacar whispered, pointing to the rubble. "Once people would have entered there to be screened for security purposes. Then they would have entered the main building."

"We should take a better look at the Vault itself," Rioletta suggested. "The fire doesn't seem as bad as I'd expect at this point."

"There's very little inside to burn, other than wall coverings," Sanctacar said. "The exterior is made of stone, and it's supported with forged metals. Nevertheless, at some point it will undoubtedly collapse."

Rioletta frowned. "The damage to the entrance hall is more minimal than I would have expected, as well. Surely Rudon, or Losino, has better explosives than that."

Sanctacar looked over the damage once again. "I guess he didn't want to risk damaging the Museum itself. I'm sure he knows some of the hints and stories. Perhaps he ordered only as much damage as would render the safe exits unusable."

"Perhaps, but I notice something else. Look at the flames licking out of that window there, on the seventh story. Keep watching the tongues of flame and see if you see anything odd."

Sanctacar watched for a minute, then nodded. "I see what you mean. It's as though the flames are repeating, in a pattern. It's a Deception of some sort."

"So it appears. But is it a Deception of Rudon's or one left by the residents of Hyolon?"

"That I don't know. I'm good with Protections and Concealments in general, but not so good at Fire Skills."

"I have some knowledge of Fire Skills," Rioletta said. "One of the members of my Council is Skilled with fire and explosives. I've learned some from her over the years."

"Then let's see if we can get inside," Sanctacar said. "And let's hope we're not walking into a trap set by Rudon. He might be trying to keep people out until he can access it himself."

"Not likely," Rioletta whispered as they began to move towards the Vault. "If he prevails in this conflict, he'll just be able to walk in the front door of the Museum. If he doesn't, he knows that we know of the secret passageways into the Vault, and that we'll have them guarded. I suspect this is some leftover from the old days, a trick to protect the Vault itself in case of some outside attack or attempt at robbery."

"We have several options," Sanctacar said. "We've been accessing the Vault through a Concealed bridgeway from that building over there…" he pointed to a structure just off the plaza, "but I see that it is well guarded by Hyolonal. They certainly are aware of that passage, and it's likely it's been seriously damaged anyway, as it ran just over the foyer. So we're left with two ground-level doors."

Rioletta and Sanctacar first tried an entrance that had probably been an employee door. It was in the deep shadows thrown by the Vault and not yet covered by full daylight. But the door was a true door, locked with a physical lock: it could only be opened with a key or by physically breaking it, or perhaps by one with advanced Locksmithing Skills. Any attempt to break in would certainly attract the attention of the Hyolonal, and besides, neither of them had any kind of tool to make such an attempt.

The only other option was to try to get in through the entrance foyer. This required that they step into full sunlight, but the Hyolonal were far enough away that they managed to get to the area without being noticed. The destruction of the foyer was no Deception: a real explosion had ripped through it, collapsing the roof and bringing the interior walls and much of the exterior down. It was a smoking pile of rubble.

They clambered quickly over the junk where the front door had been and gained the comparative safety of the interior side of the north wall, which had been left standing relatively intact. Sanctacar pointed ahead at a ragged dark hole close to the tower wall of the Vault.

"There is where the entrance into the Vault tower lies," he said. "If it hasn't caved in completely, we may be able to make our way through it and up into the tower. But there's smoke coming from it. Can you tell if it's real?"

"A Deception, I believe," Rioletta said, squinting at it. "Let's get closer and then we'll be able to tell."

They climbed carefully over the piles of stone and glass and interior wallboard, trying to maintain a semblance of Concealment while concentrating on their footing. Parts of the pile were burning with actual fire and they took care to test each step and avoid hot spots and loose rubble. It took several minutes to make their way to the damaged, partially-filled doorway that led into the tower.

Rioletta stooped and studied the smoke. "Some small part of it is real, but most of it is a Deception," she told Sanctacar. "There's no need to try and break it. We'll just go through with the knowledge that it's false."

"And hope that a real collapse doesn't occur," Sanctacar said nervously.

Rioletta ducked and climbed a few steps down the rubble into the doorway. It was dark inside, made darker by the swirling smoke and the fact that only the upper part of it was open to the outside. "Sanctacar, you're going to have to lead," she said. "I don't know where I'm going."

Sanctacar had followed very close behind her. Now he pushed past hesitantly and put a hand upon the wall. Rioletta grabbed his shirt in the dark and they went forward a step at a time. There was debris upon the floor, and from time to time they tripped over it. Wires and other objects hung down from the ceiling or stuck out from the walls, catching at their hair and clothes. As they proceeded the heat increased and then a light began to grow, orange and flickering, accompanied by the heavy, choking odor of burning textiles, wood, and paint.

They stepped into an open room, lit only by flames crackling up the opposite wall. The heat was so intense that Sanctacar put an arm up before his face. Dark brown and black smoke rolled across the ceiling in ominous waves and the fire seemed to pulse.

"It's a Deception," Rioletta shouted at him over the roar. In actuality, the heat, noise, and light were so intense that she was not sure of her own deduction.

"Some Deception! I've never seen one like this!" Sanctacar shouted back "The door to the stairway lies beyond that wall of flame. If we can't get past it, we can't access the hidden doors above that will lead us to the Museum."

Rioletta stepped boldly past him, demonstrating a lot more confidence than she felt. She walked towards the wall of flame. The heat became even more intense. The ceiling lowered with black smoke. It was almost impossible to force herself onward: the fear of fire was primeval and the roiling smoke was terrifying. She crouched involuntarily as she crept forward. But the pattern of it was that of a Deception, although unfamiliar in form.

Finally she stood before the sheet of flame. She slowly raised one arm and extended it into the fire. It felt as though her flesh was beginning to sear and crack, but she saw that her shirt did not catch fire. She drew her hand back and examined it. There was no mark; the skin was not even red. And she also noticed that despite the heat she felt, she was not perspiring.

She scrambled back to Sanctacar and showed him her arm. "It will be painful to go through, I think. But it will be quick and we won't suffer any damage."

"If all of the fire is a Deception, and none is real," Sanctacar said doubtfully.

"There may be true fire above, but this is not. We'll have to go quickly."

Sanctacar drew a deep breath and took her hand. They approached together through the stifling heat and smoke. The sound seemed to grow louder, rushing and roaring like a flood coming down a canyon. They paused briefly in front of the sheet of flame, then with a quick look at each other, they ran through.

The doorway was not visible through the fire, and Rioletta relied on Sanctacar to guide her. But his estimate was off, and although he himself passed through the doorway, Rioletta ran full on into the frame and fell backwards into the Deception. The pain was like nothing she had ever felt before. It was as if every nerve in her body was being burned from the inside out. She felt as though she had lost control of her limbs, and groveled on the ground.

A second later she lay sprawled on the floor of a corridor. Sanctacar had dragged her free of the sheet of flame by one ankle. He collapsed against a wall; the air here was much cooler and the billowing smoke was gone. Both of them gasped for breath.

"Well, that was unpleasant," Sanctacar said finally. "Sorry about the misjudgment."

Rioletta rubbed her head and shoulder where she had slammed into the doorframe. "I think I'll be okay. Where do we go from here?"

"Up, but remember, the flames we could see from outside were on the sixth and seventh floors, which is where the passageways are located. There may be more of this."

Up they went through the first floors of the Vault. Each staircase ended at the floor it accessed, and the next staircase started from the opposite side of the building, which meant they had to pass through all the corridors or hallways or offices in between. It was an empty building, and there was virtually no furniture of any kind, although there were partial walls and dividers and the floors were covered with the remnants of ceiling tiles and wallboard. Some floors were virtual mazes, while others were huge open expanses.

When they reached the sixth floor, the fire began again. This time it sprang up in unexpected locations, difficult to predict. It would suddenly roar up a room divider, complete with heat and rolling smoke, or explode out a window where the glass had been broken. Rioletta and Sanctacar negotiated the maze of corridors to the far side, and there they were blocked once again by a sheet of flame.

This time it licked up one side of the staircase. They bolted up the steps, searing pain burning one half of their bodies as they clung to the far wall. The seventh floor was half on fire, much like the first room they had entered on the ground level. Once again the ominous black smoke rolled across the ceiling, sometimes lowering almost to the floor. Huge tongues of flame shot out the broken windows, and the heat was intense. There was a Darkening Deception on the room as well.

"Through this is where the passageways start," Sanctacar shouted. "If those in the Museum managed to make it into the Vault, they would have been confronted by this fire."

"Are they not able to see Deception?" Rioletta asked.

"You have to realize that you're better at it than most. You are from Andolith, and your people are known for that. I wouldn't have risked the fire downstairs had you not shown me it was a Deception. Those in the Museum were here to see the explosion and probably believe that the fire and the risk of collapse is very real."

They darted through the last sheet of flame and into a huge room with several chambers opening out of it. Sanctacar approached a fireplace with a fire apparently burning in it. He reached through and up into the flue, then pushed the back wall of the fireplace aside. It slid from view into the wall. The two of them crawled quickly through and into the passage beyond, and Sanctacar closed the door behind them.

It was a relief to be away from the noise and heat of the Burning Deception. The hallway they entered stretched to the left and right and appeared to be a meditation room or sanctuary of some type. There were several desks and chairs in the narrow space, and niches in the wall with heavily-jeweled reliquaries, swords, and goblets in them. Sanctacar turned left and approached one of the niches. He lifted up on its frame, and the entire box slid up into the ceiling. Once again, they clambered through and this time entered a long corridor with a narrow, steeply slanting ceiling. Rioletta guessed that they were just under the roof of one of the side walls of the plaza, heading towards the Museum.

At the end there was a steep upward staircase. Sanctacar touched the bottom step with the mutter of a Skill, and the entire staircase lifted up, revealing a downward stair beneath. At the bottom they stepped into another narrow hallway perpendicular to the corridor. This appeared to be a display hall: there were more niches, most with weaponry of one type or another, and several large paintings of battle scenes. Sanctacar opened one like a door. A small ladder descended from it, and they climbed up and out onto one of the upper floors of the Museum itself.

"Do you have communication with Hyphanden?" Rioletta asked. "We should contact him and let him know we've successfully entered the Museum."

"Of course," Sanctacar said, fingering a talisman about his neck. "He seems busy, though."

"How so?"

"There seems to be a battle going on at the Council-house," he replied, and paused. "Things go badly for Gomphos at the Security House as well, very badly."

Rioletta felt a jolt of adrenalin. Stolen was with Gomphos. "What can you tell?"

"They're scattered and pinned down by a large force of Hyolonal and a number of Rogues. Several of them are injured. We'd better find our people here quick and bring them back out so we can join one or the other of the efforts," Sanctacar said. "Come, I have an idea where they might be."

Chapter Nineteen: The Battle for the Security-house (Stolen)

Stolen slipped through the streets of Hyolon towards the bachelors' estate, employing all his Skills in Concealment and Stealth. Although he remained on high alert, he wasn't particularly afraid. He knew it was often easier for one person to slip by unnoticed than for a group, and he was very familiar with this area of the city. But he was also looking forward to the opportunity to engage with Rudon's forces, and he imagined even confronting Rudon himself.

The bachelor's estate was a long, sprawling complex that had perhaps at one time belonged to an extended family. It had many bedrooms and two kitchens, as well as stables and a big yard. There was also a large central room, and there Stolen found the remaining bachelors and some others of the community gathered already.

Gomphos had been assigned to lead the group to the Security House to free Cayon and Caladoc. Stolen looked over the collection of twenty-two individuals. A few of them, like Gomphos, were true Outcasts, Sorcerers who had been banished from their Councils for practicing the Forbidden Skills, but most of them were others of the Skilled who had been encouraged to leave their homelands for one reason or another. A few, like himself, were people who simply would not be accepted elsewhere.

Stolen stepped quietly up next to Anseri, a young Outcast of Kyelon. She was a particular friend of his, small in stature and like him, Skilled in Concealment and Stealth.

"Stolen! Are you joining us?" she whispered.

"Yes," Stolen whispered back. "What have I missed?"

"Not much," Anseri replied. "Gomphos has been going over the layout of the Security House and the area around it."

"I'm familiar with it already," Stolen said. Gomphos gave him a look, and he quieted.

Stolen shifted his weight impatiently while Gomphos talked. He wanted to get going. He had been depressed, for reasons he couldn't really figure out, since Mynador and Kwistocta had told him about his parents. He had agreed to use the information as necessary to save Hyphanden, but now he didn't want to talk about it. His mother had been dead for most of his life, and he would never get the chance to find out what she had been like. His father was a powerful Sorcerer, it was true, but an unethical and dishonest one. He felt a great deal of anger when he thought about Arvindahl. Arvin could have sent him away somewhere to be fostered by a Skilled family, but had instead disposed of him to further Rudon's relationships. For the first time in days Stolen felt motivated to do something, and what he wanted to do was defeat Rudon.

Finally the group left the bachelor's estate and headed south towards the Security House. Gomphos planned to engage the rogues there himself with a few of the most Skilled while the rest of the group took on the Hyolonal. Anseri was chosen to go ahead and find a lookout on a nearby building. They would not move in until her signal.

As they neared the Security House, Anseri put a hand on Stolen's shoulder. "Good luck, and stay out of harm's way if you can." She slipped quietly off into the dark and disappeared.

Stolen stood quietly with the rest of the group. He could feel his heart pounding. He could hear the sounds of a battle from somewhere beyond the next row of buildings. He knew Cayon and Caladoc were alone at the Security House, but he also knew they were powerful and Skilled. Over the last year they had learned to Throw Skills, and they had the advantage of being in a protected position. But he also knew that nobody can Throw Skills forever, and they were undoubtedly becoming tired. He was impatient to go to their aid, and it was difficult to wait.

Finally Anseri's signal came. Gomphos clutched his talisman and whispered to the rest of the group.

"Anseri reports that a number of Hyolonal are dead, scattered around the courtyard in front of the Security House. But there are at least two rogue Sorcerers, and the remaining Hyolonal are well-organized. At least some of the building's Protections have been broken, and they've gained a position right up against the front doors."

"It sounds as though they're quite determined to get in," one of the bachelors said.

"Very determined," Gomphos replied. "We know there are a large number of weapons inside. That's why we've been guarding it. Remember what we discussed. Don't sacrifice yourself. If you add yourself to the casualties you will only make it harder for the rest of us. Stay organized and look around you."

They made their way forward quietly until they were right behind the Hyolonal, unnoticed behind the corners of the buildings. Then they attacked with a volley of Thrown Skills and physical strikes together. Gomphos concentrated on one of the rogues while Stolen and the others went after the Hyolonal. Stolen was good with his machete, but he also could Throw a few Skills, and he tried to balance the two to best advantage.

The rogues turned and replied with their own Skills, knocking the Hyolonal over from the opposite direction. They didn't seem to care if they injured their own troops. Several Hyolonal moved to cover them, kneeling in front of them and loosing arrows at Gomphos' group.

Stolen waded recklessly in amongst the Hyolonal and began to swing at those who were wielding only spears and more traditional Hyolonal weapons. Those ones seemed prone to flee after a few good smacks. They were obviously not among the elite who had been issued firearms and bows. However, there seemed to be a great number with more advanced weapons, and eventually those Hyolonal organized themselves into a semblance of a fighting force and began to take more careful aim. Too tired to maintain Concealment, Stolen and the others were forced to retreat to cover around the corners of buildings.

A wave of Skills emanated from a side street, and another rogue Sorcerer and a new contingent of Hyolonal appeared. Stolen attacked the Hyolonal with renewed vigor, protecting Gomphos as best he could. Gomphos staggered from a blow to his side. Stolen saw Anseri fall off to one side, but there was little he could do. He was having a hard enough time protecting himself.

Cayon and Caladoc pressed their attack from the building, but Stolen began to fear that more Hyolonal and perhaps more Sorcerers would appear from behind. He continued to fight, but he began to take blows from the Hyolonal as the groups' Protections weakened with Gomphos' injury. Finally he was forced into a stairwell, swinging his machete above his head as he backed down to a dead end at a locked door.

He heard the shouts of the Hyolonal increase. Those who had been swarming around the east side of the Security House seeking entry came around the corner in full stride, barreling through their own companions. Soon the rest of the Hyolonal also turned and fled, leaving the rogue Sorcerers at the door.

Stolen peered out from the stairwell to see what was causing the panic. Perhaps Mynador or some others were coming to their aid. Instead, he saw three huge creatures gallop into the square. They stood some twenty feet tall. Their hooves were the size of shields, their teeth like machetes. And there were others: a herd of smaller such animals, each one larger than the largest draft-horse used in the fields.

But the horses did not arrive on their own. Stolen glimpsed someone up high on the back of one of them, clinging to its neck with a rope. At first he assumed it was Cardon, but this man was dark-haired, not fair-haired. He saw the man wave a hand, and the horses responded to his command.

One of the horses paused at the door of the Security House. The rogue Sorcerers Threw a series of Skills, but the horse snapped up one of the Sorcerers in its mouth, flipped her body up, and devoured her. The rest of the horses charged by in pursuit of the Hyolonal. The man on board waved a hand again, and a deadly stream of fire issued forth, incinerating all those in its path.

After they passed, Stolen crawled out of the stairwell. A few Hyolonal who had been smart enough to hide darted away in the opposite direction. In a moment, Cayon and Caladoc appeared at the door of the Security House.

"Come on!" Gomphos shouted, waving the group to action. He gripped his side, but seemed rejuvenated by the rout. "On to the Museum! We are needed there!"

Stolen's reckless energy was ebbing, but he scrambled to join Gomphos. He cast about to find Anseri, then saw her leaning against a nearby building. She was bloodied and pale, but with Stolen's help she got to her feet and he supported her as the group followed the horses towards the Museum and Vault.

Chapter Twenty: The Battle for the Council-house (Hyphanden)

Hyphanden, Kwistocta, Creed, Andor, and Aliora hurried along the wall towards the Council-house in the dark. They had not gone far when another explosion ripped through the night. Stones and other debris rained down upon them, and they escaped being seriously hurt only by ducking under a jutting abutment of a turret on the wall.

"That was undoubtedly timed to injure anyone responding from the estates," Hyphanden said. "A few seconds later and we would have been caught in it." He motioned them onward. In a minute they came to an area where the wall had crumbled away. Beyond that was utter devastation, eerily lit by flickering flames here and there where wooden struts and joists burned. Ornamental trees flamed alongside piles of stone and rubble.

They paused for a moment to get their bearings. A hundred yards ahead, the wall had at one time risen to a turret, beneath which a staircase wound down through an arched stone gateway. From here Creed and Andor had seen Duri fighting the Hyolonal during their first visit to the city, but now it was utterly destroyed. Hadrost and Myloy had been keeping watch there, and there was now no doubt in anyone's mind that they had perished with the first blast.

Beyond and to their left the building Hyphanden called the Convention Center had stood, thirty stories high and constructed of polished stone and glass. It had withstood abandonment for more than a hundred years. Now it was a smoking mountain of broken rock, the victim of Losino's latest detonation. On either side the remains of the high arching wall they had used as a trail above the city streets lay now as an impediment to travel, rather than a passageway. Far and wide, the ground was littered and uneven.

237

They stood in silence for a long moment. Their goal was the Council-house and plaza beyond, but to get there they would have to descend and make their way through the destruction. There was no way to know how far the buckled streets and slumping structures extended on either side, or what destabilized buildings might topple at any moment. Working their way around could take a long time, and they would undoubtedly be faced with Hyolonal looking for them. On the other hand, trying to cross the rubble itself held unknown dangers.

"Well, we have little choice," Hyphanden sighed. "We must go down to get to where we need to be. Rudon will have Hyolonal and some of his rogues waiting for us, I'm sure. The only question is, shall we go into the city or try to travel through the greenbelt for as long as we can?"

"I'm for the greenbelt," Creed said immediately. "Trees are less apt to drop chunks on us, and I'm used to moving in the woods."

"Kwistocta and I are less so," Hyphanden said, "but I agree. Let's get off this wall, where we're silhouetted. We can at least travel a ways towards the plaza before we have to take to the streets. But I suggest you use whatever Skills you have at your disposal, including Concealment and Stealth."

"Neither will fool a rogue who's looking for it," Kwistocta said grimly. "But we can at least avoid the Hyolonal."

Aliora scrambled down the broken rock face of the wall. She quickly chose a route, and the others followed her. At the bottom they silently surveyed the old park. It was heavily overgrown with trees, most of which seemed to have fared well in the explosion, perhaps sheltered by the wall. There was a deep, narrow creek with dense underbrush along its banks and deadfall in the channel. Alongside the creek was an unkempt walkway of laid stone. Although it was cracked and some plant growth had forced its way through, it offered by far the clearest route.

"And the most likely to be watched," Andor whispered uncomfortably.

"They would hear us if we were crashing through the underbrush anyway," Aliora said. "There's only so much Stealth can conceal."

In places the destroyed wall had crumbled out onto the path and the trees seemed to press close. They did not dare use any light, and the overhanging limbs deepened the darkness so that they tripped and stumbled over unseen objects. They moved as quickly as they could, Aliora and Creed with bows in hand, Creed with the pistol he had brought from Andolith in his front waistband. Every once in a while they caught movement in the brush or up upon the ruins of the wall, but the route was curiously unguarded.

"I don't like this," Hyphanden whispered. "Perhaps they're drawing us in to a place where we have no escape."

"Or perhaps everyone's occupied with trying to breach the Council-house," Andor said.

"Breaching the Council-house won't be too difficult for Rudon," Kwistocta said. "He can easily Throw a Skill to open the door. We have set some extra Protections on it, but given a little time, those won't be hard to break. Then all he'll have to deal with is the leftover animation Skill inside."

"Then why all this?" Andor wondered. "Why didn't he quietly go in, stop the pendulum like he did last time, and continue with his plans while the Hyolonal loot the place?"

"He knew our guards or our Alarm Skills would detect him and immediately alert the rest of us," Hyphanden said. "He's been testing to see what he could get away with, to see if he could disable the guards quietly, but we've been too vigilant. Our Protections around the estates have held up to his testing as well, so he had no possibility of destroying us all in our beds. His only option was to create as much destruction and distraction as possible, kill or trap as many of us right off the bat as he could, and then in the confusion take his time to access the Council-house."

They rounded the corner of the wall where the greenbelt faded away to the north into unsettled lands. They would have to enter the city itself in order to reach the Council-house and travel on the streets, exposed to the rooftops above and subject to ambush from the narrow alleyways. But there was nothing that could be done, and Hyphanden was in a hurry to join the rest of the Community.

They encountered small groups of Hyolonal roaming the streets, but in the pre-dawn light their Concealments held and they passed by unnoticed. Kwistocta led them down one alleyway and up another, taking a circuitous path in order to avoid buildings she thought might be used as command posts or gathering points.

As they drew nearer to the plaza they could hear shouts and small explosions, with a background rumbling. The rhythmic swoosh and click of the pendulum on the face of the Council-house was overwhelmed or absent. Here and there a dead or seriously wounded Hyolonal lay sprawled near the base of one building or another.

Suddenly Hyphanden threw an arm out and stopped them. They drew back against a wall and gathered close together.

"A Sorcerer guards this route," Hyphanden hissed. "I can feel him, or feel his Skill – he is concentrating on penetrating Concealment. We will be as visible to him as in broad daylight. He is likely a Skill-breaker of some type, but it's not Rudon himself."

"Now we must make a decision," Kwistocta said. "Do we try to avoid this Sorcerer, and make our way around in the hopes that other routes in to the Plaza will be unguarded, or do we make an attempt to overcome him here, thus announcing our presence but saving ourselves time and possibly doing away with someone who endangers us?"

"The second," Creed growled.

"Yes, we can't avoid conflict forever," Aliora said.

But Andor eyed Hyphanden and Kwistocta. "Do you know who it is?" she asked.

"I believe it to be Fellodon," Hyphanden said. "It seems Rudon has rejuvenated his Skill-breaking powers, and doubtless promised him more for his cooperation, possibly a mind from the Crypt, which would help him regain what he lost in the Stripping. We knew him once, and he was not an evil man. I'm loathe to cause his death."

"Perhaps he can be reasoned with," Kwistocta said. "I'm willing to try."

"If he can't see reason, maybe we can disable him without causing his death," Andor said. Creed nodded and slung his bow, taking out instead his heavy-hafted machete.

240

The group split to either side of the alleyway, and Kwistocta relaxed the Concealment she had been maintaining and walked forward.

"Fellodon! Well met!" she said, raising a hand. "It's been many years since we saw each other."

At the end of the alleyway, a man stepped into view from around the corner.

"Kwistoctavrina," he said in a thoughtful voice. "But I wouldn't say 'well met'. We've been expecting you, but you're overbold to walk so openly."

"Why shouldn't I?" Kwistocta said, approaching him closer. "You and I are well known to each other. I don't fear you. I regret that you drifted away from the Outcast Community, but here is an opportunity for you to rejoin us. This would be an ideal time for you to show your true colors, and unite with us to stop this unnecessary chaos and destruction."

As Fellodon concentrated on Kwistocta, the rest of the group inched forward along either side of the alleyway. Hyphanden kept a clear path to Fellodon so any Skill he might Throw would not affect Kwistocta. Andor kept close by him. Creed crept along the wall nearest to Fellodon, and Aliora along the other wall. A number of Hyolonal, attracted by Fellodon's conversation, approached with spears and staffs at the ready.

"Rudon has given me what you could not, the opportunity to regain some of my Skills," Fellodon said. "The use of his devices has re-ordered my mind, and allows me to share Skills with others. He has promised me more. Certainly he will reward me for getting rid of you for him. You and your husband are his greatest rivals and have been directly responsible for keeping him from the prize he seeks. I'm afraid I cannot turn against him. There is too much to lose."

With that, Fellodon raised a hand, in which he held a short, knobby club sometimes used to direct Throws. Hyphanden Threw a rolling wave out in front of him and Fellodon, distracted by Kwistocta, was knocked off his feet. He scrambled to his knees, but Creed rushed in and dealt him a blow to the back of the head with the butt of his machete.

241

"Ouch," Fellodon said, looking up at Creed. Creed halted in surprise. Kwistocta stepped up on Fellodon's other side and laid a hand on his head, employing a Skill that caused him to slump to the ground.

"That should keep him unconscious for at least a while," she said. "Bashing somebody on the head isn't a good way to knock them unconscious, Creed, unless you do it hard enough to really cause some damage."

"Hyolonal!" Aliora cried. Creed rushed to aid her as she engaged the Hyolonal and nocked an arrow. His shot lodged in the shoulder of one of the attackers. Two others loosed spears, but Kwistocta deflected them with a wave of her arm, and they fell harmlessly to the ground. Andor snatched them up and leaned them against a wall, where she cracked the staves by stomping on them. Hyphanden Threw another rolling wave, and the Hyolonal, along with Creed and Aliora, fell this way and that.

"Sorry," Hyphanden shouted as Creed scrambled up and grabbed Aliora by an arm. "You'll need to learn to fight behind us. Your best use is as rear guards."

With the Hyolonal confused, they were able to rush forward and disarm them. Creed yanked his arrow from the shoulder of the wounded man with some distaste. He could not afford to lose one if it was possible to retrieve it.

They ran into the plaza and stopped short. It was a scene of total chaos. Hyolonal ran here and there, throwing spears randomly and swinging wildly with their staffs. Occasionally a shot rang out. Members of the Outcast Community were in the streets, exchanging Skills with rogue Sorcerers. At the Council-house, a huge timber on wheels had been driven into the path of the pendulum that swung in front of the main door. The pendulum, undeterred, was straining against the timber from the side, chopping away at the wood like a giant axe.

"We need to get up high," Hyphanden shouted. "There is Kerdahl on the roof."

Creed fended off an attacking Hyolonal with a backhanded slap of his machete. The group ran forward, dodging through the plaza until they reached the back of the building Kerdahl stood atop.

242

"Well met!" cried Tarbros at the door. He swung it aside. "We need your help! The Council-house is breached. It's only a matter of time before Rudon reaches the Crypt."

"Have you seen Rudon himself?" Hyphanden asked. "I have a great desire to meet him face-to-face. I would not allow him to cause the death of two of our community without retribution."

Tarbros grinned. "You're getting a little hot, there, Hyphanden! It's about time! But we haven't seen him. He's letting his crew do the dirty work, but he must be directing the scene from somewhere nearby. The rogues are sharing Skills among themselves with those devices, each adding power to the other, and the Hyolonal act in concert and respond very quickly to new threats. We're hard pressed."

Hyphanden led the way up the stairs several stories to the rooftop. Kerdahl turned, ducking underneath a railing.

"Stetsor is on the other side of the plaza with a few others," Kerdahl said. "We've been trying to keep anyone from entering the Council-house, but the Hyolonal have wedged the pendulum to allow them free access back and forth with whatever goods they desire. The pendulum was first stopped by a Skill, but when the door was opened the stray Skills bouncing around inside shot out and re-activated it. Then they wedged it as you see. A few minutes ago a small group entered. They were not Hyolonal, and one of them may have been Rudon. I'd guess it was the group he needs to open the Crypt."

"Then he is inside, and we have little time," Hyphanden said. "We cannot let him open the Crypt."

"I don't know what else we can do, unless you know how to seal the place up somehow," Kerdahl said. "We're losing the battle here."

Hyphanden stood very still for a moment, his eyes focused inwards. Then he looked directly at Kwistocta.

"I was afraid it might come to this," he said softly. "It is indeed possible to close the Council-house."

She shook her head. "No. I know what you propose."

"Would you have me ignore this information and allow Rudon access to the Crypt?" Hyphanden argued. "If I can close the Council-house with him inside it, this battle will be over. If it continues, we will lose more of our companions, and possibly all our lives if Rudon triumphs and is vengeful."

Hyphanden turned abruptly. "I'm sorry," he said. "It's my responsibility to do this thing." He turned his back on the group assembled on the roof and strode quickly towards the doorway.

Inside the top floor of the building, Hyphanden chose a dusty chair and sat down. He pulled out the small box in which Stelaphandon's mind-map was contained, and after a moment's hesitation, he unlatched and opened the lid.

"Changed your mind?" Stela asked as he inhabited Hyphanden's mind.

"We are losing the Council-house. Rudon is inside. If I close it now, we may trap him in there and prevent his access to the Crypt of Souls."

"If you close it, you will lose the Crypt forever," Stela warned. *"The minds in there will never be accessible to anyone again."*

"What will happen to them?" Hyphanden asked. "Will they be destroyed?"

Stela hesitated. *"I don't know. But in some ways it might be better if they were."*

"Then show me how to close it. We must hurry."

"You remember our bargain?" Stela asked.

"I remember, and I will keep it. I will allow you a place in my mind, and I will never put you back into the box again."

"Very well," Stela said. *"We are on the plaza, I observe. Yet the way to close the Council-house is in the Museum."*

"Then we must hurry. The Museum is not close by," Hyphanden said, jumping up. He strode quickly to the door and back onto the roof. "We must make our way to the Museum," he announced. "It's not worth expending our energy here anymore. The battle for access to the Council-house is lost. Once our retreat is noticed the focus of the attack may change. We must be prepared to fight our way there."

Kerdahl abandoned his post to join them, and they descended the stairs to where Tarbros guarded the door. They worked their way across the plaza to the south, picking up Outcasts as they went. Stetsor and his team joined them, and others fought their way to them.

At first the Hyolonal seemed to see the retreat as a victory, and they consolidated their scattered forces into a unified front to drive the Outcasts from the plaza. The Outcasts retreated quickly enough, with a new goal and no reason to stay, defending their rear flank only as necessary. Soon the Hyolonal and the rogue Sorcerers who commanded them paused. Hyphanden took the opportunity to make as much headway as possible towards the Museum, routing out a few bands of roving Hyolonal along the way. Creed gathered a few arrows, some of which he passed off to Aliora.

After a brief respite from Rudon's forces the pursuit picked up again, and this time the rogues were seeking not only to rout them, but to cut them off. Their direction had been duly noted, and their destination guessed. They were met at the flaming Vault by the Hyolonal left stationed there. Hyphanden pulled up short, dismayed by the state of the entrance foyer and the flames shooting out of the upper floors.

"Put the Vault at your back and defend yourself!" he cried.

Soon more Hyolonal and the first of the rogue Sorcerers began to arrive and the battle intensified, driving the Outcasts back over the rubble, closer to the scorching flames of the Vault. With the Hyolonal pressing them, they were overmatched and soon exhaustion began to take a toll as well. Tarbros fell with a Hyolonal spear struck through him. Aliora answered with an arrow to the assailant, but it was too late for Tarbros. A bullet grazed Creed's jaw; with his arrows depleted, he reached finally for the firearm at his belt.

Hyphanden looked up at a yell. A large group of Hyolonal were running towards them at full speed from the direction of the Security House. For a moment he thought Gomphos and Stolen's group must have been totally overcome and his heart fell, but the Hyolonal rushed past them pell-mell, not pausing to join the fray.

Seconds later it was obvious why the Hyolonal fled. Cardon's clawed and sharp-fanged horses, now grown to many times their original size, came galloping down the street. The three huge beasts were accompanied by a herd of smaller ones.

The Hyolonal who had been fighting Hyphanden's group crouched back against walls and slunk down stairwells, but they did not join their compatriots in wild flight. Moments later the horses passed, and the Hyolonal surged forth from their hiding places to resume the fight. Hyphanden's group was backed against the wall once again.

A battle yell drew their attention. Hyphanden looked up and saw Gomphos and his team running towards the Vault. Stolen, Cayon, and Caladoc were with him, as well as twenty others of the Outcast community. They set upon the rogues from the east. Encouraged by the additional resources, the Outcasts began to gain some ground upon the Hyolonal.

"Hyphanden!" Kerdahl shouted as they stood together, backs to the wall. "Where do you need to get to?"

"Stela says I must get inside the Museum," Hyphanden shouted back. "I know the route from here, but at the moment I don't know how to access it."

"There are Hyolonal on the walls between here and the Museum," Kerdahl yelled. "Soon enough they'll breach the roof, and the passageways will be cut off."

"It will be of no consequence if we can't find a way to get inside the Vault," Hyphanden replied.

Suddenly Rioletta was standing beside him. "Hyphanden! Follow me! The way is clear, but the Hyolonal are pounding through the roofs between here and the Museum! Get anyone you can inside. We may need to fight."

Hyphanden turned without questioning her. He ducked in through the smoke-filled cavern that had been the door, and slowly the rest of the group began to work their way in. It was easy enough to cut down anyone who dared step through the door. With Gomphos pressing them from the outside and the doorway a deadly danger, the Hyolonal began to falter.

Hyphanden and Kwistocta followed Rioletta as she dashed into the first of the Deceptions. The three of them stood on the other side, pulling the rest through as they staggered, blinded by the fire. Last through was Creed. They left the entrance unguarded, hoping that the flames would deter the Hyolonal.

They climbed the stairs as fast as possible. Rioletta went first through the walls of flames and onto the final floor. Hyphanden was content to follow, since her perception of the Deceptions was considerably better than his. Sanctacar and the several Skilled guards who had been trapped in the Museum waited for them on the seventh floor. But just as they entered the room the fireplace door that led to the secret passageway slammed to the side. As the doorway opened, a blast shot through it, knocking Rioletta backwards so violently that she flew through the air and landed on the far side of the room. The blast was followed by another equally as powerful, and with a yell, a group of rogue Sorcerers poured through the destroyed fireplace into the room, followed by a contingent of Hyolonal.

Fellodon, newly revived and raging, his injury contributing to his mania, was the first to burst through. The Outcasts fell back. The room was large, but still close quarters for fighting, especially with Skills ricocheting off the walls.

Hyphanden scrambled into a back corner. With his back against the wall, he took a few seconds to identify the main threats in the room. His Skill would be best used against the rogue Sorcerers, but he also realized that anything he could Throw with the power to disable one of them would kill his own forces if he was not exacting with his aim.

Aliora stood firm in front of him, warding off Hyolonal with a machete. The room was too close to use a bow. "Hyphanden!" she shouted. "You must get to the passageway! Leave us to the fight! I will guard you until you can get to the door!"

The fireplace entrance was on the far side of the big room. Hyphanden began to edge along the wall, looking for opportunities to use his Skills as he went. Creed joined them, standing shoulder-to-shoulder with his sister as they moved.

Other rooms and alcoves opened out from the main one, and the battle spilled into them. As he came to the doorway of one of the rooms, Hyphanden saw Caladoc inside, backed into the corner. Already exhausted, unable to take the time to Throw a Skill, Caladoc drew his knife and instead of cowering, threw himself forward into one rogue Sorcerer and two Hyolonal. Taken by surprise, the Sorcerer's Skill went awry, and Caladoc plunged the knife into his abdomen, taking a slash from a Hyolonal in the arm as he did. Creed leapt into the room to help him, and both of the Hyolonal fell to his machete.

247

Another rogue dashed for the door. Creed raised his machete, and Hyphanden raised a hand to take the fleeing Sorcerer down.

"No!" Kerdahl shouted. Creed glanced up, and at that moment the blast from a Hyolonal gun struck Kerdahl in the chest. He fell gasping into the room at Creed's feet. The rogue Sorcerer threw himself at Kerdahl and cradled him in his arms, looking up in agony. Confused, Creed once again raised his heavy blade.

"Stay, Creed!" Kerdahl choked. "It's Ryedanc of Herion, who has risked himself as a spy against Rudon this past year!"

Caladoc, bleeding heavily from the arm, dropped to his knees beside Kerdahl and Ryedanc. "Go!" he shouted. "We'll care for Kerdahl and keep any who enter this room at bay!"

Creed sprang back into the main room to rejoin Hyphanden and they pressed forward once again. Although Hyolonal no longer burst through the fireplace, the room was crowded with them. Suddenly the sheet of flame blocking the stairway wavered as if cooled by a blast of water. A tall, slender man jumped through, and a phalanx of rogues rushed in behind him. He scanned the room quickly, and his eye fell on Hyphanden.

The two men locked eyes for a long moment. Aliora stepped in front of Hyphanden, but with a flick of his finger, the new Sorcerer sent her tumbling head over heels into Creed. His gaze never left Hyphanden.

"Well met, Losino!" Hyphanden said, his hand going to his beltline.

Losino raised his chin, and the hint of a smile played on his lips. "It dismays me, my friend, that you have chosen to deny us access to the Crypt. Do you intend to keep it all for yourself? Can you not consider sharing it with an old companion, one whom you respected enough to match wits with in the not-so-distant past?"

"The Crypt would never have been accessed in the first place if it weren't for a pressing need," Hyphanden replied. "The minds there should not be removed and used willy-nilly. They are their own people, and we do not have the Skills to restore them to useful bodies."

"Yet it's well known that you use some of those minds yourself," Losino said. "How is it that you've suddenly developed such a conscience when it comes to others doing the same?"

"It's true that I've used one mind in particular, but I have no intention of allowing Rudon or any of his cohorts access to the remainder of the minds in the Crypt," Hyphanden said. "Those minds I kept were forced upon me, or has Rudon not told you of his behavior in the Crypt?"

"I see," Losino said. He advanced a few steps towards Hyphanden. "You consider yourself more worthy and your purpose more ethical than ours. How conceited of you, and how unsurprised I am!"

"I am not better than you nor more ethical," Hyphanden replied. "I could never pretend such, as we are all Outcasts here. But I admit that I prefer a future in which the residents of Hyolon exist in a peaceful, if uneasy, relationship with the communities around us. I do not accept a future of chaos and retribution, as Rudon intends."

"Then we must take what we want by force," Losino replied. "You give us no choice. I warn you, Hyphanden, Rudon's access to the books left here during the Dispersal have given us some unusual insight into Skills we didn't even know existed. There's still time for reconciliation. I'll consider a request to save the lives of your Council in exchange for your surrender of the minds you took from the Crypt."

Hyphanden's eyes flashed. "Only a few hours ago I hoped to open a conversation with you to forestall this violence and destruction, Losino. Now you've murdered two of my community with your fire and flames, and I regret that reconciliation will not be possible."

Losino did not answer, but with a grin he rolled a small object at Hyphanden's feet as if bowling. Hyphanden had just enough time to leap aside and Throw a protective cover over the object before it exploded. The explosion was not large, though, and the Skill not particularly powerful for one acquainted with the Forbidden Skills. Hyphanden turned back to Losino, surprised by the clumsy distraction, only to find Losino an arm's length away. A second later, Losino delivered a powerful backhand to the side of Hyphanden's face, knocking him sideways and to his knees.

Losino drew back a step and Hyphanden saw his eyes unfocus as he concentrated upon a Skill. Hyphanden drew his knife from his belt and scrambled to his feet. He sliced the air inches in front of Losino's chest as he rose.

Losino jumped back, his Skill interrupted. "You know you cannot out-Skill me, so you intend to stab me to death, is that it?" he taunted. At the same time he stepped forward again, and with one arm deflected Hyphanden's knife-arm.

Like many of the Outcasts, Hyphanden had practiced using objects to concentrate and increase his energy, and the force of a Thrown Skill emanated from the tip of the knife. He had just enough time to cut the Skill short as it streamed by to buffet others behind Losino.

Losino gripped his wrist in a powerful clasp and with his other hand clawed at Hyphanden's face as though to send a Skill directly into his skull. Hyphanden ducked and countered, and the two of them clenched each other and fell to the floor, grappling in a physical fight, Skills temporarily forgotten. They rolled back and forth, clenching each other's arms and struggling to attain a superior position. Hyphanden yanked his arm free, but Losino's assault kept him from producing any coherent Skill.

Dimly he was aware of the battle around them, of Fellodon and Kwistocta to one side and of Creed and Aliora battling the Hyolonal, but he could not remove his focus to look. The roiling smoke of the fire Deception lowered around them to the floor as though attracted by their fight.

Losino pinned Hyphanden's arms again, and with his face inches away began screaming a Skill aloud. Their eyes locked, and Hyphanden understood that Losino was trying to bore directly into his mind, to create some damage from within. He didn't know how to counter such an attack, and could only squirm in Losino's grasp, feeling the first probes of the Skill licking into his brain.

He felt an unfamiliar surge in his mind, and Losino gasped as his Skill was countered and deflected. Hyphanden yanked his knife-hand free once more. He plunged the blade into Losino's gut to the hilt and concentrated the last of his energy into it. Losino screamed and thrashed. A blast issued from within him, and he disappeared in a cloud of particles.

Hyphanden struggled to his feet, the blade in his hand, internally thanking Stela for his aide. He looked around to see what had transpired in the minutes he'd been locked with Losino. Although he could hear the sound of clashes taking place elsewhere, the main room was deserted except for numerous dead. Fellodon lay gasping in a corner, grievously wounded but alive.

Then his eye fell upon Kwistocta. She lay still and silent upon her back in the middle of the room. With two strides, Hyphanden was at her side. He fell to his knees and looked into her face. But she drew no breath, and the color had drained from her skin. Desperately, he grasped her face between his hands and willed himself to calmness. He tilted her head back and opened her eyes, and brought his own forehead close to hers, whispering her name. He screamed for Stela's help and aide once again. But it was of no use: her life had drained away, and the map of her mind was gone forever.

"No!" Hyphanden shouted in disbelief. He released her head and stared at her. Then his eye fell upon the knife he had discarded upon seeing her lying there, and in a moment he had scrambled to it. With one last agonized look at her face, he raised the knife and threw his head back, exposing his own throat to the blade.

But the knife did not descend. A powerful hand encircled his wrist, the fingers wrapped completely around, the pressure so great that the knife fell uselessly. He looked up at Creed, who stood above him bloodied and wounded, gripping Hyphanden's wrist like a vise. Creed looked into Hyphanden eyes, and did not turn to the body upon the floor.

"Let me die," Hyphanden pleaded. Creed released his wrist and scooped up the knife. Hyphanden slumped to the floor, his face in one hand, the other searching for the hand of Kwistocta. In a moment Andor arrived, and she knelt down upon the floor on the other side of Kwistocta's body. The three of them remained in silence for a minute, but the battle was not over, and it threatened to return to them from the other rooms and the staircase.

"Hyphanden," Andor said gently. "The way is open. You must close the Council-house. Rudon is in the Crypt, and all this is his doing. Close it now and rid yourself of him! Your motivation is now greater than his. Use it."

Hyphanden staggered to his feet. He laid Kwistocta's hand across her body, and turned to the fireplace door. He leaned for a moment on the mantel, and as he did he allowed Stela to come into the forefront of his mind. As a wave of Hyolonal burst from the stairway, following a rogue, Hyphanden threw an arm out in a sweeping gesture, and the blast that issued from him was like a white fire. Charred bodies fell upon one another in the doorway, blocking access for others behind.

The doors to the passageways beneath the roofs lay open, and Hyphanden scrambled through quickly. He allowed the anger to rise within him. He was not given to anger, and did not know what to do with it, but Stela was no stranger to the feeling. At the far end of the passageway he ran into the gallery, then out onto the fourth-floor balcony surrounding the central rotunda.

A huge bobbin-headed pendulum hung suspended from the very top center of the rotunda three floors above him. On normal days the pendulum crossed with its tip a graph upon the main floor. The graph resembled the face on the clock tower in the plaza, and had long been assumed to be a time-telling device. The pendulum had not stopped during the past hundred years, but now, oddly, it seemed suspended in place at an awkward angle, not in repose as one would expect of a weighted, hanging object that had ceased to swing from side to side. From time to time it twitched or bounced.

"The pendulum is attached to the one that swings in front of the Council-house door," Stela told him. *"The Council-house pendulum has stopped; thus, this one has stopped as well. You must descend to the floor. The secret lies under the clock graph."*

Hyphanden rounded the balcony and found the stairs. He ignored the works of art, the sculptures and statues, the paintings upon the wall, the play of light from colored glass windows that channeled the sun. Down each staircase he leapt, ignoring as well the desperate agony in the back of his mind: to give it a voice now would bring him to his knees, drive him crazy. It seemed to threaten to send his mind flying out of him and into the void, so powerful was it.

On the ground floor he stopped for direction. *"Can you reach the pendulum bob?"* Stela asked. Hyphanden strode to it. It hovered in the air, its cable stretched taut, just at the level of his head. He put a hand out and touched the smooth brassy metallic surface, etched with ancient and unknown symbols. It was large and appeared solid. Its weight was easily that of three men, and it was half his height in length and two-thirds that in width.

"There is a door within the bob," Stela said. *"Open it by turning the collar at the neck of the bob, where the cable enters. It is numbered. You must pass each part a specific number of times, as I direct."*

Hyphanden strained to see the numbers upon the collar. He followed Stela's instructions and heard a faint click. Stela directed him to pull up on the collar, and a small door opened in the side of the bob, its sides concealed by the runes etched upon the surface.

Inside were three keys. Hyphanden took them, closed the door, and pushed the collar back down. Stela directed him to the graph upon the floor. It was pock-marked with small slots and carvings, some resembling the runes on the bob and others the slots of the gears of the clock face. In fact, Hyphanden could see that the gears were not carved into the floor, as he had previously thought, but were in actuality functional versions of the ones upon the clock.

Hyphanden inserted first one key and then the other at Stela's direction. He worked from the outer edge of the pattern towards the center. At each turn of a key, a gear in the floor turned, grinding with the sound of rock against rock. Finally he inserted one key in the hole in the middle. At that moment, some instinct made him turn. The pendulum had suddenly released and swung directly towards him.

He dove to the floor, avoiding a strike to the head but taking part of the blow to his shoulder. The point of the pendulum raked across him, tearing his shirt and the skin beneath. He rolled out of its return path and the heavy metal bob swished by within inches.

"The pendulum at the Council-house must have been released or broken through by itself," Stela said. *"Nevertheless, we must continue. You will be able to remove one of the cogs from the pattern."*

As the pendulum gained the highest point of its arc, Hyphanden gripped the edges of the smallest of the cogs on the floor and lifted it aside. Beneath it was a hole with a ladder. He stood aside as the pendulum rushed by, then stepped quickly onto the ladder and descended. A light came on as he did so. A floor beneath, the hole opened out into a small chamber.

"The controls are here, but they are Protected," Stela said. *"You will have to break them, but I know the Skills. It will be hard on your mind, but you're lucky! I'm here to support you."*

Hyphanden moved to a small table, installed within the top of which was a control box with a series of levers. The whole table was suffused with a turquoise glow. On the far side of the table sat a model of the Council-house, the tiny pendulum with its wicked edge swinging back and forth in time with the pendulum above.

He passed a hand over the control box and without Stela's prompting caused it to reveal the make-up of the Protections upon it, and began to work to undo them. What did he care now if his mind suffered damage? In a few minutes the glow subsided and the levers sat free upon the table.

"It is the rightmost one from where you stand," Stela said, and Hyphanden laid a hand upon it.

"Wait!" Stela cried. *"Are you sure? Remember, this will close the Council-house forever. I do not know how to undo this action. If there was a way, only Trophandra knew it. I do not."*

"I'm sure," Hyphanden replied.

But still Stela hesitated. *"You do not realize what I will lose,"* he said softly. *"It has been more than a hundred years, but still I have retained some hope."*

Hyphanden stood still, searching within his mind. "Now I understand," he said. "There is a name: Alantrenne? Who lies in the Crypt? Who did Erendak place there when he leveled the accusation of treason?"

"A woman; a lover; is it not always so?" Stela said. *"But that story can wait. There is now no hope to save her. I know the torture of existence in such a state, and if Rudon removes her she will remain forever trapped in the mind of an evil, acquisitive man or some insane Rogue. This state is hardly better, believe me. It is not life. Once I gave her gifts, the finest that I could buy. Now, I choose this one last gift: release. Pull the lever."*

Hyphanden hesitated only a second. Then he laid a hand upon the machine. He yanked the lever down. Above him the gears in the floor spun wildly. The pendulum bob swung by one final time.

There was a musical twang as its cable parted, and the bob crashed heavily and skidded across the stone.

The pendulum on the Council-house model crashed to the floor at the same moment. As Hyphanden watched, the long sides of the model rose into the air and then tilted towards each other. The spires lining the top of each side meshed like a set of pointed teeth. The sides leveled out into a horizontal platform, then settled down over the vertical front and rear panels, which had moved inwards. The spires of those panels speared the windows of the sides. Then the whole thing settled slowly into a hole in the table, as though sinking into its own basement. Finally only the flattened sides remained at ground level, with the spires of the front and back puncturing them.

"It is done," Stela said mournfully. *"The Council-house is closed. Anyone inside it is dead, or will be soon. Likendhal's Key is lost forever as well."*

"Good," Hyphanden said. He turned and climbed back out of the hole and then sat down upon the floor outside the ruined clock-face pattern. He was exhausted, and any motivation he had felt was completely gone. Now he felt nothing but numb and sick. He wished for his knife, but Creed had taken it. He had not enough energy to search for some deadly thing within the Museum. He was still sitting there a half-hour later when Andor Acaladon found him, took him by the hand, and led him out of the Museum by the main door and back to where those well enough to do so were gathering horses to carry the rest to the estates of the Outcast Community.

Chapter Twenty-One: The Aftermath (Nikal)

Nikal and Cardon rode as hard as they dared through the dark after receiving Rioletta's message. With only the two of them and good rested horses, they made the journey from Dobor to the gates of Hyolon by mid-morning. They could see the smoke from the Ruined City. Columns billowed into the sky from several locations and a heavy haze rested over the vineyards of Tabor.

They pulled the horses up at the city gates and held them to a steady walk. The clop of the horses' hooves sounded loud on the old brick street. Nikal had not been able to contact Rioletta since her first message, but she had told him she would be going to the Vault and Museum.

They came first to the Security House. The area was silent and no one was to be seen. The bodies of Hyolonal were strewn around. Nikal pulled his horse close to one corpse and looked down at it.

"I can tell what happened to this one," he said grimly. "Tooth marks."

"Yes, and they're bigger than last time," Cardon agreed. "I'm afraid they're growing."

"They seem to have concentrated on the Hyolonal, at least," Nikal said. "We should ride on to the Museum. Whatever happened here is over."

They went cautiously, alert for any signs of rogue Sorcerers or Hyolonal, but other than those lying mangled on the ground, they saw no one. At the Museum they stopped and stared at the upper floors of the Vault. Sheets of flame still licked out the windows and smoke roiled out of the damaged doorway. They rode around the plaza in the eerie silence, but it was obvious that they were too late there as well. Nikal tried unsuccessfully to contact either Kwistocta or Hyphanden. With no further guidance, they turned hurriedly towards the Council-house. A few groups of marauding Hyolonal darted through the alleyways, but when they saw the two Sorcerers they fled.

The way to the Council-house was difficult going. Many of the streets were buckled and rubble blocked the alleyways and plazas. Familiar landmarks seemed to have disappeared, and they were at first unsure they had reached the Council-house plaza when they arrived.

They could only stare uncomprehendingly at the place where the Council-house had once stood. The pavement had cracked and crumbled, the buttresses had pulled away, and the two longest walls seemed to have risen out of the ground and tilted inwards, with the turrets and false towers upon them meshed like a set of immense teeth. The spires of the turrets on the front and rear wall pierced the now horizontal windows of the sides. The Council-house as a whole had sunk, leaving those things that had been the side walls level upon the ground, with only the spires sticking through them to mark the place where the building had once been.

Nikal pulled his horse around. His inability to contact Rioletta, Hyphanden, or Kwistocta now seemed more ominous. "We must head for the Outcast estates."

Cardon nodded without answering. They urged the horses onward as fast as they could safely manage through the rubble. They rounded the smoking pile where once the Convention Center had stood. The landmark of the wall was missing, and Nikal led them uncertainly until they found the neighborhood.

Suddenly a young man stepped out in front of them, leveling a spear. Nikal pulled his horse up abruptly. Several others jumped down from walls and appeared from behind bushes to surround them.

"What business have you here?" challenged the young man with a scowl. He was certainly not Hyolonal, nor a Sorcerer, although he was of the Skilled.

"I am Nikal of Dobor," Nikal replied. "I have come at the request of the Outcast Council. Who are you?"

The man lowered his spear. "Nikal of Dobor! I recognize you now. I'm Ephedril, mustard saucier of Tane."

Nikal swung down off his horse. "What are mustard sauciers of Tane doing in the Ruined City?"

"Also many from Tabor," Ephedril said. "There are perhaps a hundred of us. It was I who first saw the smoke rising at dawn from the Ruined City. My father and I were enroute to Tabor with goods to sell. We alerted the shop-owners, and we all went to the plaza to get what news we could."

An older man pushed up next to Ephedril. "A big fire in Hyolon could spread through the vineyards and even into Tabor itself. We were concerned. But, if truth be told, although we know that contact with the Outcasts is Forbidden, many have family members here, and we were concerned for their safety as well."

"More and more people began to gather in the plaza. The First Chosen could not ignore us," Ephedril said. "They appeared at the Chapel of Trees. Arvindahl told us that Hyolon would take care of itself. Fires have happened in the Ruined City in the past on occasion, and they haven't spread to the vineyards or to Tabor. He said that what takes place in Hyolon is the business of the Outcasts."

"Obviously you didn't accept his word," Nikal said.

"No. Hyolon is too close to ignore. A few of us took up what arms and fire-fighting tools we have and came here. Most of us here were supporters of the Second Chosen and Elder Council, and we are prone to disregard the First Chosen anyway. We knew Caladoc and Cayondahl took refuge here. Inside the city gates we met an Outcast named Sanctacar who led us here, and Caladoc, who is in charge here, accepted our services and set us to guarding the area of the estates."

"Caladoc in charge?" Nikal asked. "Where is Hyphanden?"

"I don't know. I'm familiar only with Caladoc. You'll find him at the estate. You may go on up."

Nikal remounted and he and Cardon urged their horses along the lane towards the gate to Hyphanden's estate. "I hope Hyphanden is all right. I wonder what happened?" Nikal mused grimly.

The gate stood open, the Protections disregarded, and a number of saddled horses grazed here and there on the lawn. Above, at the estate, Nikal could see many people going in and out. As he and Cardon cantered up the drive, they saw Stolen caring for a horse near a small group of trees.

"Stolen!" Nikal cried. He reined his horse in and dismounted. Stolen was on his feet, but it was obvious he had been injured. Several bandages were wound around his arms and a thigh, and the side of his face was scraped and poorly cleaned.

"Are you all right?" Cardon demanded, taking Stolen's arm. "Do you need medical care?"

"I'll be fine, Cardon," Stolen assured him. "I'm not seriously hurt, and I can heal myself faster than most. I've taken on the task of caring for the many horses that have arrived here, something I can do to help."

"Have you seen Rioletta?" Nikal asked.

Stolen shook his head. "She was inside the Vault by the time I arrived there. I haven't seen her since we returned, but I'm sure she's around somewhere."

"Can you tell us what happened?" Nikal asked as Stolen led the horse he'd been caring for to the shade of a tree.

"I can tell you only what I saw and what I did," Stolen said. "I don't know what happened elsewhere. Caladoc will hold a meeting soon, and we will get more information there. Come with me while I find a place for your horses. There's no room at the stable."

"Can you tell us if Rudon has been overcome or if he managed to access the Crypt?" Nikal asked.

Stolen shook his head. "I heard he was in the Council-house when Hyphanden closed it. Many here seem convinced that he is no longer a threat."

While Nikal and Cardon unsaddled the horses, Stolen told them about the nighttime explosions, the fight at the Security House with Gomphos, and the arrival of Cardon's horses with their mysterious rider.

"We ran after the horses towards the Museum and Vault." Stolen said. "Hyphanden and some of the others made their way inside. My group stayed outside, holding off the Hyolonal. Suddenly it was as if the Hyolonal just stopped. They began to mill about in confusion. The rogue Sorcerers deserted them and the Hyolonal abandoned the fight. In minutes we were left standing alone outside the Vault."

260

"Perhaps the closing of the Council-house discouraged them," Nikal said.

"The story must be filled in by someone else. Caladoc is in command right now. You'd best go to the estate, for there you will find some in need of your help. I'll tell Rioletta you've arrived if I see her."

Nikal and Cardon hurried up the drive to the front door. Nikal was relieved to see both Andor, who appeared relatively unharmed and had been put to work gathering supplies, and Creed, who was being treated for multiple wounds. Cardon was immediately conscripted to help with the wounded.

Nikal found Caladoc in one of the front bedrooms, a heavy bandage on one arm. "We chose to withdraw here to Hyphanden's estate following the dispersal of the rogues," Caladoc told Nikal. "Partly because it's large, but partly because we decided that Hyphanden should not be left alone for the foreseeable future."

"Is Hyphanden seriously injured? He's not able to take on the leadership of the Council, I see."

"He is not seriously injured, at least physically," Caladoc said. He hesitated. "Many tragedies have occurred here this day, Nikal. Not the least of them is the loss of Kwistocta."

Nikal stood stunned for a moment while the import of Caladoc's words sank in. "She is lost…for good?" he stammered, his mind turning to Hyphanden's box.

"Yes. Her body has been retrieved, along with several others. We'll gather in the great-room shortly, and the rest of your questions will be answered."

Nikal made his way into the great-room. Almost everybody from the Outcast community was there, and the rooms were crowded. He looked around for Rioletta, fingering his talisman, but he did not see her. Perhaps she'd been put to work gathering healing herbs in the garden.

To the east was a large room usually kept closed. It had at one time been a formal dining room, but Hyphanden and Kwistocta ate in the kitchen and never used it. Now the bodies of those Outcasts who had been recovered lay there, awaiting formal immolation. The door was ajar, and occasionally one or two of the Outcasts quietly went in, often carrying some small object for those who lay

261

within. Nikal stepped in cautiously, his heart pounding. None of the bodies were Rioletta. He looked for a moment on Kwistocta, but he could not bear to stand there long. He turned to the great-room again.

Hyphanden sat slumped in his large chair, facing the fireplace, his eyes blank. Around him there was frantic activity, but he himself seemed frozen. Nikal went to him and laid a hand upon his shoulder, but Hyphanden did not respond at all.

Gradually the Outcasts began to gather around. Eventually everyone who was mobile collected in the great-room and pressed into the kitchen and yard to hear Caladoc speak.

"Thanks to those who responded from Tabor and Tane, we are currently well protected and can take time to refresh ourselves and rest," Caladoc began. "They are mustering more forces from among their families and friends to bring firefighting equipment. As we are able, we will have to venture out and assure ourselves that the Council-house has indeed been closed and Rudon is no longer a threat."

"We saw the Council-house," Nikal put in. "It is certainly what I would call closed."

Caladoc nodded. "That is good news. Later we may decide to rid the city of those rogues who stood with Rudon, although I think the Hyolonal can be left alone. We will make plans as to how to hunt them down and ferret them out in the days to come. But we have suffered grievous damages today, and those I would now like to acknowledge."

He paused and looked around. "A number of our comrades are confirmed dead. Hadrost and Myloy were the first to fall, and their bodies have not been recovered. It is my hope that in the days to come we will be able to locate some part of each that we might provide with a proper ceremony. Kwistocta, Tarbros, Stetsordahl the Third, and Jamoy lie in state here. In addition, several of our number are badly injured, but currently survive: Kerdahl, Gomphos, and Cayondahl among them. Many others are also injured and should be acknowledged, including our friends Aliora and Creed, and Anseri and Stolen, and our secret compatriot, Ryedanc of New Herion. Also, several of our community members and friends remain missing. These include Dacent of Ist and Rioletta Eris of Andolith."

At this both Nikal and Cardon looked up sharply. "When was the last time Rioletta was seen?" Nikal demanded.

"She was last seen in the Vault," Caladoc said. "She was near the secret passageway in the fireplace, and was struck by Fellodon's blast as the rogues entered."

"I saw her," Creed said. "She had been knocked to the ground, and I remember seeing her lying there a few minutes later. But I was fighting, and I don't know what happened after that."

"She would have had little protection by herself," Nikal pointed out. "She can't Throw Skills, and she would have been unarmed, except perhaps for a small knife."

"But we went through the Vault as we left, and found neither her body nor that of Dacent," Caladoc said. "There is still hope that they survive and are hidden somewhere."

"If so, she is wounded or unconscious," Nikal said, bringing out his talisman. "I have been unable to contact her."

"It will be a priority for us to search for the missing," Caladoc assured him. "But right now we must attend to those who are wounded, refresh ourselves, and take enough rest that we can function when we leave the confines of this estate. Otherwise, we will be needlessly risking more lives."

"I will go out," Nikal said. "I'm not exhausted as you are. I can take a contingent of the Tabor force."

Caladoc nodded. "Then go, if you will. Be aware that most of the fire in the Vault is a Dispersal-era Deception. You can pass through it, although it's uncomfortable."

"I'll go with you," Sanctacar volunteered. "I was with Rioletta before the battle. I lost track of her when she went to guide Hyphanden inside. I've been through the Deceptions at the Vault."

Nikal borrowed several horses from Hyphanden's stables, and together with the Outcasts Dicrao and Taus, who also volunteered to join him, he put together a contingent of a number of the Tabor residents and headed quickly for the Museum. Several blocks from the Museum they found Dacent. He had suffered severe leg injuries and lost his talisman, but he lived. He had been determinedly pulling himself along the pavement with his arms, his legs dragging behind him cradled on a leather Hyolonal shield. Dicrao and several of the Tabor contingent assumed care of him, bandaging his legs as best they could before hoisting him to the back of one of the horses for the excruciating ride back to the estate.

Nikal, Sanctacar, Taus, and the rest continued to the Vault. With his knife drawn, Nikal made his way over the rubble behind Sanctacar to the doorway and ducked inside. The smoke cowed him for a moment, but he remembered Caladoc's words. He stepped over or upon the bodies of Hyolonal and passed through the first of the sheets of Deception flame. The pain was intense, and he stopped on the far side to examine himself, but there was no burning.

Taus and Sanctacar paused to search through the lower rooms. Nikal continued up the stairs and finally arrived at the burning stairway. Above that was the last sheet of fire. He hurried into it, but on the far side he was tripped up by the bodies of the Hyolonal cut down by Hyphanden. The blockage kept him in the flame for longer than he would otherwise have stayed, and by chance he saw that there was a small room or alcove off to the side, perhaps a closet, hidden within the flames. And within it, barely visible in the light from the fire, he saw an object.

Willing himself to withstand the sensation of heat, Nikal groped his way to the closet in the blinding orange glow and grabbed at what he had seen. With a firm grip, he dragged a body out of the flame and down into the stairwell by one wrist. Rioletta Eris lay before him, and she had been in the Deception fire for many hours.

As he shook off the effects of the fire, Nikal could see that Rioletta lived. She was insensible, injured physically and injured to an unknown degree from lying within a pre-Dispersal Deception intended to cause intense mental and physical anguish. He could only assume she had crawled there herself to hide from the battle, but he could not fathom how she could have stayed there. He hoped she had been insensible most of the time.

"Taus!" he cried, and the Outcast answered him, reluctantly braving the flames to reach his side. Sanctacar joined them a moment later. Together they brought Rioletta down. Nikal mounted his horse, and several of the Tabor band passed Rioletta up to him. He gripped her around the waist with one arm and allowed her head to loll on his shoulder as he carefully maneuvered his horse back through the city.

At the estate he passed Rioletta down and followed as she was brought into one of the bedrooms and laid upon a bed. Cardon and Mynador joined him, and Cardon gently loosened Rioletta's collar and examined her wounds.

As he unbuttoned the top buttons of her shirt he sat back suddenly. Nikal leaned forward and saw his talisman with the antique amplifier next to it, threaded on the chain around her neck. The amplifier now glowed with a blue light so intense it was difficult to look at. It also seemed to have molded itself around the talisman, fine threads of luminous blue spidering across the black glass. Carefully, Nikal reached out and touched it.

"What do you think?" Cardon asked. "Should we take it off her?"

Nikal shook his head. "I'm not sure what this thing is, but I know it's not an amplifier, and I now think it's possible it confers some sort of Protection. Remember when Creed was struck by Rudon's Skill at the Crypt? He should have been killed, but he wasn't even injured. He was carrying a knife from the same place as this object. Leave it on for now."

While Rioletta's physical injuries could be cured, no one was sure how to deal with whatever the mental impact of the Deception might have been, protective device or not. With Kwistocta gone and Hyphanden in no state to help, Nikal contacted Adla, and she agreed to ride to Hyolon as fast as she could to provide aid as a Healer.

"I've never been in the Ruined City, even for glass salvage," Adla reminded him. "Will I be able to find you easily?"

"No," Nikal replied. "I'll meet you at the east gate. You should be safe: there are supporters of the Second Chosen from Tabor and Tane guarding the city."

Reluctantly, Nikal left Rioletta for the time being to see what else he could do around the estate. There were plenty of chores to be done to support the large number of people gathered there. He managed to take breaks in between tasks to check on Rioletta, but she did not awaken. Cardon also checked on her frequently, between tending to others who were injured.

In mid-afternoon Nikal saddled his horse again and rode out alone to meet Adla. He figured he could wind through the neighborhood due south and intersect the east entrance road, although he had never taken that route before.

The route proved more complicated than he had anticipated. The neighborhood appeared to have been laid out randomly. Streets suddenly petered out and came to dead ends at ancient buildings the street-builders apparently hadn't wanted to raze. Other alleys curved or branched into two parts that later met again. While he knew generally in which direction he was headed at any given time, he was less sure of exactly where he was.

He rounded the corner of a triangular building and entered a tiny plaza, paved with tightly-fitted bricks. His horse whinnied and Nikal pulled up abruptly. Across the plaza he saw the tell-tale shimmer of a Concealment. He heard the clatter of hooves on the plaza's stones and drew his knife just as a horse burst into view as though parting a deep mist.

The horse continued at a full gallop directly towards Nikal, then pulled up abruptly. Sparks flew from its hooves.

"Well met!" the rider said, raising a hand.

"Duri!" Nikal exclaimed in relief, sheathing his knife. Then he frowned as he noted Duri's appearance. There was an almost manic glint in the man's eye, and his grin seemed somehow unnatural. Nikal could feel his presence, an unpleasant vibration in his mind.

"Where have you been?" Nikal asked suspiciously. "When did you arrive?"

"Just in time for the fight," Duri grinned. "Don't worry, I didn't miss a thing. I had to go back to collect Scorcha and the pack-horse afterwards." He gestured at the far side of the plaza. With the Concealment relaxed, Nikal could now see a woman sitting on another horse.

Nikal squinted. She appeared to be Unskilled. "You were here for the battle?" he asked Duri. "No one has mentioned you."

"Oh, I was here. We heard the explosions from just outside the city. I had an idea things might be going badly. I hid Scorcha and went on by myself. Then I had an interesting idea, and Cardon's horses were obliging. It was quite the ride."

Nikal stared at him, thinking of Stolen's story. "You were able to control Cardon's horses? Where are those things now?"

"I've got 'em corralled," Duri said. "That is, I stuck them back on a wall. I can call them whenever I want, though."

Nikal had many questions, but some of them would have to wait. He told Duri about the losses they had suffered.

Duri sobered at the news about Kwistocta. "I've been monitoring the Outcast Council's communications, and I learned of it soon after the battle," he said. "You might be interested to know that I returned to the Vault. Everyone was busy evacuating the injured, but upstairs I found Fellodon still breathing. However, he breathes no more, and there's no danger of rescuing his mind."

Nikal wasn't sure how to react to that admission. He could not find it in himself to feel sorry about Fellodon's death, however. "Where did the girl come from?"

"Scorcha. She's Unskilled, as you can see," Duri said.

"And you thought it was a good idea to bring her here, to an Outcast city of Sorcerers? Why not drop her off somewhere where she'd be more at home?" Nikal demanded impatiently. He didn't think much of Duri's choices.

"She, eh, seems to be with child," Duri said uncomfortably. "Don't know how that happened."

"Really?" Nikal scoffed.

"You know what I mean," Duri said. "I'm not sure exactly what our union will produce. It's possible some of my Skills might be passed on, and at the moment I'm not even sure what Skills I have."

"I see," Nikal ran his hand back through his thick hair and sighed. "There's obviously a lot for you to tell us. Right now I have to go meet Adla. You should probably go to the estate and see if there's anything you can do to help."

"I'll take another turn around the city," Duri said. "But the Hyolonal have gotten wise." He touched a device on his belt. "With this, I've been able to track down several who wore Rudon's gadget. But now they've figured it out and thrown them away. I'm

267

finding only discarded devices, not Hyolonal chieftains and rogues. The fun appears to be over."

"If you've done with tracking the Hyolonal, I suggest you turn off the device," Nikal said severely. "There are others who might be tracking *you*, and we know it's a poor idea for Sorcerers to remain in constant contact with anyone else's mind."

Duri shook his head. "I'm not so sure I can do that, Nikal. As you might have figured, I've achieved total integration with Malbec and Chasan, which gives me a great deal of power. But the device keeps my mind ordered. When I turn it off, my mind tends to re-partition itself. Only thing is, I can't control which part goes into which partition, and I end up with parts of myself stuck in with bits of Malbec and Chasan."

"Kwistocta might have been able to help you, but I don't know what we can do for you now," Nikal said.

Duri smiled indulgently. "You should try one of these, Nikal. With your communication Skills, it would be really interesting. You'd love it. It's like nothing you've ever experienced. I understand now why these things were so tempting to our ancestors."

"No, thanks," Nikal said. "I assume that using these precipitated your integration."

"True. Still, I managed to hold them apart until the day I was attacked by Scorcha's kin. All of the force of Malbec and Chasan suddenly seemed to run through me like water," Duri said in an awed tone. "It was great: Unskilled flying everywhere, their firearms twisted into knots in their hands. I started to flee, but I figured I couldn't leave Scorcha there, so I knocked those of them still on their feet into a back somersault, scooped her up, and away we went. I'm still discovering all the things I can do. With my mind open like this, it's as if Skills just flow through me, even if I never knew them before."

"Just be careful they don't flow out all over the place and damage people on our side," Nikal said. "Adla and I will be back to the estate later. Take the poor girl there and introduce her to Mynador. She's had the most contact with the Unskilled."

Nikal found the east road quickly after parting with Duri. He and Adla took a more familiar route back to the estate and Nikal led Adla in to Rioletta's room. He also fetched his belongings and set them up in the room: the bed was plenty big enough for both of them, and he'd be able to feel if anything changed overnight.

When he awoke the next morning, he was disappointed to see that Rioletta's condition had not improved. He busied himself doing what he could to bring things back to a more normal pace. A few of the Outcasts returned to guard duty, but they had nothing to report. The city seemed deserted. Those that needed more time to recover began to return to their own homes. The fires were only smoldering by late afternoon, and the contingent from Tabor and Tane began to pack up. A contingent from New Herion, summoned by Ryedanc, arrived as well, and they took over much of the patrol and clean-up.

Nikal sat by Rioletta's side, fingering the oddly changed talisman around her neck. He had a feeling he might be able to use it to help her, but for once his communication Skills failed. The feel of it was too strange and foreign for him to access, and in his mind he could see nothing but flames.

Chapter Twenty-Two: Return to Andolith (Rioletta)

When she first began to awake, Rioletta had no memory of what had happened. Her dreams were haunted by fire. Sleeping was no respite, but waking was only confusion. She relied on Nikal to tell her when it was time to eat, sleep, or move from one place to another. Gradually her mind began to clear, but as she became more aware, she began to suffer from the grief of the news of the dead.

On the fourth day after the battle, services were held for Kwistocta, Tarbros, Stetsor, and Jamoy, as well as services-in-absentia for Hadrost and Myloy. Four pyres were built in the yard between the house and the stables. Rioletta was barely strong enough to attend, but she forced herself to sit as long as she could by the pyres. Nikal and Creed pulled Hyphanden to the yard, one at each arm, and stood him before the dead. Many stepped forward to speak about those who had perished, but Hyphanden was silent.

Nikal finally led Rioletta back to her bed before returning to stand guard at the pyres. The fires traditionally burned through the night, with watchers mounding the coals until nothing but ash was left.

On the afternoon after the funerals, Rioletta lay on her bed, staring blankly at the ceiling. She heard a light tap on the door.

"Come in," she said woodenly.

Stolen pushed the door open and came tentatively into the room. "I hope I'm not disturbing you."

Rioletta pushed herself up on one elbow. The talisman around her neck swung to the side. "You're not disturbing me, Stolen."

Stolen stepped closer to her bed. "I have an idea to help in your healing, but it may seem objectionable to you. I have passed it by Nikal and Cardon, and they have agreed that it might be something we could try, although they have some misgivings."

271

Rioletta felt an inkling of interest for the first time in many days. "What is it?"

"The Andian Sorcerer Duri returned from his travels, as you might have heard. He brought several of the old devices implicated in your Charter as having led to the Dispersal. It appears he successfully used these devices to allow him to fully integrate his mind with the minds of the two Sorcerers he kept there."

"Yes, Nikal has told me something of it."

"In order to do this, he has had to learn about ordering the mind. In fact, he now knows more about Mind-sharing than perhaps anyone else other than Kwistocta. And it appears that part of your ill-health is due to the disruption of your mind caused by the false fire in which you lay for many hours."

Rioletta considered for a moment. "You're suggesting that I allow him to help me re-order my mind. But you also have such Skills, don't you?"

Stolen nodded. "But Duri is more close to what you are, and in addition, he is Andian, and understands how you were raised and the structure upon which your mind was developed."

"Of course, Creed and Andor are probably against it. It would certainly be something far from the Traditional way. It might mean an end to my serving on the Council. But I could not, in truth, serve in the state I'm in now," Rioletta mused. "I'm not sure I can recover fully by myself. Bring him here, if he's willing."

Duri arrived in the evening. Cardon, Nikal, and Stolen were also there, in the hopes that they could help if something went awry. Rioletta lay back upon the bed and allowed Duri to take her communication talisman in his hand. She looked into his eyes, which seemed to pulse from black to amber as the thoughts of others swirled in his mind.

Slowly she felt the intrusion of his mind into hers, similar to how she felt when she contacted Nikal, and growing to the intensity of her contact with Cardon. She stirred uncomfortably, but at the same time, she began to feel more present in the moment, less haunted by the past. Soon, the memories of flames and pain began to recede. They were not gone, but they seemed to be behind a wall, in which there was a door she could open at will, but also close.

"I've helped you to create a partition in your mind," Duri said, sitting back. "This way, the thoughts you do not want to attend can be kept at bay, but they have not been destroyed. You can access them when you have the time and energy to deal with them."

Duri saw back and turned to Nikal. "Take the talisman, Nikal. I'll return it to your control and reestablish the link between the two of you. This ancient Skill upon it is of Herion, and I have some knowledge of it now."

In the days that followed Rioletta began to feel a little more normal and began to be able to take care of herself. She made a point of walking around the estate several times a day, although even that much exercise tired her. She encouraged Nikal to leave her alone for periods of time so he could help the community regroup.

One day Rioletta went into the great-room where Hyphanden had been installed in his chair every day since the battle to find that he was not there. Creed and Stolen were poking around in the kitchen, throwing things together for lunch.

"Where's Hyphanden?" she asked.

Creed glanced at her and shrugged.

"You don't know? Is anyone watching him?" Rioletta asked in alarm.

"No, Rio. We can't babysit him forever. He's an adult and he has a right to decide what to do with his own life, or his own death, for that matter."

Stolen nodded in agreement, but added, "I think he went up to the tower. I wouldn't worry too much. I don't think Stela wants to die now that he finally has a new chance at life."

Rioletta went down the hallway that led to Hyphanden's room. Off the hall was a storage room with a steep stair that led to the second story. From there one could climb to the turret. She knew the turret housed Trophandra's library and personal study. She climbed the stair carefully.

The library door stood ajar, and Rioletta quietly looked in. Hyphanden stood near one of the large windows, an open book in his hand. He glanced up at the movement and nodded. Rioletta stepped in.

"What are you reading?" she asked gently.

"Just something I chose off the shelf," he said. "Stela recommended these books." He gestured to one wall, and Rioletta frowned in confusion. Three of the turret walls were covered with floor-to-ceiling bookcases loaded with volumes, but the fourth wall had a larger window and thus narrower wall space on either side, and those spaces were painted as faux bookshelves. However, this was where Hyphanden had pointed, and she could see what appeared to be a gap in the painted book spines.

Hyphanden went to the wall and placed the book he had been reading into it, then pulled out a second one, apparently from the painting.

"Interesting Deception, isn't it?" he said. "Stela pointed it out. I had read every volume in this tower, or so I thought. But these are Trophandra's most valuable volumes. The information in them will be fascinating."

"I'm glad they interest you," Rioletta said, running a hand over the smooth painted wall. She had no idea how to break this Deception herself. "So Stela is still in your mind?"

"Yes, but he has retreated somewhat. He mourns as well, you know."

"For Kwistocta?" Rioletta asked, imagining that Stela might be subject to Hyphanden's emotions.

"For Alantrenne," Hyphanden replied.

Rioletta frowned. The name was unfamiliar to her.

"She was a member of the Younger Council of Hyolon, and Stela's lover. She died before the Dispersal, though."

"She was the one Erendak put into the Crypt for treason, wasn't she?" Rioletta realized. "And so the closing of the Council-house…"

"Destroyed her forever," Hyphanden confirmed. "Yet Stela was willing to do it to save us from Rudon."

Rioletta thought for a moment. Perhaps she had misjudged Stela. "Do you know why she was accused of treason?"

"I know some. Now that I have access to these books, I may be able to find out more," Hyphanden said, gesturing to the painted shelf.

"I hope you'll keep me informed," Rioletta said.

"Do you want to know?" Hyphanden asked skeptically.

"Of course. I'm a Loremaster. I have to know."

Hyphanden closed the book. "Creed, Aliora, and Andor will be returning to Andolith soon?" he asked.

"Yes. Fall is coming, and they need to get back. Creed and Aliora are well enough to travel now."

"And you?"

Rioletta hesitated. "I'll return to Andolith as well. I don't know what I'll do in the future, or where I'll go. I don't think Andolith will be my home forever, or even for much longer. But I need to return there to make my final decision."

"You will be welcome here, should you choose it." He looked away, out the window, and although Rioletta was somewhat heartened by the fact that he seemed interested in the books of the tower, she saw that he was still not out of danger. She left him sitting on the edge of the desk, looking out over the ruins of what had at one time been tall and great.

Before they left to return to Andolith, Rioletta went to see Kerdahl, who was recovering from the Hyolonal gunshot. He had returned to the bachelor's estate, and his friend Ryedanc had been admitted to the Outcast community.

"Kerdahl, I know you and I are still Traditionals, despite what we've seen and done," Rioletta said. "But we've also used Skills that most Traditionals have never imagined using. I would like to ask you a favor. Do you think you and I could set up a communications talisman? I would like to have contact with someone else here besides Hyphanden, someone who can tell me how things are going."

Kerdahl nodded. "I understand. What shall we use as a talisman between ourselves?"

"Duri probably has many interesting things we can use," Rioletta replied.

Kerdahl grimaced. Like many of the Community, he found Duri alarming, although Rioletta did not feel that way. "He was here earlier. Let's see if we can find him."

Kerdahl led the way through one of the wings of the bachelor's estate to a den in the back. There they found Duri, Stolen, and Anseri, with a pile of the devices used by Rudon to control the Hyolonal around their feet. They were engaged in deactivating them.

"Come in!" Duri said as he saw them. He gestured to the pile of devices on the floor. "Can I interest you in a communications device? I have plenty. They're on sale."

"Actually, yes," Rioletta said with a smile. "But not one of these, I think." She explained what she and Kerdahl were planning.

"I've got just the thing," Duri said. He retrieved a thin blue ring from his room and presented it to Kerdahl. As Kerdahl placed it upon his finger, it stretched itself to the correct size and began to glow faintly.

"That's from Herion," Duri said. "I've traded for a few antiques with the contingent from New Herion and set up a deal to get more. Items from there are rare, and they'll be worth a lot of money. They also have some interesting qualities."

"Not too interesting, I hope," Kerdahl said, eying the ring.

"Mostly they enhance communications better than other such items," Duri said. "Rioletta's amplifier and Creed's knife are from there. A strange place, and one worth exploring in the future."

Rioletta and Kerdahl next sought out Nikal, who was working with Caladoc on plans for a possible Challenge. Nikal was able to program Rioletta's amulet to listen for both his calls and Kerdahl's. It took longer to guide them through the process required to connect Kerdahl's ring. Rioletta was tired when it was through, but she felt better knowing she would have first-hand information about the goings-on in Hyolon. She cared for Hyphanden, and as a Loremaster she felt connected to him.

Although she suspected she'd see Nikal again soon, the talisman was a comfort as the group left Hyolon for home. The journey back to Andolith was slow. Creed and Aliora were still weak from their wounds, although Creed was too proud to admit it. They spent a night with Betar and Luridos along the way. Fortunately, the weather was good and beginning to cool a bit in the evenings. As they rose towards Andolith, the temperature dropped a few degrees more, and they welcomed the shade of the oaks of the Riola.

Rioletta was relieved to be back in her quiet house. Although she knew in her heart she would one day leave Andolith, for the time being the presence of her friends and the people with whom she had grown up comforted her and allowed her to ignore whatever the future held. She slipped back in to routine study, supplemented by a few Council duties, regular communication with Nikal, and semi-regular communication with Kerdahl.

One day when fall was well underway, the leaves not only turned but beginning to fall in the Riola and the first snows upon the tops of the mountains to the north, she felt a familiar sensation, and realized that Kerdahl was trying to contact her. She quickly found a quiet spot, sat down, and concentrated. Soon she could hear Kerdahl's voice.

"I have news for you," Kerdahl said grimly. "Hyphanden is gone."

"Gone? What do you mean? Is he dead?" Rioletta asked in alarm.

Kerdahl paused. "No, he lives. We are connected enough to him that I believe we would feel it if we were separated from him, as we felt the loss of Kwistocta. I'm sure he lives, but no one knows where he has gone, and he will not answer our summons."

"Did he go on foot? Is he still within Hyolon?"

"His horse and tack are missing, but almost nothing else. It appears he took no travel gear. There's little we can do about it. His grief has not been assuaged over the last few months, and we must leave him to organize his life as he will. But I wanted you to know."

"Thank you," Rioletta said. The stress of the communication threatened to break the link, and she allowed it to fade away. She sat deep in thought, but she came to no conclusion. Wherever Hyphanden had gone, he had not cared for anyone to know, and there was little use searching for him when his direction of travel was not even known.

Several days later, Rioletta walked the edge of the Riola with the intent of circling the village and climbing the Contemplation for a morning meditation and to catch the first rays of the sun. But as she rounded the clearing near the road to Matbor, her eye caught motion in the woods, and focusing into the gloom she saw a large, dark horse. It was saddled and bridled, but not tied, nor was there a rider in view. Rioletta recognized the horse at once. It belonged to Hyphanden.

Stilling herself so as not to startle the horse, she walked quietly into the woods and took it by the reins, which dragged on the ground. The saddle was cold and dewy. The horse had not had a rider for some time. A deep suspicion came to her.

She ducked under the horse's neck and mounted. Hyphanden's stirrups were slung much too low for her, but she did not pause to adjust them. She urged the horse into the forest and along the old familiar track, north from the village and up over the wooded rocky ridges in the Syrola, rising towards the distant peaks.

It seemed to take longer than she remembered, but finally she was there. The clearing of the Lefollah opened before her, the central stone gleaming white in the morning sun. Hyphanden lay sprawled on his back at the base of one of the Lefollah, his shoulders supported by the trunk, his head lolling.

Rioletta threw herself off the horse and ran to him. She was relieved to feel that he lived as she took his hand, but she was horrified to see that he was wrapped in what appeared to be tendrils or slender branches sprouting from the trunk behind him.

"Hyphanden!" she cried, shaking him. Slowly he opened his eyes and gazed languidly up into hers, but he made no move to shake himself free of the tendrils. Rioletta felt the presence of Leaves around her, and she heard the cracking that signaled the waking of the Lefollah.

"What are you doing?" she whispered urgently. "Come away, Hyphanden. You cannot stay here."

"But that is what I intend to do," he said, pushing himself up slightly. "There's nothing for me anywhere else. There is only pain, both my own and Stela's."

"You can't just stay here in the northern woods, Hyphanden. Winter is coming. You will die of starvation and cold."

Rioletta felt breath on the back of her neck, and knew that Hope was bending forward from her place in the grove. She heard the hissing Lefollah speech, but she refused to turn and look.

"He will not starve nor will he die of the cold," Hope said. "We will take him within us, and nourish him and keep him warm as we did Stolen."

"Why?" Rioletta demanded, but she asked it of Hyphanden, not of Hope.

"I only want to forget," Hyphanden replied. "I cannot take the pain. I cannot live if I cannot forget."

"We will nourish him and keep him warm," Hope repeated. "We will let him sleep. We will cause him to forget. In exchange he will provide us with what we have sought these many years: a bloodline to reinvigorate our own."

"No!" Rioletta turned suddenly to Hope. "That is not acceptable!"

"It is not your choice," Hope said. "He carries one within him who denied us our bloodline a hundred years ago. It is just. And if he stays, we will release your people from the bargain we made: that the girl Shushte would be brought to us when she is of age."

"Exchanging one unacceptable bargain for another is no bargain at all," Rioletta shouted at Hope.

She turned back to Hyphanden. "Hyphanden, you don't truly want to forget. I've seen death myself, both of my parents and many other people I know. The pain seems unbearable at times, but with time it becomes a thing you can live with. I understand that you want to be free of the pain, but you don't truly want to forget Kwistocta. You want to remember her and the time you had together. Now it seems intolerable, but in the future you will be glad you remember, and it will give you joy and comfort to look back on those memories."

Hyphanden stared at her. "I murdered Losino with my own hands," he whispered, "a man I once played games with in my great-room. I allowed Fellodon to live, and he murdered my wife. I condemned Rudon, a man I knew for thirty years, to what was likely a slow and terrible death. Are these memories you think will give me joy and comfort in the future?"

He shook his head and lay back against the trunk. He closed his eyes. "To forget or to die; to become a part of that which we have been. This is what is offered me; this is what I accept."

Though Rioletta repeated his name, Hyphanden answered her no more, and the tendrils from the bark slowly grew thicker and thicker as she watched until he was almost covered with them. After a while she could no longer find his wrist to check if he

279

lived. Finally she rose and found his horse. She did not turn back to bid the grove farewell.

Epilogue (Rioletta)

The winter in Andolith was cold and long. Despite the poor weather, the members of the Integrated Council traveled frequently, mostly to West Ford and Matbor but also to Dobor.

Over the course of the winter, a subtle shift occurred in the management of the Council. Morcah began to take on more and more responsibility, and his decisions reflected the Younger Council's sensibilities. Although Rioletta refused to vote in matters of consequence, Morcah called upon her frequently as an Advisor, and she provided him with what information she could, gleaned from the books and documents she had accumulated as well as the Charter and its traditional supplements. Sometimes the questions were hard and serious, and at those times she often glanced at the little dog talisman on the shelf as she made her way out the door, laden with books. But the dog's eyes were nothing but stone.

The consequences of the battle for Hyolon were many, and Rioletta took advantage of her relationship with Stetsordahl the Elder to track what was going on in Tabor. Following the fire and destruction in Hyolon and the defection of several hundred Tabor residents to the aid of the Outcast Sorcerers, the First Chosen began to face more political opposition. Stetsor worked diligently behind the scenes to encourage dissatisfaction. As the winter began to loosen its grip, he called for Rioletta to visit him in West Ford once again. When she returned, she met with the Council to tell them the news.

"The Second Chosen are about to make their move." Rioletta looked around at the assembly. As usual, Morcah, Pateret, and Andor sat close to her at the front of the table, and Ladon sat with them. Amidon and Boradon sat further back, with a seat or two in between them to indicate their displeasure with the state of affairs.

"This news should not travel beyond this room until the announcement has been made," Rioletta continued. "The Second Chosen will make their Challenge on the equinox."

"The time seems right," Ladon said. "Tabor is awash with rumors. When I met with the Matbor Council last week, I overheard several travelers. They were discussing rumors that Arvindahl knew about the threat in Hyolon beforehand, but refused to entertain the notion of sending help."

Rioletta nodded. Many in Tabor considered Hyolon an historic resource, if one they never visited due to the danger. They were incensed that some of the most important buildings were damaged or destroyed when there was at least the possibility that the battle could have been averted. "Stetsordahl has also encouraged rumors about Arvin's first expulsion, and stories of his illegal liaison with an Outcast he drove to suicide."

"Did Stetsor tell you what the Second Chosen's platform will be?" Morcah asked. "It may affect our willingness to help them."

Rioletta unfolded a piece of paper upon which she had taken notes during her visit to West Ford. "Here it is: they will enter a formal Challenge, with the promise that if affirmed, they will retain the Council of Tane as Advisors; they will abolish the unpopular practices of Outcasting and Skill Stripping in favor of other sanctions; they will open communications with the Outcast Council in Hyolon and broker a deal for protection of the historic parts of the city, perhaps even tourism, although in deference to those Traditionals who won't accept re-integration of the Outcasts they promise not to withdraw current warrants; and they will cease to press for the annexing of Dobor."

"Entirely reasonable," Morcah said, and Andor and Pateret agreed.

Ladon did not agree aloud, but he did not disagree either. "Of course, the First Chosen will dismiss them as not having standing to issue a Challenge. But with Stetsordahl backing them, they will have a greater chance."

"Stetsor is holding his grandson, killed in Hyolon while supporting the Outcast Council, as a martyr," Rioletta said. "He was popular amongst those of his generation. But there is another thing to discuss."

Rioletta turned the paper over. She addressed Morcah directly. "Cayondahl and Caladoc will issue the Challenge. They have requested that Charnia, recently experienced with the administration of a Challenge, and myself, recently experienced in the winning of one, travel to Tabor to act as advisors. I'm willing to go if the Council agrees."

Two weeks later, Morcah, Charnia, and Rioletta set out for Tabor. This time Rioletta saw the Main Hall of the Council-house from a different angle, since she sat upon the lowest tier of the stage just below Caladoc's table. The final vote reinstated the Second Chosen by a large majority. The First Chosen were deposed for a second time, and immediately removed from the Council-house. Upholding their promise, the Second Chosen refused to Outcast or Strip their rivals, and they were allowed to continue to live in Tabor upon signing an oath of fealty guaranteeing they would not incite their followers. Half of the First Chosen signed it; the others, including Arvindahl, fled the city.

As Rioletta, Morcah, and Charnia returned from Tabor, the winds shifted and began to blow warmer. The ice melted from the roofs in Andolith and the Andian soon began to flow. On a clear morning, Rioletta stepped out onto her porch in the early light, relishing the warmth of the sun. There was still snow in the woods beneath the trees of the Syrola, and a light skiff of snow frosted the clearing, where it had blown during a windy night.

Suddenly she noticed faint tracks leading directly to her door. She looked around quickly, but no one was in evidence. Someone had approached her house but possibly, seeing that she was not up, had decided not to bother her. Her curiosity piqued, she grabbed a coat. She could not see where the tracks continued, but she could follow them backwards to see from whence they came.

They led her not into the village but away from it, towards the line of dark trees. In the deeper snow beneath the branches there were clear tracks, and those led back through the forest to the north as far as she could see.

Rioletta turned back to the village, her heart pounding. A brisk walk brought her through the central plaza, past the Council-house, and into view of Ladon's house. She could see two men seated on the narrow porch before his door in the sunlight. Ladon sprawled in one chair, his broad shoulders and long legs obvious even from a distance. The other man was thinner and taller, darker of hair and clothing.

283

Rioletta's steps brought her forward almost at a run to Ladon's door, and she stopped there and stood wordless, not daring to believe it. Hyphanden looked up at her with an expression of some amusement.

"Well, Rioletta, you were right," he said, squinting at her in the sunlight, as though his eyes were not accustomed to it. He reached down to the side and picked up a bottle from where it sat on the floor of Ladon's porch. "I didn't want to forget. And the Lefollah did not take my memories from me, but they did allow me to sleep. Time has passed now, and it makes it somewhat easier to bear."

"I thought I would never see you again," Rioletta said.

"I apologize. I caused many people concern in my own grief. I hope you'll forgive me," Hyphanden said, reaching for her hand.

"Of course, Phando," Rioletta said. "I understand. Maybe more than anyone else. But what of Stelaphandon? I don't sense him within you. You seem to be all yourself."

"The Lefollah were able to create a partition in my mind for him. I promised that I would not put him back in the box, but I did not promise that he could stay in the forefront of my mind. He is aware, and he experiences what I do vicariously, but I remain in control. He and I share certain experiences in our lives, and I find him a comfort."

"It seems the Lefollah have given you a peace no one else has been able to, and for that I'm grateful. Will you return to them?"

Hyphanden laughed shortly and shook his head. "No. They've done all they can for me, and I've fulfilled my part of the bargain. Call it the Third Accord if you like. I know everything I've ever wanted to know about the Lefollah. But it's not within my destiny to become as they are."

"What will you do now, then?"

Hyphanden looked down for a moment. "I'd like to go back to Hyolon, at least for a little while. I would like to walk around, place my hands on material things: my books, the kitchen table, even the box where the last of the minds from the Crypt remain. I've missed the things I've accumulated. But eventually I think I would like to travel. I've seen little of the world or even the region. If Duri and Stolen are around, perhaps they'll join me. I think we'd make an interesting group. I think I will not stay in Hyolon, not at this point."

"Many changes have occurred over the winter, both in Hyolon and elsewhere in the region," Rioletta said. "Cayondahl and Caladoc have returned to Tabor as part of the reinstated Second Chosen Council."

"Ladon has told me," Hyphanden said. "But he does not have news of Hyolon."

Rioletta smiled. "I have some. Kerdahl did not return to Tabor. He remains as Leader Pro Tem of the Outcast Council in Hyolon. Communications and trade are of course much better, although the warrants still remain in name. Duri will soon be a father, and it remains to be seen what that union will produce. Scorcha lives in an Unskilled community near Tabor, now. But Duri spends much of his time away. He and Stolen have taken proprietorship of Porbruten's shop in Race, and I think you'll find them amenable to other travels as well. You may also be joined by Anseri, who has become a special friend of Stolen."

"Many changes, then, as you say," Hyphanden said with a smile. "So tell me: what of Dobor? How are Cardon and Adla and Justah, and how is Nikal?"

"Cardon is fine, and settling in to Dobor. Things go well between him and Adla, or so I hear from Justah, who has a communication talisman connected, now, to mine. As for Nikal, I've been able to see him several times this winter." She glanced at Ladon. "I have no specific plans to leave Andolith at this point, but we'll see what the future brings."

"As will I," Hyphanden said, raising his eyebrows.

"Will you be back this way, do you think?" Rioletta asked. Many things had been taken from her during the last few years, and having regained one whom she thought was gone forever, it was difficult to accept that he would soon leave again.

Hyphanden sat forward and took her other hand in his. "Of course. I'll need to discuss what I find in my travels with my friend the Andolith Loremaster, one of few in history who has mounted a successful Challenge and one who seeks knowledge for knowledge's sake. Do you still have the little dog talisman?"

"Of course."

"Well, I think it will work again for you. But don't worry. I'll be back this way regularly. I have children here now, and I'll need to check on their progress from time to time."

Rioletta raised an eyebrow. "Children?"

Hyphanden gestured. "Progeny, whatever you want to call them. I've engendered a new line of Lefollah, and I'm curious as to what may develop."

"I'm not sure what to say to that," Rioletta said. "Congratulations, I think."

Ladon laughed. "Sit down and let me bring you a drink."

Rioletta pulled another chair around on the porch so she could see both of the men, with the sun not in her eyes. Ladon returned with a bottle of stronger stuff than she was accustomed to drinking in the morning. The three of them sat in the first day of spring, while new life sprang into being in the woods around them there and far to the north, in the grove of the Lefollah.

#####

About the author:

K.A. Krisko is the author of a number of fantasy fiction novels and literary short stories. She grew up living in national parks, where her father worked as a ranger. Her mother, a William and Mary graduate in English Literature, encouraged her to write, read, and recite poetry competitively. Her father took her on star walks and taught her about lightning. Later she became a ranger herself, and worked in parks from Texas to California. She now lives in northern Colorado with her two Australian Cattle Dogs, Page and Carter. She enjoys walking and hiking with her dogs, skiing and snowshoeing, and reading and writing.

Other works by K.A. Krisko:

Novels:
Stolen (Book One of the Stolen Trilogy)
Crypt of Souls (Book Two of the Stolen Trilogy)
Cornerstone: Raising Rook (Book One)
Cornerstone: The Delving (Book Two)

Short Stories:
The Snow Deer and Other Stories (short story anthology)
One Wet Dog (stand-alone short story, also included in
Happy Endings II)
Almost A Dog (in Happy Endings I)
The Possessed RV (in American Blue: Real Stories by Real
Cops)
Mother Bear (in Wisdom of Our Mothers)